A
SIGN
of
HER
OWN

A SIGN of HER OWN

SARAH MARSH

PARK
ROW
BOOKS

As is true in many books of fiction, this book was inspired by events that appeared in the news. Nevertheless, all of the actions in this book, as well as all of the characters and dialogue, are products solely of the author's imagination. Where the names of real people, companies and places appear, they are applied to the events of this novel in a fictitious manner.

PARK
ROW
BOOKS™

ISBN-13: 978-0-7783-1078-5

A Sign of Her Own

Park Row Books
22 Adelaide St. West, 41st Floor
Toronto, Ontario M5H 4E3, Canada
ParkRowBooks.com
BookClubbish.com

Printed in U.S.A.

Recycling programs
for this product may
not exist in your area.

For my mother, Hilary Marsh

"I fear me this—is Loneliness—
The Maker of the soul
Its Caverns and its Corridors
Illuminate—or seal—"

Emily Dickinson

Prologue

Bird

YOU HAVE eyes like a hawk, Mr. Bell once told me. You miss nothing.

To most people, I miss everything, being in want of a hearing sense.

Watch my lips, he would say. Watch closely. That, in the end, is what he thought my hawk-eyes were for.

1

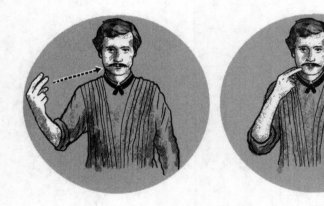

Watch

TODAY'S MISTAKE is a jar of peaches. It sits on the parlor table, the halves inside plump with sunshine. Mr. Bell, who has unexpectedly come to visit, doesn't seem to notice the jar at first. He stands by the hearth, too agitated by his enthusiasm to be seated. My fiancé, Harmon Bardsley, stands only to match him, but can't keep his words apace. I leave my careful watch of their lips and look at the jar because of the word I've seen. Surely I'm mistaken. The men aren't even looking at the jar, so why would they be discussing the peaches?

Peach. Its shape floats on Mr. Bell's mouth. The pinch of the *p*, followed by a rounded push of the lips, sending the last syllable hard across the tongue. My hand nearly reaches for my pocket, as if the feather from our lessons might still be found there. It's been a long time since I thought of the feather. I would balance it on my knuckles and make it quiver with the puff of my ps. Puh-puh-puh. I stop myself just in time, folding my hands against my skirts. Why has Mr. Bell come?

For now, Harmon leaves me to my guesses. Mr. Bell is arrived in England, and I suppose it is natural to look up old acquaintances. Never mind my surprise that he should still call me one. He's simply here to congratulate us on our engagement. Aren't those his words I see? He stands in the middle of the room with more statesmanship than the last time I saw him, saying Marvelous news and Marriage is the happiest situation. Adding to his height is a new girth—new, I suppose, since his own marriage—and I think for a moment of Mabel. Does she feed him floating islands every night? Beef slathered in gravy? But it's not only his girth that shrinks the parlor. His voice, although it's beyond my reach, gives invisible inches to his shoulders. Meanwhile Harmon, with his thinness of wrist and waist that marriage hasn't yet had the chance to fatten, has lost his usual flow of words. Yes, yes, he says. No, no.

I try to keep my eyes steady on Mr. Bell. Distractions won't help me now, although upstairs there's a letter speaking against him that I know I should have burned. Harmon has no idea about the letter, of course, and surely Mr. Bell doesn't either. But his next look sends a quiver of alarm right through me. Surely not? I think, as he lowers his chin and his face becomes still with intent.

Peach, he says. He would like some peaches. Nay, he needs some Peaches. Mr. Bell, all the way from America, his name in all the papers, and here he is, asking for my mother's peaches.

Is it some English custom that I'm yet to learn of? It's true that my mother's preserved peaches were the best, coming straight from our orchards in Pawtucket. I gaze at Mr. Bell, feeling once again the lock of our eyes, as firm as hooked arms. I want to look away, but I can't stop looking at him if I'm to understand his speech. Mr. Bell says a few more words and amongst them I catch Boston. Like it was in Boston, he says.

I'm out of time. It is Mabel, I decide. Mabel Bell has been reminiscing on her home country and the jar of peaches on our table—even if he seemed not to notice it—has prompted Mr. Bell to recall her homesickness.

Of course, I'll offer Mabel Bell this friendly token of comfort. Without any further hesitation, I reach for the jar as I gather letters in my head—*h* for horse, hammer, hound—and feel for the starting *fr* on my lips.

From home, I say, trying to give the *h* its punch of air. Taking a breath, I add, I hope Mrs. Bell likes them.

Mr. Bell looks surprised. Thank you, he says, accepting the jar. He gazes at the peaches and says, Ah yes.

Taking out a small notebook, he writes: "Speeches. We are talking of speeches! A speech."

Warmth creeps up my neck and I lower my eyes, but Mr. Bell holds up his hand, as if he can command the halt of my blush.

He says, An error. It is understandable. What I said—

And I watch him say Speeches as his eyebrows lift with a question. It's my voice he wants, same as in Boston. I try to focus on his question but all I can think is that of course Mabel Bell doesn't want the peaches. She isn't homesick, she doesn't think back to those days. Yes, I say, when I realize both Harmon and Mr. Bell are waiting for my answer. Yes.

Yolk, Yum, Yield. I drop my chin as best I can. At least the hiss at the end is easier than a hiss at the start. Cakes beat the lonely Scone.

Yes, I say, although other words are stirring in me. I know they'll bring no good. Yes, I say for a third time, hoping its clean strike will banish them.

Excellent, he says and reaches for his hat. His visit is concluded, but my relief is dimmed. Will he relate this anecdote to Mabel? She'd never have made such a mistake herself. I think to stall him, reaching for my notebook so I can inquire after Mabel's health. Does she keep well with the child?

Before I have a chance, Harmon starts up a lively stream of words. They wash toward me with only a few outcrops of sense. The Telephone. Is he talking of the Telephone? Harmon would hardly pass up the chance of this topic. After all, he keeps every newspaper article about the Telephone Fever that has swept the country and has cataloged the Telephone's appearances at societies and conservatoires and even down a coal mine. He makes one last clutch at Mr. Bell's attention.

To our surprise, Mr. Bell's face darkens and Harmon stops his spiel. He glances at me with an anguished smile, as if my lack of comprehension might offer him a rescue line. Oh my dear, he'll say, I forgot! Then he'll start repeating himself or fetch a notebook. But both of us are frozen by Mr. Bell's next word.

Liar, he says. Liar! He swivels round so I have no hope of catching the rest of his words, but my blood has run cold. Did I really think he would visit without making any accusations? Perhaps he knows about the letters after all, or else suspects me. My thoughts start hopping around for defenses to plead, but Harmon is patting the air with his hands and shaking his head. Papers, he's saying. Believe. Nobody believes everything they read. Nobody!

The Times, I think. There were articles in the papers. They are the cause of Mr. Bell's distress, not I. He's the one who stands accused of lying.

Mr. Bell's celebratory mood is gone. No, he says, and Nothing and Never. The leaden push of *n* against the soft palate. Nuh. He will have nothing more to do with it. Nothing More and Never Again. Nuh-nuh-nuh.

Harmon's stance is growing more confident as he starts to talk. This, he knows, is his moment. This is how he can step forward to the great inventor. I watch his lips and imagine what he might be telling Mr. Bell. Hasn't he said it to me before? He thinks it's outrageous, he'll be saying. A clear infringement of Mr. Bell's patent rights. I fancy he even mentions the Western Union. And as for the Western Union! he might say. He can hardly imagine the stress the lawsuit must have put the Bells under, particularly with Mrs. Bell in her present condition.

But he is talking about the speeches again. Certainly we can help. At this time of need.

Mr. Bell's face is slackened with his attention. I feel a snag of surprise. I've seen that liquid gaze before, when my voice was his goal and not the Telephone. He attended to my words with a contained assessment of their imperfections. Is he bending Harmon to his will as he once did with me? Now he attends to Harmon's words, and the reassurances that bloom within them. He gives his slow nod, the one that makes you feel that you have given him the gift of satisfaction. Yes, you are right, he says. Thank you, yes.

A sudden laugh rounds his cheeks and jumps inside his shoulders. He fetches his hat and extends his hand to Harmon in farewell. It was good to see us. Is this what he says? He heartily congratulates us on our approaching betrothal. We must call on Mrs. Bell, of course, we must. I watch his lips for all of these sentiments. And he won't recount this error, or any of my past ones for that matter. He won't call me a liar. Those days are long forgotten.

Goodbye, I manage, although my jaw feels made of wood.

After his departure, I turn to Harmon and put my questions onto my fingers. What have I agreed to? Although deep down I already know. To offer up my voice, like old times. Harmon fetches our notebook, which is our usual method for communicating complex matters. While I wait, I begin to feel the lapping waves of fear. Haven't we just started to settle into this new life? Harmon puts the notebook between us, but goes to pour himself a rum-and-water, deliberating. What can he have to ponder? He knows nothing of what happened in Boston. Still, I must wait for him and his reassurances, same as he offered Mr. Bell. I watch the lip of the rum bottle clink against his tumbler. Glass on glass. *Clinking* is a word my mother taught me. Clink-clink, she said, knocking her glass against mine. To your future.

Impatience rattles through me. I take the notebook from the table and search for some space, flicking through the pages that suggest the happy times to which my mother had raised her glass. Our sentences laced together in uneven lines, some of them smudged with hasty fingerprints or stained with the ices that we ate in Regent's Park. Harmon calls them our conversation books, and it's true you might see ease in our carefree scrawls, just like the chatter of a couple walking arm-in-arm. Harmon has learned to buy notebooks that fit the size of his pockets, although there are many times when he prefers the finger alphabet for expediency. He knows that his thin-lipped mouth does little more than flicker, and only his most shapely words are decipherable. It is unfortunate, he once said, when your eyes are sharp for what your ears are not. I told him his lips were to blame as much as my ears, and he laughed.

I present Harmon with a clean page and wait while he pens the explanation neither man offered earlier. Mr. Bell, he writes, is often visiting schools for the deaf-and-dumb. Their teachers are interested to learn more of his methods. And just recently, he had a request for a paper from the Royal Anthropological Society. How better to explain it than with a demonstration from a former pupil? What an honor, Harmon writes, when he is so in demand and has been invited everywhere to demonstrate his new Telephone. Am I aware of the kind of company that Mr. Bell keeps? Just think, he writes, you will speak before a society of Anthropologists. What will come next? The scientists, or even the nobility, of his new acquaintance?

"We must help him," Harmon writes. "His old work is surely a relief. His detractors are everywhere. His mind is turning to the deaf-and-dumb children again. He must have so little time. We can help Mr. Bell promote Visible Speech. He said you could speak about the Telephone. After all, you were there from the beginning."

No, I want to tell him. I cannot speak for Mr. Bell like I once did. Why has he asked me? Is it my forgiveness that he wants? Or does he think there is nothing to forgive? My speech would be a confirmation of the fact. I remember the way he looked at me, saying Peaches, peaches, as he scooped me into his gaze. Once Mr. Bell told me things he didn't dare tell anyone else, not even Mabel, and I won't tell them to Harmon now, not from loyalty to Mr. Bell, but because of other loyalties, about which Harmon knows nothing.

Besides, there's the business of the letters. The first one arrived two weeks ago. I knew the sender, Mr. Crane, from America. He'd written: "There is a matter concerning the inventor Mr. Bell with whom I believe you are acquainted. The rightful ownership of the Telephone patents has come under scrutiny and I write to request the assistance of your talented eyes."

My talented eyes gazed at the letter and knew to burn it. Wouldn't I lose everything if I agreed and Harmon found out? Ever since my mother's death I have depended on my stepfather's goodwill and his promise to my mother to vouch for my safe-keeping, a burden that will transfer to Harmon, as his nephew, in three months. Mr. Crane's letter went into the fire, and I hoped that was the end of it.

Harmon is looking at me. Is everything all right? he asks.

I think of all the Yeses I've said today and wonder if my hisses were clean enough.

Yes, I say, and take up the pen. "The only problem," I write, "is that I didn't know about the Telephone when I studied with Mr. Bell. I read about it in the papers like everyone else."

I'm surprised at how my lie thrills me. If Mr. Bell can dismiss the past, why shouldn't I remake it as I please? But Harmon's face is fogged with noncomprehension when he looks up from my words. "No," he writes. "He must have told you something."

He hands me the notebook and his gaze slides into me, but he's only seeking an answer.

"It was a long time ago," I write back.

Harmon studies me. He can't understand my hesitation as his ideas thunder toward this newly glimpsed prize of Mr. Bell's favor. His head dips down to the book, the pen. "It was three years ago."

I disregard the notebook and the formal penning of Harmon's suggestion. Instead, I fix my eyes on him and keep his on me as I spell on my fingers, Mr. Bell might not be happy with my speech. I can't help hoping that Harmon will agree, and I will be freed from the task on this score. My voice has not stayed the same, I add, without his instruction.

He looks baffled. We will use Visible Speech symbols, he spells back. Your voice will be perfect.

He makes the gesture for "perfect," his index and thumb pinched into circles. The gesture is the same as the sign used in the language of signs, but I'd never tell him this. Harmon permits the sole use of finger-spelling as the proper method for communicating, since it is basically English on the fingers. The true sign language, however, he disregards as being primitive. He himself has a knack for rapid finger-spelling that springs with precision. I watch his streaming words while thinking of my mother's clink-clink. Wasn't she usually right about everything?

I switch back to the notebooks. "He did tell me about a device," I write, "to help deaf children. It was called a Phonoautograph. I think it gave him the idea for the Telephone."

My heart stalls when Harmon reads the words. But is there so very much in them? I don't know anymore. And yet Mr. Bell has come back. Harmon treats the suggestion with irritable disappointment. But it'll have to do. All right, he says. His lips push forward. Is he saying Good? His mouth doesn't retract after one Good. There must be at least two. Good-good.

Good, I concur, trying to picture Mr. Bell's symbols for the word as I puff a *g* from the back of my throat. Summertime is when we will be wed, but already I fear that Mr. Bell's visit has changed everything.

That evening I sit down to start on my speech, but it is Mr. Crane's second letter that I fetch instead of a clean page. This one I couldn't burn. I turn the pages slowly, anticipating the painful swoop my heart will make on reaching the last paragraph. For three pages, Mr. Crane writes of the Western Union, and the bitter squabble of rivals now that the Telephone looks to be valuable. They want evidence, to impugn Mr. Bell's character, and Mr. Crane fancies that the talents of my eyes might collect it for them. A lip-reader, a spy.

"I must inform you," he writes finally, "that a debt is due to me. I believe you are acquainted with the 'debtor' who is beholden by a sum of thirty pounds, which was placed in your keeping. I am happy to discharge this bill upon completion of the original service for which I am owed."

Panic drained me on the first reading, but now I stare at the word, *debtor*, suspended by tiny curved-ink wings. His debtor is Frank McKinney. Mr. Crane knew perfectly well how to ghost his name onto the page, but why would his debt be placed in my keeping?

The sidesteps of a memory. Frank standing in the print shop, handing me pieces of movable type, while signing on his free hand. What was he telling me? Instructions? An anecdote? My memory adds his smile, slanting across the workbench at me, and remorse seizes my shoulders. I cast down the letter. Mr. Crane might hold a debt over Frank, but what right does he have to ask me to discharge it? And this from a man who clearly has his own crooked interests in mind?

Still, my best course was to write to Mr. Crane so he wouldn't write again. But what should I tell him? Yesterday, I might have replied that I hadn't any contact with Mr. Bell, and our acquaintance was severed. Today, however, the great man himself was in the parlor, offering a renewal of his friendship.

"Dear Mr. Crane," I write. "You may discover that your letter comes at an opportune time, but allow me to inform you that I do not barter in the business of deceit and lies however you feel yourself to be owed. Those deeds you believed me capable of in the past can have no bearing on the person I have become since my engagement to Mr. Harmon Bardsley. I beg you do not write again."

When this letter is sealed, I turn to the speech for Mr. Bell. It ought to be simple enough. A fresh page and newly inked pen to make a tidy little account, which Harmon will translate into Visible Speech so I may give a corresponding declamation to Mr. Bell and his audience.

Liar. The word bounces into my thoughts. But it is Mr. Bell who stands accused, who risks losing the fortune promised by his invention. At least his lawyers will know what to do, mustering testimonies, letters and dated sketches that confirm each of his steps toward the Telephone.

But I have little to muster for myself. No lawyers or records, and even my voice will be coded by Visible Speech symbols. Only this pen knows how to speak.

2

Lesson I
əl, əlɹ, əl, ələl
[me, my, ma, mama]

I WAS called Ellen Lark in the days when I knew my name without needing to look for it. Back then my name came around
doorways, down staircases, across fields, from the stoop where
my mother stood hollering news of our dinnertime. I didn't need
to see any person to know I was summoned. I heard my name,
looked about, came or went accordingly. My name lived in the
air like all the other words I knew. It danced from the mouths
of my playmates so frequently that sometimes I knew only that
it had been uttered and not who had done the uttering.

Then came the fifth winter of my life. I can remember my
mother's handwritten sign hanging from the portico to warn

away visitors. Scarlet Fever was clearly written upon it although the letters lacked the usual flourish of her copperplate. I lay in the blue room, tucked under a Nine Patch quilt. My mother must have told me the rest. My tongue turned the color of strawberries and under the cotton nightdress, my skin glistened with smeared lard. The doctor did not know if I would live or die. Every hour my mother readjusted the red ribbon that secured a slab of fat salt pork to my neck. This was to take away the fever's heat. The first time I stirred from the delirium was to protest that I minded more about the ribbon than the pork. Not a week before it had secured the wrappings of my birthday presents.

That winter it snowed heavily. In a daze, I watched the forming drifts. I wondered why my own mama had fallen into some quietness, although her mouth moved as it did before. When I asked her about it she began to cry. She folded over the quilt and sobbed with a weight I'd never suspected of her. I thought it was the snow. It soaked up every tiny vibration. Not only the shouts of passersby, but the voices belonging to my mother and father, and my sister Mary who I watched hurling snowballs down in the fields. Their words were trapped out there in the drifts, and no longer in their mouths. Like every child, I had a warm imagination.

The snowdrops had burst from the ground by the time I was recovered. Springtime ladled sun onto the muddy rivulets in the lane. But I stopped looking around when I was spoken to. I didn't flinch when my mother dropped the pans. My eyes were drawn to people's faces until I was called out for my rudeness. But I watched their lips like you might study the stars. Speech glittered in a cosmic confusion until at last I could pick out a few words and join them together in a pattern. I saw Baby for the neighbor's newest arrival. Pawtucket for the name of our town. School for the place Mary went every weekday. But I couldn't see my name anywhere. Ellen. It had vanished. Even when Mama stooped right down to me, she barely opened her mouth to utter it. There was a flick of the tongue behind her teeth but that was it. Ellen!

I was a hole in the sentences she spoke about me.

In time, she started calling me La-La which was easier to see in the mouth. I became a note in a lullaby or a tonic sol-fa.

A note of consolation.

If I felt terror or grief, I don't remember it. The silence was short-lived. Hearing people little realize the truth of it. For years they've looked at me as though I live within its cage. But my eyes were busy the minute the meltwater had flowed from Pawtucket. Mary clamoring for her school boots. The ponies looping the meadows in a canter. The wind brightening the elms next to our house. My eyes turned hard on the world and filled my head with a different kind of noise.

At that time, we lived outside of Pawtucket by three miles or so. Father had gone to the war and Mama tended the orchards that flanked the back of our house. In summer people came to pick fruit. I skipped with the girls and ran from the boys. I didn't think of what I lacked: only of what I wanted. If I saw a huddle of children, I pushed my way to the middle and tried to figure why they were gathered. If the children started up hop-scotch, I watched their feet until I knew where to put mine. If they laughed, then I laughed too and felt happy enough. A few children even picked up some home-sign. If they teased me, and gave me nicknames, I never saw them.

It was one of these summers that I finally understood my difference. We were canning the peaches for the soldiers at Camp Arnold. Women had come from town. We gathered around the truckles and planks that had been assembled into benches outside the north barn. I knew a few names. There was Mrs. Cain and Miss Gemma. Everyone else was a smile, apron and knife. My job was labels. I was to carefully paste each label and pass them to Mary for binding with cloth at the jar's neck.

I was talking to Mary because I couldn't use home-signs while pasting. At that time, I still used my voice. Mary didn't have any trouble with it. But other children came our way, and some of them didn't know me. I looked up from the jars and there was a row of mouths stirring as if a brisk wind had gusted through treetops. One child spoke and then waited, and when I didn't reply, another child took a turn. Words hopped between them, and they came closer. Finally, I got sense of the eldest, Celine Vester. She was regal and apt to float about in tulle and bustles, no better than the words I was clutching after. She bent close so I smelled her rose-soaped skin even atop the sweetness of the peaches. She said, Why do you talk like that?

I said: Like what? The other children burst out laughing.

Mary put down the jars. Celine Vester wasn't so very much older. She said, I bet you can't do this. She spanned her indexes the breadth of the group and shook her head.

Then she lifted her fingers and started teaching them the manual alphabet. That turned them about. It was a good trick of hers. Most children loved to discover the speed of their fingers, and none were as fast as Mary and me. But I kept my voice tucked away for the rest of the afternoon, and for a good while longer too.

Mama kept up my English. She spoke to me with special care. Her words dug brackets about her mouth as if her remarks were an aside just for me. They were never too large or small: they fitted my understanding perfectly. Her style of speaking was smooth and connected. She related an anecdote in a steadfast manner, always giving me more words, not less, from which to guess her meaning. She knew how to phrase things so they would be more easily understood. She said "twenty-five cents" instead of "a quarter" and "half a dollar" instead of "fifty cents" because fifty looked like fifteen.

In time, the lines stopped fading from Mama's mouth and became permanent.

She turned my father's workshop into a library: him being gone such a while. She boxed up his engraver tools and lined the shelves with children's stories and nursery rhymes. Mama was British, and I loved best of all her collections of children's stories she'd brought to America when she married my father. She sat for hours with me, reading the books while pointing at the words. I could read before the fever, so I guess she wanted to stopper up that English in me by putting more words into my head before they could leave. I rested against her so the story murmured in her shoulder. While Mary was at the schoolhouse, I sat alone with those books. The words inside them never ran from me. They didn't hide or mock me or shift shape. Each time I opened the book, I found them on the page just as before. Large and inked and certain.

Those books didn't have much use in the yard or fields. Home-sign was our daily mode. It was a kind of talking which came so naturally to us that Mary and I hardly thought of it. She was raven-eyed and quick-handed: she had spark in her and didn't care to labor. If hands could speak faster, so be it. Our signs arose as inevitably as the red maples and skunk cabbage in the lanes. A fist held high was the sun, while a C-shaped hand tapping your palm was a cake. A thumb and index snapping together was the beak of a bird. We pointed at things until we found a common sign for them, and then we stopped pointing.

We went into Pawtucket on Fridays. Mama dressed me in my best plaid with a blue jacket and matching ribbon for my hat. I followed her like a duckling, feeling as cheery as the shine on my boots. She was the tallest woman anyone knew, although height did little for a woman apart from make her strong at hauling fruit tubs. It troubled her not a jot. She walked into town like she was a Boston Brahmin though we were lower bred than that. Her bright hair crowned her with another inch of radiance, and I traveled so easily in the wake of her skirts I might have been sailing on her back.

I tried awful hard to look like a child who belonged in a plaid dress. I remember one visit to Mr. Paul's dry-goods store. I wanted a bobbin or some such and told my mother. I suppose I should've known better, even then, to both be wanting and putting all that want on my hands and face. It was only a few signs, hardly a frenzy. But someone got sight of me. A blonde lady with a bouncy jaw. She was acquainted with Mama but you could see it was a glancing sort of chat between them. She saw my moving hands and said My! Wasn't I a little savage? I only knew it because I saw the word on Mama's lips. She repeated it as if she was confounded. The woman started laughing as if a savage-child might be a curious kind of pet, there was no harm in it.

The next week Mama bought me a gold pen and a fine notebook with feltine covers and marbled end pages. Usually, I carried a small slate.

That gold pen was the loveliest thing I'd ever owned.

Oh, people said, when I applied the lovely pen to the page and let my writing flow forth.

My pen flashed Ohs onto their faces. If they thought me spoiled, Mama didn't care. I'd worked hard at my calligraphy. Mama said: how would she afford all the ink? But she was smiling from start to end of that sentence.

For a while I had my gold pen and it glittered in my hand. And why shouldn't I have some small vanity? But I guess I showed it off too much. One day some children gathered around me as I waited outside the liquor store for Mama. There was that switching of smiles and words between them. I felt the warmth of their cluster and a corresponding hop of hope within me. Was this some kind of invitation to play? I readied my eyes to catch any clues but they seized me from behind and pinned me while stealing from my pockets. There was a well on the edge of the town, and I chased them to it. But I was younger and slower, and by the time I reached the well, the children were skittering at the end of the street, having already committed their crime. The pen was uselessly sunk to the bottom of the well shaft, dulled into oblivion by the black water.

That was the last time Mama took me into Pawtucket.

So I was back to chalk, slates and my hands. When children came by the orchards with their parents, I started to hang back in the barns. I watched them flit with Mary between the trees while Mama packed peaches into crates. Mary had friends of her own from the schoolhouse who would come for her on Saturdays, and they'd walk down the lanes together. They readied their bonnets and ribbons as though they fancied themselves off to a ball. If I went with them, I stayed behind or ahead of their huddle, making an examination of the verges for flowers. On those walks, I contented myself with endless posies.

My grandmother, Adeline Lark, sent cures from Boston. Mama always referred to her as Adeline, as if to indicate a distance she intended to maintain. Mama went to the post office in Pawtucket to collect her packages: small brown bottles of strange-scented fluids that tasted of chamomile and chalk. Adeline folded recipes into letters that said "Poor Ellen," and called me a deaf-and-dumb child, and described what must be done about me. Mary said my grandmother disapproved of my father's marriage to Mama, and that was why she never visited. In fact, "Poor Ellen" was the only reason she wrote at all.

Mama never replied to the letters but nonetheless she mixed those cures in the kitchen after Mary and I had gone to bed. She baked onions in tobacco leaves and juiced them. She stirred bay salts with spring water and sweet almond oil with camphorated spirits. She dropped the liquids into my ear at the next bedtime and secured their coolness with a wad of cotton. I got used to the feel of that medicine trickling down the silent channels that ran into my head. It was followed with the firm, reassuring stamp of her good-night kiss. But the cures leaked a sour idea past my eardrums and into my core: there was something wrong with me, and no one knew how to fix it.

The next day Mama watched me closely until it was apparent I was not going to jump at a single one of her clatters.

Adeline recommended a doctor who came to us all the way from Connecticut. He sat me in our parlor while he lit a candle. I was told to look out the window but I couldn't help sliding my eyes to the candle and the metal rod he was holding to its flame. He smiled at me and crossed to the chair, then I felt searing pain behind my ear and a swell of sound heave through me. Mama had to hold me firm while he did the next ear. She clamped my forehead to her chest so I felt the thunder of her heart against my face while the pain came newly from one side of my head and merged with the pain on the other burned side.

The next week the doctor returned to examine the blisters. He rang a silver bell at my ears then gave me a boiled sweet wrapped in paper patterned with forget-me-nots. He shook his head at Mama and folded the bell inside a square of black velvet, which he slipped into his bag. He said a word that looked like Asylum, which I had seen in Adeline's letters. I looked at Mama. She kept her eyes on the doctor and didn't move to disagree with him.

After the doctor left, she stopped sealing nighttime tinctures into my ears. Adeline still sent her letters and recipes, but Mama threw them in the trash. She began to talk about the Asylum instead, which was a large school in Hartford. There I'd be able to learn a skill and get some sort of education. The pupils used the sign language, so I'd have no trouble taking my lessons. They lived at the school, which was bigger than any building in Pawtucket so I conjured up ten schoolhouses next to each other and each one was filled with children like me. But my mind always stalled when I tried to imagine the sheer amount of hand-talk that must take place along that many benches. I'd not known any children apart from Mary who talked on their hands.

I pestered Mama to tell me about the school. Would they really all talk like myself and Mary? She shook her head and said, Not just the same. Their signs will likely be different.

It took me a moment to ascertain her meaning. Certainly, Mary and I had made up our home-signs entirely but there was sighted logic in them. How could there be another way of translating the world with your eyes? I didn't like the idea of Mary and my mother being unable to understand what the Hartford children would teach me, but since it was some years until I could attend, thoughts of the place soon drifted away and I forgot all about it.

Mama started using more of the home-sign I used with Mary. She added our signs to her English, her face providing ample accompaniment. She put creases of dismay about her eyes or blew out her cheeks in amazement. Your father, she told us, taps cipher into the telegraph wires. And she pressed her knuckles to her lips, sealing a secret against them. Secret codes, she continued, about the enemy.

She often talked about him in this way, as if she could paste over his absence with her signs and words. She'd met him in England on an island called Wight, when he'd been on vacation one summer. Summer, yes, but I married your father in a thunderstorm, she told us, as her fingers pawed rain into the air, followed by the zigzag lightning strike of her index.

I copied her sign, my finger ripping through the air. His new name, I signed. It was better than the usual *F* we referred to him as on our fingers.

Stupid, Mary replied, wrinkling her nose so her eyes went small. She had grown tall over the summer, new curves under her shirts and skirts, but her home-signs were as boisterous as before, even if shades of bored irritation were apt to stir through her. Lightning? she signed. He isn't quick coming home. Lightning!

Her flying finger caught me in the chest. I jabbed back and soon we were chasing each other around the table. Mama was laughing. He will come soon, she said, then you can see if he likes the name.

I watched for him on those days, when the rain lashed at the panes. But our father didn't come back even when the war ended. First he was waylaid in Pittsburgh. Then he took up with a merchant as a traveling salesman. Mama explained it to us, resolutely, as if she didn't dare let us, or herself, doubt him.

But if she loved to regale us about his life, the news of his death didn't appear on Mama's hands or lips. Instead, she kept her face straight as she spelled it out on my slate, before wiping the chalk away, as if she couldn't bear to see her own words.

I thought it couldn't be true, if you could erase a statement as easily as that. It was the same kind of fickle as I saw on hearing people's mouths. I kept my eyes alert for more information. But I only saw tight words on Mama's face that were directed at the visitors who came from Pawtucket. They were words that made her look like a different person.

It wasn't until many years later that I had a full picture of what happened to Father when Mary wrote me about it. One morning, he'd left town and followed a telegraph wire into a hug of nearby oaks. Local boys playing at Indians found him the next day. Wire was in his hands and some around his neck. An accident, my mother had told us. He was trying to run a line out of the woods. But Mary told it differently: he didn't even have a pair of pliers with him to make the installation.

He came home trussed up in a coffin. When I saw him, I found myself searching for the face I had memorized from the photograph we kept in the parlor. All I could think about was how long and soft his eyelashes looked above his sleeping cheeks. I cried shuddering tears because I couldn't bear to see the parishioners drawing in their pale expressions, closing their eyes, trying to be as still as they could. I wanted to break apart their silence and calm with the sound I felt in my chest. What use was sound if it could not do that? But the mourners kept their glances pinched as Mary pressed me and my sound to her side.

After his death, the letters from Adeline thickened in our mailbox. This time they didn't concern me. Instead, it was Mama's debts she wished to advise on. At first Mama threw those letters in the trash more readily than her proposed cures. After a while, she started reading the letters before throwing them away and eventually she stopped disposing of them. But her face was bitter as she filed them in her writing desk. Your grandmother, she remarked, thinks she can take better care of you both than I can.

Glenn King, who often bought our peaches for his father's grocers in Providence, started coming by weekends while Mary loitered in the doorway and you could tell she used raspberry juice to brighten her cheeks. He said that a mute was like a monkey, and wrote his ugly words on my slate. I had to run into the kitchen to wipe the board clean. Mama pleaded with Mary to make a better choice but she replied, Adeline thinks it is an excellent match, which made Mama pale with fury. Soon Mary was to be married, her sights set on town life in Providence although Glenn King wanted to buy orchards of his own to serve the nearby mining camps.

Mama seemed to forget about the school in Hartford. Wasn't I needed around the place to assist her? We were busy early each morning when the canning season came around. Mama started talking about a trip to England to see an aunt of hers, and I thought she meant to take me with her. For a while she seemed content again, and I was content alongside her.

One morning Mama and I were doing speech-reading drills. Usually she sat me before some text or another. On this day it was *Robinson Crusoe*. There was fat sunshine coming through the windows and pushing cheerful squares of light up the walls.

Mama perched opposite me, her long fingers splayed across the book's covers. She tilted forward, her face dropping close with her words.

I will read this page, she said. You just write it.

I picked up my pen, but I felt dull inside. The books she recited were different from the ones she read to me as a child. She didn't go slow and point out a word here or there. I couldn't rest against her shoulder. The story didn't breathe and rise within her chest. When she started on our drills something happened to her whole face that flattened the sense right from her.

Mama started to read, and I jotted down whatever words I spotted. I hated the work. It was slow and irksome. My back ached as much as my eyes, and it was impossible to sit still for the entire hour.

Eventually, I fetched a line about how Crusoe had been on the unhappy island for ten months but I could make no sense of the next part about his Condition. Mama repeated the sentence slowly, breaking it into fragments so I could see the full shape of each long word on her mouth.

But they were like fishes in a pool of water. I watched their narrow backs flash and dart away from me. Then I flung down the chalk so that it broke across my slate, spattering white dust. I said, Let me read the book for myself and I will know it much faster.

Only Mama could easily understand my voice by then, but her face was as straight as a tallow. She looked at me for a while, then picked up her hands and started spotting her speech with home-sign.

She said, When you go to school everyone will use the sign language, so we must keep up your English. Or you will come back, to the real world, and understand nothing. How will you work?

I stared at her, and she repeated herself twice, thrice. But I saw her words clearly enough. It was the attendant thought that slowed my response: I wasn't going to England with her.

Mama placed her hands on the pages of Crusoe as if she were taking their pulse. She said, This is what I can do for you. Do you see?

Her safe, regular words. I didn't know if she meant the speech-reading drills or sending me to the Hartford school. I thought of the liquids she'd poured into my ears so many times, followed with a kiss. I wanted that warmth from her again, not these drills. And I wanted her to stop feeling so torn and unsure about what she should do for me. Every time I thought she'd forgotten about my condition, it cropped up again, and I was furious at myself for missing the clues, or thinking it was gone from her mind.

I will not be away long, she continued. No more than a year.

She glanced around and paused. Then she stood up and left the room. I was used to people coming and going with no clear reason. Was coming back? I looked again at *Robinson Crusoe*. Suddenly I was angry with the book, because I knew I couldn't be angry with Mama. Didn't she only want the best for me? I looked down at the open pages and examined the passage she had read. My head felt tight like a band had been wound about my temples. Why hadn't I seen even one of those words? All her cures pooled cold and useless inside me, and now I must be sent from her. I wanted to get it right. To mend what the bay salts and blisters couldn't fix. But I didn't know how I'd ever do it.

I picked up the book where it lay open on the table and pressed back its covers so that the spine broke. I felt it snap in my hands like a hapless bone. Then I read the page through three times, my thoughts moving more clearly. When Mama came back, she didn't notice the damaged book. Although I'd achieved nothing, I felt the satisfying burn of my victory.

We might never have bothered with Crusoe again if Adeline hadn't arrived one morning without warning. She came by a coach-and-pair, which had Mary spluttering an announcement in the doorway. Mama scarcely had a moment to tidy herself and us before my grandmother was in the narrow hallway with two gentlemen behind her. She entered our parlor and her eyes skipped about the room in a display of fleeting interest. She was slender like my father but darker-haired with narrow shining eyes. She had the busy, calculating manner of someone always on the cusp of a smile or remark but electing to withhold it.

Mama said to me, You remember your grandmother.

I didn't especially but I waited while she took out a notebook and wrote two names: Mr. Benjamin St. John Ackers and Governor Orr. She let me read the names then held her hand toward each of the two men.

This is Mr. Ackers. Governor Orr. They have come to see you.

She was speaking carefully and made no home-signs whatsoever.

Both men had huge beards, and their greetings did no more than waggle them. At least Mr. Ackers's face rounded a little with his smile but the Governor's cheeks were as limp as pancakes as he gazed down on me.

Adeline crossed the room. She leaned forward but she was standing with the window behind her so the stoop of her head only darkened her face further.

I missed her question. She stretched a patient smile across her words as she repeated them but this only made it harder. I managed to grasp School from her sentence. Then I had to take my best guess. She was asking me if I went to school, or wanted to go to school, or had ever been to school. The best thing I could do was supply a straight factual answer and hope it addressed whichever angle her query was slanting from.

I am going to school next Fall, I replied, trying to bite an F into my bottom lip.

Mama smiled at me but it was a hopeless sort of smile. I hated to see it. Adeline drew back, while Mr. Ackers nodded, and Governor Orr looked at me as though I was a piece of furniture that should hardly have spoken at all.

Mama handed Adeline the notebook, but my grandmother raised her hand at it. She took a book from her bag with red fel-tine covers and gold flowers embossed upon its spine. I ought to have minded the slight at Mama but I felt myself go soft with longing. It was the prettiest notebook I'd ever seen. Adeline's face squeezed in a conspiring smile as she opened the book, pulled a chair to the card table, and began to write. She wrote for two whole pages. Then she handed me the book, stood up again and started to talk. She was talking at me but it must have been for the gentlemen's benefit for I had no idea what she was saying. Was I meant to read what she'd presented me in the pretty notebook?

I dropped my eyes to the page, although it felt like a rude in-attention. I could feel her towering over me, the smell of prim-rose tincture drifting across my face and shoulders along with her speech. "These gentlemen have traveled all this way to see you," she'd written. "Mr. Ackers has a daughter of his own who is in a similar predicament. He is traveling across America to learn the best methods of teaching his child. I told him about your mother's remarkable achievements. I said you could speech-read as easily as drinking a glass of water. So he had to meet you himself. How do I know this? Your sister tells me in her let-ters. And I can see for myself that you are a child with a clever manner which is not unsatisfactory. Mr. Ackers introduced me to Governor Orr who has told me about a school for children like you. If the gentlemen are impressed with you, they might recommend a place at the school. So I want you to do your best for the gentlemen. Do you understand me? If you understand, then close the book and leave it on the table."

I finished reading before Adeline was done speaking. I didn't know which school Adeline meant but wasn't this what Mama had already arranged? Hadn't she told Adeline about the Hartford school? And in the few weeks that had passed since we'd read *Robinson Crusoe*, Mama had persuaded me that I'd like the school better than going to England, where I would know no one. It was filled with children like me, and besides, she'd not be gone long. But Mama seldom wrote Adeline and perhaps Mary had also neglected to tell her about the arrangement. And I thought: any hairline crack in Mama's plan might have me going to England yet.

I closed the book and slid it a few inches along the table, toward Adeline.

Adeline paused in her talking. She smiled. Then she finished her sentence and the Governor stepped forward.

He didn't get very far before Mama stood again. She was saying difficult. It is very difficult for her.

She said Difficult so many times that indignation began to creep through me. The gentlemen talked on and Mama kept saying Difficult. I tried to latch on to their speech to calm myself but their words slipped from me like grabbing at a bar of soap. I didn't want Mama to apologize to these men, not when she had tried so hard for me. I didn't want her to make excuses, or explain on my behalf. Suddenly it seemed like the most dead-end of kindnesses.

I opened my mouth and said, I would like to go to your school.

Adeline looked at Mama. I didn't like her smile. See? it seemed to say.

I felt bad for Mama although I wasn't sure why. Our plan all along was for me to attend school. Did it matter which one I went to? But there wasn't time to ask her questions, because Governor Orr came properly forward until I was level with his waistcoat pocket and needed to look up. He pressed his beard into his necktie as he considered me. His beard started moving.

I tried to quell my panic and resisted the urge to look at Mama for an answer.

He dipped his hand into his waistcoat pocket and shook it about inside, while leaning toward me with his eyebrows lifted over his words. A question. Was he asking me what was in his pocket?

For a moment I was too surprised to answer. There were hardly many options. It was a small pocket, not large enough for cigars, pens or notepads.

I carefully gathered my answer. Coins, I said, wondering if I'd said it too loud, or not loudly enough.

He drew his hand from his pocket to reveal several cents nested in his palm.

He turned to my mother, and I supposed he said I must surely have some hearing because Mama shook her head and said, She has none. He looked back at me, and his brow was crosshatched, while the coins glinted in his fleshy palm. His mouth and eyebrows moved: a second questioning of me.

I said, My father always had coins in his pocket.

Governor Orr looked at my mother. She was smiling and my heart swelled. She was pleased, even though the governor hadn't understood my speech. She repeated my words and as I waited, I felt an old memory tipping in on me: sitting on my father's lap and going through his pockets, while he tried to bounce me on his knee. And now Mr. Ackers was saying Bravo. He patted his own pocket and said something that made Mama laugh.

The Governor looked at me again, his interest sharpened.

Let's try this, he said.

He took out a small bell. I was familiar with bells. Doctors often rang them at my ears. This was a pretty one with fruit branches wound around its handle. I wanted to take a longer look at Governor Orr's bell but he slid it past my cheek and ear. His arm and wrist shook as if he was vigorously polishing a window just behind my head.

He looked at me. Hear that? he asked.

I shook my head and he nodded, satisfied.

He said something that looked like Reason and Hearing so I guessed he was engaging my mother in the matter of my history. I watched as Mama related the familiar story of the scarlet fever, and the deepening gravity in both men's expressions.

The Governor was talking again, issuing instructions it seemed, since Mama crossed the room and drew up a chair. Then she folded her hands firmly in her lap and said, The Governor would like to see your speech-reading. We have agreed that you and I will talk awhile so they can watch how you do it.

Her speech was careful, her manner the one she reserved for me. Had Mama said something about the Governor's beard? I was mighty relieved that he or Mr. Ackers wouldn't be the one to test me. Right away Mama settled into steady, regular speech. She picked up a conversation we'd had just that morning about canning peaches. She meant to make me a lively sight for the gentlemen in all the ways a bright child should be. I stood there beaming at my mother and as soon as she'd finished, I quickly wrote down everything she'd said in Adeline's red notebook. Mama fetched it and handed it to the men.

Mr. Ackers peered over his shoulder and appeared to say Astounding but Governor Orr did not seem much impressed. Mama looked crestfallen, but she forced a smile when she turned back to me. She said, The Governor thinks we are very familiar with one another. She paused before adding: He would like to read to you from a book.

I felt a stab of alarm but it was too late to do anything. Governor Orr was perusing the bookshelves. He spotted *Robinson Crusoe* by the window and picked it up. His eyebrows: This one?

Mama's mouth opened. Was she going to say, Not that one? It was too hard. But the Governor was flipping the pages. Was he going to read it to me? Then he must have remembered about his beard, for he handed it to Adeline.

My relief didn't last long. She opened the book and let the pages spin between the covers. Finally, the pages stopped, neatly divided on either side like parted hair.

Adeline started speaking. She held the book as if she stood at a pulpit and was addressing an audience larger than the four ones us in the cramped parlor. Her pale throat seemed to lengthen as she read.

At first my eyes could take nothing from her speech. Her words popped like bubbles on her mouth. Then I picked out Unhappy Island. That was the line my mother had read me a few weeks ago. Next, I spotted Condition and Deliverance. A feeling of sureness arrived with me like the setting down of a heavy case. It thumped through me with relief. The book had fallen open where I'd cracked the spine. After that, my mind was primed to see the text. I could remember the rest of the passage and matched it neatly to Adeline's lip-shapes. When she finished reading, she snapped the book shut with one hand and dropped her eyes on the red notebook. Go on, she said.

I glanced at my mother, whose smile had vanished into the sinkhole of her worry. Did my mother want for me whatever it was Adeline was suggesting? The last time Mama had wanted the same as my grandmother, my ears had been blistered. Still, I was a burden on Mama for all the worry I caused her, and the way she must protect me. And I wanted to impress the men. Hadn't I once been called a savage? I wouldn't stand for them to think it, and for Mama to have to explain things away with words I could only guess at.

I picked up the pen and started to list the aloes, wild sugar cane and tobacco. I could even remember one line intact: "And I firmly believe that no human shape had ever set foot upon that place."

I liked to think of Crusoe on his untouched island, putting names to what he found, his eyes being all he needed in that strange place which was entirely without words except the ones he carried in his head. I wrote slowly and deliberated over my sentences so they shouldn't guess I knew the passage already.

When I finished, I took the book straight to the Governor. Mr. Ackers didn't cease smiling, his teeth visible through his beard. Was he thinking of his daughter when he looked at me?

Governor Orr read my words. His shoulders jumped twice as if huffed laughter had dislodged them but his accompanying frown suggested his disbelief.

He looked at Mama. His beard moved. Mama looked at me with wary confusion. She said, The Governor thinks you have quite a talent.

I dared smile. Governor Orr was still talking. Mr. Ackers was examining the book and saying Extraordinary. Mama nodded cautiously. Yes, she replied. We practice day and night. But she glanced at me.

Everyone was talking now, and there was no point trying to work out what they were saying. My satisfaction at my performance began to fade, leaving a dismal inkiness in its wake. I tried to push it aside. Hadn't I done what was asked of me?

Governor Orr sat down at the card table and took up the notebook. He wrote down the name of a school I'd never heard of and its teacher, Miss Roscoe. "You shall be one of the first children in this country," he wrote, "to study under the Oral method in a public school. This Oral School is the first of its kind in this country."

He waited for me to finish reading, his gaze cushioned with sympathy. He moved his mouth a little and I saw Questions. Did I have any questions?

I looked at Mama. She was hovering behind the Governor and didn't come toward me. I sensed the rift I'd made by reeling off Crusoe from my pen-nib and smiling smugly over it. I wrote, "Will I learn how to be useful?" I was thinking of dressmaking or one of the other trades taught at Hartford. That was what Mama meant when she said useful.

Governor Orr laughed. He wrote, "What is more useful than speech?"

He turned back to Mr. Ackers and started talking again. I waited next to the table, not daring to look at my mother and letting myself take peeks at the pretty notebook instead. Had it betrayed me? I wasn't sure. Then the scent of primrose fogged about me, and Adeline's hand pressed down on my shoulder. She was so close I could feel the hum of her words across my cheek, the spread of her warm, salty breath. Perhaps I did not seem as pleased as I ought, because she frowned as if she was taken aback. She said, Don't you want to be like other girls?

I felt my head go up and down. Nodding. Adeline smiled and her hand was like a sandbag on my shoulder. I tried to think of Celine Vester and the girls who talked and laughed so easily with Mary but I felt anger flush through me because Mama was still standing in the corner, and she looked as if she didn't know what had just happened. And there I was nodding at Adeline, as if we'd colluded to bring it about.

3

Confidential

TWO WEEKS after Mr. Bell's visit, a third letter arrives from Mr. Crane. After I finish the morning tasks, I excuse myself from the house, taking the letter with me. My stepfather, Mr. Holmwood, lives in a backwater of Kensington, in a two-story terrace wedged between the huge villas with their adjoining mews houses, and the railway cut-and-cover, which is so close we all feel the regular rumbling of trains under our feet. Today I take the northerly streets directly to Hyde Park, avoiding the museums and the old grounds of the International Exhibition, where I used to walk. I'd no idea the Bells lived so close, although I've never once seen them there.

"Deceit and lies," I read in Mr. Crane's letter when I finally find a bench, "are only my line of business insofar as I seek to uncover them. If you do not think you can assist me with the outstanding debt I have described, perhaps you can advise as to where else I should make my inquiry. Is it your stepfather or fiancé to whom I should address myself?"

There's no mention of Frank, but the ugly paragraph boils through me. I can't have Mr. Crane go to either man with debts that I can't easily explain. The envelope is still padded without the letter inside, so I upturn it, causing a handful of clippings to scatter into my skirts, with a note amongst them. It reads, "Consider, if you will, these claims about Mr. Bell. Minor charges, or would you disagree?"

Small items, carefully scissored from *The Times*. One article claims that Mr. Bell's Telephone cannot be the subject of a patent because the telephone is actually fifty years old. Another letter names the true inventor as one Wheatstone who used wooden rods to conduct band music and later the ticking of a clock. A third writes of Faraday and another of Reis. All of them state that Mr. Bell's device is little more than an improvement on what has gone before, and question his honesty in taking the credit.

I return the clippings to the envelope, feeling restless and exposed, as if Mr. Crane knew I'd read every one of them. I try to recall what I know of the inventors Wheatstone, Reis and Faraday. None of these men were on Mr. Bell's lips or in his notebooks when he first told me what he dreamed about creating. My mind goes back to the schoolroom in Boston and the worry burning in Mr. Bell's eyes. He was so tired, up all hours of the night. A night owl, everyone called him. He scarcely dared breathe a word of his idea to anyone else. Wouldn't they just laugh at him?

To my alarm, I feel the tug of that old trust between us. None of these men, I'd like to answer *The Times*, had caused the human voice to flow along a wire. None of them had delivered conversations, declamations, singing. I flick through the articles again and other remembered words begin rising in me. Current, electrician, harmonic. Some of these words Mr. Bell had to write down, and occasionally he tore up the paper afterward.

Trousered legs and a pleated skirt appear next to my knees. I look up to find a perplexed couple. The gentleman is speaking, wagging his eyebrows and nodding his chin at the remaining space on the bench. I shift along to let them sit, realizing how my thoughts have strayed. I may have been Mr. Bell's confidante once, but I wasn't any longer, and didn't wish to be one again.

I put the letter into my bag. The woman on the bench has turned to me and is saying something so I take out my notebook and show her the first page, which gives an account of myself. She reads Deaf-and-Dumb, and the alarm jumps in her neck and cheek, although she smiles when she wasn't smiling before, her eyes uncertain. I turn to a clean page and offer her the pen, but she waves her hand—there's no need, never mind—and shakes her head saying, Just the weather!

Is it just something about the weather? I wait but she bobs her smile and turns away. No matter, my thoughts are full of Mr. Crane, so I get up to leave. How am I to be rid of him? It's no use writing another letter. I'll need to meet him in person and explain the impossibility of the task. He must understand that this debt isn't one I can ever repay, nor can Mr. Holmwood.

When I return to the house, Harmon is back unexpectedly for luncheon. Mr. Holmwood is waiting in the dining room, his white hair that I combed this morning already poking up in tufts. I'll be one minute, I tell him, thinking of the food waiting under the domes in the kitchen. Our former housekeeper, Mrs. Ketter, was never late with a meal, although Mr. Holmwood isn't one to chastise. He raises a hand: he rarely speaks these days, one side of his face given to immobility. To Harmon I spell: I was reading a letter from my grandmother.

Good, he replies, looking pleased since he could never understand the trouble Mama and I had with Adeline. He holds up an index finger. That reminds me, he says and wags his hand. Come, he means.

I half turn to Mr. Holmwood. But Harmon is saying Quickly and Won't be long. Besides, my stepfather has drawn the daily papers toward him, and doesn't seem hurried, so I follow Harmon to the study where yesterday evening's copy-work has been left on the desk. Is he going to chide me for the mess? Copying provides a small income of which Harmon is ashamed, but I can fair copy two brief sheets an hour for a much lower fee than any clerk in this city. Harmon tells me that I won't need to be copying for long. Once he's promoted at the Department Store, I shan't have to work again, although my skill with the pen and ledger may have some application for the store's administrative affairs. He even promises to find a replacement for Mrs. Ketter, although he quibbles over the need while pretending money has nothing to do with it. His only arrangement has been the spinster down the street who comes daily to escort me to the market even though Mama taught me everything I needed to know, and Mrs. Ketter showed me how to go about it.

On top of my copy-work is a new pile of papers that I don't recognize. Harmon points at them and spells, Business letters. I need you to make copies.

His fingers are crackling with the words, and his eyes have a bright bounce in them. I've seen the look before: an enterprising new idea has come to him. It is the same tendency that troubled his own father, Mr. Holmwood's brother-in-law, who was a tradesman in china and glassware with a successful shop on New Bond Street. Before he died, he handed the reins to Harmon's younger brother, insisting that Harmon lacked business acumen and was prone to flights of fancy. Angered, Harmon found a position in a Department Store on Oxford Street instead, but soon was dissatisfied. Then he wanted to organize a lecture series for a German man who claimed he was a world-leading mesmerist. Next it was setting up his own company to sell the latest gaslights. Neither came to fruition, and it was Mama who tried to reassure him. It was a good position, she said, and a man with his kind of energy would surely rise in it.

I try to think what Mama would tell him now, and make my advice like hers. I only manage: What about the clerks at the store?

His face is dismissive. He says something like, This isn't about that, and waves a hand at my suggestion. He takes his notebook and begins to write, "Mr. Bell's Telephone Company is renting out wires and instruments and I plan to establish the first Telephone franchise in this country."

I stare at his words, and then at Harmon. He laughs a little and says, Don't worry. He takes back the notebook. "The Telephone is a marvel," he continues, "but now we must create its business uses."

My hands jump up but I stop myself, switching to the pen instead. I try to match my words to his: strident, certain of themselves. "But surely," I write, "businesses prefer a written record. Even the Post Office Superintendent thinks it cannot replace the telegraph."

Harmon shakes his head, and his assessment arrives with me in fragmented paragraphs as the notebook goes back and forth. The Telephone provides speed and personal connection. Mr. Bell is a fine inventor and educator but not a businessman, whereas Harmon has turned around the fortunes of a Department Store. Well, that of his floor at least. Harmon will lease lines and instruments from Mr. Bell. He will bring on board shopkeepers and other department stores. "And we must think further afield," he finishes. "Physicians will readily see the Telephone's use for emergency calls. Pharmacies, lawyers. The list goes on."

I take the pen from him. For a moment I think of pointing out that Mr. Bell has already surrounded himself with fine businessmen, Mabel's father to start with. Instead I write, "I don't think that the Post Office will allow private telephone companies. This isn't the States."

Harmon gazes as me, baffled by my resistance. I feel a skip of panic. How can I make him understand that I don't want to renew my acquaintance with Mr. Bell? It is best to leave alone what can't be undone. I try to forget how I rooted through Mr. Crane's letter only a few hours ago, hoping for a mention of Frank.

"Unlikely," he replies with matching tidiness, "as the Post Office does not have supremacy on this matter. Private companies are free to operate, so we must start immediately. I want copies of every letter that I send logged so I have it on record."

I take up my fingers. I don't have time, I tell him. When am I meant to do this? In the evenings I must finish my copy-work, then I sit with Mr. Holmwood.

The man is half-asleep by then, he replies. The evening is perfect. He winks so a dimple appears in one cheek, and says Yes? Hmm? with a nod that sends a wing of his auburn hair sliding forward. He picks up the letters and holds them between us like an offering but it only serves to end the conversation, his hands being too full of paper to reckon with any demur of mine. And once I take them, I won't have my hands free to answer him either. This is a new tendency of his, to stop and start conversations as he sees fit. He closes a notebook when he decides he is finished, he turns away with a word still on his lips. Is it simply impatience, forgetfulness? I think back to our early days before Mama's illness, and our long walks in Hyde Park together, talking all the time on our fingers. When he showed me around his floor at the Department Store, his fingers danced with letters as he relayed the queries of the shop-floor assistants and my replies to them. Soon he became my most regular interpreter. He sat beside me at lectures and social calls. He would spin other people's speech and mine through this flicker of finger-letters. He didn't mind the attention, the opposite in fact. Shy Harmon; I gave him new confidence.

I take the papers and put them on the desk again. Then I spell emphatically, Problem, smacking the *M* into my palm. You don't know how the Telephone works, I continue in a smooth stream, before lifting my palms and pressing the corners of my lips firmly downward. A what-to-do?, if not quite a rebuke.

Ah, wait. He's raising an index and taking a card from his pocket. I feel a tremble in my arms as Mr. Bell's writing comes into view. Then the card is in my hands, his sentences between my thumbs, as if I'm holding one of our class notebooks again. His scrawl is the same attempt at tidiness frustrated by his evident haste. It reads, "You are cordially invited to a DEMONSTRATION of the new TELEPHONE which shall be exhibited from the DEPTHS of THE THAMES."

There follows a place and date: tomorrow.

I give back the card, hoping Harmon won't notice that the tremble has reached my hand. How will it help? I spell. The Telephone will be in the river.

Harmon takes the notebook and writes, "Your speech, do you remember? I will write to all the schools for the deaf-and-dumb, and offer our services. Mr. Bell desires to do justice to Visible Speech in this country, but he has no time. We will help him, and he will return the favor."

I keep my eyes on the page, not daring to lift my face in case he can see what is twisting inside me. I am a trading token. That is his plan. My Visible Speech for Mr. Bell's Telephone. Mr. Bell already has my voice, I want to reply, inside the Telephone. Not just mine, but all his pupils. Hadn't our voices plucked at the strings of Mr. Bell's attention, enlivened his belief in the value of speech? He picked up a wire and dreamed a voice might travel inside it. He told me of it and bade me not to tell a soul. And I kept his promise, until I saw that it was already broken.

I agreed to one speech, I say, using my voice. It comes out

roughly with my unused consonants, forgotten vowels. Then I write, "You want us to travel the country? We're not even married."

Harmon's head nudges back. The dimple that appeared earlier seems sunk into his cheek. His face grows long, longer. There is a sharpening light in his gaze, an ugly look that sends my thoughts skittering. But then the blue of his eyes is calm again. I almost see the stumble as he catches himself and something firmer sets his face.

Kindness. Kindly. He is affecting sympathy. His finger-spelling becomes smooth again. I know you don't want to speak, he spells. You know I have no problem with your voice. But you know Mr. Bell's system, and this is what your mother would want for us. To advance ourselves. Mr. Bell's friendship will help us.

He spells all the words except for the ones that denote the two of us. *I* and *Us*. *You* and *Yours*. *Ourselves*. For these, he taps his chest, slides an index between us, and jabs his finger toward me. Jab, jab. *You, You, Yours*. A shortcut, but it conveys his insistence.

My heart stalls on his mention of Mama. He hardly refers to her these days. Six months have passed since her death, and we acted as if it was better to let time quietly seal up my grief, and that of old Holmwood. Confusion spins through me, and I lapse into the question he wants me to ask myself: Would my mother tell me I should do this? In a drawer upstairs there's a letter from Mama which I was sworn not to open until the eve of our wedding. It's not the first time I've thought about it, but now my desire for her advice is stronger than ever. Mr. Crane, Frank, Harmon. They lean in, crowding around me, pointing me at Mr. Bell in different ways so I feel like a weathervane, and don't know which direction to turn.

Fine, I reply, before I can stop myself. I consider snatching back the word, but I'm too stunned by what I've agreed to. A snappish all-right at Harmon; have I answered yes simply to his plans or yes to Mr. Crane as well?

Harmon smiles. Did I only imagine that brief ugliness of his anger? He flips both thumbs like a youngster, smiling now. Rich, is the word I see on his lips. Does he say that one day we will be rich, as will Mr. Bell?

After dinner I sit down with his letters, counting six. Three of them are to the principals of the schools in Bristol, Exeter and the Old Kent Road, London. One is for a physician acquaintance suggesting a Telephone wire between the man's residence and his office so he can learn of emergencies more quickly. Another is addressed to the boss of his Department Store with a similar suggestion. The last is to Mr. Bell and requests the support of the Bell Telephone Company, and informs him of the schools he has contacted, offering us to demonstrate Visible Speech. Along with the letters there is also a new logbook. He wishes to record not only his business correspondence, but every favor we have granted Mr. Bell, in our arrangements with the schools. It's a side of Harmon I try not to notice; his meticulous score-keeping.

I start on the copies but I can't settle. A different kind of regret stings me all over and makes me feel afraid. Harmon used to send me letters regularly, and they weren't like these ones. Instead he told me about his day and asked about mine. He slipped the envelopes under my door every night. The next morning, I propped my replies against the pepper mill at breakfast. He read them and laughed in all the right places, or so I guessed as I measured the way his eyes moved down the page. Mama smiled her appreciation from across the table. Sometimes he tucked them in his pocket, as he wished to reread them on his lunch break. That evening, there would be another letter filled with more anecdotes about the customers at the Department Store. "One lady," he wrote, "came in with a ferret and I was certain it was a stole until it looked at me and squirmed." Another letter: "I

thought of you today when a gentleman asked for some earrings
to match his wife's eyes, and I realized that in all the department
store we do not have any earrings that would do yours justice."

After Mama died, the letters became fewer. I hardly noticed
at the time, and Mama's absence allowed him to move closer to
me in other ways. With Mama gone, and old Holmwood unable
to manage all of his affairs, Harmon was practically head of our
small household. I was as good as his wife already. He still wrote
notes of a practical nature, but they didn't seem worth keeping.

And now I can't bring myself to copy his business letters. My
hand ghosting his words across the page will make me complicit
in the things I don't wish for, arrangements I want no part of.
Instead, I open the logbook and enter the details of the business
letters before sealing them into envelopes. I leave them ready
for posting, with no copies made.

The next day, rain is drifting across the Thames Embankment.
A crowd of twenty-odd gentlemen is assembled behind the railings while farther back onlookers pause in the street, drawn to
the sight of Mr. Bell. He stands by the river, dressed in a diving
suit and waving a gloved hand next to the vast copper dome on
his head. Breathing tubes are looped to the helmet's side. A ladder is secured to the railings where a second diver is lowering
tubes into the water, readying Mr. Bell's descent. His boots look
so heavy I wonder how he can even lift his feet. A pale smudge
of nose hovers behind the window of his helmet. Of his lips,
there's nothing to see. I look around for Mabel although in her
condition, in this weather, she's surely keeping indoors.

Between the shuffle of brollies and shoulders is the Telephone.
An assistant is giving a talk, but I only catch the words: Voice
and From the Depths. A wire connects Mr. Bell's butterstamp
handle to a black wooden board, then trails across the table, over
the railings and into the water, running parallel to Mr. Bell's
breathing tube. The tube is fat like an intestine, whereas the

wire is as thin as hair. They will make an exchange: air will go into the river, and his voice will come out of it. Mr. Bell will be vanished, and yet there will be the sound of him, like some ghostly essence.

As I watch him waving his hand uncertainly in the vast helmet and suit, Mr. Crane's request seems absurd. Even if I should see enough of Mr. Bell's words, what is he likely to reveal here? Every public occasion is a demonstration or explanation: not a confession. His job is to promote the Telephone, to represent the fruits of his labor. He won't be telling them how business isn't treating him kindly. That the Germans are making telephones more cheaply on the continent, and another company has secured the German patent. He won't mention the other patents he's losing in Europe, and how soon the continent will be flooded with cheap telephones not owned by him. Not a word about the debate in *The Times* or the Western Union and their legal case. His patents taken from him, his name teetering at the edge of history, his chance of a fortune washed away with it. His reputation hangs in the balance but he will smile and smooth his troubles away as he explains his invention in a manner that will stoke nothing but fascination. In short, nothing of use for Mr. Crane.

Now Mr. Bell is astride the ladder, ready to enter the water. The canopy of umbrellas is broken apart by waving arms and hands. Mouths open with well-wishing cheers. Slowly Mr. Bell descends until he's gone from sight. A few people rush to the railings and peer after him, before turning to the crowd and confirming that he is indeed underwater.

Everyone clusters around the Telephone. I half expect riverweed and rusted nails to come out with his voice. The crowd is restless, chattering to each other as the assistant passes around the butterstamp handle, each person hoping to be the first to hear Mr. Bell's voice.

When it reaches me, I slide a finger into the small hole in the receiver's base. Hope quivers across my shoulders. How would Mr. Bell's voice feel? A tingle, a shiver, a tremble? To my surprise, I want the Telephone to know me, to curl Mr. Bell's words into my palm, like a child placing its hand in its parent's. I make myself as still as possible, waiting for the Telephone to recognize my touch.

But there's nothing. I pass on the receiver, ignoring the odd looks from the assistant and the crowd. Harmon clasps my hand against the folds of our coats. I suppose I must look crestfallen.

The gentleman who has the butterstamp receiver raises his palm. His eyes narrow as he pushes the receiver against his ear. Yes. Yes! It's Mr. Bell's voice.

There is laughter and commotion. Everyone wants a turn with the Telephone. I watch Harmon take his. A song, I see him say, but his face strains at the earpiece. Perhaps the water has swirled Mr. Bell's speech into a broken, burbling melody. He has become part-merman, blowing bubbles into the ears of this distinguished crowd, teasing them. But they mask their disappointment: it is a marvel all the same.

You are probably right, I spell, ignoring the interest of the assistant at my finger-flicker. He might have a piano down there.

Harmon smiles. Then Mr. Bell heaves himself up the ladder, water streaming off his suit. His assistants help him over the railings. Together they lever off his helmet, and he stands blinking in the rain.

Headache, I see him say. I have the most awful headache.

His words sail so easily into me that I'm jolted with surprise. I can't help glancing around the crowd. Did anyone understand him? But he's still some distance off, waving at his audience as the assistants remove his diving suit. The cheer from the crowd hums across my shoulders. Since I ought to look like I too am celebrating, I knock my palms together with them, while watching Mr. Bell closely. Here he is, at another successful demonstration, smiling at his admirers, and yet he's unhappy, even unwell. And no one in the crowd has a clue. I can't help feeling victory's snap of pleasure. For a moment, I've more sense of him than anyone else here, however their ears may serve them.

Headache, he says and rubs at his temples.

I turn to Harmon and take out my notebook. I don't want Mr. Bell to see our finger-spelling, since he surely knows the British alphabet from his early years in Scotland. He was teaching even back then. "He has a bad headache," I write as gray spots of rain appear on the page. Harmon frowns, concerned.

"It must be the water pressure," he writes back.

Liberated from his diving suit, Mr. Bell enters the crowd to receive praise and questions. His face is pale. Harmon takes my elbow and tries to ease us through the throng, but every time he finds a gap someone steps between us and we have to wait. Peeved, he asks, What else is he saying?

I try to watch Mr. Bell but the gentlemen surround him, and I've only an interrupted view of his face. I write, "He is telling them how much rubbish there is in the Thames."

Harmon shakes his head with as much disgust as if I'd told him drowned babies were down there among the riverweed. Terrible, he says. Quite terrible. What else? he spells.

But Mr. Bell has spotted us. He says Excuse me to the gentlemen and comes over before I can answer.

What did you think? he asks, and adds You, Finally and See.

We have finally seen the Telephone. His head is turned toward me, as he makes his words clear. I feel relief to understand him. Half of it, I say, and Mr. Bell laughs.

It was very dark down there, he replies. I saw nothing! I feel quite awful.

You should take a rest, I say, but he waves away my suggestion. Rest, he says. No. And adds something about how little time there is. I can't help smiling, and he notices. What? he asks. Ah, I always say that.

He smiles and the swerve feels dangerous, even though Mr.

Bell looks pleased. I'm almost thankful when Harmon starts talking. A letter, he says, so I guess that his topic is business. At first he glances at me while he talks, trying to stitch me into the conversation with the needle-like dips of his eyes. But soon he has forgotten himself, his lips are too quick and he stops looking at me at all. I watch for mention of a Telephone Franchise. Surely he is smoothing the conversation in that direction. Isn't that why we are here?

And Mr. Bell is listening to Harmon. He nods, smiles, nods again attentively. Certainly they make a motley pair, with Mr. Bell expanding into comfortable statesmanship, while Harmon looks like he fuels on nothing but water and the agitation of his thoughts. Harmon isn't a calm influence by nature, but his manner is clever and deferential, and he's generous with his admiration. People of a certain type like having him around, and I now see that Mr. Bell is one of them.

I feel restlessness pawing at me like an animal. How long will they talk for? Harmon doesn't look like he's stopping anytime soon, and neither does the drizzle. I shift on my feet, trying to adjust my posture as I feign interest, make some nods, smile at what appear to be timely moments. I'm practiced at this. I mustn't burden Harmon with my incomprehension and task him with fixing it. But still I can't help my boredom.

Mr. Crane's proposal drifts into my mind. I had understood Mr. Bell better than I'd hoped, even when no one else did. Headache, Mr. Bell had said. I feel awful, he'd told us, as if here amongst everyone we alone were his confidants. Perhaps even in this crowd Mr. Bell will break from his spiel of promotion. Could I bring something to Mr. Crane that would be enough to satisfy him? A new thought has troubled me lately. What if Frank simply could not pay the debt himself after what happened between us?

Then I see Mr. Bell say Headache again. Harmon says, You must try not to think of it, and Mr. Bell is saying Health and

Nervous Excitement. His health, he is saying, followed by Skin. Is there some trouble with his skin?

He waves an index at the river and tells Harmon the doctor didn't recommend it. A salt bath, a spa town, not a filthy river.

They laugh, and Harmon is asking him: Why?

Mr. Gray.

That's the answer I see on Mr. Bell's lips. The reason for his poor nerves, his health and his skin is Mr. Gray. He says Mr. Gray several times and looks quite troubled.

Elisha Gray. One of the inventors from the Western Union's stable. It can't be. I blink it away. Mr. Bell discussing in idle chat his rival Mr. Elisha Gray as the cause of his headaches? I know I've made a mistake. The shape lingers in my thoughts as doubt spirals around me. What other words look like Mr. Gray? I used to play lip-reading games with Mama where you had to tell certain words apart using your wits alone. Paper, baby. Egg, ache. They looked the same on the lips so what mattered was how they were framed. But most words have no match, no twin, however hard you try to find one. My eyes strain as I watch for more words, this time on Harmon's lips.

Mystery, Harmon is saying. That surely makes more sense for two people who don't know each other so very well. The cause of Mr. Bell's bad health is a mystery.

I wait as the words tumble between the two men. Mystery, Mr. Gray. Then the conversation moves on, leaving me with a memory, as fragile as a scent, of their shapes. The words are almost similar. What if I didn't make a mistake at all? Mama always said to trust your first instinct, and there is nothing to lead me astray, like the jar of peaches when Mr. Bell first visited us. There is no reason that I should think of Mr. Gray, unless it was what Mr. Bell said.

My mind skips to Mr. Crane. I can't help composing an answer to him in my head. "If you would agree to meet," I'll write, "I should like to discuss in person the matter of your proposal.

I have already gathered some information, but first I need good reason why you should be worthy of it."

Frank. He's the only good reason. I can't bear the thought of his debt, which is becoming more like mine as each day passes. I seal up Mr. Crane's letter in my thoughts, thinking it's just a fancy, of course I shan't be sending such a letter, but when I turn back to the men, Harmon is talking about the letters he has written to the principals of the schools, and the speech I will give to them, and the anthropologists. He is saying my name, that I have written many pages.

Mr. Bell looks at me and I feel the rain's chill go through me for the first time that evening.

Well, something short, he says. His thoughts have worked creases around his eyes.

He doesn't trust me after all, I think.

I take out my notebook, feeling in need of its safety. "We are so happy we could come today," I write, and present the notebook so that he is forced to drop his gaze to the page.

Yes, he says, and then Harmon is saying Goodbye and Mr. Bell is saying the same. Before we turn away, he catches my elbow. The touch surprises me: a habit he has with deaf people, but it burns like a brush with a candle flame. Harmon's eyes skip down and up, but any judgment is forestalled by Mr. Bell's next remark. You must call on us, he says. My wife would be thrilled.

Oh, I say, forgetting the notebook. Thank you. Thank you, I repeat because Mr. Bell isn't smiling, instead he's watching me closely, as if he's reaching for something in my face. I square my shoulders and present myself openly to his search, but I can't help the tightness that traverses through me, finding an outlet in my grip on the notebook.

He starts speaking carefully. My wife can offer advice, he says, on your wedding. Setting up home. It must be difficult without any womanly advice. She misses her own family greatly, he adds.

I try to unhook my stare from his face without much success.

Did I see his words correctly? Surely, he remembers this isn't the first time he has sought to give me advice on my marriage?

A shadow of anxiety passes through Mr. Bell's brow and jawline. He is waiting, I realize, for my answer. The reference to my mother's absence feels like a knife pressed against the balloon of my resolve. He didn't give his condolences, I realize, on his first call, or were they among all the other words I missed? Something inside me starts to tear. I think of pointing out that we shall not be setting up home on par with the residence they have in Kensington, but instead I take up my notebook and put down my finest hand. "Please thank Mrs. Bell," I write. "I am much in need of advice."

4

Lesson II
ᴐſ, ᴐʃʌ, ᴐſ, ᴐʃʌ
[pea, pie, tea, tie]

MY NEW home was Miss Roscoe's Oral School. It was a roomy house on the edge of a small town, surrounded by flowerless gardens. The tall gate marked a new boundary on the world I'd just left. Miss Roscoe called it the hearing world. Whenever one of us pupils asked when we'd live in it again, Miss Roscoe would say, When you can speak like a hearing child, and I cannot tell you apart.

For now, we were apart. Twelve pupils in her constant care. "Mutes," "Semi-mutes," or classed as "Only Deaf." I was a Semi-mute since I had learned most of my speech as a young child but was losing clarity, shedding my consonants like strands of hair. Most of us were born hearing although a few pupils had been born with no hearing at all. These children were the "Congenitals."

Regardless of our classification, everything at the Oral School was to be done in English. We must always say our words carefully and read them on Miss Roscoe's lips. We took every meal together like a family at white-clothed tables and said, Please pass me the butter. We played like siblings in the playroom and said, May I have the doll. On Sundays, Miss Roscoe took us through the gate for a stroll around the town. People came to their windows to see us. Sometimes they waved from behind the glass, and we waved back. Those days we were victorious.

Miss Roscoe was both mother and teacher. She was a slow-moving woman with slack cheeks atop which her green eyes were set like stones. She flushed easily when she was hot or annoyed, and we tried to annoy her as little as possible. She had the talent of standing stock-still while she was speaking and only smiling when she knew it wouldn't interfere with the patterns of her speech. She smiled into her own silence.

Each morning, she handed us pocket mirrors. We huddled over them, studying the way our lips moved. They needed to move just like Miss Roscoe's moved. If we could match our lips to hers, we thought maybe we could match ourselves to the world outside.

Words were spooned into us, and then drawn out again, inspected and repeated. We learned nothing of History or Geography, and little of Mathematics. There was sewing and woodwork, but mostly Words. English words, flickering across Miss Roscoe's face.

We listened to the murmur of Miss Roscoe through long hearing tubes or placed our small hands on her throat, taking turns to feel the hum of her steady, regular speech which died as soon as our hands dropped away.

Once she gave us red balloons. Like this, she said, and her

face disappeared behind the balloon. She seemed to be kissing it. We glanced at each other to see who dared laugh at the sight of our teacher's head replaced with a balloon. Theresa Dudley was the first to understand. She grabbed a balloon and pressed her face to it. Then she laughed and passed it to me. I felt my voice humming on my lips and between my hands. Soon we were throwing the balloons about the place, catching them and putting our voices and laughter into them.

Gentlemen came to visit us. I remember the stream of top hats and untrimmed beards that made a jungle over their speech. We searched for clues in their sentences as they rang bells at our ears and looked into our mouths. We were used to sitting still for long spells while they discussed us with Miss Roscoe. After a time, we'd be sent back to our rooms.

Miss Roscoe told us that our school was the first of its kind, a pioneering school. Soon there would be many schools like ours across the country. You are the first and best, she'd tell us. Think of the poor children in the asylums being taught like monkeys.

She wrinkled her nose in a grimace so we smiled at her and each other. Her pride made us proud too. Over the years, she carefully impressed an understanding on us: using signs marked people as belonging to an inferior class. Apes and Redmen used them if we needed any further proof. She called them the de l'épée signs but after she wrote the word on the board for us, she struck a line through it. We, children of the nineteenth century, deserved far better. She, and the gentlemen who took an interest in our little school, would ensure that we received it.

Some of us, it appeared, deserved it more than others. Miss Roscoe had clear favorites. There was Pearl Adams who could do declamations and recite poetry. Mae Turner and James Brook could hold a conversation when seated three yards apart. They did these tricks for the gentlemen while the rest of us watched from the rows at the back. We knew Mae was a Semi-mute and

James was Only Deaf. The born-deaf pupils never took the stage. They were instructed never to speak outside of the school's gates.

I was the best speech reader. Sometimes I had to stand in front of the gentlemen and read Miss Roscoe's lips. She never gave me anything as hard as *Robinson Crusoe*, and usually it was a simple text we had studied in class. And by now I knew her lip patterns as well as Mama's. All those years of drilling with Mama had paid off, but there were many times when I feared that Miss Roscoe would discover I was simply guessing at her words, and matching them to exercises we had already done.

Take a page from Miss Lark's book, Miss Roscoe told us in our speech-reading drills. A few pupils looked at the workbook on my desk. Should they tear a page? Miss Roscoe liked to present English in its usual expression. We saw mustard that couldn't be cut, thunder that could be stolen and chickens that you mustn't count. We rejected them, thinking we were mistaken. When we learned those sentences were indeed as we'd seen them, we felt cheated.

No, Miss Roscoe explained. I mean that Miss Lark is very good at this exercise. She has sharp eyes. Like a hawk.

I flushed in front of the class, as if Miss Roscoe had described a secret power in my possession. Perhaps I wanted to believe her, and when my friends changed my sign name that evening, I didn't object. It used to be the E-shaped hand from the manual alphabet, waved slightly in the air, which Mama had circled on an illustrated card sent to us by the Reverend at our local church. Now my friends changed it to a snapping thumb and index at the mouth, the sign for a bird. A Lark, or a Hawk, I didn't know which one they intended. Eyes sharp, but wasn't that true for all of us? We were all watching the world, reading every little detail around us.

As for our hands, we made them fly in the hallways and our dorms. It was our own school argot, comprised of our home-signs and the de l'épée signs that some of the older children knew from spells at the deaf-and-dumb schools. But we kept our signs from Miss Roscoe's sight, or at least we tried. We knew we looked like the asylum children, a horde of monkey-children jabbing at each other, thumping our chests, sweeping circles in the air. We feared being caught, and the small cupboard where we'd be confined, to chalk out endless lines, or the hours of being made to sit on our hands in the corner of the classroom, heeding Miss Roscoe's threats to tie them down, if we tried to use them. If the gentlemen visitors saw us, we feared worse. And although we loved each other like siblings, we didn't put much store by our signing. Once we left the school, we'd never see each other again, so what use would our signs be then? You couldn't use signs out there in the hearing world. Miss Roscoe had told us they'd earn us nothing but disdain. It was the secret language of the Oral School, and one day, like all childish things, we'd leave it behind.

At first, I longed for Mama and Mary. Every month Miss Roscoe dropped letters onto our desk, but with each one it became clearer that my mother wasn't returning from England. "The house and orchards in Pawtucket have gone to your father's cousin," she wrote. "Please understand that I'd no choice. Your grandmother has promised she will help you and Mary. I had debts to Adeline too and you know how exacting she is about such affairs." I wasn't sure I did know, but Mama was writing to me like I had more summers on my years than I did, and I wanted to be worthy of her confidence. "Of course, Mama," I replied. "The food here is very nice."

Then she started writing about a gentleman called Mr. Holmwood. "He is a kindly man with a large house in London not far off from where the Queen herself lives. Fancy that! Did you know the Queen can use some signs, like you and Mary?" Finally, there was a letter explaining they had married. "Mr. Holmwood's health is poor, and he is in need of care whilst I myself cannot come back to America readily. Please understand my little La-La. I have no place to live and would be entirely dependent on Adeline who does not care a whit for me, as you know. But trust that she will ensure you're taken care of until one day when you can join me."

"One day" was a shimmer of a notion. As I read her letters, I strained to interpret her meaning. Next month, next summer, next year? But the months passed, and Mama kept up a cheerful tone and "one day" assumed no clearer dimensions.

The first Christmas I went to Mary and Glenn King's farm in Ohio, but it was a long journey for which Mary had to fetch me, and once there Mr. King fastened his gaze on me so tight I barely knew where to look. Mary had a child already and another on the way and was relieved when I told her I would stay at the school the following year, so she needn't trouble herself escorting me on another long trip.

Adeline visited me instead. We sat in the garden under a bare chestnut tree while she fixed me with her narrow gaze and nodded, questions on her lips. How were my lessons? My meals? My heart went hollow as I gave her a sequence of careful replies that amassed into a single message I knew would be reported to Mama: I was happy here and making progress, so she wasn't to worry about me.

On one of these visits, Theresa Dudley and Pearl Adams walked past. They had their arms linked and were talking to each other. Apart from their expressions of intense concentration, you wouldn't know them for deaf, unless you heard their voices, I supposed, but I couldn't, and it seemed Adeline couldn't either at this distance. She was watching them with interest, a smile hooked into her cheeks. Theresa had been at the school for many years. She was born-deaf and knew the de l'épée sign language from the Hartford school before coming here, but since her father had helped found the Oral School, Miss Roscoe had only praise for her speech, even if she wouldn't present her before the gentlemen. Theresa's signing was the best we had seen, although of course Miss Roscoe never saw it. We all loved her stories at nighttimes when we managed to get enough moonlight through the gap in the curtains.

But only last week Miss Roscoe had announced that Theresa was leaving the school to study speech with a professor in Boston. Since then, Theresa had stopped signing with us and took up with Pearl who, of all of us, cared least for our hand-talk. They went around the school like this, watching each other with so much focus you wondered how they didn't walk into the walls and doorways. We tried not to mind, although we missed Theresa's stories.

Is that the girl, Adeline began. But I missed the words that followed, apart from one that looked like Bell.

One Fall day, my mother came for a visit. She stood in the yard with her arms as wide as the open gates. Her bonnet was capped with a huge green feather, and she looked so strange in her fineness that I didn't know whether to run to her or not. Eventually she had to fetch me from where I stood rooted, circling her arms around me so I breathed in the jonquils of her perfume. Any resentment for her decision to stay in England flowed right out of me.

She picked up my suitcase. We will go to Boston, she said.

Boston? I asked.

I thought but didn't say: Harbor. Boston Harbor. A steamer to England. Either that or she meant to Adeline's, but my grandmother could have collected me herself.

The pupils were ranged on the steps to bid me farewell. I waved at their surprised and sullen faces, remembering the times I'd been the one waving at whichever pupil was departing through the gates. Now I was leaving. My shoulders felt wide with happiness.

Mama laughed at my performance. Come on, she said.

She sat close on the train all the way to Boston. If the judder of the carriages disturbed the other passengers, it didn't trouble me. Our speaking was easy like old times. I watched her lovely lips and she smiled at all my answers. I waited for her to tell me we were going to Boston Harbor to catch a steamer to England, but she took a brand-new feltine notebook from her bag, and on the first page, wrote "Mr. Ackers." She pointed at the name. Do you remember him? she asked.

A knot tightened in my stomach at the memory of transcribing Crusoe, his aloes and sugar canes. I nodded.

She fetched a letter and handed it to me. Inside was one brief side of efficient copperplate.

"Regarding a suitable teacher," it began, "please allow me to recommend Professor Bell of Boston University who is having notable success in the field of deaf-mute education. If you find his methods suitable, I would be happy to act as your daughter's sponsor. England is lacking in suitably trained educators of the Oral method, and I am considering setting up a teacher-school to address the issue. Should your daughter's education proceed well, we would welcome her demonstration of Professor Bell's methods here in England."

I read the letter three times. Wasn't Bell the name of the professor Theresa Dudley had gone to study with? I gave Mama back the letter. I said, It is a kind offer.

It is exceptional, she said, and let the word sit heavy on me. No one refused Exceptional.

She squeezed my hand and shuffled along the seat until she was pressed right against me. The train was too thick with vibration for me to know what movement was hers, what was breath, speech, or the beat of her heart. I felt a hot scramble of desperation, as if I was trying to climb out of myself but couldn't get hold of any rungs. How could I tell her I didn't want this? I wanted only to join her in England. But Mama smiled on through the shuddering motions of the train. There is still time,

I thought. A few days together and Mr. Ackers's offer could become less exceptional. She could change her mind.

First, she said. Let's see about Mr. Bell. He might be an awful humbug.

Humbug was a big press and smack of her lips. She contorted her face so I laughed. Yes, I said, measuring the feel of my voice like Miss Roscoe had taught us. An awful humbug.

The parlor of the house in Pemberton Square was filled with gray-haired dignitaries. Councilmen, legislators and educators, I supposed, like the ones who visited the Oral School. My mother found us seats near the front where a stage area had been cleared in the bay window. There was a blackboard and three empty chairs. I stared at them and looked around for Theresa. My reservations had been replaced with curiosity. Was one of the chairs for her?

Everyone turned to get sight of Mr. Bell when he entered the room. He was slender-framed in the way of nervous young men, and on first sight not especially tall. His forehead sloped to his hairline as though it'd been pressed gently by a palm, and his dark eyes skipped across the crowd with a measure of uncertainty. He didn't look like the great professor Miss Roscoe had described or the one whose methods Mr. Ackers had so admired. But neither did he have the smooth confidence of a humbug. I glanced at Mama, trying to hide my hope that he was a disappointment. She just smiled back and patted my hand. And no one else looked surprised to see this restless, doubtful figure take the stage.

Mr. Bell took a small bow. As soon as he was upright a change came about him. He began speaking, drawing himself up with confident ease, one arm scooping circles of emphasis and his hand occasionally slicing downward. From this distance, his lips made no more than a tight twitching movement, but when I glanced around I saw how he had the audience's tranquil attention. Their fascination was only heightened when he picked up a stick of chalk and wrote a long string of symbols on the blackboard. He labeled them: "Visible Speech."

Then he raised a hand at the door and said, Ladies and Gentlemen. Allow me to present—

Three girls came into the room and sat down in the bay window. The eldest girl had bright chestnut hair, which she kept patting at her temples. Next to her was a younger girl who fixed her eyes on her folded hands in her lap. But it was Theresa who I couldn't stop looking at. She was in the finest dress I'd seen her wear, and looked paler and older than I remembered, her eyebrows floating as if she was fearfully astonished.

I tried to catch her eye, but Mr. Bell began talking, so I looked at my mother's notebook as she scribbled down his lecture. Between glancing at her written words and Mr. Bell's spoken ones, what I understood was this:

The three girls were Miss Isabel Flagg, a scholar of the Boston School for the Deaf, Miss Alice Jennings, the daughter of Reverend Jennings of Auburndale, and Miss Theresa Dudley, daughter of the Hon. L. J. Dudley of Northampton. They had been studying Mr. Bell's system of symbols for only a couple of months. As a result, they had attained power. Power over the instrument of speech. Such power that they could produce the elementary sounds of foreign languages, as well as English, by merely knowing these symbols.

He wished that special attention be directed to the case of Miss Dudley since she was a congenital deaf-mute.

After all the years at Miss Roscoe's school, Theresa finally was on the stage. The pinch of her face beneath those wavering brows suggested she wasn't altogether happy to be there, and my stomach began to twang with matching nerves. It was the same with all our performances at the Oral School. We prayed that we'd each do well, and Miss Roscoe would be pleased.

Mama was writing fast but she couldn't help her glances at the girls. There was a bewildered softness in her cheeks and jaw. It was evident that she was filled with more than ordinary hope about Mr. Bell.

Suddenly, I hoped that Theresa would perform badly.

The girls sat waiting for their cue. I could see no evidence of any notebooks. No bulge in their skirt pockets. Nothing propped up in the shadows under their chairs. Perhaps Theresa didn't need slates or notebooks anymore. Behind them the symbols hovered on the blackboard in rows of truncated circles and bars, like some sort of planetary code.

I looked down again at Mr. Bell's words in my mother's writing. "Power over the instrument of speech."

The audience were equally disbelieving. In the front row, heads began to shake and turn to one other. Smiling, Mr. Bell held up his finger, waiting for the hum in the room to stop.

He spoke and my mother wrote, "This is the system invented by my father. It is called Visible Speech."

He bowed his head at the girls. I saw him say Miss Dudley and would she honor us?

Theresa crossed the stage. She looked so different, as if she'd been wound up tight, her face oddly immobile. Arriving at Mr. Bell's side, she smiled at her teacher in a small flush of trust.

Mr. Bell turned to the audience. My mother wrote, "He freely invites us to dictate words in any language!"

People began calling out words. It looked as though a gust had blasted Theresa. She struggled to compose herself. I glanced around and saw what she did: the open-shut of numerous mouths, the visible excitement. On the stage, Mr. Bell wrote the new symbols so quickly, trying to keep up with the calls, that the bob of his hair shook furiously. His first piece of chalk snapped, and he needed to fetch another. By the time he was finished, the side of his hand was whitened, and a blade of chalk dust bisected the length of his sleeve.

He raised his hands. I saw him say Thank you and That is

Plenty. He turned to Miss Dudley, his own eyebrows lifting with a question. Miss Dudley?

Theresa looked at the blackboard, opened her mouth and moved her lips. The patterns made by her lips were different from her usual speech. They looked crisp, like a hearing person's. I couldn't shift my eyes from her mouth and its fluid, clean-cut shapes.

Then I looked at my mother because she wasn't writing anything. She was too busy watching. Her expression hovered between rapture and disbelief. Sorry, sorry! she said, when she saw me looking. She picked up the pen again. "She's speaking German! Now Japanese, says Mr. Bell. Zulu! German again, but with a French accent!"

I looked at the faces around me. There was no tightening of the eyes, no frowning or confusion, or any sign that Theresa couldn't be understood. Theresa looked into the audience, beaming with her own success, and didn't see me.

Mr. Bell thanked her and addressed the audience again. My mother wrote, "Slow, but you see how the articulation is perfect. The best thing," she continued, "is that Theresa does not know she uttered words at all."

That stalled me. I looked at the symbols loitering on the blackboard but could make no more sense of them than Arabic or Mandarin. But Theresa had the power of speech. How could she not know what she said? I looked at Mama, but she was watching the girls again, her cheeks glowing from the candlelight, and something worse: exhilaration.

"Relative Pitch." My mother underlined Mr. Bell's next words in her notebook.

Now Miss Jennings stood on the stage moving her lips and soon the audience was clapping. She stepped down and Miss Flagg was taking her place. The other girls smiled and exchanged glances. Mr. Bell rolled onto the balls of his feet, his hands sweeping up like hoisted flags. My mother's arm drifted on the page as she watched Mr. Bell make his announcement. "A song!" she dashed down. "Miss Flagg is going to sing!"

There were new symbols on the board. As Miss Flagg read them Mr. Bell moved his hand, sliding it through the air like a conductor. The shape of Miss Flagg's words varied in the length they remained on her lips, her chin was raised, her throat moved noticeably, her chest expelling some of the words with more force than others.

"And to think that she cannot hear her own voice!" my mother wrote. "It is a sweet song," she added.

The audience began to stand up. As they rose, the girls broke into smiles and reached for each other's hands. Mr. Bell looked so pleased I thought he would have swept his pupils into his arms had propriety allowed it. The pounding of applause made the floor shake under my feet.

Mama put down her pen and rubbed her wrist. She was still watching the girls. Desperation twisted inside me like the onset of nausea. I wanted to fetch her back to me. I wanted her to tell me I didn't need to speak like Theresa or sing like Miss Flagg. To scoff and say, Humbug! A charlatan. The worst sort of quackery. But she watched the stage, while easing the soreness in her arm. I looked at the symbols again. Their strange half-moons and hooked lines were like the mystery of Crusoe on my mother's lips, all those years ago. I stared at them until my eyes smarted. Then the girls were leaving the stage and filing out of the room, their exit as neat as their entrance. The demonstration was finished.

Truthfully, I was relieved that Theresa hadn't noticed me. I felt newly shy of her. Mr. Bell stepped down from the stage, disappearing into a circle of gentlemen, so that only the bobbing curl of his hair was visible as he nodded, receiving, I supposed, their praise and questions.

Perhaps my eyes were tired from watching the demonstration. Or it was the strain of swinging them between my mother's notebook and Mr. Bell's speech. My throat ached with thirst. The scratch when I swallowed, the dull throb in my chest. My thoughts were packed in tight like a pocket of stones. As my mother fetched her coat I noticed a brooch on its lapel, of four silver lemons. I started thinking about our orchards. One year she'd planted a lemon tree but nothing grew on it. Mary said it was lonely and so she planted three more, one for each of us, my father included. The lemons grew all summer, and we finished the year with bottles of homemade lemonade in our pantry.

How strange it was, therefore, that one of the men talking to Mr. Bell should be speaking of lemons. Lemonade, this gentleman was saying, leaning toward Mr. Bell. He had a wiry gray beard like a wolfhound's coat, but I saw his discussion of Lemonade all the same. This was what the girls needed, he said, and the other men agreed, and Mr. Bell smiled. Lemonade. They talked at length about Lemonade.

I was confused. Why should the girls require lemonade? Was that where they had gone? For refreshments?

My mother said, Stop staring, but it was too late. Mr. Bell had seen us. I felt my mother's alarm at my side, followed by her collecting breath. With Excuse Me on his lips he stepped away from the group and came right up to us. From this close distance, I saw each of his words clearly.

You are attentive, he said.

I knew I was often guilty of what Adeline once termed my bluntness. But how is one to get by on limited information without venturing a guess or two? So, before my mother had a chance to offer an apology for my intrusion, I had burst out: It isn't the season for lemonade!

I knew I had missed both taps of n and d so all that expired from my tongue was a long vibrating *ay*.

The gentlemen standing behind Mr. Bell looked at each other.

What was the girl speaking of? Shame snaked through me, and Mama's gaze pressed into my cheek like a hot coin.

But Mr. Bell understood. He leaned forward. I did not say Lemonade, he said, and fetched a small notebook from his pocket. Inside he wrote "Illuminate."

I stared at the word.

He continued writing, showing me his book between sentences, "You are quite right with your error... For Lemonade and Illuminate look similar... And I was just discussing with these gentlemen the similarity of many words in speech...and the difficulty they present for the speech reader... You have illustrated my point perfectly."

I felt a confusion of pride swirling through my embarrassment. I glanced at my mother to see if she'd read Mr. Bell's words, but he'd started engaging her in the business of our attendance. The demonstration, he said. Enjoyed it. He hoped we had.

My mother, to compensate for my folly, gave profuse reply. I saw mention of the tears to which she had been moved. But I'd not seen tears. Surprise at her lie bumped through me, and I felt shades of resentment for what now felt like her efforts— the picnic on the train, calling Mr. Bell a Humbug—to keep me on side. She gave an account of our names, our reason for coming, and of Mr. Ackers. I watched as she said, my daughter, she has been at an oral school for four years, but still, it is hard for people to understand her speech.

She tilted her cheek away from me as she spoke, but not as far as she might have liked, since Mr. Bell was directly in front of us both, so I caught enough of her words, and all of her meaning.

I see, Mr. Bell said.

He folded a card inside a letter which he handed her. He said how he took private pupils. I clearly had some talent for speech-reading. These were his terms and fees, but he would be happy to write to Mr. Ackers directly. He must go now. It was a pleasure meeting us. He nodded at my mother, his smile warm and agreeable.

In the hallway, people were pushing toward the door. If they knocked into us, I felt unsteady for other reasons. My mind cast back over the train journey and the Thank-Yous I'd issued to the men who carried our cases, the cold chicken I'd requested from the vendor, when I'd spoken to the conductor as I fetched my ticket. All that time Mama was forming an assessment about my speech; her praise for me was as false as the tears she'd confessed to Mr. Bell.

Now she was stooped under a wall sconce, opening the letter. I saw the first few lines. "Mr. A. Graham Bell begs to announce the opening of an Establishment for the study of Vocal Physiology; for the correction of Defects of Utterance and for Practical Instruction in 'Visible Speech.'"

It was fine penmanship. I thought of his symbols, shining at me from the blackboard. Theresa, her mouth moving with speech lifted straight out of the hearing world.

I took my mother's notebook and under her words that were Mr. Bell's words, I wrote, "I want to learn Visible Speech."

My mother glanced at the page and her nod was business-like as she tucked away the program and looped my arm through hers. We shall discuss it, she said. First, bonbons!

For the next few days, we didn't talk about Mr. Bell. We ate bonbons in Fera's Confectionery, waltzed across marble floors at Lorenzo Papanti's dance school and joined the crowds for the lyceum lectures at Tremont Temple, which Mama transcribed for me. We strolled amongst the bare nubs of winter shrubbery in the Public Gardens and talked like everyone around us was talking. There was no one else listening or watching to tell us it was otherwise. But after a while, it began to seem that we didn't talk about Mr. Bell because we didn't need to discuss the matter. It was already decided. The future was taking shape within the gaps of our conversation. And wasn't it an exceptional opportunity that only a fool would refuse?

Mama showed me her letter to Adeline with the terms of the arrangement. I would stay in Boston under Mr. Ackers's sponsorship for six months or until such time as I was able to exhibit my learning of Visible Speech. Then I would join her and Mr. Holmwood in London.

I nodded my agreement, and she sealed the envelope. If I hated that I'd be away from Mama for a second time, I couldn't blame anyone but Mama herself, and I was right in league with her.

5

]⋋ ∃[,]⋋ ℧[℧,]⋋ ∃]⋋℧

[I may, I need, I might]

ADELINE LARK lived in one of the beetroot-red houses in Boston's South End. It was called Little St. Clouds, by herself at least, after the hotel on Tremont Street, whose awnings could be glimpsed from the fifth-floor windows. The parlor was even longer than the one at Mr. Bell's demonstration, and was filled with books, ferns and ornaments along with two stuffed weasels by the fireplace, and a stack of dirty teacups. This would be my new residence in the hearing world. I tried to assume a haughty dignity, as if I was perfectly serene despite Mama's recent departure, but I could only achieve it by sitting rock-still and not touching a thing on the tea table.

My grandmother was talking so I tried to fix my eyes on her

words. It was something about Rules. She paused and waited. After a moment it was evident she was waiting for me so I said, Yes, of course.

A twitch ghosted through her features. Pay attention, she said, nodding her head slowly with each syllable. I nodded and wondered how near my mother was to Boston Harbor. Less than an hour had elapsed since our farewells, but already it felt longer.

She gazed at me. You are tired, she decided.

I said, I have a new notebook, and fetched the one Mama had bought me the day before. But Adeline dropped her eyes on it as if I'd pulled a dirty handkerchief from my bag. Her mouth sagged to match the limp extension of her hand as she held it out for my notebook. Then she wrote, "I will show you to your room."

Her writing was unnecessarily large as if she perceived me to have a problem with my sight or mental capacity. Thank you, I said, but she flinched.

I followed her up four flights of stairs. I couldn't help but cast my eyes around the huge house. Japanese leather on the walls glinted under a series of glass-and-crystal sconces, which lit our way from one flight to the next. I tried to picture my father as a child running along the narrow hallways, skittering down the servants' stairwell, but he seemed so wild and unrecognizable in my image of him that the thought was no comfort.

One object gave me pause. It was a bronze cast of the Roman god Mercury. I was remembering something Miss Roscoe had told us about Mercury being the God of Communication. Adeline saw me halt. She came over to me. You like it? she asked.

I dropped my eyes. Miss Roscoe told us that Mercury was also the God of Thieves since he was a trickster. We sensed a warning from her, but didn't know what it was for, or about, or why it was needed. It was yet another sum that didn't add up, but that we had to leave alone for lack of other options.

On the uppermost floor, Adeline bade me put down my case.

She fanned a hand at the room that was to be mine. There was a brass bed, a washbasin, a single desk and a Boston rocker. Next to the sash windows hung a colored lithograph of some marigolds. The view was to the rear and revealed endless fire balconies being crisscrossed by stray cats. There was a string of servant bells in the landing outside my room. I hoped Adeline would remember to think that if those bells rang, I'd not hear them. That gave my stomach a twist. Was anyone else up here in case of a fire? I'd never been so high as a fifth floor before. I crossed to the window and was relieved to see a small drop onto the fire balcony below.

Now that we were stationary, Adeline jotted down the names of the other people resident at Little St. Clouds. The two lodgers were Mr. Dupont and Mrs. Baylis, and the latter's great-nieces, Eva and Rhoda Day, were staying on vacation from Trenton. She handed me the paper. We dine at eight, she told me, and held up eight fingers. I nodded and wondered if I'd ever see the finger alphabet again.

I had several hours until the appointed dinnertime. My first in the hearing world without Mama or Miss Roscoe to guide me. I unpacked my notebooks and rearranged them on the desk several times. I studied the cheerless marigolds. I counted the cats on the fire balconies. I wished I'd brought more books and wondered where I could get some. I started a letter to the Oral School but hadn't much to report yet, and I'd already written about Theresa and the demonstration from my lodging rooms with Mama. I was so relieved when eight o'clock finally arrived that I almost skipped down the stairs to the dining room.

The lodgers were already taking their seats. The fare looked simple but the table was set with huge decorations: candlesticks and tall platters arranged with moss and fruit. The fruit had been glazed but the skins were wrinkled and the sheen looked dusty. Adeline sat at one end of the table and Mrs. Baylis's great-nieces on either side. Rhoda was a tall, sour-looking girl, with a ropy-looking plait pulled over her shoulder. Eva had bright eyes and an immovable smile, which was tiled with broad, healthy teeth. Both girls paused when I came in. Adeline waved a hand and introduction in my direction, then they said Good Evenings and continued their conversation.

At the other end was Mr. Dupont who I'd learn was spending a semester at Boston University. Mrs. Baylis, meanwhile, was visiting from New York. She had white hair plaited and smoothed into a bun, and spongy features. Everything was plain to see on her unadorned face, and I was relieved when Adeline indicated for me to sit next to her. Then there was a sixth gentleman-guest whom no one had introduced to me nor had Adeline written down his name. His extensive beard concealed his speech so I didn't fancy my chances of ever finding it out.

As soon as I sat down the diners disappeared behind the ornamentation. The Day sisters flitted between the candlesticks while the beard of the gentleman-guest levitated above the silver platters. Here at least was something to write my friends at the Oral School: in the hearing world candlesticks the size of small trees are commonplace dining decor and plates are stacked threefold high to bear fruit, whether that fruit is fresh or not. One must have a strategy—every deaf-and-dumb person knew that—which I could advise them on as well. I carefully took out my notebook and pen and placed it alongside my place mat.

As she was next to me, Mrs. Baylis was the only person in clear sightline, so long as I turned my head. She noticed my book and smiled but did not reach for it. She said Evening and Welcome and Was I very tired?

A little, I said, and opened my notebook to ask her about herself but just then my plate of food arrived, and I had to sit back from the table, the notebook flipping closed again. Mrs. Baylis started on her food straightaway so it didn't seem polite to request her attention. But after chewing a few mouthfuls of the hotchpotch, she said something. I slid the notebook to her so she could write it down.

"You don't look deaf-and-dumb," she wrote.

I looked up. Her smile was kind. I didn't know what to say. Thank you? Her lips moved with words that seemed like Very Pretty. When I didn't respond she took the pen again. "Do you know that hand-talk?" she asked. "I saw a performance at one of the Deaf Mute Asylums, it was a hymn I think, and it was astonishingly beautiful."

I replied, "I attended Miss Roscoe's Oral School so I don't know much of the sign language." It was truer to say I wasn't supposed to know it, but this didn't seem a distinction worth clarifying to Mrs. Baylis.

Ah, she said, and patted my hand when she finished reading. She took the pen. "Of course. You are not like them." She continued, "After the performance I saw them talking on the hands in the corridors and it was quite different." I looked up from her words and she grimaced to aid my understanding, while she flapped her hands in impression.

"It is an expressive system," I wrote, "in the same way hearing people have the tones of the voice. That is how you get the finer meaning."

Yes, she said, but looked unconvinced.

"Soon I will start with Mr. Bell at Boston University," I continued, writing as fast as I could to keep her attention from drifting to her hotchpotch. "So I shall understand about tone of voice myself." Then I wrote for a little while about Visible Speech.

Her face ignited with wonder. A miracle, she said.

If I felt a nub of guilt toward my friends at the Oral School, I let the feeling slip away. This was the hearing world and there was no place for the sign language within it. That was the entire point of Miss Roscoe's teaching and if I didn't learn how to get by here in Boston then how could I go to Mama and Mr.

Holmwood in six months? I didn't dare think of the cost of my sponsorship.

The cook came in and out with more dishes. She slipped me a piece of paper after the second course introducing herself as Joan, and asking if I would like trifle or blanc-mange? I was so happy to see some clear words I almost replied that I'd gladly help her bring them up. But I didn't know how to explain my leave of the table and supposed that it wouldn't fare me well in the eyes of Adeline, so I wrote my reply very formally—the trifle, please—although the smile I sent with it was a real one.

Then Mrs. Baylis was tapping my shoulder. Eva Day wanted my attention. She was waving a hand. I smiled at her although my heart set up a quick patter: she was still behind a candlestick, and I couldn't send my notebook easily across the table. There was a mountain range of plates, dishes and tureens between us.

Mrs. Baylis wrote it for me: "Eva says that your grandmother has told her you are very good at reading lips!"

I looked across the table at Eva's lips again, which were moving only slightly within the frame of her smile. She shifted so the candlestick was to the left of her face but it was still distracting. I didn't know if the candlestick or the smile was the greater problem.

You are smiling, I blurted out in explanation, but all that did was bring down her brow in a degree no less severe than that shown by Adeline.

The smile flickered with words that I knew too well to miss. Never Mind, she said.

The School of Oratory was located in the University buildings on Beacon Street, just along from the Athenaeum. Its facade was tall and narrow, the doors were black, and in spite of the large number of windows, it looked like a place that did not have much association with daylight. If I was impressed by its spindly grandeur, I was unsettled by its austerity. Adeline liked it better. The sight almost cheered her. Perhaps she thought it suited the task I was about to begin. Come on, she said, taking my elbow.

It was not Mr. Bell who opened the door but a woman. She had a triangular face pinned in the middle by her puckered lips, giving her a look of abiding consternation. After a few words with my grandmother, she whisked a notebook from her skirt pockets. Her name was Miss Lance, she told us, and she was Mr. Bell's assistant. I saw her lips say Oh dear, dear, as she glanced over her shoulders, into the hallway. "Mr. Bell has not arrived yet," she wrote. "Usually he is very prompt but come upstairs anyway." We followed her through the dim corridors and up the stairs. There were windows on each level, looking over the Granary Burial Ground. I was relieved to see some trees, even if they had their roots among the dead.

I looked around for other pupils but apart from a few teacherly types there didn't seem to be anyone else in the building. Surely I wasn't the only pupil here. Nerves crunched through me: I'd not been taught alone once at the Oral School. We stopped outside a room, and she raised a finger—one moment—and knocked twice, her ear held to the door. No, I saw her lips say. Not there. Let's go in. She waved a hand.

The room was sparsely furnished with green flocked walls and two chairs placed opposite each other. If it hadn't been for the mess of papers on the desk, and the blackboard smudgy with a previous lesson, I would have thought of a dentist's waiting room. I struggled to contain my disappointment. Was this really the place where the three finely attired girls at Mr. Bell's demonstration had studied?

The door flew open and in came Mr. Bell. He said, This terrible mess!

Hastily he gathered the papers. When he finished, his eyes rested on us. His words were clearly shaped. I saw him say something about his suspicions, followed by a second utterance of

Terrible, and two opposites Early and Late, each which came with a tap of his finger; the first one on his chest, the next one toward us.

I suspected he was saying, I'm terribly late but I hope it is you who are terribly early.

His lips took a blade's edge care with each word and leaned toward me in a very exact degree to show me where his attention was focused as he put his words between us, like arranging items on a table, although there was no force or strain on his face. I was flushed with relief to understand him.

Adeline was not impressed. She said, I'm afraid we are right on time!

Mr. Bell extended his hand to one of the two chairs. Please, he said.

I took a seat as Adeline left with Miss Lance. He reached for a notebook and spread it across his knee, but didn't write anything. Nor did he say anything although it seemed at any moment he might. There was a barely contained restlessness in the way he sat. His eyes settled on me, and I couldn't help smiling at the warmth and bustle of his consideration. It was as if a tuning fork had been struck within my being and he was listening without me needing to say anything at all. I thought I might break into laughter if he didn't say something soon, and that might even be his intention.

After a moment he said, Tell me how you came to Boston.

It was like I'd settled into a plush sofa, and I felt a greedy stirring to see more of his clear, steady words. I told him about Miss Roscoe's school and Mama's visit from England, and Mr. Ackers's letter. But I said more than I'd meant to, and his eyes started to show a faint strain so I guessed my voice was becoming slack. I stopped abruptly.

He picked up his pencil. "My estimate," he wrote, "is that you lost your hearing at six or seven years of age."

He turned the notebook to show me his words. In the slope

of his penmanship, a more orderly, and perhaps older, professor presented itself than the one seated opposite me.

I was very pleased at his guess. Actually, I said, although Actually was not a word I could really say at all. I was four.

Why had I not started with Thank You? I was quite well rehearsed in Thank You and it would have been better form besides. But Mr. Bell didn't frown or look alarmed. He took up the notebook again and wrote, "Let us discuss your modes of communication. You read lips and use notebooks. Do you know the manual alphabet or de l'épée signs?"

I hesitated, before answering, I know the American and British—

But I could not say Manual Alphabet easily so flashed ABC in the air with my fingers. My mother is English, I finished.

This interested Mr. Bell. English? he said, not bothering with the notebook. I'm from Scotland. He smiled at my surprise. His lip-shapes, I realized, were similar to Mama's. Surely that was one reason I'd understood him more readily: his accent must be British. I supposed it was the first thing people learned as soon as he opened his mouth. I felt a kick of betrayal that neither my mother nor Adeline had thought to tell me.

He bent over the notebook. "I would permit," he wrote, "the limited use of the American Manual Alphabet in this classroom but not the de l'épée signs. There will be no signs of any kind in the place of speech."

He turned the page, and I nodded to show my understanding. I'd not expected his rules to be any different from Miss Roscoe's and who would I use hand-talk with besides? There were no other pupils to draw into conversation.

He continued writing for some time, pressing the pencil harder than seemed necessary. We would use a notebook, he wrote, as it was the most effective way of conveying the material. In time, we would progress to viva voce and speech-reading. Some of the terms were quite technical. In the lesson we would only speak or write. Did I understand? At home I must practice very hard if I expected to see any kind of improvement.

I read his words and nodded again, wishing that he would put down the notebook and speak to me again with that careful, clear manner. It was not so different from Mama's way of talking to me. But he kept his head bent over the page and wrote, "This book is intended to record the progress made by Miss Ellen Lark in gaining complete command over the movements of the vocal organs." He continued down the neatly ruled page: "Plan of Daily Instruction."

I didn't understand half of the things he wrote but made a note of the main headings for they seemed like impressive things to tell Mrs. Baylis over dinner. I would study two strands, these being Articulation and the Culture of the Voice. The last one consisted of Timbre, Duration, Force and Pitch. Every day I would need to study the elementary symbols and take a reading lesson with Roman letters.

You are curious?

I realized I was leaning forward in my seat in my attempt to read his handwriting upside down. I brought my finger and thumb together with less than an inch between them: a little. Then I remembered what Mr. Bell had said about not using my hands, and put them back in my lap.

He didn't notice, or chose not to. Instead he took a piece of unwrapped chalk directly out of his pocket and rose from his chair. Mr. Bell, I said before I could stop myself. Your pocket!

I blushed at my outburst, fearing that I was no better than Adeline for my judgment although I knew that I already liked his disordered ways. Mr. Bell peered down at his pocket, inserting a finger into the lip and drawing it open so he might see inside.

White, he said, laughing. Like the moon!

He looked at me with awful seriousness. Several pupils, he said, have looked horrified. Now I know why—he finished, tapping the side of his head to signify this new knowledge. I smiled because I could see his own smile starting to crinkle his eyes. I wondered if he'd chosen Horrified on purpose. I'd have no chance at spotting a word like Aghast.

I took the notebook. "There is a groove in the blackboard," I wrote, pointing at the board when he looked up from my words.

Good idea, he said but he didn't cross over to the board, and reached for the notebook instead. "My landlady will admonish me," he wrote, "for my pockets. She already cuts my candles in half."

I frowned and blinked, meaning to convey my bewilderment. I signaled for the notebook, "But light is so precious at this time of year," I wrote. "Why would she do that?"

"It is for my own good, so I go to bed before midnight. But sometimes I think my mother has a hand in it. She is always advising everyone on my health."

I was delighted at this unexpected idle chat. Wasn't this the kind of trivial subject that people told me it was no matter to miss? Then I wondered what was wrong with Mr. Bell's health. Was this another fact that Adeline and Mama knew which I was only learning? That is a late hour, I said, trying out my voice again.

Not as late as five o'clock in the morning.

Surely not, I said, making my best show of being shocked.

He seemed pleased. Ah, but those are the best hours!

Now he did rise from his chair and step to the blackboard. I felt a grab of disappointment at his departure, but he put the chalk in the blackboard's groove and took out not one but three more pieces of chalk from his pocket, placing them in a line. He turned in time to catch my smile. Gratified, he began chalking out a picture. When he finished, he stood back to let me examine his creation.

It was a cross section of a face. It showed the cavity of the mouth, sealed off by the teeth at the front with a wide-open throat at the back. The tongue was in the middle like a soft muscly foot. The teeth didn't fan around the mouth, but protruded like a pair of spikes from the gums.

"It's a face," I wrote.

Good, he said, and started rubbing away some lines while leaving others. Soon I began to see them: the horseshoes and vertical dashes of the symbols I'd seen the girls read at the demonstration.

He pointed at the curved line where the tongue had touched the teeth, and instinctively I touched my own tongue against my teeth. He was sitting down again with the notebook while gesturing at the symbols behind him.

"Good," Mr. Bell wrote. "Now push the air through your throat. Good. You just said 't.'"

Next he pointed at the horseshoe that replaced the lips, and I closed my lips.

"Add voice through your throat. Excellent. You just said 'b.'"

B was made of two symbols, a curve for the lips, and a line for the throat, to show that air was passing through it.

He wrote how you could combine the elementary symbols to make more complex symbols. All the consonants had a horseshoe curve that represented the position of the tongue while the vowels had a straight line for the aperture of the mouth. There were glides, hooks, crossbars. Tiny squiggles indicated suction, tones, trilling and even inflection.

He pointed again at the curved line meaning "lips" and I lightly touched my lips together. But next he drew a small line inside the curve. "That means 'shut'," he wrote, so I shut my lips more firmly. I kept my lips clamped together as he closed off the curved line with a new line at its neck, so it was a semicircle. "This straight one means 'voice.'" Next he made the line wavy, like the outline of a nose. "This is nose. So you have lip-shut-voice-nose. Go on."

I tried to push a sound through my nose.

"There is no voice coming out through your nose."

He showed me his words, and I released the seal of my lips, feeling my breath collapse inside me. I couldn't help my disappointment, or my wish that we would go back to our earlier chatter in the notebooks. Does your mother suggest cures for your health? I would ask him. For I knew all about cures, that endless quest.

He reached into his other pocket and this time took out a white glove and canary feather. He held up the glove, which had been marked on the fingers with letters from the alphabet. Not this, he said, and stuffed it back into his pocket. That is for the children. This, he said, holding up the feather.

I didn't think the feather seemed any less appropriate for a child than a labeled glove, but I didn't say anything. Instead I wrote, "Who are the children? Do they come here?"

"No, I teach the children at the Boston school. I've always loved teaching children. But also, I am a tutor for a child in Salem. That is where I reside, with the boy's family."

I revised the image I'd made earlier of Mr. Bell living in a shabby boardinghouse with a landlady who mercilessly severed his candles to save money. Surely this was a family of some means if he resided as their child's tutor, and they had a genuine concern for his night-owl habits.

Here, he said, raising the feather. A downy puff of barbs surrounded its quill while the rest was a smooth yellow oval. He held it under my nose and lifted his eyebrows to indicate I should try again.

"The feather will move," he wrote, "when the sound has passed satisfactorily through the nose. That is not bad. Now try 'P' from the lips. This is the basis of a universal alphabet. It is called Visible Speech. Every letter, and every part of a letter, has a definite physiological meaning. In this way, you can represent any sound that the human mouth can make, so that another person should be directed how to utter it."

But the triumph I'd felt on ruffling the feather had faded. I saw again those girls talking on the stage, speaking languages from around the world. Was this how they had begun? Their first lesson, making a *mmmm* sound through their noses and blowing a feather from Mr. Bell's palm?

Mr. Bell was watching me. He wrote, "One day your voice will move more than a feather, I can assure you."

I thought of asking if I might move a roomful of gentlemen to their feet. I thought of the Day sisters, the long evenings sat in the parlor with not a word to be grasped. If I conquered the feather, might I move Adeline to laugh or stir Mr. Dupont to a response? Could I fold myself into a tête-à-tête with Mrs. Baylis or cause Mama's face to slacken in astonishment? Theresa had done it, hadn't she?

I took the feather and placed it on the back of my hand. Pursing my lips, I made a firm *puh* along its barbs, my breath spilling over my wrist.

That is excellent, he said. Visible Speech is not easy, he added, leaning in as though others were in the room who must be kept out of earshot. But I think you will do very well.

6

ӨГѠ ОГОЈ ӨЈ⋏ Ɫ ОЈ⋏

[Bid papa buy a pie]

I KEPT the feather in my pocket like a talisman even though it could do little but tell apart my *B*s and *P*s. At night I practiced with my head resting on the pillow, the feather and its telltale barbs a few inches from my lips. Puh, puh, puh, I said while Adeline's boarders slept in the rest of the house. The feather didn't grimace or puzzle at my utterances. It fluttered, as if stroked by my words.

Soon there was an ivory plug as well as the feather. I needed to bite down and not let it fall from my teeth while I spoke. Mr. Bell gave me a small book called a "Progressive Indicator" which was filled with symbols. Closed and open horseshoes, lines with hooks at each end, 3s that were not threes and *W*s that were not double-Us, and elongated s-shapes like the raised heads of a snake.

"Read this line," he wrote, and glided his pen across my Progressive Indicator.

I read it carefully. "Read the next one," he said.

I watched the flash of his pale wrist as he worked his pen across the page. He wrote, "Look at the two symbols. Name them. You see they are the same except that the breath is divided in this one. It is very important to do this perfectly."

When I tried to divide my breath, he wrote, "The voice must stop here." He drew a line in the notebook.

I interspersed his instructions with my questions. "What is this dash?" I asked, pointing at the line inside a horseshoe.

"That is throat-sound," he wrote, "or what we call the voice."

Buh and Duh had throat-sound while Puh and Tuh had none. It made me think of the river in Pawtucket that ran freely all the way to Slater Mills where it met with wheelpits, sluices, dams and spillways. Throat-sound flowed up from inside you until it was chopped and spliced and segmented by the busy factory of the mouth, departing from your body as words.

Words like *purr* and *curr*. I purred, I curred, until his pen attacked the page again. "Take in plenty of air and make the vowel long. You need not shut your mouth when you take in breath. Let the air go in through the mouth and nose."

Next came *curt* and *pert*, *Turk* and *kirk*. I tried to feel the symbols exactly in my mouth, matching myself to them. Mr. Bell treated the words as if their purpose was no more than instruction, but I couldn't help sentences arising in my mind. The Turk was curt but I didn't know what a kirk was to be pert.

Kirk, I said. Pert.

Good, he said. His pen again: Err, fir, her, fur, turf, earth, firth, Perth, eat, eke.

"Do not put the tongue between the teeth," he wrote. "Do

not sound the voice until the tongue is in the right position. Do not move the tongue till the voice has stopped."

My tongue went back and forth like a rower at the oars. It tapped the teeth for Earth and stoppered all breath in the throat for Eke like a plug dropped into a sinkhole, releasing it again in a small explosion. Eke, eke.

I wanted to master Visible Speech. I wanted to please Mr. Bell and have Mama and Adeline pleased because of his approval. But I also wanted him to put down the notebook, the indicator, the feather and ivory plug and wander off into conversation again. I waited for those moments when he'd look up from the notebook, a blade of interest slicing along his gaze, and I would smile, knowing that he was about to waver off course.

Now it came. He tapped Perth but when I started to repeat the symbols he held up his finger, and asked, Do you know where Perth is?

I shook my head. And I don't know what a kirk is, I said.

He fetched a map, which he spread over the table and planted his finger in the middle of Scotland, withdrawing it to reveal the bold lettering of Perth amongst a litter of place names.

I leaned over the map. Perth, I said. And kirk?

A Scottish church, he replied, leaning forward as well. When we have finished our lessons, you will know all about Scotland.

He was close, his shoulders tipped over his homeland. You must miss Scotland, I said but he shrugged. In Brantford, he said, there are Scots everywhere! Some of the towns around there even look like Edinburgh.

I smiled. Edinburgh especially was a generous word to spot on the lips. How long had it been since I'd understood anyone so clearly? Mr. Bell was unlike any teacher I knew. He was so strange and curious with his shabby broadcloth suits, quick movements and bright eyes. I didn't know where our conversations might turn, and yet I could follow each diversion because he never broke eye contact and knew how to take my understanding with him. There were very few people with that talent. Even in this drab room, with the plain notebooks and chalk dust, it was thrilling.

My mother was happy to return to England, I said, after my father died.

He looked at me, and I wished I could take the words back. But he said, I understand, and added something about his brother. His brother had died, which was why his family had left London, where they had lived after Edinburgh.

I studied his words and tried to summon their shapes again in my mind because I was sure I'd seen Died and didn't want to take a wrong step on such a topic.

Your brother, I said. I'm sorry.

My brothers. Two brothers. He held up two fingers. My only brothers. They both died of—

But I missed the disease that had taken his brothers, same as I'd missed the plural *s*. Two brothers, not one. I started to nod but it was no use hiding my confusion from Mr. Bell. The great white plague, he said, repeating himself. Tuberculosis. And he did something he'd never done in our lessons before, spelling the T and B on his fingers.

I was hasty with my condolences for a second time, embarrassed that I'd caused him to spell out the situation so exactingly, even bending his own rules about adhering to speech and notebooks. I thought of his parents, and their concern for his health made sense. He was their sole surviving child.

The air must be much cleaner in Canada, I said. I wanted to add how I'd been sent away from my home too, and that was also in the name of a cure, and everything depended on what Mr. Bell could do with my speech and lip-reading if Mama was to be happy.

He smiled. That is exactly what my mother said! She was right, of course.

He hesitated, as if this was an admission he hadn't meant to make. He seemed younger and newly uncertain. I smiled at him, and picked up the notebook, thinking to smooth over the moment. The kirks in Perth, I said, are in the firs and turf.

His chin lifted with laughter. Perfect, he said. He took the notebook and added, "In Canada the Scots put maple syrup on their porridge, and that I am very happy with."

Soon Mr. Bell only had to write down the most difficult phrases. The pages of our notebooks became a constellation of words hinting at varied subjects. East Wind, he wrote. Courtesies, Sermons, Physiology. Every night, when I finished my Visible Speech practice, I would turn to these pages and piece our conversations back together. It was like meshing real, tangible words into a net that could be drawn tight on my loneliness at Little St. Clouds. I carried our conversations in my head as I went about Boston. I thought of them as I watched people walking together, their cheeks turned to one another. I didn't envy them like I might have once done. That was how Mr. Bell and I talked. We were hardly different.

But I was careful writing to Mama and Mary. I didn't want them to think our lessons wandered away from Visible Speech, or that I had an infatuation. He was my teacher, and several years older, although I didn't know how many. The Day sisters had other ideas and were merciless gossips, having heard from Adeline about his shabby suits, ill-combed hair and interest in afflicted people. Mr. Bell was the ceaseless word on their lips. They thought nothing was higher than romance, and that I should not be setting my stall too high anyway. To them, Mr. Bell sounded perfect.

I ignored them. I didn't think any man had confided in the Day sisters like Mr. Bell had with me. I remembered his brothers, and how he had trusted me with his sadness, and I felt a new kind of responsibility.

But I selected some conversations to describe in my letters to Mama, meaning to demonstrate how I was maturing from the girl she had collected from the gates of Miss Roscoe's school.

"His own mother is deaf," I told her, "so he has seen firsthand our struggles. It is natural that he should see the true use for his father's Visible Speech symbols." In another letter, I wrote, "Mr. Bell tells me that he always walks from the train station to his parents' home, even if it is the middle of the night! It is many hours across the hay fields, but he loves the solitude. Nonetheless he says that the worst thing he can imagine is to feel that solitude in a room full of people."

I signed off each letter with my name in Visible Speech.

Mary's replies were rushed and apologetic, having been composed between one baby's feed and another child's tantrum. She usually managed to include some strident but hasty, half-spelled-out advice, such as "Remember, a pretty voice isn't the most useful thing in the world." She was hauling fruit tubs in Ohio, despite her hopes of escaping rural life in Pawtucket, and I ignored her remarks. Besides, Mama's letters were full of praise, and more than anything I wanted her to bring good news to Mr. Ackers so that I could join her in London.

"It thrills me," Mama wrote, "to think of all you are learning. Keep at your lessons thoroughly and you will be with us in London in no time at all. Mr. Bell sounds like a most unusual teacher. Mr. Ackers tells me that he is exceptionally talented at the piano and famous for his declamations of Shakespeare as well. When he was only a boy, he made a speaking automaton! I suppose his father being a philologist gave him the idea."

I read her letters several times, storing inside of me her praise for whenever my Visible Speech practice felt too exhausting.

I wrote letters to Miss Roscoe and my old friends at the Oral School too. I told them to have hope. The hearing world could be mastered through study. I included easy samples of Visible Speech and gave the English translations and how they could be practiced. I knew Miss Roscoe would pass the letters around the classroom, although she didn't permit direct letter-writing between her pupils. It was the only contact I could hope for with my old friends.

7

∩ʃ ʃϖ l ◖Iᴙ3ʃᴄ◖ ◖ϖʃᴙ⸋ᴙᵧ
[She is a perfect treasure]

ONE EVENING at Little St. Clouds, Mr. Dupont strutted through the parlor. When he spotted me he came over and dropped himself lightly on the sofa. I was looking through my notebook and its assortment of jotted-down phrases. Mr. Dupont looked at my book, and leaned forward as if to take it, then hesitated, unsure of the correct form. I smiled, turned to a clean page and handed it to him. Thank you, he said, and grasped my pencil too.

I expected some remark on the day but instead he wrote, "I had the good fortune to meet Professor Bell at the University today. He spoke most highly of you."

I was more pleased than I allowed myself to show. I wrote, "He is a generous teacher."

"Yes, he told me all about his fascinating Visible Speech system. His knowledge of the Human Voice is impressive, but did you know that he was awarded the professorship although he does not have an academic degree?"

Mr. Dupont's eyes betrayed a close keenness for me to fully digest this fact about my teacher, although I didn't care one whit whether Mr. Bell held a degree or not. I tried to remember what field Mr. Dupont specialized in but only remembered it was to do with French Literature.

"The School of Oratory has an excellent faculty," he continued. "There is Professor Raymond who is the Delineator of Shakespearean Character, Mr. MacKaye who lectures on Aesthetics and the Dramatic Art and Mr. Bashford who is most knowledgeable on Rhetoric. And of course, Professor Bell who specializes in the Instruction of Deaf-Mutes. A noble cause, everyone is agreed, but a curious addition to the faculty."

He showed me these words rather than let me have the notebook. I felt irritation rip through me. Mr. Bell was certainly a curious person but I didn't like the way Mr. Dupont had conveyed it. When my eyes reached the bottom of the page, he shifted the book back onto his knee and continued: "His father, Professor Melville Bell, is a truly great scholar. Did you know he was the one who invented Visible Speech? But he had different ideas for its uses such as diplomats acquainting themselves with foreign languages or imperial states diffusing their mother-tongues to the most remote of dependencies. He is such an estimable philologist! It gives cause to wonder what he has made of his son's work with deaf-mutes."

He gave me the notebook with a faultless smile and waited while I read as if each faculty member's name ought to stun me while the grand schemes for Visible Speech would pinpoint the lowly use Mr. Bell had put it to: namely, myself. I skipped over the words quickly and wrote, "Are you one of the esteemed faculty members yourself?"

He glanced at me, hesitating. Then he wrote "I am making a course of study with Professor Raymond."

I wrote, "Well, I am sure you can hope for a similar greatness in time."

His face puckered, and he penned his next words almost as if he meant to assault the page. "Miss Lance," he continued, "says she has nicknamed him the Night Owl because he does all his work in the small hours and sleeps until midday as a result! He spends half his time in a mechanic shop so that he comes to the School with oil on his sleeves. It is a most irregular way to conduct a daily schedule."

I was about to reply, but Eva and Rhoda Day came over before I had the chance. I supposed they were amazed that I'd stirred this moody boarder from his silence and had the audacity to make our conversation out of their reach. Eva said, What are you talking about?

Rhoda peered down at my Progressive Indicator. Russian, she said. That's Russian.

I shook my head but she said Uncle. Something about her uncle knowing Russian. Then she pointed at the book and said, Read us some.

I was still feeling hot all over from Mr. Dupont's onslaught in my notebook, but I read out a line: She is a leering little charmer.

Then I looked at Rhoda and said as tidily as I could, Is it Russian?

Rhoda burst out laughing and clapped her hands. Again! she said.

A leering little charmer, I repeated. Then I read:

A writer of pretty lyrics.

A person of discretion.

The man is a drunken wretch.

My gaunt old aunt told us all.

Mr. Dupont stared as if he didn't know whether to be astounded or appalled that he'd even considered a tête-à-tête with me. Who was I calling a drunken wretch so immaculately? Could, I wanted to ask him, the esteemed professors of the Oratory School pull off a feat as impressive as that?

The next day I arrived for my class to find Miss Lance on the doorstep talking to a young woman about my own age. I had seen her once or twice before, chatting away to Miss Lance, and assumed she was one of Mr. Bell's student teachers who belonged on the upper floors of the building and studied alongside Miss Lance. Neither of them had spotted me so I waited on the sidewalk. The girl had a mirthful face with large, clever eyes. Her hair was so long that its ends swirled on the bustle of her dress. Watching her I realized she was far too well dressed to be one of the teacher-students. But she couldn't be Mr. Bell's pupil either since she spoke and understood Miss Lance so easily.

I hung back, not wishing to interrupt, but Miss Lance spotted me. She turned to her companion and said, Mr. Bell's next pupil is here.

The woman glanced at me. Good afternoon, I said. Her gaze flickered, her smile was uncertain. Good afternoon, she answered, cutting the words quite crisply.

Miss Lance must have heard a noise because she looked into the hallway. The young woman didn't react. She only turned when Miss Lance said, Excuse me, and set off down the hall. I considered her again. I said, Are you Mr. Bell's pupil?

She frowned and a word that looked like Pardon folded her lips.

Pupil, I signed, then rang my hand at my ear. Bell. I pointed at her with my fist, keeping my finger tucked politely inside, so I wasn't pointing directly at her.

She gazed at my hands then looked at me. There was a red tinge in her cheeks. She smiled and shifted uncomfortably. I felt heat rise in my own cheeks. If I'd forgotten Mr. Bell's rule about the sign language, she clearly hadn't. Shame squeezed me. It was simply what I'd done with the pupils at Miss Roscoe's school as soon as Miss Roscoe was out of sight. Was this fine young woman going to tell Mr. Bell?

I'm sorry, I said, using English again. Her smile twitched with bewilderment. She said something in reply. I smiled and nodded, but of course she knew that trick of pretending. We both glanced down the corridor for Miss Lance, but couldn't see her and had to turn back to each other. The moment seemed to swell like a bee sting. I started searching for pen and paper. I managed to find my pencil but my notebook had slipped to the bottom of my bag. My hapless search seemed to stir my companion and shortly she was offering her own notebook.

Here, she said. She wrinkled her smile almost apologetically. The notebook was of a very ordinary kind and she flipped straight to the back pages. She paused as if she didn't know what to write. Then she scribbled something while supporting the book against her palm. I couldn't help wondering: which conversants did she relegate to the back page? The last page was finite. It suggested your expectations of a conversation's length. Or was her notebook so full of words in spite of her easy speech that the back page was the quickest blank page to find?

"I'm Mabel Hubbard," I read, when she turned the book. The words sprang off the page, knocking aside our awkwardness. I had an urge to sink closer toward this possibility of comradeship that seemed to be extended along with her name. "I'm studying Visible Speech with Professor Bell. I traveled here from Cambridge on the stagecoach. My mother frets, but I like the journey."

I looked up and she handed me her pencil with a half-shrugging smile that seemed to say, Well, go on, take it, you might as well.

I wrote my name and added, "I'm staying with my grandmother in the South End."

I hesitated before putting down the South End. It was hardly Cambridge or even the Back Bay, and wouldn't Adeline want me to give a more prepossessing account of myself? I could imagine Adeline's reaction if I described Miss Hubbard and her place of residence. And I'd never held another deaf person's notebook before. At Miss Roscoe's school we were supposed to speak, and anything we did write was on a slate. I desperately wanted to know what conversations of Miss Hubbard's the notebook contained. Was Mr. Bell in there? Had he penned his ranging and roaming conversations in her notebooks, too? Did she know about his brothers, his life in Canada, his lonely moonlit walks across the hay fields? Before I could stop myself, I wrote, "You are very talented with your eyes. I saw you talking so easily to Miss Lance."

She laughed. "I lost my hearing when I was four," she wrote back, "so I learned English like other children."

I lifted my eyebrows to show my enlightenment. Well, that explains it, I meant to convey. I wasn't going to say that I also lost my hearing when I was four, but never talked to Miss Lance so easily as that. Perhaps she had known Miss Lance a long time. I smiled, hoping to win her over. After all, wasn't the back page a place for jokes and banter? And she had turned to it because there might be informality between us. Perhaps my earlier mistake of attempting signs was rectified.

"Cambridge is a pleasant place," I wrote back, although I'd never been.

"Do you know it?"

But Miss Lance returned with apologies on her lips and ushered me inside. Goodbye, I saw Miss Hubbard say, although I thought I spotted the slide of relief in her face. It was only in the corridor that my prickles of panic returned. Would she mention to Mr. Bell that I had used the hand-talk? I'd forgotten how my tendency to gesture was a habit buried deep inside me. I'd humiliated Miss Hubbard with it, suggesting that she was akin to myself. As I followed Miss Lance upstairs, I wondered if I could write her a note asking that she didn't mention it to Mr. Bell.

Miss Lance must have noticed something about my mood, for at the top of the stairs she wrote down Mabel's name and showed me, saying: That was Miss Hubbard. Then she wrote, "Her father has campaigned widely to establish articulation schools for deaf-mute children. I believed he visited your little school several times."

I thought back to the gentlemen who'd visited us at the Oral School but they blurred together, a mass of whiskered faces, and I couldn't recall anyone who'd borne a resemblance to Miss Hubbard. Did she go there? I asked. I don't remember her.

Oh no, came the reply.

Of course not, I thought. Probably she had private tutors. Still, I wished that Miss Lance hadn't interrupted us and hurried me inside.

As I followed her up the stairs, I wondered about Miss Hubbard's speech and speech-reading. Did those words from her mouth sound as much like a hearing person's as they looked? I knew I couldn't be as good as Miss Hubbard. Mr. Bell never reacted to a misspoken or smudged word when we wandered into conversation, but Adeline was still prone to wincing, and Eva Day frowned openly at me. Doubt rocked through me as we waited at Mr. Bell's door. I had no way of knowing the truth, other than by the constant mirrors of other people. Mr. Bell's praise was the greatest mirror of all, as he measured this part of myself of which I had no idea, and never would: my voice.

Inside the classroom, he was bustling with his own private thoughts. It was plain that he was in a good mood. He crossed over to his desk and said, Ah! for no clear reason. Then he came back and circled his chair before sitting in it, which he did with a little flick of his wrists, placing his palms with extravagant smoothness on his knees. He appeared filled with equal amounts of merriness and distraction for which the only outlet was these detours and flourishes. I calculated I must be his fourth pupil that afternoon. There was no doubt about it: he was feeling revived after his last one, and that was Miss Hubbard.

Good afternoon, he said, and I answered: It has been a long afternoon for you, I think?

Long, yes, he said, as if he had just remembered. Yes, four hours. But for me the afternoon is like the morning.

Your landlady does not trim your candles anymore?

He smiled. I have bought some new ones, he said. She doesn't know where they are. He tapped his nose and winked, so I couldn't help the smile that broke in me. Now then, he said, and fetched our notebook.

My heart sank and I felt the burn of my impatience as Mr. Bell marked out the day's Visible Speech lesson. He drew three cuts of the human head on a clean page in my notebook and wrote under them the consonant *r*.

I didn't like *r*. It was hard to see on the lips, its movement depending on its placement in the word. In Arm or Barb, the lips didn't pucker and the *r* was invisible. But in other words, like Fear and Moor, you could detect it slightly in the wrinkling corners of the mouth.

"There are three symbols for *r*," Mr. Bell wrote. "You are familiar with the first two which gives us words like Reef and Shirt. Today I wish to pay attention to the third symbol which is a wide variety of the *a* sound, heard before *r*, as in Air, Care and Bear."

He showed me the symbol which looked like a skinny, elongated *c*. "The cavity between the tongue and gum is slightly smaller, while that behind the tongue is larger."

He wrote a list of words with Visible Speech next to them. Then he covered up the words and bade me read the symbols.

I did so, trying to keep in mind the words I knew I must be reading: Air, Fair, Rare.

He watched me. I read them for a second time while thinking how Miss Hubbard had sat in this same chair not more than fifteen minutes before me. Would I talk with her again? Now that I knew she was Mr. Bell's pupil, I realized how Miss Lance had made no effort to introduce us. I started to wonder about his other pupils too. Usually there was such a throng of university students in the corridors that you couldn't identify Mr. Bell's deaf pupils. Or, had I been passing them by all the time?

Mr. Bell showed me his next word, which was Azure. He had written, "This word similarly begins with our widened 'a' sound, and it ends with 'glide' symbol."

I strained my concentration but it was like trying to swerve a fast-rolling cart. When did anyone have occasion to say Azure? It was a word I'd scarcely seen in books. Did people use it in common daily talk?

Azure, I said, feeling the long slide of breath from my teeth.

No, he said. Try again.

Azure, I said for a second time. Could Miss Hubbard say Azure? Four years old, same as I. Was it the scarlet fever that stole her hearing too?

"Too far forward," Mr. Bell wrote. "The tongue is lifted so that the sound passes easily into the consonant."

I took the notebook and wrote, "Mr. Bell, forgive me, but what use is the word Azure in ordinary conversation? Is it something people say very often?"

Mr. Bell looked at me and blinked. Then he laughed. Azure, he said, with a musing nod. He pointed to his eyes: Azure eyes? Out the window: Azure sky? He spread his hands; You're right. What does one call Azure?

"Lapis Lazuli," I wrote. "That is Azure. Some birds I have seen in books. A kind of jay and a magpie. But wouldn't it take a poet to talk of the sky and oceans in that way? I have never seen Azure in a conversation but maybe I do not know what to look for and people are saying Azure all the time. Is that true? Mr. Bell, can I tell you that I would be very afraid to say Azure if I didn't know whether it was commonly said. We have had many conversations now and I do not think I have seen Azure in one of them."

Mr. Bell was laughing. I stand corrected, he said. As you know, I am a great believer in usefulness.

I watched his lips. Believer. Useful. What did Mr. Bell believe? That one day Visible Speech would have me talking amongst my peers and taking ready sight of their speech like a hearing person? Or would I be just good enough, and how good was that? Every lesson he pushed me toward this goal, but he never said how near I was or how much further I had to go. One day, he'd promised, I'd move more than a feather, but when would that day come?

I remembered Mary, and how our home-signs were our first response, the quick burst of instinct lifting our hands. She talked to my eyes and didn't bother with my ears. She was my first teacher, I realized, not my mother. Most of the ideas I had of the other children in Pawtucket, the goings-on in our lane, the whole world in fact, were because of what she told me with her hands. Suddenly her absence appeared like a huge hole that I felt I would stumble into, if I wasn't careful.

But I wasn't careful. In a rush, I said, Mr. Bell, do you think signs can be useful? More useful than knowing how to say Azure, perhaps?

He looked at me. I saw the flicking *L* and press of the *P* that Miss Roscoe's lips had made that day she struck a line through the French word on the board. The de l'épée signs? he asked.

It was too late to take back the question. I nodded. He paused before picking up the notebook. "It depends what you mean by useful," he wrote. "Deaf people may like signs because they are easy for them, but that ease is dangerous. Signing isolates them from society. It isolates them from their own family. Therefore, signs are only useful in a very limited way. Deaf children especially should be kept apart to avoid the temptation."

It took me a while to read his words. Temptation. Was that the name for the instinct that had made my hands jump when I'd met Miss Hubbard?

Miss Lark, he said, when finally I looked up. Do you disagree? Then he took his notebook. "We have worked so hard," he wrote. "Your mother the same. Think of your sponsorship. This is because we believe you can belong in the hearing world. You question it now?"

His sternness wasn't unfriendly, but there was an obvious puzzlement in his face that loosened a coil of guilt in me. He was right. What was all our work for? I knew from Miss Roscoe's school that signs had such a hold on your mind that it made you want to give up on spoken English, however hard you tried otherwise. That was why she put us in the cupboard, or tied our hands down. Perhaps that was why Mabel Hubbard was so good at speech-reading. She'd never had the chance to be tempted. I thought of her on the doorstep, and all the times I'd mistaken her for a teacher-student. She didn't exude loneliness: far from it.

I question Azure, I said eventually.

He smiled. You are right on that point. Everything will be ordinary blue from now on!

Blue eyes, I said. Blue skies.

Exactly, he answered. Plain blue is good enough for me.

I smiled but I couldn't help the thought: plain blue, just so long as it is uttered perfectly.

Soon afterward my lessons were moved to the evenings. Mr. Bell said he was teaching more pupils and his timetable was becoming full. I didn't see Miss Hubbard again, although I kept a lookout for her. But the building was nearly empty at that hour, even Miss Lance had gone home. If I regretted not seeing Miss

Hubbard, I liked that Mr. Bell opened the door himself. He was
at his most cheerful in the evenings. And sometimes it was as if
we were alone in the School of Oratory, our classroom soaked
in the twilight that pinked the sky outside the windowpane. I
imagined our conversations rising through the stillness of the
deserted teaching rooms, as if we were the life of the place.

One evening, on the last lesson before the summer vacation,
Mr. Bell turned and looked out of the window. He said Gardens. You will be walking in the gardens.

Gardens? I asked. You mean the Public Gardens?

Gardens? Mr. Bell repeated, surprised.

I thought furiously. What looked like Gardens? He had been
looking at the window, and it was dark beyond the panes. When
he said Gardens again his lips flashed with another word: Darkness. He meant that I would be walking in the darkness. I
laughed.

What is it? he asked.

"I thought you were musing on whether I'd have to walk in
the gardens," I wrote. "I couldn't understand why you were so
worried. But you meant darkness, the dark."

Mr. Bell picked up the mirror. He said the two words although I did not know which was which on his lips. Gardens,
Darkness, Gardens.

Putting down the mirror, he said, I would never have spotted that.

The admiration in his gaze sharpened into interest, and I felt
a buoyant lift in my chest that had me sitting taller in my chair
as I said, My mother and I used to play a game with words that
look the same.

A game?

Yes. I reached for the notebook, because I was uncertain of
how to say the next word clearly. "Eye-puzzles," I wrote. "We
called them eye-puzzles. So, for instance, one person makes up
a sentence with a word which looks like another word and tries

to trick the other person into thinking it's the other word. So here I could say, Do you like walking in the darkness after dinner? And you must reply, and if your reply is incorrect—perhaps you say, Yes, I love to take an evening stroll in the garden—then I have won. I will make my voice silent when I say the key word so you must try your best to speech-read me. Of course it doesn't matter what you do with your voice upon my turn."

I see, he said. Let us try. You go first.

I told Mr. Bell that I had a really bad ache at breakfast time, making sure I couldn't feel anything of my voice when I said Ache. I had to repeat the sentence slowly several times, and then he said, Ah! I see. Had it gone off?

I laughed and wrote "Ache" on the page. I win, I told him. Ache not Egg.

He laughed, shaking his head. Ache, Egg, he said a few times. My turn, he said, and thought for a moment. I know. Ready? The maid left a smudge in the bathroom.

I replied, Perhaps you should hire a better maid. Did you hope I'd see sponge?

Yes, he said, laughing. How did you know I said smudge and not sponge? Are they not identical?

You must question the easy answer, I replied.

He looked at me, still smiling. I remember, he said. When I first met you. You thought I was talking about lemonade.

The word glittered on his mouth. Lemonade. Illuminate. Panic jumped through me at the memory of my mother's brooch, and the mistake I'd made in front of all those gentlemen.

No, he said. Don't be embarrassed. You are extremely good with your eyes.

Ex-treme-ly was a lovely word, with the lips pushed forward in their desire to be emphatic.

Thank you, I said, feeling a rush of pleasure.

Then he said, You have eyes like a hawk. You miss nothing.

I looked at him, remembering what Miss Roscoe had told

the pupils at the Oral School, and how later they had changed my sign name, to a larking hawk-eyed bird. But we all knew that we missed so much on people's lips, and surely our eyes had better uses.

Then my name was on Mr. Bell's mouth again, requiring my attention.

Miss Lark, he said. Let me tell you something. He took up his notebook, so I knew the matter was a serious one. "It is my greatest regret," he wrote, "that my mother never learned to lip-read. Nobody thought it worthwhile. When I meet people like you it astonishes me. I wish she had learned when she was younger. Her struggles would have been much less."

I read his words. He was astonished. He was aggrieved. Did he blame himself, or even his father, for his mother's suffering? All the solitude that cloaked her throughout her life could have been dispelled.

He sat back, his shoulders spent of sighs. I didn't want to tell him that lip-reading was exhausting, and I made all kinds of embarrassing errors, because he'd just told me that I astonished him.

Wait, he continued. I have an idea. He sat forward, energized again, and started rummaging through the papers on his desk. He took a thin stack, turned over the last leaf, and wrote on the back: "This is a paper I'm writing on the subject for my journal, *The Pioneer*. Did I tell you about it? I don't know what to title it. Perhaps you have some suggestions? The truth is, I hardly have time to write at the moment with all my work."

He gave me the journal papers and I flipped through them. It was filled with articles on Visible Speech, education conventions, textbooks for instructing deaf pupils, new teachers enlisted in the cause.

He took the paper back and continued writing. "I would like to compile a list of words that look the same to the eye. These are known as homophenous words, just like Ache and Egg. There are surely thousands. The list of homophenes will accompany an instrument I am creating to help the deaf."

Mr. Dupont's words came back to me: the oil on his sleeves, the mechanic shop. Was this instrument the reason for his late nights?

He continued, "I should like to include an account of the art of speech-reading. I shall publish it in *The Pioneer* and then no one shall doubt what can be achieved with speech-reading. You shall be its author. What do you think?"

Well, I said, with a little laugh. A paper! But the hesitation was a false modesty, for already my thoughts had galloped on toward that prize: my name in a scientific journal, a place where my words would have equal weight with Mr. Bell and his peers. I could scarcely hold the idea in my head. Hadn't it been a long struggle to get to where I was now? All the cures poured into my ears and the blistering behind them. The endless months and years at the Oral School, watching Miss Roscoe's lips and our own in our pocket mirrors, day in and day out. From the woman who had called me a Little Savage and the children who had chucked my pen to the bottom of a well, to Mr. Dupont monopolizing my notebook. But now I, Ellen Lark, would be published in a scientific journal. Perhaps Mr. Bell was right to compliment my lip-reading? After all, I could mostly understand him, aided by our notebooks, and had no trouble with my mother, or even Adeline on most days, at least now that I was familiar with the variety of her grievances. And a little bit of lip-reading could take you further than none at all. A paper would lay down all my ideas, and other people like me would take heart—and even lessons—from it.

I said, Of course I will help. Then remembering Mr. Dupont's words, I asked, Is the instrument at the mechanic shop? I should like to see it.

He laughed. I don't think your grandmother would approve

of you going to a mechanic shop. No, he said, and took up the pen to jot his next words. "It is in the Institute of Technology."

He wrote the name of the Institute in the Back Bay with such a flourish that I couldn't help wrinkling my mouth with admiration.

Well, you could come, he said and peered at me. Then he wrote, "Do you assure me you are of sound scientific mind?"

I picked up the pen. "Mr. Bell, do you tease me as we sit in the first university to admit women?"

He smiled and shrugged. "I warn you that you may be one of the first women in the Institute's workrooms," he wrote.

I smiled back and wrote, "I don't care a jot. What are you making in the mechanic shop?" I didn't see why Mr. Bell needed to get oil on his sleeves in such a place if he had the Institute to work in.

To my surprise, he leapt up. I'll show you, he said, laughing at my alarm. No, not the mechanic shop. We shall see about your scientific mind.

He tapped his temple, and I watched Scientific appear on his lips. It didn't have much shape, but I knew to guess it from our earlier conversation. He crossed to the door and beckoned for me to follow. In the room next door there was a piano. Mr. Bell lifted the lid on the keys and the soundboard to reveal the strings. Come here, he said, and rest your hands here, on the strings.

The piano's darkness was striped with silver wires, each one soft with dust like an animal's coat. It hadn't been played for some time. I wanted to clean the wires, but instead placed my fingers lightly on them.

Mr. Bell played a few notes. You can feel them? he asked.

I nodded and closed my eyes. It was just possible to feel the difference between each note he played.

But when I opened my eyes, I realized that I was no longer feeling the notes of the keys, but Mr. Bell singing. I laughed to feel the song thrumming in my fingertips, the jangle in my skin

that seeped into my bones and reached as far as my wrist. Mr.
Bell's face was a comic sight as the oval of his mouth lengthened; surely he was making his notes sink and rise.

Let me guess, I said to him. You wish to put a voice in a wire?

He was still bent into the casing. He pulled himself up, but
his head hit the propped-up soundboard. His mouth parted only
briefly, but my hands still resting on the strings felt his cry. He
stood with his eyes scrunched shut, rubbing his head with two
fingers. He opened one eye, then the other, as if to check I was
still there.

A voice, he said, in a wire. I—

For a moment he looked astonished, his mouth hanging open
on his *I*. I didn't know what I'd said to cause it. He made a circling gesture with his hand, but even that seemed to stall midair.

I have been thinking about that, he began. Then he started
patting his pockets, but he'd left the notebooks next door. Wait,
he said, and dashed from the room. When he returned, he closed
the lid over the keys and bent over it as he wrote: "I am working on a Multiple Telegraph. The problem with today's communication is that you can only send one telegram down a wire at
a time. It is slow and cumbersome. That is the great challenge
of our time. How can you send multiple messages? My idea is
based on Acoustics. When you sing to a piano wire it will repeat the note, whatever the pitch. You can do the same thing
with a telegraphic instrument. If you send many signals at different pitches, then you can send many messages at one time.
Since there is only one air, therefore there only needs be one
wire. I call it a Harmonic Multiple Telegraph."

Before he showed me his words, he winked at me. You mustn't
tell a soul, he said. Do you promise?

I made a mock-grimace and held out my hand for the book.
I promise, I said, then read his words about the telegraph. But
it wasn't his idea that quickened my pulse at first. Instead, I was
remembering my father. After the war, he had worked in tele-

graph stations all over the East Coast before winding up in Pittsburgh. I knew little about his work, or what had driven him
into the woods that day, with wire in his pocket. It was out of
respect for Mama that I never asked. I wished to step away from
the piano, and its funereal wires laid out so straight and oblig-
ingly. Of all the things I was expecting Mr. Bell to reveal to
me, it wasn't the telegraph race. I tried to think of something
to show my enthusiasm.

What about the voice? I said. Isn't it voices that you know
about? Our voices, I added.

Mr. Bell looked at me. Had I misunderstood him? He hesitated, so I thought he was going to answer my question, but
instead he tore out the notebook's page, crumpled it and put it
in his pocket. He lowered his chin, so his eyes shone out at me,
and said, Tell no one!

I laughed, although I felt startled. Of course, I said.

But who was there for me to tell? Mr. Bell rubbed his head,
and said, The doctor says I must stop all this work. It brings
on the worst headaches. Crashing into pianos doesn't help. He
smiled at me. Well, Miss Lark, he said, then wrote: "When I am
back from the summer vacation, we shall go to the Institute to
see my new device for the deaf. Never mind all this telegraph
nonsense. I will write to you over the summer."

I shall gladly come, I said. But as we turned to leave, I was
sure he was repeating something to himself. A voice, he seemed
to be saying. A voice.

Downstairs Miss Lance was in the hallway looking through
Mr. Bell's class timetables. I forgot these, she said, when she saw
myself and Mr. Bell. I came back for them.

Excellent, Mr. Bell said, and started talking about gardens
and darkness again. His words to Miss Lance were quick on his
lips, and I couldn't catch them. I started to feel a prodding finger of panic that this was how Mr. Bell normally spoke to peo-

ple. This was his natural pace and speed, and I couldn't follow any of it. But shortly he turned to me and said, Miss Lance can take you to the stagecoach.

Oh, there's no need, I said. It's not very dark yet.

I looked at Miss Lance but there was a stiff expression on her face. It startled me. Had I wronged her somehow? Thank you, I said, although I wanted to say goodbye to Mr. Bell properly and wish him well for the summer vacation in Brantford. Watchfulness was burning in Miss Lance's eyes, but Mr. Bell didn't seem to notice. He said, I shall see you after the summer, Miss Lark.

Outside it was already too dark for lip-reading, although the sun hadn't fully set. Neither of us felt compelled to pause under the gas lamps, but when we reached the stagecoach stop, Miss Lance took out her notebook, and used her upturned satchel to rest it on. When she finished writing, she gave me the book with a smile that was conciliatory before I'd even read her words.

"When you return from the vacation," she'd written, "can I suggest that you ask Mr. Bell to keep to teaching Visible Speech in your lessons?"

I stared at her but she took the notebook again and carried on. "He likes to talk. Indeed, he likes to sing! I hear him from outside the classroom but then most people can hear Mr. Bell from a mile away. I don't think your grandmother would be pleased to learn his attention has wandered. I recommend that you stick with Visible Speech lessons. Visible Speech can only be learned through intensive rote practice."

I'm improving my speech-reading, I told her, although I knew she must have heard some of our conversation around the piano, or even Mr. Bell's singing to the wires, my delighted laughter.

Miss Lance's smile twitched. My dear, she said with her voice, then continued with the pen, "Let me tell you something. Mr. Bell's interest is in humanity not people. He's fascinated by mankind, but doesn't really see men or women—individual people— if you take my meaning."

I didn't know what she meant at all. How could you care for all people and not for any one of them in particular? I remembered Mr. Dupont again, and how Miss Lance had told him about Mr. Bell's odd working habits. Clearly, she wasn't of sound judgment to reveal such things to a person like Mr. Dupont, who could scarcely mask his disdain of Mr. Bell. I asked her, Did you advise Miss Hubbard of the same?

She gazed at me. Well, no—she began.

It was clear to me, then, that it was Miss Lance who had favorites, not Mr. Bell. She had been plainly joyful when chatting with Miss Hubbard. And why not, with her distinguished family? But she saw nothing fruitful that might come from my conversations with Mr. Bell. I burned to tell her that I'd been invited to write a paper for his journal, but decided against it. I'd not have Miss Lance meddle with things.

Her eyes went past my shoulder, so I guessed the stagecoach was pulling up. I thank you for your advice, I said, but I do not need it. I wish you a good vacation.

I turned and called out my stop to the driver. Usually, I used my notebook, but now I wished to make an assertive departure. But the driver frowned at my words, shook his head and cupped a hand about his ear. I could feel Miss Lance waiting in case she was needed. I hated, then, this dependency that others saw in me, and how I couldn't loosen myself from it. I tried again but the driver shook his head a second time, so I was forced to flip open my travel notebook which had the words Tremont Street inked large. He nodded and waved me inside. Miss Lance was still stood on the sidewalk, watching me go. I climbed the steps and sat myself facing away from her, keeping my shoulders tall as if the confusion hadn't happened.

8

Alone

THE TURRETS of St. Saviour's rise high above the street junction but there's no sign of Mr. Crane. When I reach the church's steps, a group flocks through the doors. They are busy signing and don't notice me standing on the pavement. I want to wait and watch them. Mr. Holmwood's housekeeper, Mrs. Ketter, used the sign language. Our friendship grew out of the long hours we spent together, and the British signs she taught me, which were different to the American ones. I haven't seen anything of it since she left us three months ago.

The group doesn't stay on the steps for long. Glancing at the sky, they open their umbrellas against the rain, and resume their

signing one-handed beneath the canopies. Shortly they're away
from the church and out of sight. I feel the pang in my chest
lengthen, like string being drawn from me.

Inside, St. Saviour's is lit by tallows still burning from the earlier service. There are more candles than I've seen in a church
before and the pews have been elevated so that the rear rows
have sight of the twin pulpits. There is no choir or organ, and
no pillars. This is a place where sight cannot find darkness. At
St. Bride's, Mr. Holmwood and Harmon always ensure we have
a seat at the front of the congregation, but here it doesn't matter where you sit. Everyone can get a clear view of the priest's
sermon.

I breathe in the smoky sting of the candles and the coolness
of the flagstones. Why did Mr. Crane suggest this as our meeting place? Did he suppose it was familiar to me? Or perhaps he
saw another convenience of deafness: our invisibility. Here is a
building in plain sight on Oxford Street which few have cause
to notice. We could slip inside St. Saviour's, same as he wishes
me to slip into Mr. Bell's orbit again.

I didn't refuse his choice of location. It was suitable enough
for an unaccompanied young woman. But as I cast around, I
know I'm looking for more than Mr. Crane. This is where Mrs.
Ketter came. Every Sunday and Thursday evening, she'd come
to St. Saviour's and return to Mr. Holmwood's house in high
spirits. Sometimes she would tell me about a new journal in the
library, or that week's theater play in sign language, or the de-
bating society's chosen topic. But she was careful not to say too
much. Harmon had made his views clear when he allowed her
to keep the evening off that Mama had agreed to before she
died. "Her daughter Miss Lark belongs in hearing society," he
wrote her, "and your position in Mr. Holmwood's household
rests on that understanding." He showed me the letter so that I
would be clear on that understanding, too.

I search out the door that surely leads to the library. Adeline always said it did not serve a woman to be curious, but I can't help myself. I long to see the library and club rooms and compare them to the images I've crafted from Mrs. Ketter's occasional descriptions. But no sooner have I taken one step toward the door when it opens, and Mr. Crane appears. His casual manner, as if he had exited that door a thousand times, prompts a spark of alarm. Is he known at St. Saviour's? Are others here involved in his contact with me? I try to brush the notion aside. No doubt Mr. Crane is some sort of meddler in the community, that's all. He's poking about the church with no good intentions.

He folds and wags his hands. Welcome.

A British sign, same as Mrs. Ketter's. I gaze at him, unable to respond. He's older than I remember, although I only saw him briefly in Boston. His features are uneven and unhappy. There's too much restless light in his eyes and his thick-lipped mouth won't stay still, as if he's constantly tasting his words before speaking them. Brilliantine has been combed through his thinning hair, the stiffly plowed lines set against the mobile unease of his face.

He bobs his head and indicates the pews. I walk down the aisle while he follows. I seat myself quickly since I've never liked people walking behind me where I can't see them. He sits himself over a yard away, too far for passing a notebook. I take off my gloves and lay them across my lap. The cold of the church slips about my wrists as I lift my hands to ask him if he knows the sign language, and my coat sleeves draw back, revealing an edging of my white cuffs. It's dark with ink from last night's copying. Embarrassed, I pull down my sleeves again but Mr. Crane has already seen the stains.

You are fond of letter-writing, he remarks, in quick signs.

I'm a copy-clerk, I tell him. The fact of this work might be a less seemly reason for my carelessness than keeping up my correspondence, but suddenly I desire to confound him.

My cousin's daughter is a copy-clerk, he signs. She works for a merchant house. But she will be married soon. Like you, he adds, and his lips curl with what I can't tell to be smile or smirk.

Where is the firm? I ask. Since my mother's death, and Mrs. Ketter's departure, I have longed for any kind of task or business that will take me away from the house. Mr. Holmwood keeps to his rooms most of the time, and Harmon has long days at the Department Store. Now I picture being set upon a high stool amongst the boxes and crates of a merchant house, copying invoices and receipts side-by-side with the other clerks. But it's a tall order for a woman to be clerking, let alone a deaf one. Besides, I also will be married soon.

Old Broad Street, he signs. Perhaps some small crack has revealed a glint of my loneliness, because he's watching me with interest. I try to seal myself up again, but I can't help the way curiosity curves through me. His signs are fast, tucking and turning as he explains precisely the location of the merchant house. They are placed in the air according to the rules of the eyes, not those of English. He uses space to set out his meaning, placing the merchant shop just off Old Broad Street, and along from the Stock Exchange, and behind a busy costermonger market. His features move with his signing, adding expression to his signs. Some of them are too quick for me, and I miss a few.

How did you learn signs? I ask, unable to help myself, even though he has summoned me here to deceive my husband and outwit the Inventor of the Telephone, not to make idle chat in the pews of a church.

My parents are deaf, he replies. It was my first language. I learned English later.

But you are hearing? I ask, bringing my brows down, tilting forward into the question.

He touches his finger to his ear, his mouth: yes, hearing.

Your parents brought you here as a child? I ask. The signs come quickly to me, I can't resist them. My arms almost feel hot from the release of the language locked in them, as if some unknown friction between different parts has slipped and caused the whole of me to judder into place. My British signs aren't perfect although I am far better in the British sign language than the American one. I spent every day with Mrs. Ketter for nearly a year. Our stop-start signs became an almost fluid stream. Then Harmon found a way to end her employment, and I learned not to think of them anymore. Instead, I folded my anger into my grief, hoping time would free me of both.

No, he replies. I first came here when I was twenty. Before that I lived abroad for a long, long time.

Boston, I think, remembering the occasion I saw him in the print shop. Did he know the American signs also? I thought he was a hearing customer, and then when I later learned his purpose, I supposed he conducted his business with Frank by letters. How close had they been? Was he part of Frank's community?

The idea must snag in my face because Mr. Crane raises an eyebrow, pulling up a corner of his mouth. You've never been here? he asks.

I shake my head.

Why not? Here we all see God's word. Everything clear, everyone signing, he adds.

I hold his gaze, trying to push away Harmon's reasons which line up in my thoughts. From the way Mr. Crane is looking at me, I'm sure he can guess them all. It is an oralist's reasoning, nothing surprising, and in the vein of Mr. Bell and others like him. The church fostered a clannishness among deaf people. It turned them into a social class of their own. Deaf children would suffer, locked away from the hearing world until it was too late to learn how to get by in it. Finger-spelling English words was one thing, but the sign-gestures were another, being quite crude in appearance and simple in conception. It wasn't proper for the kind of society Harmon planned to keep.

After a moment, I sign: There is no one to accompany me. My stepfather is hearing. We go to St. Bride's.

I almost mention Harmon but stop myself, even though the guilt I thought I'd feel about coming here is strangely absent.

You are here now, he signs. Alone. His index finger swoops out from behind the palm of his other hand, like a person appearing suddenly in the wilderness.

I look at his solitary finger, capped with a squarely cut nail. My breath seems to quiver, same as his finger. I slip my gaze to Mr. Crane and try to fix him with it like he did me. This wasn't my plan. I'd meant to be firm. To hand him my report and tell him what I needed in return. I straighten myself and ignore the way both his eyebrows slip upward in a matching movement that hints at his amusement. Before I can sign anything, his thumb strikes down his palm.

Let's start.

Wait, I begin, remembering my report on the demonstration in the Thames. I should be the one to start, not him. But Mr. Crane has opened a notebook which he flattens on a list of words. He shuffles closer so I can see them, and my eyes swoop on the page before I can stop myself.

"Telephone."

"Vibration."

"Reed."

"Harmonic."

"Current."

Words that Mr. Bell once spoke and wrote for me. In a column are the corresponding Visible Speech symbols and their familiarity creeps through me, tingling the shapes of words across my tongue and mouth. Telegraph, I say. Transmitter.

Mr. Crane's eyes squeeze with his smile. He taps the column with the Visible Speech. You can practice them in a mirror, he signs, so you can recognize them when you're watching Mr. Bell. What? he asks, because I'm smiling.

Mr. Bell told me the same, I reply. He always advised mirror-practice.

Mr. Crane is watching me, and I notice the thin length of his neck above his shirt collar. A crane, I think, and in my mind's eye, I give him a sign name, a beak-shaped hand held to one side, so you can see the full length of lower arm, like a bird's long neck. Crane. A bird's name, like mine. Has circumstance made us fly together? But I push the idea away, and look at the list again. What is Mr. Crane's interest in Mr. Bell's fortunes? Are the Western Union really paying him so much that he'll risk getting this close to Mr. Bell's ire? Or does he suppose to use me instead because Mr. Bell's fury will be knotted by his old affection for me? My thoughts feel like one of Mrs. Ketter's cheesecloths, wringing out murky, sour water.

Why don't you get the information yourself? I ask.

I can't get near to Mr. Bell. The Union needs someone whom Mr. Bell trusts. Someone of your talents.

I watch his lie spinning off his hands and sputter a laugh from my lips. Talents. Lip-reading. If his parents are deaf surely he knows it can't be done.

Perhaps my laugh has come out loud, but his face shrinks like a prodded animal. I sign, I don't know why the Western Union cares about the Telephone. Everyone in England says it is very quiet. People must shout and talk slowly so it is not convenient and easy like the telegraph.

I make my fists into the butterstamp Telephone and do my best impression of hearing people mouthing slow English. I've seen them do it enough times to me. They complain that they cannot put up with being slow-spoken to like this, but they think deaf people ought not to mind it.

But it is getting interest, he replies, and the Western Union own most of the wires in America.

Have you used it? I ask, and press my fists to my ears and mouth for a second time. The Telephone.

Once.

What was it like? But immediately I feel a snap of shame that I want to know the answer.

Mr. Crane grows cautious and in his wariness he looks more like a hearing person again. He signs, It was quiet. You're right. I couldn't really hear anything. They played a song. It took me a while to recognize the tune, but then I realized what it was and I could understand it fine.

I laugh. Lip-reading is similar. If you know the topic, you can guess some of the words.

Guessing, I want to say, is a kind of trusting. Holding on to words with as much faith as you can muster that they're the right ones. And now Mr. Crane wants me to trust Mr. Bell's words again.

Mr. Crane is watching me closely. Your guessing, he signs, is very good.

I stare at him. Is that what he wants me to give the Union? Guesses? And he would be content to know that that's all they are? Mr. Gray and Mystery flicker in my head. I remember the way Mr. Bell and Harmon stood on the embankment, their lips dancing within the flexing cages of their expressions, as I tried to read their conversation. Mystery, Mr. Gray. I had to reason my choice and trust it, as if it wasn't a guess at all. That was the lip-reader's art.

I take out my account of the evening by the Thames and hand it to him. He pinches his lips in mild surprise before taking it. I sit stock-still as he reads, my thoughts becoming flinty and painful, and I wish he would hurry up. Eventually he lifts his eyes to meet mine.

Elisha Gray, he spells. A Western Union inventor.

I know, I reply. Mr. Bell is concerned about him, not the other inventors. He said his health is getting worse, he is suffering and the reason is Mr. Gray.

More pleasure enters my signs than it did for my pen: I almost persuade myself of what I've seen as Health brushes from my chest, its worsening drawn out by one little finger dropping away from the other, ending in a generous, double-handed shake of Mr. Bell's Suffering.

Mr. Crane nods, still staring at me. Suddenly I worry that I've gone too far. He doesn't believe me. I shift in my seat and ask, Is he part of the Union's legal suit?

He collects himself. Did you know, he replies, that Mr. Bell and Mr. Gray's patent applications arrived at the patent office on exactly the same day?

He spells out patent and then makes the sign for a paper form. I tell him that yes, I did know, although I can't think where I learned about it. Harmon? The patent was awarded to Mr. Bell, and he finished his first properly working Telephone not long afterward.

It is very strange, he continues, driving both indexes under his chin in opposite directions so they make a cross. It stays there, this cross of his hands, his head nodding above it in consideration of the strangeness of the events. When patents arrive on the same day, the officer should declare an interference.

But they didn't, I finish. Mr. Bell was awarded the patent.

Mr. Crane is nodding but it's my report he's conferring his approval on. This is good, he signs, and his thumbs flick up in a strong, firm motion, his final conclusion.

But I have matters of my own that must be addressed. I make the largest, most strident signs I can manage, matching his. I have given you information, I sign. Now I want something in return.

To my alarm, Mr. Crane laughs. He looks about as cheerful as I've seen him yet. Sweet, he signs. You don't understand how debt works. I am owed, not you. But I think I know what you want.

He roots in his pocket and produces a small package. Go on, he nods when I hesitate. It is light, with something hard-cornered and flat inside. I unfold the paper but it takes me a moment to realize what I'm looking at, and then I feel as though the cold of the church has slammed through me. A rectangular object glinting dully in my palm, like a wearily opened eye. The smoked glass. It was a gift from Mr. Bell the first time we went to the Institute together, but later I gave it to Frank, entrusting it into his safekeeping.

How did you get this? I ask.

Mr. Crane has a patient smile ready on his face, as if he had foreseen this moment.

Frank, he replies, gave it to me.

As Frank's name slices down from Mr. Crane's nose, I feel a matching blow like an axe's blade. His palms draw neatly to himself. To give, to receive. I want to reach out and pull his hands away, break apart this act of giving, un-gift what should not be in his possession.

As payment, Mr. Crane continues. He thought I could sell it now that Mr. Bell is famous. He rubs his fingers in his palms. There's an ugly shine in his eyes. Money.

But it doesn't belong to you, I tell him, my arms swiping out from a cross as I refute him. When Mr. Crane shrugs, I ask, Will you sell it? You cannot sell it.

No, no. How would I explain how I got it? He's smiling again.

I take the glass from him and fit it along my palm. The line scratched through the faded soot waves across its length. I try to focus on the line, but it feels as though it's swimming in my palm. I gifted it to Frank McKinney with a promise: I would never do anything more for Mr. Bell. A promise that I broke once, and then again, because that first break is the one you can never fix.

I turn the glass over, almost wishful that it might reveal something, or give me a clue. But the back is smooth and clean. There are no marks or signs of damage. Frank has taken care of it. He was full of bluster, and yet he was also one of the most careful people I knew.

I realize my eyes are stinging. Do you need a handkerchief?

Mr. Crane signs, dabbing excessively at his own eyes in imitation of my burgeoning tears. But he doesn't offer one, laying his hands on his knees instead.

Anger tips through me, but it's my error for what I've shown Mr. Crane. Sweet, he'd signed, like I was a child. I quickly press my tears to my ink-free sleeve, then tell him: I'm keeping this.

But you gave it away. He pauses and ponders the glass deliberately. I don't know. Maybe it is worth something.

What do you want for it? I have ten pounds I can give you.

He laughs for a good while. I need more than that—I am owed. Frank thought I would get thirty pounds. Enough to clear the debt.

He drives his finger hard down his raised forearm—*debt*—but he's still laughing. An image comes to me, of Frank pleading with Mr. Crane to be off his back. He had spent all the money from Mr. Crane on lessons with me, and Mr. Crane had seen no return from it, nothing to help him get information on Mr. Bell. He couldn't pay the debt, so gave Mr. Crane this early token of Mr. Bell's newly famous Telephone instead. I had only seen Frank plead once before, and that was in Philadelphia, in his efforts to stop me doing what I did. If I'd left him in impossible circumstances, then his debt should become mine.

I switch my eyes back to Mr. Crane. I will help you, I tell him. But my stepfather can't find out. His nephew will not understand. We will be married soon. He doesn't know—

My hands drop from signing, and I look at the altar, sensing Mr. Crane's nodding next to me. Does he see all the things I have never told Harmon? Does he know I have nowhere else to go if we do not marry?

His nod is minute acknowledgment, carried by the air, and the deal is done.

I take out my pocket watch. Time is getting on, and Harmon will be home soon, and Mr. Holmwood will start to wonder where I am. I thrust my finger at the list of telephone components. You will have to add Mr. Gray, I tell him. And Mystery. I need symbols for both.

Mystery?

I ignore his puzzled face and sign, Also I want the glass. I don't wait for his permission and fetch a handkerchief, carefully wrapping the glass inside. As I tie its corners I turn my shoulder from Mr. Crane like a petulant child. I don't want him to see the relief that floods me to have the glass back, even though I'm not sure what has been saved.

I put the smoked glass in Mama's travel case, and try to forget about it. Harmon has given me more business letters to copy. They pile up on my desk alongside the pages of a botany guide sent by a friend of old Holmwood's who wants five copies. I start on them after clearing away dinner and sitting with Mr. Holmwood. It's gone eleven o'clock by the time I get to Harmon's letters, my wrist burning with soreness.

Most concern the Telephone franchise, encouraging more interest from local businesses. There is a letter to the Bell Telephone Company about the lease of instruments. A few are replies to schools for deaf children that have expressed a tentative interest in Visible Speech. Harmon writes with an almost belligerent confidence. "I can offer a demonstration," he tells each principal with little variation, "by one of Mr. Bell's former pupils but you would be wise to make haste with arrangements since demand is high at the current time."

Taking my pen, I try to start on the first copy, but I can't bring myself to replicate even one of his words. Instead, I take eight new envelopes, label them with the recipients, and fold sheets of plain paper inside. I file them in an empty drawer, to all appearances businesslike. A drawer full of blank copies. Harmon's memory is immaculate. He won't need to refer to them. Besides, it's almost midnight and I'm too tired to care. The task is done within fifteen minutes.

Soon afterward, I lie in bed watching the crack under the door for the telltale glow of his candle. But it's late, he won't come to my bedroom. I dangle my fingers to the floor and press the tips against a strip of floorboards by the wall. If Harmon passes my door on the way to his own, I'll feel his footsteps. A little prayer builds up in me that tonight he'll pass on by, although that never used to be my wish. The air swills cold around my fingers. I think of the smoked glass lying under all my letters, its scratched line shining through the tangled layers of words. A promise returned to me. But what am I to do with it? Several trains go under the house, sending up their deep-earth rattle. The trains have been the one constant since Mama died. I start to think I can smell an extinguished candle from somewhere.

I think back to our early correspondence. It was only when Mama became ill and took to her bed that I started taking my letters to Harmon's room directly, sliding them underneath his door. There didn't seem any point waiting until breakfast. On the fourth or fifth time of doing this he opened the door just as I was ducking down. I straightened up, blushing, and there was a strange light in his eyes, but also nervousness. Thank you, he said, and neither of us knew if he should close the door or not.

I said good-night and went back down the corridor. But the next night, I took him another letter at the same hour. He was ready this time and received it with a small bow that didn't break his gaze. Soon his replies were coming under my door as well. All the time Mama was getting sicker, and the doctor told us that she would likely die soon. My letters to Harmon, and his to me, were all that kept me together. Back and forth they went, becoming longer and more urgent. "These days are so precious," he wrote. "We must hang on to what we can." And I clung to that urgency, as if it was throbbing life itself.

A week after Mama died, he came to my bedroom door. In my grief and confusion, I didn't know what he was doing there. We will be married soon, he spelled. I deliver myself in place of a letter. And I still didn't know why he was stood in the door-way, with those points of light in his eyes, and the rise and fall of his chest beneath his shirt. I stared at him until something seemed to collapse that drawn-back bearing of his shoulders. He apologized and left. The next day he refused to look at me. I was afraid. Had I done something wrong? Was our promise to Mama receding from him already? That night I went to his room. I don't have a letter, I spelled, and he stood back to let me in.

The floorboards are silent under my fingertips. I roll over, letting the night angle its darkness about me. But I can't stop the question in my head. If Mr. Bell had never visited us, might we have managed a happy life? I think of Mama, clinking our glasses: the sound, she told me, of breakable glass.

9

Lesson III

ꟼ0 ɘ⅃3 ɘí ɘⅉ∪⅃ ⅃ ꟼ⅃ɒ

[It gave me many a pang]

THE SUMMER I met Frank McKinney was one of the hottest I can remember. Boston stewed in sunshine. Dust from the land-fill pits in the Back Bay spread across the Common so at times the trees appeared to be standing in a golden mist. No more relief could be found outdoors than indoors. The residents sat about Little St. Clouds fanning themselves and switching from the front and back parlors as the sun tracked round the house.

I collected homophenes for Mr. Bell's paper. I watched the boarders' conversations and made a note of any confusions. I fished out Lung and Luck from Mrs. Baylis's remark about walk-ing in stormy weather. Was it good lungs or luck you needed?

Moat and Bones from Adeline's comment that once she had visited a castle in England surrounded by ancient bones. Gold and Cold from what was making Joan's head feel heavy. As soon as I spotted one, I made a note in my daily notebook or on my slate. Later I would take them upstairs and write them into my essay. I also wrote down the conversation in which they had occurred, and how I had teased them apart with the lip-reader's skill, so I could explain them to Mr. Bell after the summer vacation.

Unlike Adeline, Mama was thrilled with Mr. Bell's request for my essay in *The Pioneer.* "I have told Mr. Ackers all about it," she wrote, "and he insists that you ask Mr. Bell to send several copies to London once it is published. You must send a copy to Miss Roscoe too." The thought of Mr. Ackers and Miss Roscoe thumbing their way through my essay opened pride in me like a stretched scroll.

One day I accompanied Joan to Quincy Market and she bade me wait in the Public Gardens while she called on an ailing aunt. I settled myself on a bench under some trees near the Lagoon. Nearby a group of people had gathered around a board which was mounted on a wooden stand. It read:

> Frank McKinney, Silhouettist.
> I am Deaf and Dumb.
> Likenesses Taken.
> Two cents each.

I stood up and came closer. The board was covered in hundreds of silhouettes, each one cut from black paper. I marveled at the jumping dogs, dancing girls, and the figures on bicycles, each thin wheel spoke evenly cut.

Their creator, Frank McKinney, stood five yards away, slightly apart from the group who had stopped to admire his work. He was a stockily built man, a few years older than myself, his hair longer than how most men wore theirs, parting at his crown in

two waves. Shreds of black paper surrounded his feet, and more
floated from the sheet he was holding, his fingers lightly locked
in the bows of his surgical scissors. As they ducked around the
paper, he kept glancing at four women who were posing in front
of him. They stood in profile, their hands raised in comic gestures, as though they were acting out a pantomime, trying their
best not to laugh as they held the pose.

When he finished, he opened up the silhouettes like a string
of paper dolls, and the women flocked over to see. Frank smiled
and took a bow for his work, and that set off laughter in the
group. They left with the silhouettes, waving as they went.

I should have moved away, but my whole body felt turned
in the direction of Frank, his silhouettes, the bold words "Deaf
and Dumb" shining out from the board.

The clouds shifted from the sun and my shadow sprang across
the ground. It shot toward Frank as if I was a sundial and he was
the correct time. Noticing it, he looked up and raised a palm,
indicating the tall stool where I might take my seat. With his
other hand, he tapped the board, and the word, Likeness. Then
he pointed at the stool again, his eyebrows lifting with his question. Was I interested in giving my custom? He picked up his
scissors and waited, still smiling.

We were in a public place, and anyone might see us. I should
shake my head and move on, pretending to be no more than
another curious bystander intrigued by the mute silhouettist.
Instead, I thanked him in signs. I told him I was no good at sitting still. Not even for a minute. But these—I fanned my hand
at the silhouettes—were beautiful.

Surprise opened his face. The fingers of one hand were still
laced into the scissors, so he signed on the other hand. He asked,
Are you deaf or hearing?

Deaf, I replied, supposing that my signs must not have been
very good for him to even ask the question.

He put his scissors away and came closer. Which school? he asked next.

I hesitated. Had he gone to one of the schools where they used the silent language? What would he think of the little oral School where it had been banned? I decided he probably wouldn't know of it in any case, so I may as well tell him.

He patiently waited until I reached the last letter with my fingers then his smile flared like a struck match. I know that school, he told me. He gave his chest a gentle thump. Myself, Hartford. Do you know that one? Big school, everyone signing.

He puffed out his cheeks, spun his circling indexes, blew apart his arms to show the size of the school. His fingers sprang, even as his arms kept a sure tuck about the space in which his hands turned. His whole face moved with the meaning imported to his signing, whereas I knew my signs were strung together in a fashion that was too much like English.

I know Hartford, I signed. My mother wanted me to go.

Really? Why did she change her mind? He touched his forehead with his index finger then held his hands in front of him and switched their places.

I hesitated. I couldn't think how to explain about Adeline and her views, although probably he was familiar with them. It is a good school, I replied.

He nodded. For speaking, he signed. Right? But before I could answer, he asked, Can you speak?

His eyes were direct on me, there was nothing in his face to show his question was anything other than asking for a fact to be made apparent.

Yes, I replied. But not clearly.

Frank turned the corners of his lips down, as if he was considering this.

I forget my manners, he signed, after a moment, spelling Manners on his fingers, a shadow of English slipping across them. What's your name, he asked.

Ellen, I spelled back, before adding: Lark.

Morning bird, he signed. He flipped his hand up for morning, then turned his fingers into a snapping beak. Bird.

My sign-name, I told him, and showed him. It was the first time I'd used my sign-name since arriving in Boston, and I felt a skip in my chest to feel it on my hand again.

He tapped the board and flashed his name on his fingers. Frank McKinney. Then his palm struck out straight from his nose: the sign for frankness.

Are you? I asked. Frank?

He smiled and looked at me with the same directness as his hand slicing from his face. My heart capered like a gusted leaf. I smiled back and tried to consider him with an open equanimity like he was giving me. He was neatly dressed, in spite of the shreds of black paper caught in the laces of his shoes. His eyes were brightly brown, and there was a softness in his face that seemed to add up his features into a smiling aspect even when he wasn't smiling. He stood steadily and his arms moved quickly, while his torso remained broadly facing forward, making small, decisive shifts with some of his signs. He was one of those people who looked as if he was always ready to present himself, even before he knew what or whom he was presenting himself to.

I knew I should leave. Joan would be back soon, and we would go on to Quincy Market. But his signs were such a draw on my eyes, it was like every muscle in my body was bending my attention to them, and I couldn't move my feet away if I tried. And I liked the easy flip of his smile, and his unflinching manner.

He signed, Hearing people say deaf people are always too direct. But hearing people are the opposite, talking, talking, never being clear, wandering from the point. They say it's a good thing. Yes, I'm frank.

I laughed. Same, I signed. People call me blunt, B-l-u-n-t, same.

He nodded. I've seen you here before. You're always writing

and walking, doing both at the same time. One day you'll walk into a tree or a gaslight.

His signing showed me walking into a tree, then a gaslight, falling backward. I couldn't help a second smile. His teasing made the space between us feel smaller, the sun hotter on my neck. I lifted my hands to tell him about the essay for *The Pioneer* but before I had a chance, we were surrounded by children. They were shouting Look and Shadow Man at each other. The younger ones tugged on Frank's sleeve, raising their hands into what looked like duck beaks making Quacks.

What do they want? I asked Frank.

He spelled on his fingers: Shadowgraphs.

He flapped his hands at the children—All right, all right—and turned around his board so that the plain wooden backing faced the sun. Some of the children started jumping up and down, clapping their hands. Frank positioned himself between the sun and the board with his own hands raised. In quick flicks of his fingers and wrists, he deftly arranged a succession of handshapes. His palms open and interlocked were a dove's wings, his fingers sticking up made a rabbit's ears, or hanging down formed an ass's tongue. He even took the toy telescope a child was holding, which became the tall hat of a speculator. The shadowgraphs hovered on the board and the children called out their names. They shouted Goose, and Bearded Goat, and Farmer, the last one being a man with the brim of his hat upturned.

Some of the children seemed to be shouting out requests, saying the same things over and over. The words were simple on their lips. Dog. Devil. But Frank just moved on to another shadowgraph. So I started spelling them for him: d-o-g, d-e-v-i-l.

His eyebrows lifted but he gave a small nod. He made a barking dog with a tooth in its jaw. Then a devil with a warty chin, hooked nose and long pointed ears.

We worked our way through a whole farmyard and fairy tale of characters. Finally, Frank stepped in front of his board, placing his whole body where the shadows had been. He swiped his hands through the air to show he was finished making shadow-graphs. Instead, he pointed out a tree, and made his arms wave, like the tree caught in the wind. The children looked very hard at the tree and then did the same. Next Frank pointed at a stage car that was rolling down the road. The children did their best imitation of that too, their arms shunting circles at their sides for the wheels. Frank was nodding—not bad, not bad—making a show of being impressed. He looked around, searching out something else for the children to copy.

Ah ha! His eyes lighting up. He pointed at a post which was about waist height. That, can you do that? His pointing finger asked the question. The children pulled themselves erect and stood as still as they could.

Perfect! Frank signed. The children grinned, but this made them wobble. Frank shook his head—No wobbling! He pulled himself up equally straight and made his eyes motionless at the distance. Soon the children were wobbling all over the place in fits of laughter. Frank slackened and waved his hand at them. The show was finished. His hand dropped away from his lips—thank you—and the children copied him. They ran off, still touching their fingers to their lips—thank you, thank you.

Frank turned to me. They liked that, he signed. You could understand them, he added. Lip-reading. You are good at that. Did they teach you at your school?

Every day, I replied, and grimaced to show him how I felt about all our ceaseless drills. Suddenly, I didn't want to leave the Public Gardens. Could he tell? Smiles slipped between our glances, like the swans weaving on the Lagoon's waters. Curls of giddy lightness unwound in me so I had to look away.

Frank started packing up his bags. He looked up as I dithered next to his board. Finished for the day, he told me. He pointed at me and made his face into a question. Which way are you walking? His flat palms walked like feet.

I pointed out the gate onto Tremont Street where I was meeting Joan. He turned over his two index fingers, tapped his chest. Same, he signed. I'll escort you. He held out his left arm and rested his right hand in the crooked elbow where mine would go. *Escort*. But then he dropped his arm: he didn't mean that I should actually take it.

Thank you, I replied.

We set off together, crossing over the bridge and wending through the flowerbeds. Do you mind the children? I asked, thinking of the parents that had also gathered, entertained by Frank and a simple idea of sign language as some sort of gestural spectacle.

He shrugged. I like children, he signed. Your family, he asked. You are the only deaf one?

Scarlet Fever, I was four, I told him, spelling out the illness that wiped sound from the world. I wanted to tell him more— about the snow, and how after the illness I didn't know that I'd lost my hearing, only that I was constantly getting everything wrong. But my signs were muddled. I kept switching between spelling and hand shapes, and there was no fluidity in my meaning.

Frank nodded. I supposed he had guessed from the English shapes I was apt to put on my mouth that I wasn't born deaf, just as I had guessed from his lack of lip-shapes that he was.

I asked him all the same, holding out my fist to him.

Born deaf, he signed. Three brothers, all deaf. Parents same. Uncle, aunts same. Actually, one aunt, she is hearing. My father is a teacher at the Hartford. Two brothers are also teachers.

His signing was faster again, there was pride on his face. I felt a scratch of panic that I wouldn't be able to follow. Are you a teacher? I asked.

In Boston? He laughed. The only school here is an oral school.

O-R-A-L, he spelled and I dropped my eyes. At Miss Roscoe's school we hadn't questioned that our signs were complicit, hidden, even when Theresa Dudley told us about the deaf schools where everyone signed. I couldn't imagine a whole family of deaf people, all signing.

I'm a printer, he added. He spelled out the words and followed with the signs: he had trained as a printer and bookbinder.

A bookbinder? My excitement must have showed because he laughed again. All deaf people same, he signed. Always writing, writing so hearing people can understand. Like you and your notebook.

He made the movement of a pen and hunched a shoulder to show me bending over my book as I wrote, while staring ahead, concentrating on a point in the distance, as the pen still hurried on. His eyes were tight and watchful, his hand flying from left to right.

My pride spilled through me, and I resisted his effort to make me smile. It wasn't idle notebook-scrawling but important work for Mr. Bell. I told him, I'm writing an essay for a journal of science.

I wished that I was skilled enough to make my signs appear lofty but, as it was, I didn't know the signs for either Essay, Journal or Science and had to finger-spell all three of them.

An essay? Frank made a sign I didn't recognize. My temples were starting to ache from watching his signing so closely, but I couldn't help making a note of it. An essay. That's what I was writing. He looked impressed: I noted that readily too. What's your subject? he asked.

I spelled out the title in full but I must have made an error because Frank frowned. So I just dashed my V-shaped hand in front of my lips.

Lip-reading? His head cocked backward, and his index finger snagged in the air by his temple. He still didn't understand.

I started trying to explain about Mr. Bell, Visible Speech, *The Pioneer*, but I didn't get far with the long string of my

finger-spelling before Frank stopped me. Mr. Bell? he asked.
You know him?

He made a sign like the ringing of a bell at his ear.

His sharpness surprised me. He's my teacher, I replied and
returned his question with an emphatic sealed fist in the air:
did he know him?

He hesitated. I've met him a few times, he signed.

He looked preoccupied. We reached the Maid of the Mist
and his gaze drifted through its watery plumes. I waited, but he
didn't explain. The easy mood between us puckered like cold
skin, as if we'd stepped right into the fountain. What was his
hesitation? Had Mr. Bell taught at the Hartford School? I supposed it was likely. Hartford wasn't so far from here, it was one
of the largest schools of its kind in the country and Mr. Bell's
methods were considered pioneering. It was likely he'd been
invited once or twice. Did he not care for Mr. Bell's methods?
That seemed likely too.

I tried again to explain about my essay but there was too much
in my head I wanted to say and too little in the repertoire of my
body to match it with. I stopped and took out my notebook instead. Then I wrote that the purpose of the paper was to enable
deaf people to study and therefore be aware of the most common homophenes that arise in speech—you might say the words
that are likenesses of each other—to help limit the misunder-
standings that so frequently occur for people of our situation.

I handed the notebook to Frank. Had I written too much? But
his eyes quickly skimmed the text. He signed, Let me check I
understand. You are writing an essay about how to speech-read?

I nodded firmly. He considered me, and signed, All deaf people are different, as if this concluded the matter.

A moment ago you said we were the same, I began, but I
stopped when he stepped close leaving only enough space to
make small signs. His gaze landed so heavily I felt as if every-

thing I'd just been thinking was knocked away, leaving only the spidery lightness of one of his silhouettes.

Don't tell Mr. Bell you saw me.

Plaintiveness stretched his gaze so his eyelids flickered. English questions went through my head. Why would I? Why shouldn't I? But my English and my signs were all tangled, and I had no hope of deciding what it was I should say, let alone how to say it in the silent language. I nodded my head although I didn't want to collude with his secretiveness.

Thank you, he replied.

We were both relieved when the children returned and started asking for more shadowgraphs. Frank went through his cycle of shadows, and I interpreted their requests, and by the time we were finished, the conversation about Mr. Bell was almost forgotten. When the children finally were gone, he walked me to the gate on to Tremont Street, where I would wait for Joan.

We stood for a few moments. This isn't your gate? I asked.

No. He smiled. Goodbye. I'll see you again, writing your paper.

But this time he didn't imitate my fervent concentration and I wished he would so I might laugh and amend the turn our conversation had taken.

Goodbye, I signed and walked through the gate. My thoughts were a jumble of confusion. When I looked behind me, Frank was headed up the hill to the Common. By the Maid of the Mist the children were making shadowgraphs on their own. The sun was low in the sky and as Frank walked by the fountain, his own shadow briefly consumed their doves and speculators. They called and waved for him, but he didn't turn back.

As summer wore on, I waited for Mr. Bell to write me about the new semester. I checked the boardinghouse's letters every day, but there was nothing from Brantford. I began to wonder if I had dreamed Mr. Bell's request. Eventually a note came from

Miss Lance. My lessons, she informed me, had been moved to morning-times.

I stared at the note as sunshine spilled over the paper, and the white cloth of the breakfast table. The Day sisters turned to each other with knowing looks and Mr. Bell on their lips. All summer they had teased me about the essay and said it was like having a spy in the house because of how I wrote down everyone's words. I gave up explaining about *The Pioneer*.

It's from Miss Lance, I told them, trying to hide the fact I minded. But the Day sisters were right to see that I cared. My evening lessons with Mr. Bell had hardly felt like lessons at all. Our conversations had moved freely, or so I thought. I'd never talked to anyone in that way before, my mother aside. I still thought of the piano wire, and the feel of his voice in my fingertips, like his words had jumped right into me. Had I made up the whole thing? Mr. Bell hated mornings, and surely Miss Lance knew it. I remembered her warning that I ought to keep to Visible Speech in our lessons. Perhaps she was plotting timetables even at the stagecoach stop.

I folded away the note and returned to my toast. The Day sisters made their faces straight, as if in imitation of my own. Rhoda Day reached out to pat my hand. It was kindly meant, so I smiled at her. Then Mrs. Baylis arrived and started talking about some kind of Dazzle or Tassel which had either been Displaced or Displayed. At first I thought she meant the sunlight, and then the curtains as she crossed the room and fussed at the strings that replaced the broken tassels. The boardinghouse was starting to become shabby. I gave up trying to ascertain her meaning, but as I took out my notebook and wrote down these new homophenes, my resolve tightened. I would finish my essay for Mr. Bell, and he would publish it in *The Pioneer*, and it wouldn't matter whether my lessons were morning or evening-times, he would be so pleased.

★ ★ ★

At the first lesson, Mr. Bell didn't show up for a full fifteen minutes. Miss Lance felt beholden to wait with me. She sat in Mr. Bell's chair with her hands folded in the skirts of her dress. It was a middling gray color that matched the middling brown shade of her hair so that in the dim classroom, it seemed a determined effort to blend the two colors into one. Her features were delicate and every now and then a quick smile would escape like a jet of released air, and you glimpsed an appealing prettiness. Her eyebrows lifted as she talked, as if she was making the biggest possible space on her narrow face for her words.

Mr. Bell is a night owl, she said. Night owl, she repeated when she saw my frown. Night. Owl. Someone who prefers the nighttimes.

Yes, I said, once I had grasped "Night." I know what night owl means.

Mr. Bell, I thought, would never have confused my difficulty lip-reading a word with a lack of knowledge. But my abruptness only caused Miss Lance to give me a sympathetic smile. She straightened her face and then continued, Well, he is even more of a night owl these days, so he must cut back on his teaching.

Her face didn't lend itself to expressiveness, especially while trying to speak steadily, but she attempted to convey just how much Mr. Bell needed to reduce his teaching load by scrunching up her cheeks and bringing her brows down. It was an awkwardness that brought Frank McKinney into my thoughts unbidden, and the natural liveliness of his face matched to his hands. But I pushed the thought aside, as I had done all summer. I'd not seen him in the Public Gardens again.

And I felt sorry for Miss Lance having to make excuses for Mr. Bell like this. She was never late for a lesson herself, and was always at the door to receive his deaf pupils as well as his other teacher-students. I pictured her studying hard into the night, same as myself, getting ever closer to her goal of becoming a fully qualified teacher. Did she talk to hearing people about her work with this same solemn expression? My impatience for Mr. Bell to arrive became even stronger.

So when she said something about inventing, I replied: I know about it. My words must have rushed out with ill-mannered roughness because she jumped. About what? she said, looking confused.

I hesitated. I was sure she was talking about Mr. Bell's inventing work but Mr. Bell had told me not to tell a soul about the Harmonic Multiple Telegraph. She must mean his work in the Institute and the device for deaf people.

Before I could respond, Mr. Bell arrived. Miss Lance looked about as relieved as I felt. Guilt nudged at me for the hard time I'd given her, but it didn't last long for Mr. Bell was smiling at us, and saying Good Morning and he was sorry to be so late.

I stood up to greet him, but Miss Lance started talking. She was speaking rapidly and he answered in the same way. His speech was a narrow muscular twitch within the panel of skin made by his beard. I watched as carefully as I could but none of his words would appear for me. Was this his normal speaking speed? Had I forgotten how to lip-read him over the summer? He didn't look changed in any other respect. He wore more or less the same suit and hadn't even acquired a suntan.

Finally, he sat down. You are the morning lark, he said, and his words were clear again. Calling me to my lessons.

Relief flooded me. I glanced at Miss Lance who was leaving the room. It was not my idea to have you rise so early, I said as carefully as I could.

He smiled, ruefully I thought, although I didn't see why he couldn't change the timetables himself. It was his school after all. How is your progress on the essay? he asked.

I have finished it, I said, feeling pleased to be able to tell him this. Then I said: I added the last homophenes last night. Quick and Wig.

Wig! he said. I knew about Wink, like a winking eye, but did not think about Wig.

The corners of his lips pulled wide on the vowel. As well as Wig, there was Wink and Wing and Wick, which all looked the same as Quick. I felt impatient for him to have the paper and fetched it from my bag. I could feel my smile trembling as I handed it over and wished it wouldn't.

It is not only the homophenes, I told him. I wrote the essay like you asked. About how important context is for the lip-reader, and having a wide vocabulary—

I stopped because my voice was starting to feel loose, and I could see that familiar pinch of assessment in Mr. Bell's eyes. He took the paper and read out the title. The Art of Speech-reading, he read, with a Survey of Homophenous Words in the English Language.

He looked up. By Miss Ellen Lark, he finished, keeping his eyes on me so that my own name felt like a crown he meant to place on my head. I look forward to reading it, he continued, but you will have to give me a week or two.

Of course, I said, but as he placed the paper on his desk, I couldn't help the soft drop of disappointment like a coat slipping from an overloaded rack. I had pictured him reading it during our lesson, issuing the invite to the Institute there and then. The essay wasn't so very long.

Mr. Bell was reaching for the notebook. His movements were slow, as if his sleeve was filled with stones. He looked as if he'd only woken up about five minutes earlier. My earlier annoyance at Miss Lance softened. If anyone was going to have the difficult morning lesson with Mr. Bell, I was glad it was me.

The following week Mr. Bell failed to turn up at all. He had told Miss Lance the day before that his headaches were too severe in the mornings. I watched Miss Lance convey this reason to me and explain that she would be teaching my lessons instead. I examined her face for any kind of satisfaction at the arrangement. Although Mr. Bell seemed prone to headaches, I didn't believe this was solely his decision. But Miss Lance was focused on making her speech clear and kept her face neutral, although her pale eyes kept blinking above her careful mouth.

All through that lesson and the next four lessons with Miss Lance, I tried to keep up my spirits. After all, I knew the reason he was so busy. He had trusted me to understand his situation, so I tried to be understanding every time Miss Lance led me up the stairs. But her lessons were tiresome. She followed the Visible Speech primer exactly. She never wavered on the instructions or allowed detours. She took so much care chalking the symbols on the board, it was like watching someone arranging priceless china, so deliberately that you couldn't help the searing temptation to rip away the tablecloth.

At the end of each class, she wrote a report of my progress for Mr. Bell. I could hardly bear to watch her writing it. She seemed determined to prove her teacherly credentials to Mr. Bell by delineating each of my difficulties. "Miss Lark struggles to produce accented syllables," she wrote. I wanted to point out the symbols I was sure I'd mastered, but she already suspected me of being proud. That same pride made me sit still and say nothing as she listed my failings.

On around our fifth lesson, Miss Lance was about to take me upstairs when she glanced back at the door again. Her face was crosshatched with surprise. When she opened it, Miss Mabel Hubbard was waiting on the doorstep.

Am I late? Mabel asked as she stepped inside, noting Miss Lance's concern. She saw me in the hallway and looked at Miss Lance who was resting her fingertips on her jaw and saying, Oh! I must have given you the wrong time.

I glanced at Mabel. It would be a long journey for her back to Cambridge whereas if I returned in the afternoon, Mr. Bell might be around. I said, I can come again later. It's not far for me.

I smiled at Mabel but she was looking at me as if she was scrutinizing an outside scene from a window, trying to determine some distant detail. I was about to repeat myself when Miss Lance held up her hands. No, no, she said over the tops of her fingertips.

Mabel swiveled her head neatly. Even her confusion shivered with beauty as she turned between us and a ripple of shine went up and down her hair. Her thinking eyes made for a lively impression.

Miss Lance said, Today you can have your lesson together. Her eyebrows strained higher than ever.

I felt a knock of surprise. I supposed she didn't want to turn one of us away over her error, but she had never suggested I meet any of Mr. Bell's pupils before, let alone take classes with them.

Then she started saying something about a problem. There was a problem with the usual classroom. We needed a different room? We needed more chairs? She waved up the staircase and said, Go ahead. I will be one minute. Then she went down the corridor, presumably to fetch some item—was it chairs?—which I'd missed her telling us about.

I looked at Mabel. After you, I said, indicating the staircase. I didn't want her to see I hadn't understood Miss Lance and didn't know where we had been instructed to go.

Mabel hesitated. She said, Please, you go first.

We gazed at each other for a moment and Mabel broke into a huge grin. I don't know where! she said, making a shrug. Do you?

No, I replied, as friendly relief rushed through me. I have no idea.

Mabel craned her neck down the corridor, looking for Miss

Lance. She shrugged again, then pointed at the staircase with a questioning face.

I smiled. After you, I said again, but with a mock sweep of my hand. This time she laughed.

We went up to the first landing where there were three closed doors. Mr. Bell's room was another floor up. Mabel paused at the nearest door. Since there was no use in cocking an ear to listen, she knocked to give fair warning to the people inside, eased the door open, and quickly shut it again. Her smile wrinkled into a comic line as she shook her head gravely. Not that one! That one? And she pointed at the next door.

I saw her game. We would go through the whole building like this. I went over and knocked the same as she had done. Inside was a room full of Oratory students, their faces turned in shining rows with all eyes on me. The teacher must have left his post at the blackboard to open the door himself, because he stopped mid-room when I made my abrupt entrance. His lips moved with a question.

Sorry! I said, and my exclamation bounced in amongst all those faces like a ball, breaking the wall of expressions into a wash of surprise and disdain. I couldn't help the rupture of a laugh as I turned to back to Mabel, who had a whatever-shall-we-do? smile on her own face.

The third door was locked so we ran up the next flight of the stairs, skipping Mr. Bell's room. Then we tried the floor after that one, but each room was filled with students and teachers who varied from smiling to disgruntled on our interruption.

We were breathless and heaving with laughter by the time we reached the top floor. It appeared to be deserted, all the rooms empty but with no sign of Miss Lance's things or evidence of being a Visible Speech classroom. Mabel dropped into one of the battered-looking chairs. I didn't want to go back downstairs to Miss Lance, and she seemed equally disinclined. She said something, and it looked amusing, but I missed it. The rules of our game were gone, and we were in freer territory where she might be saying anything. I locked my eyes harder onto her words, feeling that old desperation inch up inside me. She repeated herself but it was no use.

I took out my notebook and offered it to her. To my relief, she took up the pen gamely enough. She wrote, "I expect Miss Lance is regretting not sending one of us home! She has lost both of us now."

Another laugh jumped into my throat but I tried to seal it in with my mouth. I didn't want to give Miss Lance any clues as to our whereabouts, although she was probably already on the trail of disgruntled professors. I sat down next to Mabel and took the notebook, never more grateful for the silence offered by the page.

"I was at Miss Roscoe's school," I wrote. "Your father visited it many times, I think."

She frowned as she read my words so that I feared my stumble. Had my appeal to some kind of connection been too conspicuous? I wanted Mabel to like me. It was partly because of that lonely, unique feature of ourselves that we shared, but it was also because of the lively family life I pictured for her in her busy home in Cambridge. I couldn't help the needling desire to glimpse something of it, when my own family had been so shorn. And weren't we both Mr. Bell's best pupils? I had even been chosen for sponsorship by the esteemed Mr. Ackers. In that respect, if not much else, we were equals. Mabel might be the better lip-reader, but Mr. Bell was going to publish me in *The Pioneer.* I wanted to tell her about the essay, but feared she would take it as a boast. And Mr. McKinney's scorn still hovered in my mind although surely Mabel, unlike Frank, would approve.

"I don't recall my father telling me about that one," she wrote. "I had instructors at home although I went to school in Germany when we lived there."

My disappointment that she didn't know Miss Roscoe's school, and had no need to know of it, vanished into the cloud of my astonishment. "A normal school?" I wrote back.

She smiled widely, evidently pleased, and wrote, "Yes, I learned to speech-read German."

My astonishment didn't abate. I stared at her, then finally was roused to take up the pen. My fear about boasting disappeared and my pen hurried across the page. "I am writing an essay," I wrote, "on the art of speech-reading for Mr. Bell's journal *The Pioneer*. Perhaps you could help me include some notes on acquiring second languages?" I paused, then added, "When I first saw you, you understood Miss Lance so easily I thought you were studying to be a teacher like her."

But she only seemed mildly pleased at my invite. If anything, she pursed her mouth slightly as if she was tasting a sour flavor. "Miss Lance talks to us like we are 'cases,' don't you think?" she wrote. "Whenever I meet a teacher of the deaf, I watch them to see if that is what they are thinking."

I looked at Mabel with her treacle hair pooled across her shoulders and her eyes emanating the same velvet warmth as the chair's fabric. Hidden pride glinted inside her, and I knew it was the same as my own. It was the endless tug and pull between not wanting to be a "case" and knowing that you needed special consideration and should be grateful for it.

"Mr. Bell doesn't talk to us like that," I wrote.

Mabel smiled. "No, he doesn't. He talks about so many things, it is hard to keep up! Sometimes I think his classes are harder even than German, but much more fun. I'm always sorry when we must turn back to Visible Speech. Do you know he is only twenty-nine? I thought he was at least thirty-five."

I read her words slowly. She might have been writing about my own lessons with Mr. Bell. But how did she know his age? Twenty-nine was still many years our senior, but she seemed to think it was significantly less. And what were the various "fun" things he talked to her about, and was it the same as what he'd discussed with me? For a moment, I struggled to write anything back. I didn't want to lose this mood of commonality between us but my desire to tell her what passed between myself and Mr. Bell, and have her tell me the same, was flaring inside me.

"I didn't know that," I wrote, "but Mr. Bell and I also keep our study of the symbols brief. In fact, I believe soon we shan't even have lessons in the classroom anymore. I am to accompany him to the Institute of Technology in connection with my essay."

As soon as I handed the words over I regretted them. I had harbored his promise all summer, not even mentioning it to Adeline or the Day sisters when they teased me. Now I realized it had sustained me in the manner of a secret. Mabel's politely impressed smile didn't seem worth having relinquished it.

"There is something I've always wondered about Visible Speech," she wrote. "It is fine if you have the symbols to read in front of you, but when it comes to the things you want to say yourself, you must try to remember what your words look like in symbols before you speak them. But how can you do that for every single word in a dictionary?"

Mr. Bell's first demonstration crept back to me like a stray dog I'd been trying to ignore. The best part, he'd told everyone while indicating his three pupils, is that they don't even know they're saying words at all.

But Mr. Bell was going to publish my words.

I started writing, "At least with Visible Speech—" when Miss Lance appeared at the top of the stairs. Her cheeks were pink, and she was saying something about having disturbed every professor in the building.

I closed my book and Mabel stood up. Her smile was winning. She said, We got lost!

Miss Lance gazed at her. Her disbelief at our misdemeanor twitched into hesitation. She couldn't reprimand us, Mabel in particular. Her eyes lingered on Mabel, trying to fetch up a smile, and I couldn't help my prickle of envy. It was evident that Mabel was the star pupil as far as she was concerned.

Well, this way, she said, waving her hand, and we followed her down the stairs.

The new classroom—which turned out to have about twenty chairs in it—was in one of the rooms with a stiff latch that we'd mistaken for locked. The rest of the hour followed much like any of my lessons, although I paid more attention to my companion's reckoning of Miss Lance's tiny and precise symbols than I did my own. Throughout the lesson, Mabel sat perfectly still and upright. She scarcely demurred, the symbols causing her no effort.

As the lesson dragged on, I felt our conversation among the sunlit dust motes of the School of Oratory's upper reaches slip away. The symbols clustered at my eyes like tiny dark weights, trying to pull me under. Mabel waited patiently until Miss Lance finally said to me, Yes, that's it, and then she smiled, and I saw she meant to be encouraging.

After the lesson finished, we went downstairs past the closed classroom doors and Mabel sneaked me a smile, recalling how we'd knocked on them all. At the front door, Miss Lance took out her notebook, perhaps fearing another misunderstanding, and wrote, "I will write to you with new times. Mr. Bell is only teaching afternoons at the moment."

Mabel looked at me and said, I do not mind the mornings.

I gazed at Mabel. Had I seen her meaning correctly? She would choose a lesson with Miss Lance over one with Mr. Bell? Doubt plowed through me. Did her lessons with Mr. Bell not matter very much to her? Was her own life full enough in spite of what she lacked? I felt a hot rub of shame that I had made so many boasts to her when no doubt she had seen plainly my loneliness shining through each one. Surely she had plenty of her own friends, and they were hearing people of a similar standing to her family. My thoughts turned black: her kindness to me had been like hearing people's kindness.

Miss Lance pursed her lips then glanced at me. I guessed her dilemma. She disapproved of the carefree style of Mr. Bell's lessons with me, but would prefer to have Miss Hubbard as her own pupil in the mornings. After a moment, she nodded. All right, she said. Miss Hubbard in the mornings, Miss Lark in the afternoons.

I kept my nod functional to show simply that I'd understood the arrangement.

Mabel turned to me to say goodbye, since her stagecoach stop was different to mine. I was surprised to see that she looked anxious, her smile trembling into carefully modulated words. I watched her mouth, hoping to find some expression of her pleasure, or desire for us to meet again. Whatever she had said, Miss Lance didn't feel the need to relay it to me. She took her favored pupil's elbow, and they went off in the opposite direction.

In our next lesson, Mr. Bell hardly looked better for it being past the lunch hour. His smile barely lifted the moon-colored hang of his cheeks. His eyes were small, shadows circled them. I couldn't help my concern. As we took our seats, I asked, How goes the night owl?

Mr. Bell laughed. Is that what Miss Lance calls me? he said. Well, I really must congratulate her. She has been doing a marvelous job. Then he said, I'm sorry I haven't been able to teach you. The night owl is not as bright as the morning lark, it's true.

I smiled, and wished I had some words of reassurance, although it looked like what he needed most of all was a proper night's sleep. Truthfully, I was also relieved to see his exhaustion. Miss Lance was right. He was working hard into the small hours, and it was no wonder he had been unable to take my lessons in the morning. Here he was, exhausted, and yet smiling at me as well as he could manage.

The morning lark, I told him, advises going to bed at sundown.

He shook his head, made a scoff. I have too much to do, he replied.

Let me help you, I said. The question was out before I'd even thought about what I meant.

Help me? he asked, and his look of genuine surprise sank into me like teeth.

Well, I said, trying to brush aside my hurt and meaning to remind him that in actual fact he had already asked for my help with *The Pioneer*. I took out my notebook because suddenly my voice was feeling unsteady. "I am very thorough at copy-work," I wrote. "Every week you have to write out the Visible Speech exercises for your pupils and there are so many new pupils this semester." I paused before adding, "There is also my work for *The Pioneer*."

Mr. Bell looked like he had forgotten my essay altogether. He read my words once, then nodded as he appeared to read them through again. I waited, my breath feeling bundled in my chest.

I'm sorry, he said. I haven't had time to read it yet.

His eyes were settled gravely on me as if to slide along his apology, but it felt instead like a small shove.

Of course, I said, feeling my lack of other options. I understand, I added effortfully, and made a silent farewell to all the carefully collected accounts I had hoped to discuss with him. Of Cold and Gold, Tassel and Dazzle.

Good! he said. I will read it as soon as I can, he added. This week, I expect.

The prospect of our Visible Speech drills loomed toward me. Is it the Telegraph, I tried in an attempt at deflection, that keeps you up all hours?

Ah, he said. As a matter of fact, yes. He began talking, but his speech was faster than usual. I watched his words carefully, but every time I managed a few, more would rush along and knock them from my grasp. I saw Telegraph and Harmonic, because

I knew to expect them, given my question. There was something about the summer vacation and a voice. A human voice. But his words slipped and slipped, and the more they fell away from me, the more I became distracted by the idea that most of the time I could understand him because he talked to me like I was a "case," as Mabel said all teachers of the deaf did. Or was it just the summer vacation? Had the summer made him forget our way of speaking? Or had my eyes fallen out of practice? These thoughts ballooned in my mind until there was no room at all to concentrate on his lips.

Mr. Bell, I said. Please. You are talking very fast.

My request seemed to spin around us in the long pause that followed. He frowned as if he was the one who didn't understand. I said, Just a little bit slower. I am quite tired today, although I'd slept perfectly well the night before. Then I watched the awfulness of his expression gathering, as if now he remembered who I was: a pupil, a deaf girl, someone with whom he could not talk naturally or freely. I was like any one of his other pupils, in fact, whom he must take through a carefully prepared lesson. I wanted to say No, he only had to talk like before, and then we could discuss the Telegraph to our hearts' delight. But it was too late to take my request back, and the truth was stark enough: I had not a clue what he was on about.

He took up the notebook, and I didn't know if I felt relief or disappointment that he had to resort to it. "I have this headache," he wrote. "It's because I can't keep to normal hours like most people."

I nodded. Again, I opened my mouth. What was I going to say? Mr. Bell, it must be terribly hard. You must rest more. The morning lark wins out, you must rise before ten. I tried to think of all the people I had seen making heart-to-hearts and imagine the responses that tipped from one heart to another, and the kind of thing that should tip from mine.

What I said was this: Mr. Bell, did you know that Pain has thirteen homophenes?

He blinked. It does? What are they? he asked.

Pain, I said then wrote down the rest, starting with Bait and Maid.

To my surprise, he laughed. Thirteen! he said. You found thirteen. Miss Lark, I must apologize. I do declare, he said, that thirteen is a triumph. I'll write it for you. "Triumph." Here are the symbols. Triumph. Say it with me. Triumph!

A triumph, I said. I liked how the long "Tri" of the first syllable ended with a firm thump of air on the lower lip, as if a decisive victory had been awarded for one's efforts. Triiii-umph, I said again.

A triumph. Do you know, Miss Lark, what I do when something is a triumph?

I shook my head.

Please stand, he said. Do you promise not to laugh?

Laugh? I said. I won't laugh.

Good, he said. Now please stand.

I cautiously rose to my feet.

We shall commence a war dance.

A war dance? I asked, taking a chance on what I'd seen, since the words also looked like Audience.

A war dance, he repeated, and reached for the notebook. "I learned it from an Indian man who lives near my parents' home in Canada. A fine fellow. Now, I want you to follow me."

I got up and followed Mr. Bell around the room, crouched low, stamping from foot to foot. At first, I felt foolish, but soon in spite of myself I was laughing, like I said I wouldn't. Even the walls of the room seemed to reverberate with the shared stamping of our timely feet. My body filled with the shake of the floor and the room, and with the laugh in my chest, and his laugh too.

When we came to a pause, and I'd straightened up, Mr. Bell was looking grave. He wrote, "I told you not to laugh, Miss

Lark." He looked so stern that cold worry rose up my back until the corners of his smile puckered. You have a rare talent, he said.

For speech-reading?

For dancing!

I have never done a war dance before.

You dance like you have won many battles. He took the notebook again, and wrote as if he was making a formal invitation. "Miss Lark, would you come to the Institute of Technology with me? I would like to show you some equipment I am developing to help the deaf. This is not the Telegraph, but the other aspect of my work. I would appreciate your opinion."

Should I point out that he had already promised a visit? He was making this invite sound like the first. But perhaps it was an expanded gesture to compensate for failing to read my essay. That hardly mattered now, I thought, if he wished for me to go to the Institute. He would get to my essay in the fullness of time. For now, he wished for more direct advice, outside the confines of our lessons.

I said, I shall check with my grandmother. This time next week?

I didn't think Adeline would approve of me going to the Institute of Technology. What place did a young woman have in those halls? She decried anything that fell outside of her narrow jurisdiction, but if I went in place of my lesson, she'd have no way of knowing.

Perfect, he said. Your lesson will be my lesson.

I laughed. For one hour, I said, I will be your teacher.

Exactly that.

As I was leaving the school, Miss Lance asked me, What was all that noise? I couldn't help seizing her hands and squeezing them, as if vestiges of Mr. Bell's war dance still possessed my wrists and fingers. She looked quite taken aback, more so when I said, in perfect Visible Speech: A triumph!

That's what the noise was, I told her. A triumph.

10

ⴹⵀⵔⵓⵍ ⵊⵓⵓⵍⴸ‑ ⴹⵍⵞⵓ
[A mighty achievement]

THE FOLLOWING week I walked into the Back Bay. The air was clear of the landfill dust that blew over the city on murkier days. I enjoyed picturing Adeline's impotent jealousy for the new houses which were grander than anything you found in the South End. Ahead, the recently laid streets were spotted with newly planted saplings, before turning into empty land which stretched towards the swampy recesses at the far end of the Bay.

I turned down a side street, and it wasn't long before I spotted the Institute. It was a huge building, fronted by columns and a wide flight of steps. There was no sign of Mr. Bell. I looked up and down the street, wondering if I should wait at the steps or go through the doors. I felt conspicuous standing alone but

didn't know how to give an account of myself should I be questioned inside, even though I was clutching my notebook. I began
to worry that this was another appointment Mr. Bell wouldn't
keep. I'd never been in such a vast building, and I didn't know
how to prepare myself. I even started to wish I had persuaded
Adeline to bring me.

I checked my watch again and turned to go, just as Mr. Bell
tapped my shoulder. Miss Lark, he said. Are you leaving?

I smiled but found I hadn't a reply. Standing in all this sunshine, Mr. Bell seemed different from the man who taught me
in the gloomy confines of the School of Oratory's classroom. He
cut a taller and younger figure, one who was at ease with the
impressive building behind him as if he had just stepped from
his own front door. Suddenly I felt shy. The Back Bay felt huge
around us, and the passersby too close on the sidewalk. I didn't
know how loud or quiet to make my voice. I started opening
my notebook, which was one of my finest, and the pen I'd bor-
rowed from Adeline without asking. "I was counting the streets,"
I wrote. "Do they really run all the way to the letter Z?"

Mr. Bell laughed so that two passing gentlemen glanced at us.
He, for one, didn't seem to care about his own volume. I don't
know, he said, but I wouldn't try to find out. It's a filthy trip.

I watched him bite Filthy into his lower lip, his grimace of
distaste. "That cannot be true," I wrote. "They are naming the
streets after English Lords." I pointed at the next street down,
Clarendon, and arced my finger to the following one: Dartmouth.

"Exeter," I wrote, "is after Dartmouth. But surely, they will
not get much further than I or J. We will have to hope there
is a limit to human progress and they don't fill the bay all the
way to Roxbury."

He was smiling. You're right, he said, and added how he
couldn't very well let me go any further since I'd fall into the
marsh, and then what would he tell my grandmother? This way,

he said, raising a hand to the doors. But he paused before going further. He turned to me again, and said, You can speak, Miss Lark. Speaking is not just for our lessons.

I smiled and said Yes, I will, since I didn't know how to explain how overcome I'd felt. And now that I was climbing the steps with Mr. Bell, the hollowness of that uncertainty began to loosen and disappear, like the bay at the end of the street.

We climbed the steps slowly for Mr. Bell was telling me very carefully about how he had given a Public Lecture at the Institute on Visible Speech and educating the deaf. The attendance was not large—probably a trifle over four hundred—but the finest minds in Boston were there. One of the professors invited him to give a second lecture and he had been promised a full house, plus free access to the Institute.

When we arrived at the huge doors, he waved toward the long marble floors that skimmed away from us. In here, he told me, are the finest scientific minds of Boston.

The air was chilly and smelled of the stone walls. Occasionally someone walked across the halls or nodded at Mr. Bell, who seemed his more agitated, excitable self again. He walked quickly, smiling readily at anyone who greeted him, looking at the doors we passed as if he was mentally rehearsing which estimable scientists they belonged to. I had to walk fast to keep up.

Here, he said, finally. Inside, the room was lined with benches which had been laid out with apparatus. I tried to take in the array of objects: tubes, funnels, fans and a box containing a candle and set of revolving mirrors.

He took his notebook and wrote, "Acoustics." These are all apparatus concerning acoustics, he said, pointing at the word. He showed me a few items, explaining each one carefully. Then he moved into view an object that looked like a microscope, except in place of an eyepiece, there was a large cone.

This is what I wanted to show you. Here. This is—He switched to his pen. "The Phonoautograph," he wrote.

He opened a small pouch and placed a piece of smoked glass in my hand. It was crisscrossed by two scratched lines. I had no idea what the lines meant, but I liked the feel of the glass, like an ancient tablet.

He pointed at the cone, then moved his hand downward to show a small stalk that dangled beneath it. You speak into the cone, he said. Which moves the stalk, and writes a word on the glass, here. See?

I nodded, the notion beginning to formulate in my mind. This was a different kind of visible speech, a device that could make a sort of text out of spoken words.

He was writing a long paragraph into the notebook. "This is my apparatus to help the deaf," I read, when he had finished. "I have often wondered if some simple apparatus could be contrived to bring the vibrations of the speaker's voice to the hand of a lip-reader. Then some of the ambiguities of lip-reading would disappear. What you have in your hand are some examples of the Phonoautograph. Those lines distinguish *P* and *B*. The top one is Paper, the bottom one is Baby. They are homophenes, as you know. Tell me, what do you think? Should it be useful?"

I looked at the panel of smoked glass, setting it along my palm so I could compare the lines. Paper, Baby. The lines were mysterious but it was a kind of mystery that could be grasped equally by deaf and hearing people alike.

Mr. Bell leaned forward. Well? he said. His dark eyes were speckled with his interest in my opinion.

Well? I said. Well, I—

I dropped my eyes to the glass again, thinking of all those hours we pupils had sat in our classrooms, issuing words with no idea if we were right or wrong, nothing to go by apart from the expressions of our teachers. I was so used to my ears being measured with bells, my eyes being tested on lips, and my speech being assessed with constant readings. I was used to doctors or educators nodding at me, then turning away to tell someone else—Mama, Miss Roscoe—their verdict. I was familiar with the way people listened to me with that deepening look of concentration, which at some point would turn into unease or disdain. I was used to expecting them not to try to talk to me again. And here on this glass Mr. Bell had made speech visible. Only it didn't look like very much at all.

May I try it? I asked, nodding toward the Phonoautograph.

He hesitated. The device is not complete.

I was puzzled. I said, But how did you make this? I held up the glass to him.

It needs one more attachment. He looked at me as if he was doubting himself for bringing me here. Miss Lark, I can show you, but it may not be to your liking. He took the notebook. "You shall need to have a strong constitution."

I laughed at his words. "Mr. Bell," I wrote, "I thought we had established that I am of a sound scientific mind. Isn't that why you asked me here?"

He said, Yes, but... Then he trailed off, lifting his palms as if they could hold up the weight of his explanation, before he dropped those too, and looked at me again. All right, he said.

He fetched a small box from under the table and moved it along the workbench so that he was a short distance away. He opened the lid and reached inside, and appeared to fiddle with a piece of foil, keeping his hands within the box. Since the box wasn't very big, this covert operation caused him some difficulty. I went over to him, ready to inquire after what he was doing, but he raised his hand to stop me; too late, for I spotted the gray and lumpen item inside. My body became stiff and a sound came from me, as Mr. Bell quickly wrapped up the ear in foil which was surely taken from a human cadaver.

Miss Lark? Forgive me, have I alarmed you?

I was smiling hard and trying not to think of the gristle and the hairs that protruded from it. I shook my head, and said, I am perfectly fine. Please, continue. But my throat felt tight, and I wasn't sure my words came out as anything more than a squeak. Mr. Bell peered at me, more worried than I had seen him before. My experiments, he said. This is for my experiments. You understand? Then he wrote, "I shouldn't wish for your guardians to think I leave the ears of cadavers on the table for my students to see!"

I burst out laughing. I will not tell them, I said, and I plucked my lips into a solemn line of promise.

Upset, he said. Was I not very upset by the sight of it?

I assured him I was not upset. A moment's alarm aside, I could look calmly at a dead man's ear, and ask was he really using it for that instrument?

His shoulders sank. Well, you see. I must attach it here.

He pointed at the narrow end of the Phonoautograph cone, then lifted the foil package, the ear tucked discreetly back inside it. Shall I? he asked. You wanted to see it work. Inside this ear there are membranes, bones. Membranes, he repeated, when I hesitated. Sound makes them move—

He was struggling to explain, having lost his composure. I said, I see. Nature is always the best teacher.

He smiled. Yes. Yes, that's it exactly! Sometimes we must look to nature. Wait one moment.

He spent a while fiddling with the foil package so that it was suspended below the cone with the stalk of hay or bristle protruding from it. Then he placed a new piece of smoked glass under the stalk.

I shall not ask you to speak into it, he said, and before I could protest that I didn't mind the ear, he lowered his lips to the cone.

Watch, he said, and lowered his head further, speaking a few words into the device as he pulled the smoked glass under it so that the vibrating bristle dragged across its surface. A shaky pattern appeared.

See that?

I squinted at him. It must be your words, I said. But it doesn't look like words.

It is your name, he said.

I gazed at him. My name? Did he know that my name was no more than a brief flick of the tongue, twice if my surname was included?

I can't see my name, I told him, after a moment. My mother called me La-La.

He smiled. La-La, he said, which startled me, for I had not seen that pet name for years, and did not expect it from Mr. Bell. I dipped my eyes to the glass to hide my confusion. Truthfully, I didn't recognize anything familiar in the line on the glass either, but it calmed me to see the scratched line that wasn't so different from an inked line, to examine its crags and peaks, hinting of other worlds like the script of a foreign language.

May I have a turn? I asked. I do not mind the ear.

His nod was a small acquiescence. He placed a new piece of smoked glass on the cone and turned the instrument toward me. But now that I was looking down the funnel of the cone, through the membranes and bones of the cadaver's ear, my thoughts dropped away, as if I was kneeling into a cavern.

What shall I say? I asked.

The first thing that comes into your head, he said, tapping his own head to show his meaning.

Theresa Dudley. She was the thought that arrived with me. I remembered her standing with the other girls at Mr. Bell's demonstration, reading the Visible Speech symbols on the blackboard. Where was she now? Had she found the illumination I had muddled for lemonade? As I poised myself over the cone, I felt doubt creeping into me that it might be the case. But Mr. Bell was waiting. I straightened again and took up my notebook, writing down the word "Lemonade."

How do you say this in Visible Speech? I asked, showing Mr.

Bell and keeping my face utterly serious. I would make this into a game and then my disappointment, or his, wouldn't matter.

He narrowed his eyes and chuckled. Lemonade? All right, he said and jotted down a line of symbols.

I bent over the Phonoautograph and read the symbols into the cone as Mr. Bell pulled the glass under the tip of the stylus.

Lemonade, I said, and watched as intricate curves appeared in a waving line.

There, said Mr. Bell, taking out the glass so I could hold it. Your voice, he said.

I stared at the mark. My breath, the action of my lips, teeth and tongue, that I had practiced every day for more years than I cared to count, set out before my eyes.

It needs some improvement, he continued. In his notebook, he wrote, "I can't have a real human ear. I must create the instrument with the same kind of artificial bones and membrane."

I looked at the Phonoautograph. I was awed that I had commandeered the ear, and the stylus, and something real had appeared that I could see with the same equal sight as Mr. Bell. But in that lurked a misty suspicion that it would be no more than a clever trick. Were deaf people supposed to carry one of these contraptions around every time they wished to get clarity on a difficult lip-reading word? I remembered Mabel's doubts about Visible Speech. An impressive feat of creation that was cumbersome in practice. But I couldn't tell this to Mr. Bell, and besides, I hated to feel the lapping waves of my own disappointment.

He seemed to be waiting, so I said, Would it not be heavy to carry around?

Puzzlement wrinkled his lips and brow, as he replied, It will be in the schoolroom.

I see, I said, fearing my misunderstanding. I looked again at the device, and the foil package with the ear, trying to summon up some praise. The bones in the ear seem so large, I tried instead, for the voice alone to move them. Smiling, I added, First a feather, now bones!

But Mr. Bell didn't smile. He was looking at me as if I had said something strange. I started running over the words I'd spoken, trying to picture the Visible Speech symbols for Feather and Bones. But he was saying, Yes. The idea struck me too. Yes. It doesn't seem possible. Heavy bones, a small membrane. And the voice can move them.

His eyes didn't shift from me as he spoke out these phrases, his head tapping forward on each one, interspersing them with Yes, Yes, as if he was giving each statement a tick. I waited, unsure what I should say next.

Miss Lark, he said eventually. There was something bright squeezing in his eyes that seemed to match his smile. Can I tell you something?

I nodded. Of course, I said, with a little shrug I meant to be carefree, although I was starting to feel dizzy. I'd never been asked so many times for my opinion, or confidence.

It is something I have dreamed of although I can tell no one, he said, then reached for the notebook and wrote a few words which he presented to me. "The electrical transmission of speech."

The memory of his voice under my fingertips. It startled me. I could almost feel again the thrum of his speaking in my skin, coming all the way from the other side of the piano, and the end of the instrument's string. The piano, I said, without thinking. Then I remembered our lesson in which he had tried to tell me something about the human voice, and what he had done in his summer vacation.

See, he said, laughing. You understand. Then he wrote, "But no one else thinks it is possible or sensible. The Multiple Telegraph is what businesses want. Who needs a Talking Telegraph? They will think it a foolish idea." Foolish, he repeated, when I looked up. A fool's idea, a flight of madness!

I watched his string of *F* and the pressing *M* of his Madness, although I wasn't sure if he was repeating the words for my benefit, or running away in an imaginary dialogue with all the people who would laugh at him. He looked rueful for a moment, latching his hands behind his back. His lips started moving again, but I didn't catch any of his words. I was about to ask him to repeat them, when he pulled his watch from his pocket and said, Well. The time.

No, I wanted to say. Tell me more about the voice in a wire. Ask me again what I think. But it was true that the hour was finished, and he was starting to get that harried look in his eyes, all the things he must do crowding in on him.

Instead, I said: Mr. Bell, let me help you with the school. Miss Lance said there is so much to do with the exercises, the timetable. Then you will be able to focus on the Telegraph work. A talking one! I added. Why not? I think you could do it.

Mr. Bell smiled, but it was tentative. He said, Thank you, and nodded a few times, as if considering my proposal. Yes, that would be helpful. His manner became brighter, as he added: Didn't I say this would be a useful lesson, Miss Lark? For me, he added, leaning forward so I laughed.

Good, I told him. I will come by tomorrow and collect the work.

He picked up the smoked glass which he placed in my hands. I would prefer illumination to lemonade, he said, making the two words very clearly, with the pushed out-*tion* on the former distinguishing it from the latter. Keep this safe for me.

I took the glass carefully, pinching its edges where some of the soot had already rubbed away. Lemonade, Illuminate. Hadn't I come so far from that error? It wasn't so long ago that I sat in the rows of Miss Roscoe's schoolroom, and now I was in the Institute of Technology, a building I had feared entering, but would leave carrying a little piece of its secrets in my pocket. And I would keep the glass safe for Mr. Bell, until he found his own way to illumination, his fool's dream, the Talking Telegraph.

I lifted the glass so the window light shone through the scratched line and Mr. Bell laughed. Words moved on his lips. He said, That is illumination.

Or so I thought.

I kept the smoked glass with Mama's letters, inside an old music box and nestled between the bundles of envelopes. I wrote Mama of the trip to the Institute, but kept the details sparse, only wishing to convey that my essay for *The Pioneer* had led to the invite. I didn't mention that Mr. Bell hadn't actually read my essay yet. I made no mention at all of the cadaver's ear or what Mr. Bell had told me about a Talking Telegraph. I supposed Mama would find the idea strange, and even scoff at it, as Mr. Bell said most people would. I didn't see what was so absurd about the notion. Most of my life the voice had seemed like an impossible thing that others made look so easy. Why should it not go in a wire as well? And Mr. Bell knew the human voice better than anyone.

The copy-work I collected from Mr. Bell was various. Mostly it concerned Visible Speech exercises for his pupils, which he must prepare in advance of our lessons. There was also a flyer for his evening classes aimed at adult "deaf-mutes" and a short report on Visible Speech he needed to send to a few schools for the deaf. I hoped to be given the class timetables because I wanted to see who his other pupils were, and if Mabel still took the morning lesson with Miss Lance. But either they didn't need copying, or Miss Lance had held on to them.

One afternoon I had finished all the week's copying and was in the kitchen helping Joan make preserves. These days I did my Visible Speech practice after everything else, and as quickly as I could, because it was so tiresome. I stood at the table, dipping a wire basket of figs into a kettle of hot lye to prepare them for preserving. Dip the Basket, I said as they went in. The hard part was moving my mouth from one position to the next, and it took several attempts before I managed Dip with its little punch of air from the hard palate, and Basket with its hiss on the teeth and click in the throat, by which time the figs had been quite ruined.

Before Joan could complain, Adeline came into the kitchen. She was wearing her traveling dress. She stood at the door, opening and closing it while her cheeks lifted in a wince of displeasure. I supposed the hinges made a sound because there was nothing wrong to my eyes.

Then she beckoned for Joan. My travel case, she said. Please bring it to the front door.

When Joan was gone, Adeline sat down at the kitchen table and patted the place next to her for me to join her.

I'll be gone for a while, she said. To see friends.

She started tugging at the buttons on her sleeves as if to loosen them. Her plaid traveling dress was no longer her best and she minded it. She said, Business has been too slow.

I nodded, wondering if the conversation was over. I was no longer sure if she was fussing at her sleeves because they were too tight, or because something was on her mind. Eventually she clasped her hands on the table and said, Mr. Bell. She waited until I nodded to show I'd grasped his name. She continued, He isn't teaching you. Miss Lance. Isn't she a student teacher?

I tried to settle the alarm bouncing in my chest. I said, Miss Lance taught a few of my lessons. But I believe Mr. Bell will teach me from now on.

Her long gaze seemed to drive her further back in her seat, away from me. Was something the matter with my voice?

I started saying, My essay—but Adeline raised a hand. Don't mention that paper, she said. You have been stalking my boarders all summer. The point is: I don't see why we should pay Miss Lance the same.

She had to repeat herself twice before I understood: she was concerned about my board. Mr. Ackers paid for Mr. Bell's fees, but Adeline rented all her rooms in the house, apart from mine. My room was perfectly serviceable for tenancy as far as she was concerned, even though we didn't have many boarders at present.

My mouth opened and she raised her eyebrows in a matching movement, which made me shut it again. She reached for my slate, glancing distastefully at some banter I'd had going with Joan. She wiped it clean with a rag and wrote, "I suggest we pay half for Miss Lance and the other half will cover the cost of your board."

No, I said so that surprise jumped on to her face. I wanted to tell her that it was Mr. Ackers who gave us the money for Mr. Bell's fees, but Adeline knew that well enough, so likely she was planning not to tell Mama that she was keeping half of the fees for my board. No doubt she reasoned that Mama still owed her from my father's debts that Adeline had helped settle. Fury started to bubble inside me as I stared at the slate. Adeline would never let go of old scores. Hadn't I helped Joan enough around the house to earn my board? And was I supposed to keep this new arrangement a secret from Mama? I began to tell her instead that I would find the money for my fees. My lessons needed to be with Mr. Bell, since Miss Lance wasn't half the teacher, and it was what Mr. Ackers had requested. Besides Mr. Bell needed my help with his work.

Your help? said Adeline, but she wasn't sufficiently interested to inquire further. She said, I don't like the man. Have you seen how he dresses? She touched her dress, her sleeves, and said, Broadcloth. Sleeves covered in chalk. Nervous, she said, yet too familiar.

Then she looked at me. Besides, your voice hasn't—

My breath tightened as I searched her face. Had I missed some words or was her comment left dangling? I hated her smile, matched by a flat look in her eyes. I looked at Joan, who'd returned with Adeline's case, but she was busy with the ruined figs, fussing at the sludge as if it could be revived.

Was that what Mr. Bell thought of my voice? He invited me to the Institute and told me about the Telegraph because he didn't think there was much point working on Visible Speech. I thought of Mabel in our lesson with Miss Lance and how she had uttered every word to Miss Lance's absolute satisfaction. I began to feel scooped out, as if my blood were being replaced with air, until I remembered the smoked glass. Mr. Bell had given it to me and asked me to keep his dream safe for him. Besides, I had let my own Visible Speech practice become slack. I resolved to double down on my studies again.

Copy-work, I said. Surely there was copy-work I could do to cover my board. My voice came out like a sudden rainstorm but I didn't care how I sounded to Adeline or Joan, or anyone at that moment. I needed Adeline to relent on her proposal. I told her everything would be all right, she didn't need to worry, she didn't need to change my lessons with Mr. Bell. I would find the money for my board. I would—

Adeline held up her hand, her face pinched. Enough, she said, and added something that looked like We'll see but it was so slight on her lips it can't have been more than a murmur.

At first, I found copy-work to pay for Mr. Bell's classes. I copied flyers and pamphlets for Mrs. Baylis's meetings on topics relating to the woman question. One of Adeline's friends wanted a collection of letters from a deceased uncle copied, so I spent several days copying out the man's thoughts on the Duties of the Wife. I wrote a new sign for the window of Little St. Clouds, in hope that my fine script would make our boardinghouse stand out from the others in the street. Joan said we could devise a menu and I put that in the window too. By the time Adeline came back, there would be new boarders, the dining room would be busy, and I would have earnings of my own to give her.

Sometimes I joined Mrs. Baylis's soirees and passed an advertisement along the rows while the speaker was lecturing on emancipation. While I waited for a response, I tried to attend to the speaker. If they'd written a pamphlet, then I could read that at the same time for an approximation but otherwise I was stringing together my best guesses at what was spoken.

At one of these evenings, there was a woman who kept glancing over her shoulder at me. She was about my mother's age, with dark curls scooped up in combs. I became uncomfortable. Did she see my straining eyes? I tried to straighten myself and look fascinated but the only thing I knew about the speaker was her name, and that was from the flyer.

Afterward, the woman came up to me. We were standing next to a huge fern that partly concealed us. To my surprise she started spelling out my name.

Are you Miss Lark?

Are you deaf? I asked, failing to hide my amazement, since she had nodded throughout the lecture like everyone else.

She smiled, shaking her head. Hearing, she signed. I saw your note. My name is Augusta Tanner. I would like to ask for your help.

She was using signs in an English pattern with the clear lip-shapes of a hearing person. All my exhaustion from trying to follow the lecture slipped away as I watched her.

My nephew told me about you. You have met, I think. Frank.

I felt a little leap in my thoughts, like catching something midair. Frank? Your nephew?

Right. His uncle is my husband. That is how I learned the sign language, twenty years ago now. I see you know a little?

Some, I replied. Hope was tumbling into confusion, and my whole being felt poised to see her explain what she had to do with Frank. But I didn't ask her, I couldn't; I'd turned myself away from thoughts of him.

Augusta spread her hands. Well. Frank would like to learn speech-reading.

I stared at her and laughter bounced from me. Three people turned their heads, but Augusta Tanner didn't move. If anything, her smile became firmer.

I waited until the guests had looked away again. Frank doesn't believe speech-reading is possible, I signed. He told me himself.

He has changed his mind. We can offer you a generous fee.

She held out my advertisement and flipped it over. On the back was written a sum that was almost half the fees for one of Mr. Bell's lessons.

I couldn't remove my eyes from the paper. When I looked up, she was smiling. You agree? she asked.

I'm not qualified, I told her, spelling out the word and shaking my head.

She frowned. A paper, she signed. Frank told me. Published in a journal, right?

She was so easy to understand. Her lips, her hands working together as a perfect pair, slotting notions into my mind. I felt my resolve beginning to collapse and had to gather myself. No, I cannot, I told her.

You cannot?

Thank you for the offer, I signed, and stepped back into the crowd, allowing myself one last glance over my shoulder to where Augusta stood by the fern looking down at my advertisement. She tucked it inside her bag and went back to her seat.

In the week that followed, I was restless for my next lesson with Mr. Bell, wanting to take my mind off Augusta Tanner's proposal. I wished I had not finished all his copy-work already, so I could distract myself with that. But I would have to wait until our lesson to deliver it and fetch more. I made some studies of the smoked glass, copying out the line of "Lemonade" and trying to figure which parts of the line denoted which letters. I threw myself into practicing my *R*'s in Visible Speech. But still, I thought about her proposal each night. Of course I couldn't accept. Adeline would find out and use it as a reason to end my tuition. It was clear she wanted me gone from Little St. Clouds and didn't think that Mr. Bell could do anything for my speech.

But as the week passed, the sum that Augusta had shown me kept playing in my thoughts. I couldn't stop thinking about both the money or Frank, as he'd stood before the delighted children, and flicked shadows from his hands. Temptation began to take root in me, seeding useful rationales. It was a fine sum that would please Adeline, even if she didn't know how it had been obtained. And Frank didn't have the chance of learning Visible Speech or lip-reading like I did, so couldn't I help him? Even Mr. Bell would approve, if he did find out. Perhaps he could quell any outrage of Adeline's at my deceit. But then my reasoning fell at a final hurdle: where would I teach him?

11

⸂ℳℨℽ
[Azure]

MISS LANCE opened the door at the School of Oratory. I knew before she had said anything that Mr. Bell wasn't there. Is it a headache? I asked with a smile, meaning to make light of it, and show that I was familiar enough with Mr. Bell to make such assertions. Her smile turned down the corners of her mouth. Something like that, she said.

Then she glanced down at the pile of papers in my hands. Are those the exercises? she asked.

I let her take the papers from me, trying not to mind that Mr. Bell wouldn't see how carefully I'd copied the text and symbols in the exercises. No doubt Miss Lance would take charge of administering them. At least I had paid particular attention to the reports he was sending to the three schools. Surely he would deal with those himself.

As I took my seat, I asked, How is Miss Hubbard?

Miss Lance looked up from the symbols she was chalking across the board. More *R*'s, I noted, so Miss Lance, not Mr. Bell, would see the benefits of my practice.

She is well, I believe. I don't teach her in the mornings anymore.

She turned back to the board, leaving me with the jumble of her words. Had I seen them correctly, and in that order? She had definitely said something about not teaching her, and she had also said Morning. She must mean that she taught Miss Hubbard in the afternoons now. But I couldn't stop the thought that lengthened like a shadow. Surely she didn't mean that Mr. Bell was teaching her in the mornings? Mr. Bell, who couldn't rise before noon?

We drilled *R*'s for a whole hour. Miss Lance didn't let me move on from a single word until I could say each one perfectly. We worked through the list, switching between the exercises on paper, and her symbols on the board. I could barely think by the end of the lesson, as if all the cells in my being had been pulled into alignment with my thoughts, which thundered with the symbols. Occasionally, I balked, my entire weight straining against them, and the greatest task was trying not to wonder how long until we finished.

At the end of the lesson, Miss Lance handed me a note. "Thank you again for the copy-work," she had written. "It is appreciated. I will ask Mr. Bell to leave out next week's work, and you could collect it?"

Of course, I said, looking up from the note. Miss Lance was smiling at me. Thank you, she said again, but it had the effect of overdone gratitude and made me bristle. It's no trouble, I said, as brightly as I could. I wanted to add: it is for Mr. Bell and the Telegraph, so you do not need to thank me. But I said farewell and she cheerfully bade me the same.

★ ★ ★

When I came by the School of Oratory the next afternoon, Mr. Bell opened the door and said, Thank goodness. I laughed, and said, Your headache is better?

No! he said. It is much worse. But you have been a life-saver. He turned to the secretary where a neat stack of papers was waiting. I have more exercises, some reports—

I watched the list trail from his lips, but only gleaned a general understanding that he had a great many things to do. He handed the papers to me, and said, I must go now. I have some gentlemen to meet at the Institute.

About the Phonoautograph? I asked him. Or the Multiple Telegraph? I had been practicing these names using my best guesses of their Visible Speech translations. He looked impressed, so I added: Or the invention that will talk?

His shoulders sank. Ah Miss Lark, he said. That one will never talk.

Before I could mind my bluntness, I said, You gave up already?

No, he said, then reached around in search of some paper. I gave him a sheet from the copy-work, and he turned it over and wrote on the back.

"I spoke to some electricians about the human voice telegraph idea but they do not think it is practicable. They think the fundamental principle is sound in theory but they don't think the voice will generate a strong enough current over useful distances in practice. At least it will take many years. I must focus on the acoustic Multiple Telegraph instead. However, I am not an electrician and all my work suffers for my lack of expertise in this area."

He gave me back the paper, and when I looked up, he shrugged as a final finishing comment. There you have it, he said.

I looked at his words—his defeat—again. I felt as if he was tossing away everything he had told me at the Institute and the promise that he'd asked me to keep for him. I remembered the piano wires, and his surprise when I had asked if it was a voice he meant to put in a wire. It was an instant, a connection that traveled wordless, but one I could feel in my fingertips, the shiver of a half thought between us. I'd felt it again at the Institute when I looked at the bones in the human ear. I didn't know anything about electricity, but how could a few electricians dismiss the entire thing, and say the human voice wasn't strong enough, before the idea had barely had a chance? I was surprised at the flush of my indignation. I had understood something, but now everyone was saying that my understanding was wrong, or not enough.

I said, You cannot give up just like that. Do you know how many times I have practiced my *R*? Reap, I said. Read, reef, rye, ripe. Dyer, fissure, azure. See? Azure, I said one more time.

He laughed, although he didn't tell me my words were perfect. I didn't mind. I cared more to see him smiling again. The teacher who had stood on the Institute steps seemed like a distant memory. He was pale again, his eyes touched with the red of tiredness.

Without really meaning to, I said, My grandmother thinks I should have lessons with Miss Lance.

Why?

I paused. Miss Lance is an assistant, I said. She hopes we can pay less.

I wanted him to say that it wasn't the case, Miss Lance would still cost us the same, and besides, it was important that our lessons together continue. But his initial surprise slipped into distraction. I see, he said. Right, well. Next time, Miss Lark.

Next time, I said, and went through the door. I didn't want to keep him from his meetings, although I felt pinches of disappointment through the loosening swirl of my shame. My betrayal of Adeline's financial situation, which was also my own, hadn't yielded any reassurances.

That evening when I started on the copy-work, I realized

he'd given me back the paper with the note about the electricians and the human voice telegraph. I folded it away, meaning
to return it with the completed copy-work. But then I changed
my mind and put the paper away with the smoked glass instead.
Mr. Bell wouldn't need the original papers, and I felt a desire
to keep this one sheet. I remembered how he had stood in the
hallway, words streaming from his lips about everything he must
do, and I'd missed almost all of it. I wanted to keep this small
piece of what I knew was real between us, because I had seen
it with my eyes.

By the time Mrs. Baylis's next soiree came around, I both
hoped and dreaded seeing Augusta Tanner. But when I settled
myself, Frank was sitting with his aunt near the front. He was
neatly groomed, the waves of his hair combed back. He turned
and nodded and a smile arrived on my face before I could stop it.
There was a space next to Augusta and he pointed at it. Join us?
I thought I might say yes but then I shook my head and averted
my eyes before he could continue. I had a pamphlet about the
speaker, but I soon realized it wouldn't be enough, since this
woman had a mouth like a washing line, her words pegged to it
with a gentle flutter and not much more, and I couldn't match
anything to what was in her pamphlet. But it was surely a serene wisdom that came out, for ripples of nodding traversed
the audience.

Augusta started interpreting the speech. Her signs were too
fast for me to follow and there was no longer even a hint of English about them. It was the fluent de l'épée sign language. She
saw me watching and slowed down, but the angle was awkward.
Frank was probably garnering more of the speech than I was,
and he wasn't even a woman. Whatever pertinent points were
made about my female condition were lost on me. I regretted
bitterly all my boasting about my speech-reading skills and the
essay I was writing. Not even Mrs. Baylis offered to make me

a transcript or a few notes. I fastened my eyes onto the speaker's face and grasped sight of a few words, trying to hang on to these precious finds while other words swirled around them, sometimes distilling into a misty gist, other times knocking everything down to confusion.

It wasn't long before I was exhausted, and frustration only ruined my concentration further. I got up, thinking I would go outside and see what new pamphlets had been put out in the hallway. As I browsed through them, a shape thickened on the edges of my sightline. Frank was standing a few yards from the parlor doorway. He reached and turned up the flame in the wall-sconce. The yellow light slid across the walls. He looked at me and then glanced around, as if he'd forgotten why he'd left the lecture. His eyes arrived on the Mercury statue.

Do you like it? I asked.

He considered it and shook his head. No.

What are you doing here?

He opened his hands, his brows dropped. Men are invited, right? he signed, and took out a notebook. "Don't you think it is a similar situation for deaf people?" he wrote. "If we wish to speak something in public, we have to find a man to say it for us."

I felt a jolt to switch my eyes onto his neat, flowing English, after watching his signs. His handwriting swept along the page, with exact gaps between each word as if they had been placed with the same care as type. I was surprised to find myself hoping he would put the notebook away and continue with his signs instead.

You have your aunt, I signed. She is not a man.

He smiled and replied, So who will speak for both of us! Did you understand in there? he added, indicating the parlor.

I nodded several times—yes, I understood—and his face crinkled with teasing suspicion. Good, he signed. It was interesting, wasn't it?

Very interesting, I replied, putting the emphasis into my face, like he had done. I tried to dredge up some gleaned snippet, but only managed: an interesting perspective, and made my hands into the V-shapes of seeing, but my accompanying nods were starting to feel overdone.

He threw up his hands. So teach me! You have a talent.

I can't teach you here, I told him.

How about my uncle's apartment? We will gladly welcome you there. It's above the printing shop.

How will I get there?

Say you have a lesson with Mr. Bell.

It was my turn to pause. Did he know that I walked alone to my lessons? And he was asking me to lie. This blunt fact shimmied between us as I stared at him, although I knew from Miss Lance that Mr. Bell would be away for a while on business. He stiffened and rubbed his chest. I'm sorry, he signed.

His eyes shifted over my shoulder. I turned to see Augusta Tanner hovering in the corridor. Behind her the guests were rising in their seats, the lecture finished. She took a step forward but stopped when Frank took his hat from the hatrack.

I held up my palm to him. No, all right, I agree. Next week.

He smiled. Next week. All right!

He skipped his eyes to Mercury and made a V-hand travel toward the statue while his head and shoulders drew back in wary caution. Watch out for him, he signed.

Why?

Sneaky, he replied. I don't like his expression.

I laughed—it was a statue, after all—and he twitched a smile in acknowledgment. He joined his aunt and they paired into silhouettes as they went down the steps and toward the dim evening outside. I wanted to call out to them, and stop the matching fading I felt within myself at their departure.

The following Tuesday I went to J. M. Tanner's printing shop, which was on a side street off Washington Street's busy thoroughfare. I peered through the windows. Inside, the walls were lined with hammers, spikes and cutting wheels on long wooden handles, and loops of cream thread hung from nails. The counter was empty and shone from a recent polishing. Frank came through from a back room, and stooped down to a chest of drawers, taking a sheaf of vellum from the lowest drawer. He was dressed as he was for the soiree. Tucked and trimmed, and his hair was pushed back, although he didn't wear a jacket.

I was surprised to feel my heart quickening, but I took a breath and pulled on the doorbell. The pulley wasn't like any other I'd seen, and it caught Frank's attention immediately. He looked up, waved at me and crossed to another doorway, leaning through the frame. Augusta appeared, and came quickly to the door. Her dress was simple, and her face was instantly open with welcome as she ushered me in from the cold. The doorbell, I saw once I was inside, was a flag that bobbed up and down.

Frank remained in the doorway at the back of the shop. Good afternoon, he signed. He was standing exactly in the middle, as if he'd measured his precise framing within it. A printer's eye, or a silhouettist's.

Good afternoon, I returned, suddenly conscious of the care I'd taken with my own hair that morning.

Upstairs the Tanners kept a modest apartment. The parlor was full of stools in various states of repair with a few half-upholstered chairs ranged among them like misplaced beasts. My work, Augusta Tanner signed before weaving her way between the stools to the far side of the room. She turned and smiled, This way.

Giant's Causeway, Frank told me, when we'd crossed the room. My father's family is Irish, he added. I'd like to go someday. He made a picture of the Causeway, its rocks rising in huddled pillars from the sea.

Augusta narrowed her eyes at Frank. Frank likes to imagine, she signed, that he's someplace far away.

True, true, Frank signed, and started reeling off a list on his fingers: Biarritz, Rome, a Nile River cruise. A Fjord cruise also—

Augusta interrupted him by opening the door onto a small study that looked across the narrow street outside. The dimness of the room was in part due to the mass of telegraph wires above the street. There were several bookcases filled with papers, and a round mahogany table in the middle with a plate of Italian pastries in the center. I'd never seen a study before with a round table. It suggested a social function, rather than a place of solitary work.

Augusta turned up the lamps, pulled out the chairs and told Frank, Finish before dinner. She slapped his shoulder when he replied, Do you mean the lesson or the pastries? Turning to me, she signed, Be careful, Frank has many stories. Her hands pawed gently at each other, as if she was teasing stories from them like the teasing of wool.

I laughed and reassured her that we would be done before dinner. I skipped my eyes to Frank, meaning to show my firmness. He slid the plate of pastries toward me. They were shelllike, intricately ridged with dozens of fine layers, and snowy with sugar.

He signed, These are from the North End. My aunt teaches English to the Italians. Naples. Do you know it? There is a deaf Latvian family too. I teach them our American signs.

Do they teach you the Latvian ones? I asked.

Yes, very different. All sign languages are different.

He offered me the plate again. No, thank you, I said, making my refusal as crisp as I could on my lips.

He looked at my lips but kept the plate raised in front of me. The pastries did look very fine. I helped myself to one, and Frank smiled, nodding: Good! The sweetness and melting softness of its layers soaked into my mouth, and the sugar was quickly everywhere. My fingers were dusted white, the sugar drifting down into my lap. I told him, Stop watching, turning a V-shaped hand toward myself, to show his watch of me, and then waving his eyes away.

But he was still smiling his approval. Very good, he replied, Eating and signing at the same time. He was laughing at me, at the sugar. Then he took up a pastry and started eating it with one hand while spelling out words on the other. It was the first lines of "America the Beautiful." Sugar drifted beneath his flickering fingers like a veil.

Show-off, I spelled back.

He took a handkerchief from his pocket and dabbed his mouth. I had to collect myself and remember what I'd set out to do. The notebooks. I took out two notebooks. The first I would use to instruct him, as Mr. Bell did with me, while the second contained Visible Speech exercises. I didn't intend for Frank to see the symbols. The mention of Mr. Bell had soured our last meeting, and I didn't want to make the same mistake twice.

He looked at my notebooks. The one with Visible Speech was practically in my lap I was holding it so close.

Do you have a secret written there? he asked.

Wait and see.

Frank sat very still with a questioning politeness as if he was waiting for me to explain why I had come to the shop in the first place. I tamped down my annoyance. Turning to a new page, I marked out the margins and numbered the exercises in roman numerals in the fashion that Mr. Bell used. "Let us begin by reading some sentences so I can see how your speech-reading is," I wrote.

He nodded, so I opened my Visible Speech notebook and read the first sentence.

Frank didn't respond. Then he asked, Was that the sentence?

Yes, I nodded. Try again.

But on the second reading, Frank just shook his head. A dime? he asked, spelling the word.

Almost, I told him, feeling pleased. Dime and Time were in

my list of homophenes. I wrote, "The word wasn't Dime but Time. They are homophenes which means they look the same. If you can guess any other words in the sentence, you will appreciate that I said Time not Dime."

Frank shifted forward as if he was ready to apply his attention for a third time. Appreciate, I saw him say. But when I repeated the sentence he shook his head and shook out the circle-shapes of his hands. Nothing! I saw nothing but Dime or Time.

"Short," I wrote. "Did you see short? The sentence is 'Our time is short.' You cannot have short dimes."

You're coming every Tuesday, he replied cheerfully.

I ignored him. "Let us try the next exercises. For this we will use natural thought associations. I will read some sentences which all relate to the first sentence 'Our time is short.' You will use your knowledge of the first sentence to guide your comprehension of the ones I'm about to read. It is important to understand that speech-reading is not about spotting every single word in a sentence. It is about piecing together clues."

He read my words and looked up. Do you really believe that? he asked.

Believe what? I replied, although his question yanked at me like a tugged rope. What choice did I have but to believe it?

Frank paused, watching me. He read my instructions again, then signed, It is like doing a jigsaw puzzle in your head but you can't touch any of the pieces.

I watched him. He was sitting opposite me in an arrangement of respectful lines. The breadth of his shoulders, his straight neck and tall brow. His gaze locking me into this geometry, and between us the rise of our hands. There was so much easy information in the flow of his signs, whereas lip-reading was a matter of papering over the absences, because the details of speech were minute and often hidden. I wanted to forget the notebooks, the symbols. Something of me was bending toward him, even when I stumbled in understanding. But Frank wanted to learn speech-reading to better get along in the hearing world. Wasn't that why I was here?

Speech-reading is possible, I replied, then asked, Are you ready? I began to read:

How much time do we have?

Only half an hour.

That isn't long enough.

When I finished reading the symbols, I looked up to find Frank leaning across the table with his eyes fixed on me and his brow sunk so low it was almost a glower. He sat back and put his hand to his temple. My head hurts, he signed.

What did you see?

You said we didn't have enough time, he replied, then shrugged. You could come on Thursdays as well.

I hadn't seen anyone with a smile like his before. It appeared first in his cheeks and spread with the same sort of ease he had about himself, reaching across to me like an invitation.

Pay attention, I said, in English.

He narrowed his eyes on my lips. Pay attention, he repeated carefully. Then he made a sign, driving his flat hands down from his temples like the blinkers of a horse. *Concentrate.*

I picked up my pen again. "You will see that in learning to speech-read guesswork matters as much as sight-work. Both the eyes and the mind must be trained. It's true that the eye will have many challenges because lip patterns are obscure and fast. But thought is quicker than speech, and the mind is nimble."

It took me a long time to write this, although I hastened my pencil as much as I could. When I looked up, he was gazing out of the window.

I tapped the table. He read my words carefully, giving them a great deal of consideration. To my surprise, I found that I minded their long winding English. The to-and-fro of note-books was starting to feel cumbersome. Frank glanced back to

the window and pointed at a couple standing on the street outside Little St. Clouds.

What are they saying? he asked.

I looked at the couple who appeared to be arguing. The
lady's chin was jutted toward her companion's face—her husband, I supposed. His brightly furious eyes quivered above his
pinched smile.

I have no idea, I told Frank. Then I wrote, "It isn't our business."

I think I can guess what they're saying, he replied. Look at
the way they are using their hands. Hearing people use their
hands even though they don't like our signs. Always using gestures. I think they're arguing about the size of their wedding
cake. Him, the expense! Her, but she must have one!

I couldn't help looking back at the couple. I didn't see any
words that looked like Cake.

Frank was laughing at me. He shrugged. Why not?

A cake? I signed. No. Then I wrote. "They're discussing
their eight-year-old child. She is too disobedient. The woman
blames her husband."

Frank tipped forward in his seat. Really? You saw that?

Yes, I replied, wagging my fist, although all I had seen was the
word *daughter*, something that looked like *eight*, and the woman
pointing repeatedly at a space about the height of a child's head.
But the grip of Frank's gaze was so strong all my will was bent
on returning it.

At that moment a child came running toward the couple.
Indeed, she could have been eight years old. Her parents drew
apart and looked about as if they had only just realized they had
been arguing in public. We watched the woman sweep down
with her arms extended to the child while her husband's face
darkened at the display.

Frank looked at me, and I couldn't help my kick of pride.

Clever guesswork, he decided, but I thought he looked impressed. I couldn't otherwise explain the interest in his face.

You just need to concentrate, I told him, making the same tunnel of focus with my hands as he had done. But after I'd struck my flat palms forward from my temples, the fingers of each hand hovered in front of my face, framing Frank and his smile, which was strung between my fingertips like a hammock. Not a thought was in my head except that I wanted to hold him there, hold his smile.

Are you concentrating? he asked.

I dropped my hands, feeling heat in my face and hoping he hadn't noticed. Frank leaned across the table. Teach me, he signed. I want to learn.

It soon became apparent that Frank wasn't at all interested in learning. Each lesson followed the same pattern. I opened my Visible Speech exercises and commenced with a reading. Frank was usually game for a second attempt, but never a third, at which point he would start on some diversion or other. One lesson it was a story about his latest trip to the North End, the next lesson it was what he had for dinner the night before.

I couldn't understand what he wanted since he was paying nearly half of what Mr. Bell would charge and yet learning next to nothing.

You are always thinking of distractions, I told him, and made my eyes wander around the room. Are you always like this? I asked, looking at him again.

He looked at me, then shrugged. Depends, he replied, and an image came to me of Frank in hearing society, standing away from people and their endless talking. But it didn't seem possible for him to be withdrawn in that way.

It's called conversation, he added, smiling at me.

I flicked my eyes at him to let him know that my good humor wasn't permission for him to freely continue in this manner. He was paying me a good fee and it grated against my honesty to let the lessons slide into his diversions. I already risked enough in agreeing to the lessons, given that Adeline would be furious if she found out. But however much I tried to bring us back to the notebooks, the truth was that signing was easier.

Every time I left the print shop, I knew at least ten more American signs than when I'd arrived. The thrill wasn't only in their newness, but in feeling my hands move again like they did in Pawtucket with Mary, and in the corridors and dorms of the Oral School with my fellow pupils. It was the way these shapes, feeding the quickness of Frank's answers, could dispel the clamor of loneliness that was around me all the time, the thing that hearing people called silence.

12

ᒍᗞᏅ ᏚᏅ ᏴᏕᏂᏙᏅ-ᏴᏕᏂᏙᏕ
[Apt at chit chat]

I WAS getting so used to Miss Lance's lessons that it was a surprise to find Mr. Bell waiting for me. Several weeks had passed since I last saw him. He stood in the middle of the room, his hands looped behind his back. Good day, Miss Lark, he said. He seemed pleased.

I bade him the same and took my seat. I couldn't help noticing that he looked well, his skin a better color and the usual wave of his curl drawing him up tall with its saplike shine. You are refreshed after your trip, I told him. Already my thoughts were skipping to his inventing work. Had he made some progress toward the human voice telegraph?

His answer fell quickly from his lips. I was startled to feel my eyes swimming, having missed all of it. There wasn't even one word from which I could make my deductions. I tried to focus again, thinking I must have let myself get distracted by thoughts of his voice telegraph.

He was watching me. Did you catch that? he asked.

Unbidden, Frank came into my thoughts, his index flicking at his brow. *Understand?*

I pushed the image aside. I'm a little tired today, I said. That's all. Please, carry on. I smiled at him and added, I would like to know the reason for your good mood.

But he said, Copy-work. He hoped he hadn't given me too much copy-work. He hoped that wasn't the reason for my tiredness.

Not at all, I said, trying to shift whatever cog had become stuck between us, but feeling conscious that my *T*'s felt soft and what I'd meant as reassurance had lumped together like melted toffee. He was talking more slowly now. It seemed almost conspicuous. Hoping to smooth the conversation onwards, I added: I could never be a night owl.

He laughed. It is not for everyone, he said, then sat down and put a notebook across his lap. "I shall tell you the reasons for my good mood later," he wrote. "First, we will focus on the consonant 'Wh' in why and 'W' in way. These are frequently confounded."

He showed me the symbols for both, and I read through the list: whip, whit, wit, white, wight, what, and watch.

Wednesday, I finished. Whirlwind.

But he must have sensed my disappointment that our lesson had so quickly turned to Visible Speech, as he wrote: "Miss Lark, your grandmother must feel she is getting her money's worth!"

I tried to laugh although it did little to hide what he had plainly seen. With Miss Lance I had learned to quench the flame of doubt I had about Visible Speech so that I could get through the lessons. But now it felt fresh and raw again. Was there really any point in me learning to say *Wh* and *W* clearly? I only wanted to be understood and to understand. That was why I liked lessons with Mr. Bell. It had felt easy, at least compared to my usual encounters.

My grandmother is away, I said, after a moment.

He was watching me. Well, let's impress her on her return. We shall read the Bard.

He had to repeat himself several times. The bard, he said. Shakespeare, the bard. You do know Shakespeare?

Of course I know Shakespeare, I said, more hotly than I intended, before adding: Some. I was unsure if he was asking if I knew the playwright or his work.

He wrote, "Then let your grandmother hear you say this," and presented me with a line of text.

I studied it and wrote underneath, "This is Mark Antony, I think."

Mr. Bell put down a line of Visible Speech symbols. He said, And now it is Ellen Lark. Go on.

"The evil that men do lives after them;" I read, "the good is oft interred with their bones."

Again, he said, so I read it three times and on the last time he said, Excellent. Well, are you not pleased?

Very pleased, I said, trying to match his smile. I thought of saying: but I shall never dare read the Bard unless I have the symbols and have practiced them. Even then, it will feel like darkness and shadows in my mouth, and the only pleasure I shall have is in watching people marvel at me.

Instead, I said, Now you have promised me. What is the reason for your good cheer?

Suddenly I was desperate to be done with Visible Speech for the day. So I was already willing with my smile as he wrote, "I have found a financier for my telegraph work!"

Oh, I said in a rush, feeling that the whole earlier lesson had been flushed away with the pleasure of this news. I am happy for you. So the electricians were wrong? It can work?

For a moment he looked confused. Then he said, Oh. Oh, not that one. He wrote, "I mean the Harmonic Multiple Telegraph, not the talking telegraph. That is what's in demand. Have you met one of my other pupils? Her name is Mabel Hubbard, a fine young lady. Her father is a well-known man in Boston, and I showed him the piano wire trick. He has joined forces with the father of another of my pupils. Do you recall the little boy I tutor whose family I reside with in Salem? Together, they will finance my inventing work for the Multiple Telegraph. I feel today like a huge weight has been lifted from my shoulders."

I read through his paragraph slowly and by the time I reached the end, I felt like the weight that had gone from Mr. Bell had been passed to me. I was looking at a whole web of connections concerning his other pupils, and I'd no inkling of it, or any part in what had brought Mr. Bell momentum at last. I tried to be happy for him, but Mabel's name in particular stuck in my mind. Had he been to her house, or brought her father here to the dusty piano in the classroom upstairs? It seemed more likely that he would be invited to call on them in their fine home in Cambridge. Indeed, perhaps Miss Hubbard had so sufficiently impressed her parents with the Bard that they had to meet with her teacher.

It is good news, I said, feeling that marvelous and wonderful would be too tricky for my tongue at this precise moment. But what about your dream? I asked. To make the wires talk.

Mr. Bell shrugged. He said something to the effect of: Mr. Hubbard has no interest in it and cannot be persuaded.

Then he looked at me, smiling again. I gave you that smoked glass, didn't I? Illuminate, he said. When I nodded, he wrote, "I still hope for it, although at present I must focus my energies on the Multiple Telegraph. I trust you to keep the idea safe until then."

Of course, I said, although suddenly the smoked glass, and the shining line of my voice, seemed to lose some of the luster that our trip to the Institute had given it. I wasn't sure if I was keeping his dream safe for him, or else he was trying to keep me playing some sort of game, in which he had my trust and interest.

And Miss Lark, he added. The copy-work you do is—

I watched his next word push out his lips with a large, plush compliment. It arrived with the dropping of his eyebrows. Tremendous, he said.

I took in a breath, surprising myself with how sharply it filled my lungs. Well! I said. You will have to give me the next lot before our lesson is finished.

He smiled and stood up. I watched as he turned from me and tore the pages of the notebook on which he had written about the telegraph. He crammed the pieces into his pocket. Then he fetched a pile of copy-work and said, Thank you, Miss Lark.

But that evening as I copied out all the Visible Speech exercises for Mr. Bell's classes, I couldn't help thinking that my copied lines were not so different from my readings of the Bard. Both were tedious rote work, but one happened to be a delight for others. Why hadn't Mr. Bell's delight stirred my own, as it once used to?

I had my own classes to teach, and despite Frank's distractions, I didn't know how to teach them any other way. One lesson we were practicing the long *I* sound, as in pie. "The first movement," I wrote, "is like that for ah in palm, but then watch how the opening of the lips becomes narrow in the next movement."

Palm, I read from the Visible Speech. Pi-ee. See?

Then I read: Will you have another piece of pie? There is no rhyme or reason to this. The little girl seems somewhat shy. Please put out the light.

Frank wrote something down and showed me but I saw none of the words I'd read apart from Pie.

Try again, I signed.

He shook his head and pushed the notebook away. It's no good. I'm not very good at this. I was born deaf, I don't think in English like you do.

I attempted a long breath but it was ragged with irritation nonetheless. I've seen you use English along with your signs, I signed. Putting your signs in an English order.

Sometimes with you, yes, so you understand. I'm a printer. I print English all the time. Arrange the type, every letter in the correct order. His hands daubed out a row of imaginary type.

And true, he continued, I mix with hearing and deaf people, because of my aunt. The true sign language is completely different from English, you cannot compare them. But everyone has a different level of sign, so we have to find ways to make ourselves understood. Some people are pure sign language, others prefer the manual alphabet, others like to see some English on the lips. Deaf people learn to be flexible, unlike hearing people.

I was getting used to his jibes about hearing people, and I couldn't help my answering smiles, because each time it felt like an invite to step a little closer into his world. But now an old loyalty stirred in me like a forgotten duty.

My mother is hearing, I replied. She always looked at me, tapped my shoulder, adjusted her words, so her meaning was clear.

You are lucky, he signed. Many people can't be bothered. And I understand. He paused, leaning forward. They want the connection, he continued. They want the quick understanding, the jokes, the shared ideas. They want to find something in someone else that they recognize. They don't want to explain. They don't want to say it ten times, slowly–slowly.

I laughed at his imitation of a hearing person talking slowly–slowly, and of himself in return making a charade of smiles and nods. He started on a story about a hearing man who had stopped to talk to him at a stagecoach station, and how he had carefully matched his own expressions to this man's, hoping it would pass for understanding. It turned out the man was a street-seller and he was being asked to visit his stall farther down the street where he sold an assortment of cutlery, spoons in particular. Frank was unable to extract himself from his own pretense and left later with fifteen spoons of various sizes.

I gave them to Augusta, he signed. But I was broke for a month! I also got some honeycomb from the next street-vendor along. It was delicious.

He showed the honey drip-dripping from the comb, then his fingers flew from his lip. *Delicious*. I was still laughing about the spoons, but in the pause that followed, it was Mr. Bell who came to mind. Once I was sure that he spoke naturally with me but then I had seen his faster speed. But couldn't people speak slowly and carefully, and still let that connection arise? A few people had a talent for it or did not mind the burden like Frank said they did. Wasn't Mr. Bell one of them?

I think some people are happy to make an effort, I told him. It would save money on buying spoons, I added.

He smiled at me, his eyes narrowed. You are always defending hearing people, he replied, and angled his shoulder so that his signs positioned me on the side he had allocated for the hearing. But of course, you have a hearing family, he added, and looked at me with a kind of pity.

I held up my hands in exasperated defeat, but he continued: I am always very grateful! He touched his chin repeatedly in a string of exaggerated Thank-Yous. So very grateful. Do you know what I think? I think English ruins the beauty of sign language. We deaf mix them up because we have to, but maybe we shouldn't. Take your signs. A hearing person taught them to you, right? Methodical signs. That is not the same as the true sign language.

I shook my head, waved my hands: he was wrong. I had

home-signs, I told him, with my sister. True, she was hearing, but it was like an instinct between us, not a lesson.

I had to spell Instinct, then tapped my stomach with my fingers, taking a guess at the sign. Frank made a small nod, his reversed role as my teacher never far in the shadows.

Then the other pupils at the Oral School taught me the proper signs, I continued. Some of them had been to the big schools. But I didn't get to use signs very much.

He sat forward, his face growing long with interest although a teasing spark jumped into his eyes. Because you got caught? he asked. Let me guess. They tied your hands? You had to say Bread-and-Butter a hundred times? I-will-speak-very-good-for-you?

He mouthed the words as he signed them in an English order.

It was a cupboard, I said, feeling bluster enter my stance, as if punishment was somehow a test you needed to pass. I didn't know why I was trying to convince Frank like this.

Frank sat back and nodded, his mouth folding down. Was it a small or big cupboard? he asked.

Small, I replied, marking out the size with my hands.

That is quite small. But you know what is smaller? The world with only English in it.

He made an impression of being trapped in a tiny space, looking around for an exit, English words assailing him. I raised my hands again, only this time I told him: I give up. You wanted to learn how to lip-read English. You, I added, pointing at him again for emphasis.

He rubbed his hand on his chest—he was sorry—and got up to cross the room. He stopped by the shelves next to the doorway which were stacked high with papers.

He turned back to me. There are so many sign languages I would like to learn, he signed. Sometimes in the North End I learn some of the Irish signs. They are quite like the French signs, which are like our signs because Laurent Clerc brought the de l'épée signs from France. Do you know him? He is the father of our signs. But British signs are completely different to American signs, while Australian signs are similar to British ones. There are so many more. Some deaf people are embarrassed of our signs, but I want to know them all. You can't write them down like other languages. Deaf people are used to traveling far so we can meet up, but sometimes I feel I can't travel far enough.

I didn't say anything, because his face had grown serious, and I wasn't used to it. He turned to the shelves and lifted one of the stacks of paper. I'd thought them to be leftover items from the print shop, but Frank's face was curled with too much cautious care. He placed the pile in front of me and nodded, indicating that I should help myself.

The paper on the top was called the *Mute's Journal* printed by the school in Pennsylvania. I flicked through a few more. There was the *Deaf-Mute Pelican* from the Louisiana school, the *Mute Journal of Nebraska* and the *Alabama Banner*.

This is the silent press, he signed. My father collected them. They come from schools all over the country. The papers connect the schools, connect their graduates. The silent press is how I learned to print, when I was studying at Hartford.

He reached into the pile and extracted a few papers. *Canajoharie Radii*, he spelled. The first paper. A New York paper but the editor was a graduate from the Hartford School. Look.

He tapped the masthead: the name of the paper was printed in finger-spelling, each handshape intricately detailed.

Frank pulled out another paper called *The Deaf Mutes' Friend*. This one, he signed. More recent. The editor, Mr. Swett, was a friend of my father. He writes about his observations on the hearing world. You would like it. He went on many adventures, armed with his slate. He told his stories in sign language and then Mr. Chamberlain, another deaf man, translated them into English.

He waited while I flicked through the papers. It was the reports on the school's activities that fascinated me the most. Accounts of baseball teams and football elevens, croquet and lawn tennis. Dates for picnics, maypole dancing, summer fetes. The announcements for marriages, births, deaths, the naming of children. They listed deaf-owned businesses and hearing employers who would take on deaf employees. A world of laced connections stretched out from their pages, like wires on a telegraph-map. It made the world of my old Oral School seem tiny. And as for the marriage announcements, you'd not tell them apart from those in the hearing press. Marriages like any other, although it would have made Adeline pale with horror.

Frank was waving a hand at me. Go on, go on. Take it home, read it.

I hesitated. So far, I had kept Frank as a separate part of my life that belonged to the printing shop and nowhere else. But bringing home the journals put them on par with the copy-work I brought home from the Oratory School. The few shelves in my bedroom were already piled high with Mr. Bell's Visible Speech exercises. And what if Adeline found them? But Adeline never went into my room, so I reached for a couple and slotted them inside my bag.

There's more, he signed. No rush. Just take more. Like a library. My friends often browse these shelves.

He stood close to me. His signs, turning between us, were closer still. The afternoon sun was slanting in through the window, putting sickles of gold in his eyes. His sign for *Friend* hovered in my thoughts, the clasping and re-clasping of his forefingers. Friend. Was I one? Our lessons, I knew, were becoming less like lessons with each one that passed.

I didn't see Mr. Bell for several weeks, instead collecting the school's copy-work from Miss Lance since she was taking my lessons again. On one occasion, she paused before handing me a particularly large pile and said: Miss Lark, I think we should pay you something. But I frowned and waved the idea away, taking the papers from her. This was an arrangement I had with Mr. Bell to assist him, not with Miss Lance.

But still I wondered about our lessons. I knew he was busy, but now he couldn't keep the afternoon lessons as well as the morning ones. I thought of Mabel, and if he made regular trips to the Hubbards' home, now that her father was his financier. I guessed more pupils were coming to the school, as I was asked for more copies of the exercises each week. In spite of what I told Mr. Bell, it took me late into the evenings to get it all done. I usually sat by myself in the kitchen or parlor to finish it, where the fires were warmest. Little St. Clouds had a few new boarders and Mrs. Baylis remained, but the Day sisters had gone. I was surprised to find I missed their teasing. Soon my visits to the Tanners' printing shop were the only thing I looked forward to.

One evening there was a letter slipped amongst the papers Miss Lance had given me. I recognized the handwriting immediately. Had Mr. Bell placed it in the middle to conceal it from Miss Lance, or to prevent it falling out and getting lost? I opened it quickly, ignoring some of the Visible Speech papers that slipped to the floor.

Inside was a note which thanked me for the recent copy-work and informed me of a demonstration that he planned to hold at the Institute of Technology. "I shall ask a few of my pupils to give an exhibition of Visible Speech, but I also intend to display some of the apparatus that I have been developing. I would like you to present the Phonoautograph and shall ask you to say a word to show how the instrument works."

I knew I should be pleased. But doubt kicked me like a boot. He wished me to read only one word of Visible Speech? Would the other pupils be singing and reciting the Bard? Or did he choose me because of my scientific mind, and what he had told me about his inventions? It was an honor, surely, to be linked to his scientific work, rather than the rote learning of Visible Speech. Still, I thought, it is only one single word he wishes me to say. A word!

I turned over the page. "If you agree, please let Miss Lance know that you are happy to attend," he had written. "I may see you for a lesson before then, but I cannot say when that will be. It is a neck-and-neck race between Mr. Gray and myself, who shall complete our telegraph apparatus first. He has the advantage over me in being a practical electrician, but I have reason to believe that I am better acquainted with the phenomenon of sound than he is."

He signed off his name with the usual Yours, and no special flourish. I might have suspected him to have sent several copies of this letter to every pupil invited to the Institute, especially as I had never heard of a "Mr. Gray" before. Had he mentioned this fellow inventor to someone else, and forgotten it wasn't to me? Or was it one of the words I had missed on his lips? But then I read his postscript. "I haven't forgotten the real prize," he'd written. "It is an effort to put it from my mind, but nothing can be done for now."

The "real prize." He did not name it because he knew I would understand exactly what he meant. I felt myself relenting. I would do his demonstration, I decided, for I had no real grounds to refuse, but I wouldn't send my confirmation through Miss Lance. Instead I picked up my pen to write Mr. Bell directly. "I would be happy," I wrote, "to accept your invitation. But regarding the 'real prize' are you certain the human voice is too weak to generate a current? Were you not invited to the Institute of Technology in the first place because you knew better than anyone what could be done with the voice?"

I read over what I had written. I could still feel the insult simmering inside me that I would only speak one word at his demonstration, and that would be into a dead ear, not the living ones that attended to the many words of his other pupils,

Mabel among them. Mama would be pleased, but I didn't relish telling her as once I would have done. In fact, I wasn't sure I wanted to do the demonstration at all. Did I no longer prize speech, although it was what Mama, Adeline, and everyone had always wanted it for me? I folded up the letter anyway, and labeled it "Concerning the Visible Speech demonstration" to assuage Miss Lance's concerns should she see it. Then I slipped it in with the copy-work to return to Mr. Bell.

When Adeline returned to Boston, I gave her an envelope full of Frank's money. I'd made a note on the front. THE PROCEEDS OF MY COPY-WORK. I used Capitals for the avoidance of doubt and scrutiny. But I steeled myself for her response.

What work? she asked.

"A printing shop off Washington Street," I wrote.

She frowned. A printing shop? she asked. Suitable was her next word. Was it really suitable for me?

I wrote, "Do you remember Augusta Tanner? Her husband runs the shop. I am to help copy the invoices and business papers. I work in the parlor upstairs. It is very pleasant."

Augusta, she said, slowly. I waited tensely. Did Adeline know that Augusta was married to a deaf man? Augusta, she said again. Ah yes. I remember. She looked at me. Well, good, she said.

I smiled back: it was so easily done.

Then the lyceum series started at Tremont Temple and Adeline was out every Tuesday evening. I watched her at the front door, pocketing the program which had been printed at Mr. Tanner's shop into her bag. I waved her goodbye. Now I needn't rush back after my lessons, nor worry that she'd catch me at the door with Augusta and strike up a conversation that would reveal the true arrangement.

When the appointed hour came, I bade farewell to Joan and set off for the printer shop. As I turned onto Washington Street my step quickened and my heart felt lighter.

Outside the printer shop I always paused to admire the newest books. Usually, Mr. Tanner spotted me and opened the door. He had a friendly, workaday aspect and small gold-framed glasses which he tipped to the end of his nose as he welcomed me inside. I found his signs hard to follow but my gaze wandered so many times to his books that he started showing me his work, spreading out leather, marbled paper, revealing gilded letters, and using a simple sign or spelled word to guide my eyes along the work.

After a while Frank came downstairs looking for us. He stood in the doorway and stamped his foot.

Here, he waved. Are you giving my job to Ellen?

Maybe, Mr. Tanner replied. You turn up late.

I am always early, he replied.

Mr. Tanner looked at me. It's true, he signed. He's a hard worker.

I'm sure, I replied, thinking of Frank's endless diversions in our lessons. He was standing erect as if he suspected my doubts and intended to bounce them from his chest like a ball. Then he slackened and wagged his hand: come on, he signed, and I followed him up the stairs.

Our lessons were settling into a new rhythm. I ran through a lip-reading exercise and then he found me a new paper from the silent press.

This one here, he told me, pointing at an article. Been looking for this. 1850, the grand reunion at the American Asylum. Graduates came from all over the country to raise a trophy for its founders, Clerc and Gallaudet. Such an occasion, amazing. And here, this one too. Two hundred deaf people gathered for a celebration at a rented hall in Boston in a snowstorm. Can you imagine? They stayed until eight o'clock the next morning!

He signed the heaving crowds, the swirling snow. If I could scarcely imagine a room of two hundred deaf people, Frank did the picturing for me. All our talking was becoming the language of signs.

I started to lament the moment when I'd take out my book and turn to the prepared exercise, and his shoulders would drop patiently while his cupped hands rested on the table, the shine of the mahogany kissing their stillness.

He began trying harder in his lessons. We both knew it was speech-reading that would justify our meetings, even if it was only a sliver of our time together. We worked through the exercises and I made an exaggerated report of his progress to Augusta at the end.

She nodded politely and made her face impressed at the appropriate points of my report.

You remember she is hearing, right? Frank asked, as I waited for her to fetch her coat before taking me home.

Yes, I answered, puzzled. But then Augusta was back and it wasn't until we were out on Washington Street that I realized what he meant. Augusta could hear through the door that only a fraction of our lessons was spent reading symbols and lipreading. The to-and-fro of our practice, our dimes and times, palms and pies, interspersed with long spells of silence which she would know to be the richest talking of all. I glanced at her as we walked toward the stage-car stop, newly aware of her tactful inclination to avoid the subject. I was desperate to ask her directly. What had Frank told her about his feelings? And how much did she guess?

ꙄꙆ,ꙍꙌꙅꙆꙦꙦ
Whirlwind

One Tuesday there was a dot of ink on Frank's neck, just under his left jawline. A word smudged onto his fingertip in the print room downstairs and now jumping on the pulse under his skin. I was quite distracted by it.

Frank touched his neck. What?

I shifted my eyes. Nothing, I told him, waving my hands. He was patting his neck as if dabbing on lotion and I saw the guilty finger, capped with ink.

Ink, I spelled. There.

I was smiling but Frank leapt up. One minute. He came back with his neck rubbed pink, not a spot of ink to be seen. He sat down a little stiffly. My apologies, he signed. Busy morning downstairs. A huge order of pamphlets needs to be ready by the end of the week.

I wanted to tell him I didn't mind in the least, it was only a tiny mark. A pause sprang up between us, as sudden as a hare in the road. For a while I didn't know what to say, my head tight with a racket of formless thoughts.

There is something I want to ask, I tried, latching on to the first thing that came to mind. I couldn't organize my signs and needed to write it down: "Would you print an advertisement for me? For my copy-work services."

Now I was the one looking for distractions.

He nodded, relieved at the suggestion. You have a draft? How do you want it laid out?

Blankness dropped through my cheeks. I had no idea since the thought had just occurred to me.

You want to look at some examples? he asked.

In your print room?

There were nicks of concern at the corners of his lips. No, no, he signed. The composing room. It is quite clean. No one there right now. Apart from my uncle, he added hastily.

I laughed. Women do not usually go into the print room?

He considered this. I have met women in the print room at the large newspapers. More of a worry for the compositors though. Women have nimble fingers that can set type fast.

You can tell your compositor not to worry. You've seen my finger-spelling.

He smiled and stood up. You're getting better. This way.

Downstairs the shopfront was empty and when we entered the composing room through the back door, Mr. Tanner was not there either. Frank didn't seem to notice as he showed me around the room. There was a new bounce in his movements. I could tell he was proud of his domain. The room was large and airy, the walls whitewashed and windows looking over a small yard to the rear. Large wooden racks of type-cases stood in the middle of the room next to a flat-topped iron table that Frank called the imposing-surface. Frames were laid out on the surface, containing rows of type.

I examined the letters, the metal blocks laid out so formally and locked into a promise: of a page, an article, a book. I wondered if Mr. Bell had taken my essay to the printers yet, and if someone was spending hours setting out my words with care, binding them tight into a uniform and replicable arrangement. It had been a while, I realized, since I'd thought of my paper.

This will go in the press? I asked, pointing out the hand press that stood in the corner of the room. The elegant wooden frame of curved feet, columns and a wooden banner painted with the name "Washington Press" contained what looked like a huge iron clamp within the middle.

Frank shook his head. That is for small jobs, he replied. He pointed at the frame of set type. This here will be cast into a stereotype, which is a cylinder mold of the letters. We'll use the book and job press, in the print room.

The spelled parts skipped off his fingers then he pointed out the door of what looked like a coal house. I glanced through the doorway, the dimness of the print room revealing a huge machine with several rollers and a long flat plane on which I supposed the paper entered and exited. Rolls of cylindrical stereotype, already molded with text, waited at the base of the machine.

Frank was watching me. It's a jobbing press, just a small one, perfect for us. You should see the machines at the newspapers. Here we do some books but mainly small periodicals, flyers, leaflets, that kind of thing.

He waved a hand at the far wall of the composing room. Take a look at the adverts, he signed. Choose a style you like.

The wall was covered with samples, neatly pinned with an inch of space around each one. The top row was dedicated to programs for the Temple's lyceum series and events at the Athenaeum. Beneath them were mostly invitations, advertisements and posters. One program caught my eye. It was for a fete run by the Boston Deaf Mute Society in honor of Mr. Gallaudet and Mr. Clerc who founded the Hartford School. It described an afternoon of activities carefully arranged in lines of varying size and font: a Twenty-yard dash, Tug-of-war, Croquet for the Ladies, a Hop, Skip and Jump, a Three-legged race, and Quoits for the men.

I felt Frank at my shoulder. I printed that myself, he signed.

And this one? I pointed at the front page of a deaf journal I hadn't seen before. It was called: *Boston Silent Voice*.

His chest lifted. My first journal, he signed. The first page. Just an experiment. We will print the first run next month. I can't decide on the name of the journal.

I gently lifted the bottom of the page so it curved away from the wall like a wing. The first article was called "Success Amongst the Hearing."

Did *you* write this? I asked and couldn't help the teasing linger in my pointing finger. Is this advice for thinking like a hearing person? I added.

Funny, he signed. No, my uncle's friend. How to manage hearing people, not how to be a hearing person. That is the advice. You have to represent the community, show hearing people that they can work with us. Most people have never met a deaf person before.

I paused over the article, then tapped my chest. I was nine, I signed, when I first met another deaf person.

I was three.

Three? I asked. But your family—

Three when I first met a hearing person. Or tried to talk with one. It was my aunt's father, before she married my uncle. He came to talk to me, so I made my mouth move at him because that's what he was doing to me. He didn't know what to do and walked away. I thought *that* was a success.

He reached up for an advert, his arm rising above my shoulder. I saw the weave of his shirt and through it smelled Frank's warmth, mixed with the scent of linen. I turned my cheek slightly toward his arm, wishing to keep him close a little longer.

He dropped his arm to present me with a small advert for French lessons. What about something like this? Do you want to compose it yourself? He grinned at me and nodded toward the type-cases.

I squinted my eyes, curling a gentle threat into my smile. What if I am very fast? I asked.

I won't mind. You can compose my new journal for me. Let me get new frames.

I thought briefly of the exercise book still open upstairs in the study and then followed him to the type-cases. He was setting up a small frame on the imposing-surface.

Here is the type, 11 pt. You can make up the forme. Go on, have a try. I will make the stereotype for printing later. Fifty copies?

I thought about the money I needed to give to Adeline. The fee for Frank's lessons would pad out an envelope handsomely, but I couldn't help the nudge of guilt that I was barely teaching him a thing. It was his fault, I reasoned. Not mine.

One hundred copies, I signed. I will give you a discount on your next lesson.

He smiled. I'm grateful for that. But there's no need.

He peered over my shoulder while I started selecting the type and slotting them into the frames to make up the forme. He signed, The *d* is upside down. I know, it looks like *p*.

We both reached toward the forme, but my hand arrived at the *d* first, his hand landing on top of mine. I could feel the cold edges of the type's raised letters pressing into my palm, the warm quiver of his hand not quite resting its weight upon mine. I glanced at him, but his gaze went forward, watching his hand as if he was waiting to see what it would do. I don't know which happened first, the slow sinking of his hand or the turning of mine so that our fingers slipped together. We remained in that clasp for a moment. Then he lifted his hand away and before I had a chance to feel either regret or rebuke, he dragged an index down my open palm, tracing a line from the top of my middle finger down to my wrist. It was a feather's touch, drawing tingling shapes that fizzed in my palm. Letters. He was making English letters. I waited, trying to feel their edges without looking at them. Dime, he was writing. Time.

Homophenes. I laughed. At first I nodded with each word, letting him trace them over and over. But after a while, the words became formless, and I couldn't tell what letters he was making, or if they were letters at all. The shapes dissolved into the fiery spread of his touch, and my mind was emptied of any kind of comprehension other than the growing notion that Frank felt for me as I did for him. I didn't want him to stop, so I made up the homophenes he was tracing: Gold, Cold, I spelled on my free hand. Wig, Quick. Boat, Moan.

He was laughing, and I was laughing, and laughter always had an endpoint. Regretfully, it seemed, he folded my palm, as if he was sealing the letters inside. We both turned our attention back to the type and fished out the letters of my advertisement.

★ ★ ★

After our next lesson, Augusta Tanner invited me to stay for dinner. Frank had gone downstairs at Mr. Tanner's request, and I was helping Augusta crack eggs for the beef omelets when she turned her head toward the apartment door. I think I can hear the Reverend downstairs, she signed. She looked about anxiously. Will you check? I don't know if the food is enough.

I went down to the shop. Both Frank and Mr. Tanner were behind the counter. Frank was stood still, watching Mr. Tanner who was slightly stooped and signing in the most English fashion I had seen him use, littering his signing with spelled words. Opposite was the Reverend, his dog collar peeping through his coat. The gentleman standing next to him was leaning with one hand against the counter, and I supposed he was a customer given the open briefcase that spilled a tongue of pamphlets across the countertop. He was switching his eyes between Mr. Tanner and the Reverend as the latter interpreted Mr. Tanner's signs. He nodded hard as his head moved left and right, as if to show his certainty about what was being said.

No one noticed me enter the shop. I waited in the doorway, unsure whether to tell Augusta that the Reverend was staying for dinner or not.

Mr. Tanner was explaining how he had followed the man's instructions exactly. Then Frank interrupted, but his signing was so fast that I caught little of it. The Reverend's signs, when he explained the man's dissatisfaction, were slow and English-based, and from him I understood that the man was displeased with the quality. He wished not only for a refund on the completed pamphlets but a cancellation of the contracted work for the following month.

Mr. Tanner looked desperate. We have already started the work, he was answering. Frank was picking up each pamphlet, requesting for the fault to be identified while his customer treated the pamphlets like they were handfuls of old leaves, gathering them up in fistfuls.

Frank signed, You're damaging them yourself.

The Reverend's words, when he translated, didn't appear to match Frank's signs. He said something like: You may wish to take a little care with those. Then the Reverend stopped signing altogether, talking directly with the man himself, so for several minutes Frank and Mr. Tanner, and myself with them, looked on, and could only guess at what was being discussed.

As we waited for the Reverend to conclude the matter, and give an explanation, the flag of the doorbell bobbed. Neither the Reverend nor the customer noticed its announcement, but Frank looked across the shop. His eyes snagged on me where I stood at the foot of the stairs, then he cast his gaze to the door. Since he was engaged with his uncle, I went over to the door, letting another gentleman inside. Frank's face sprang in alarm when he saw this newest customer, and he looked at me with a rare expression of frozen panic. I didn't know what had startled him, although it was true that I hadn't seen such an uneasy-looking person before as this man. His dark hair was combed resolutely forward, making a soft ledge above his fleshy, uneven features. He saw Frank's alarm and skipped his eyes over to me, his face squeezing with interest.

I felt a tug on my arm. Augusta was drawing me away even as she kept her eyes tight on the Reverend at the counter, who was still reasoning with the customer, as Mr. Tanner waited for someone to tell him what was going on.

Upstairs she gave me the silverware and bade me set the table. I counted out nine places. I didn't know what calculation she'd made about the Reverend joining us. Most of the guests were old friends of Mr. Tanner from the Hartford School. It was the first time I had joined them for dinner, and I would likely be the youngest person there.

Who was that man? I asked. The one at the shop door?

She frowned and shrugged. Him? A new customer, I guess. Bad timing. He probably left after hearing that conversation.

Our reputation is very important to us, she continued as I arranged the cutlery. Mr. Tanner, he does the best work in Boston. But it's not cheap. Sometimes this happens. A customer finds a cheaper place and they want to switch their custom. They blame the quality. Mr. Tanner asks the Reverend to help.

She started setting out dishes of cream slaw. The table was large and round, and free of flowers, candles and any ornament that reached higher than a middle waistcoat button. Instead, Augusta had arranged winter plum blossom along the secretary for decoration. I helped her with the last few sprigs, feeling an odd gratitude for the drama in the printing shop. I was an insider already for having witnessed it with Augusta.

Reputation is everything, she repeated. We must be self-reliant but also show hearing people what deaf people can do. That is our responsibility. Customers like that man: it is unfair.

I considered Augusta as she set down the plates, placing each one deftly as if matching them to some invisible mark on the table. Sometimes I forgot she was hearing herself. I saw it only in the turn of her head to a sound, or the English mouth patterns, but even those she dropped when signing with her husband. I wondered how she would sign tonight, and if I would follow her so easily.

Augusta caught my eye and I looked away, busying myself with needlessly rearranging the breadbasket. She was watching me so I tried to smile back but my cheeks felt hot: I had the feeling she could guess at my thoughts.

Frank, she began. He is very committed to the lessons. But honestly, I don't see much progress.

More heat inched into my cheeks. I have taught him all the proper exercises, I began, but Augusta held up her hand. It's not your teaching, she replied. I don't think he has the motivation.

Why does he want lessons then? I asked and immediately

wished I hadn't because Augusta timed her smile too exactly with a knowing shrug. Then she looked toward the door again. It was soon apparent why: Frank appeared, tugging off his jacket. His bad mood was evident.

Two weeks' work lost, he was signing. That man paid a pittance to cover it but all those other jobs we had on hold.

Augusta asked, Is Reverend Keep not staying?

Him? Frank replied. No, gone. I'm happy for him to go.

His aunt stared at him. Go tidy yourself, she replied.

I am tidy, he signed, presenting his flat hands at his shirt-front.

I turned back to the table. The incident in the shop was needling him but I couldn't help minding that he had barely registered me. I'd thought all week of the composing room and the way he'd stared at his hand on mine as it rested on the type, knowing he should remove it. I felt a searing impatience for another moment like that one to present itself. And yet in our lesson, he'd been more diligent than usual. He was direct, open. There were no sides or hidden dimensions to his manner, but he didn't mention what happened in the composing room other than to hand me one hundred copies of my advert. Had I been mistaken?

After he left the parlor, I asked Augusta, Is the Reverend local to here?

Yes, he does our service. He is a very respected man.

She put emphasis into her signs as if she wished to counter Frank's flippant dismissal. She continued, Our community needs hearing people to help us negotiate our position. Frank thinks that it is a kind of dependency. But he cannot avoid it, and he knows it. No person likes a debt. But I wish he would understand that some kinds of sympathy can become friendship and trust. Haven't I tried to be an example? Frank, he is too headstrong.

Over dinner, Frank was low-angled at the table. There was an agitation in him I hadn't seen before. He went from bursts of storytelling to dropping his gaze on the soup tureen in front of him. The Tanners' friends didn't allow his spells of languor to last long. They waved at him or tapped the table, diverting him with their stories or prompting him on another of his own. But he fell back into stillness when Mr. Tanner started on an account of the incident in the shop.

I charged a good price, he was telling the group. His earlier acquiescence was replaced by hard, rapid strikes of insistence.

You know, one of his friends interjected, that deaf teachers are always paid less than hearing teachers.

You think I should charge less?

There are so many deaf teachers, argued another person, and fewer hearing teachers. Printing is not the same situation.

It is prejudice, said someone else. This was a woman called Mrs. Almena Ellison. Her signs were energetic and sweeping against the backdrop of her mourning dress. I could see what Frank meant about how differently people in the community signed. She continued, Even the best pupils at our schools can't get the kind of work hearing people get.

Hearing employers are afraid to take on deaf people, replied another man, Mr. Brooks. Like the other guests, he didn't always put down his fork while signing, making nimble one-handed signs that hinted just enough at their full shape, although I missed several of them nonetheless. They worry they won't be able to communicate with us, he continued, or that we can't do the work.

We need to give them opportunities to understand, replied Augusta.

Her signs separated out hearing people from herself, but Mr. Tanner smiled at his wife, as if he was recalling their own private opportunities. Right, he agreed. We must bide our time and hope for better luck.

Augusta turned to me. She asked, You still do some copy-work, isn't that right?

My heart quickened. Frank must have told her about the advert. Did he tell her also how I'd gone down to the print shop
alone with him to print it? I felt the prickles of a flush although
the question was simple enough. I didn't dare look at Frank.

I get a little work, I admitted. Frank didn't know that only
one job had resulted so far from my advertisements. The rest
was for Mr. Bell.

How do you get it? Mr. Brooks asked.

My grandmother has a boardinghouse, I explained. There are
always people staying, one of them runs a soiree in the evenings.

I was relieved when this wasn't queried further and the conversation changed track, as Augusta remarked on the rise of
boardinghouses in the South End. The group moved on to news
about the people they knew. They discussed one friend's weight
gain, another's decision to marry a hearing woman, and a third's
efforts to find land out in Iowa. I tried to keep up with their
signing. It was a mixed crowd, and the conversation was filled
with endless requests for clarification, which everyone was happy
to give. But I was easily the youngest and newest person at the
table, and it was a while before I felt able to interrupt the discussion as easily as the other guests. And Frank's sour mood was
like a magnet on my concentration as I tried not to look at him.

There's nothing there but railroad land, signed Mr. Brooks.

His wife, Mrs. Clara Brooks, turned to me. I had met her once
before when I arrived for Frank's lessons. She was a dressmaker
and once a year came to Boston to outfit the whole Tanner
family with any needed garments. Augusta had told me that the
couple had met at the Hartford School where they were among
the small number of free black pupils. Many of the other schools
for the deaf in the North wouldn't accept them.

Clara had graceful fingers set off by the elaborate trim of
ruffles and lace at her sleeves. He works as a boatman, she told
me. We think about moving West, but the oystering business
is going well.

She spelled Oyster and supplemented it with her two hands opening and closing like a shell. She smiled when she saw how I noted the sign and asked, When did you learn to sign?

I'm not sure, I told her. My sister and I had home-signs. She was hearing but some pupils used them at my school.

She nodded. You must learn from deaf people, she replied.

My eyes skipped to Frank before I could stop myself. At the same moment he looked at me, and the touch of our gaze felt like a bright clash of cymbals. We both quickly looked away again. I was embarrassed to find that Clara had noticed.

It is a shame Frank left Hartford early, she told me. He would have been a good teacher there, same as his brothers.

I was startled. Frank had never mentioned not finishing his studies although he had spoken so highly of his school. I looked back at him. He was studiously talking to Mr. Brooks and another guest. Was that why he worked in his uncle's shop? And none of his own Hartford friends were here?

Clara's comment caught the attention of Mrs. Ellison. She settled her eyes on me. They were a shining light gray color, in contrast to her heavy cheek and jaw, and I felt their beam like a needle in my stomach.

You are the girl who teaches Frank, she signed. You teach him lip-reading.

Everyone looked at me. I felt a note of surprise escape my throat, as if it had been squeezed from me, although no one apart from Augusta would have caught it.

That is correct, right? Mrs. Ellison turned to Frank.

Frank made a little laugh. Ellen is writing an essay on that topic, he signed, as though this was an explanation. She's an expert.

Most of the group smiled although their expressions were a mix of surprise and polite enthusiasm. I smiled back, hoping to conceal the hurt confusion that steamed through me as hot as the freshly ladled soup. Shouldn't Frank be taking my defense, since he had asked for lip-reading lessons himself? Instead, he was spending the dinner avoiding eye contact with me and the other guests to the point of rudeness. And now he shrugged away everyone's eyes again by sending them all to me.

Mr. Tanner came to my aid. He signed to Frank, Maybe Ellen can publish her essay in your newspaper? Then he told everyone else: Ellen is a very good teacher.

I felt a scrape of shame at Mr. Tanner's generous rescue.

Mrs. Ellison turned to Frank. You want to improve your skill? she asked.

Frank huffed a laugh again and replied, I don't have any skill. But Mrs. Ellison was still looking at him so he reddened slightly. I can hope to improve, he added, and puckered his face as if the answer ought to be evident.

I could make no sense of his behavior, but I drew myself up and turned to Mrs. Ellison. It is useful, I signed, as fluidly as I could, to have many options when dealing with hearing people.

Right, agreed another guest called Mr. Olive who relied heavily on finger-spelling. He took out an ear trumpet from his pocket and laid it next to his plate like an unusual piece of cutlery. That is why I have Delia, he added, tapping his trumpet. Always prepared.

A few jokes sprang up around the table about Delia, although Mr. Olive smiled resolutely through them all.

Prepare what you will say, Clara signed. Prepare how you will arrange your face, prepare your smile, your notebooks. Prepare your eyes for all that watching, all that concentration. Prepare an answer for a question that went over your head.

She made such a mime of the effort of preparing oneself for the hearing world that everyone started laughing. Frank's face cooled to its usual color, and he was almost smiling at Clara's performance.

Mrs. Ellison was only briefly diverted. But Mr. Bell is your teacher, she persisted. As you know, he does not believe in all the options. He believes in one thing: speech.

It was the first time that I had seen Mr. Bell's name at the Tanners'. An unease seemed to drift into the room, and my body felt tight, ready to jump, although I didn't know at what. Mrs. Ellison was repeating my signs and I realized I'd made an error with Options, using the sign for Decide instead of Choice. There was something deliberate about her correction.

Mr. Bell, she continued, thinks that we deaf should not use signs. He is not arguing for options. No, it must always be speech and speech-reading. He will turn our children away from the silent language. What will be the result? He will turn our children away from our community. That is what he wishes. Frank, she asked, tapping the table smartly to force his attention. Didn't he teach you the same?

Frank didn't have much choice but to respond. That's right, he replied. At the Hartford School. But I was just one of hundreds of pupils.

I gazed at Frank. Here was another thing he hadn't mentioned, although I had wondered if he might have seen Mr. Bell at Hartford. My earlier confusion gave way to cold anger. If he was so embarrassed about the lessons, he shouldn't have asked for them.

Mr. Olive signed, Oral methods are popular in Europe now. Isn't Mr. Bell Scottish?

The question for me, Mr. Tanner signed, is how can you be useful in society? You must be practical. If you can speak, like our friend Mr. Olive here, fine. But a notebook is more useful than poor speech. If you are lucky your employer might learn the finger alphabet.

True, replied Mrs. Ellison. And what about home life? I was married for thirty years. Only a marriage between two deaf people can be an equal one.

Everyone laughed. You are forgetting our hosts, signed Mr. Brooks.

Augusta smiled at her husband, and signed: It is my own fault. I forget I am hearing most days.

But you are hearing, Mrs. Ellison replied, and her pointing finger was emphatic so that even Augusta struggled not to avert her eyes. And Mr. Bell has many oral pupils, she continued and looked at me. Her eyes didn't shift from me even as she signed the multitude of his pupils. They help him to set an example to the rest of us. To forget who we are.

Augusta's smile was strained. She stood up and signed something about fetching the dessert. Mrs. Ellison was still watching me. Her signs for "the rest of us" had neatly set apart Mr. Bell's oral pupils from everyone else.

I looked down at my food. This must be what Frank believed, or he'd say otherwise. After all, he wasn't one to be shy of his own opinion. I didn't know how to respond to Mrs. Ellison, since a defense of myself felt like a defense of Mr. Bell.

Mr. Brooks glanced at his wife then said, In most places they already separate the students.

The oralists won't bother with your schools, Mrs. Ellison replied. Her signs were neat and conclusive.

Frank waved his hand at Mrs. Ellison to get her attention. They attended Hartford, he reminded her.

Mrs. Ellison didn't respond, but pushed away her plate so that Augusta could set down a clean one for dessert.

There were just a few of us, signed Mr. Brooks.

Frank said, In Hartford they sometimes divided the students according to their ability to learn speech. I had lessons in the assembly hall with all the others, but some pupils had smaller classes with Mr. Bell.

There was his name again, easily on Frank's fingertips. Now his lips curled and he continued, You know what sign name we gave him?

He ran his hands up and down an invisible set of piano keys.

Why? he signed. Because he was always playing the piano in his hotel room. Frank bashed extravagantly on the keys.

Mr. Bell is a fine gentleman, his uncle interrupted. I've seen him once or twice at the mechanic shop on Court Street when I get the parts for our printing presses. He wanted us to print his Visible Speech textbooks, but it couldn't be done. You need a special type.

Frank added, He's renting the attic there to work on a multiple telegraph.

His signs were quick and small, as if it was an inconsequential interjection, but my eyes snagged on him. How did he know about Mr. Bell's work?

Mr. Tanner continued, The Western Union is offering a million dollars to the inventor who can solve the problem of the multiple telegraph. I saw it in the papers.

Now everyone was interested in the communication troubles of the telegraph, but I couldn't join in, my promise to Mr. Bell to keep secret his work on the telegraph feeling suddenly like a burden. A slice of treacle tart had arrived on my plate, which thankfully required both a knife and fork. I busied my eyes and hands with it although I wasn't at all hungry. I'd learned so many things about Frank this evening and felt that I knew him less, not more. So I was surprised when, three mouthfuls into the tart, Frank's hand slid into view. He was reaching across the table and rapping his knuckles to lift up my eyes.

We are talking about communication breakdowns, he signed. I was telling everyone that you have some good examples. From your essay, he added, and he kept his gaze on me, as if he was trying to glide over a reconciliation.

I looked around at the guests. Everyone was waiting, and I felt the blaze of their expectation. I regretted the nervous smile that fluttered on my face but took a breath. My mother is hearing, I began. Once she said she had a hot ache at breakfast time so

I brought her a cold compress. But she had said Egg, not Ache. A too-hot egg.

Ache, Egg, I spelled on my hands, making the same lip-shape with each one, to show how I'd become confused. I continued: She put the compress on her egg, and said that will cool it down.

Everyone laughed as I showed my mother draping her egg, and relief flew through me to find that Frank was smiling as well.

For my next lesson, I arrived at the Oratory School expecting Miss Lance and found not only Mr. Bell in the hallway, but Miss Hubbard. The skip of pleasure I felt at seeing Mabel was immediately brought into check by the way Mr. Bell was talking to her.

I paused on the doorstep, even though Miss Lance waved me inside. Mabel's face was upturned to Mr. Bell's, and his gaze pooled down on her. She stood rooted within the great wash of his attention, and did not seem to mind it in the least.

Mr. Bell saw me, breaking eye contact with Mabel so that she turned as well. I spotted the greeting on his lips, and managed to return it, answering Mabel's smile at the same time. But I was still thinking of the way he had been looking at her, and was slow to focus on his speech, although he seemed to be saying something about good news.

I shall be teaching your lesson today, he said, then turned to Miss Lance with some remark about the good job she had been doing with me. He said, Will you wait five minutes? holding up the splayed digits of his hand. He went upstairs to his classroom, leaving me in the hallway with Miss Lance and Miss Hubbard.

Mabel watched him go, her smile warm on her cheeks, and I felt the cold sluice of clarity. Does she know it yet? I thought. That she cares for him?

Mabel looked at me, and Miss Lance stepped closer, remembering no doubt our misdemeanor of a few months before. Miss Lance started saying something about the demonstration at the

Institute. She stood with Mabel at one shoulder, and myself at the other, and spoke clearly, switching between us in turn, repeating herself on occasions, so we both had equal sight of her speech.

I started to feel needles of my impatience. It would be better if Mabel and I could sit down with our notebooks, but Mabel was nodding, so I followed suit.

Eventually I understood that Miss Lance was talking about Mabel's Visible Speech performance at the demonstration. Mabel would be reading a poem. I didn't get the name of the poet, although it seemed to be a Robert.

Robert, she said, then the corners of her lips sprang back on the poet's surname. The word I thought of was "Noise." But I knew there was no Robert Noise, just the silence of the ignorance she left me in.

Then I saw the word Phonoautograph and Apparatus. Since she was directing her speech at Mabel, I guessed she was explaining what my performance entailed. I knew that in Miss Lance's estimation this was the lesser performance, and my impatience flared into something worse; a desire to take Mabel by the arm and find some spot where we could talk more easily alone, leaving Miss Lance adrift in one of her morbidly slow sentences.

But I noticed that Mabel was struggling with the word Phonoautograph. Had Mr. Bell never told her about it, despite this new closeness of theirs? Instead of feeling pleased, I felt a knife of longing for Frank, and the way he had looked at me in the print shop, same as Mr. Bell had looked at Mabel.

After a moment, Mabel's look of concentration bounced loose from her narrowed eyebrows and strained gaze. She said, Oh! I'd much rather do that.

Miss Lance was taken aback. What do you mean? she said.

Mabel glanced at me, checking herself. I mean, she said, that does sound interesting.

Miss Lance recovered and started talking about Robert again. I attended as best I could, feeling I owed Mabel a compliment

similar to the one she had paid me, but I still missed the surname of this Robert, even as I raked through my repertoire of all
the famous Robert-poets I knew, which did not number many.

Mabel noticed and reached into her bag, finding an opened
envelope. She wrote "Robert Lloyd" on the back and added, "I
shall read an ode by Robert Lloyd in a British accent!"

Miss Lance pinched in her lips so that Mabel's hand quivered
slightly under her teacher's downward gaze. But she held out
the envelope until I'd read it and laughed. A British accent! I
said. That will impress everyone.

Miss Lance pulled out her watch and said something about
five minutes, and that no doubt Mr. Bell was waiting. Goodbye, I said to Mabel. I wanted to add something about seeing
her at the Institute, but the word was tricky for lip-reading, and
Mabel had folded away the envelope.

Goodbye, she returned, and Miss Lance said, Lovely, as if she
was stamping the conversation with her approval. Mabel went
with her to the door, and I went upstairs to Mr. Bell.

He was sitting at his desk with a pile of papers at his elbow.
He didn't look like he was readying himself for my lesson, but
starting on another task, or else trying to finish one. Ah! he
said, when I came in. He glanced at the papers and said something about the window.

I looked at the window. There was nothing changed about
the view. The temperature in the room was ambient, so it didn't
need opening. Did he wish to chuck the papers out of the window, such was his workload? I looked at him, to see if I'd missed
the joke.

He wasn't smiling. Instead, he was rephrasing his words carefully. Time, he was saying. A smaller window of time. Between
lessons. I have less time. A smaller window. Less time to do all
this work.

I said, I thought you said you were going to throw your papers out of the window.

I meant to jest but his smile was brief: he was preoccupied today. He turned to the pile of pupil notebooks and busied himself with trying to find mine. I could see Mabel's notebook lying separately from the rest of the pile. I remembered Miss Lance telling me she no longer took Miss Hubbard's lessons in the morning. Had Mr. Bell been teaching her, even when he hadn't time to teach me? And Mabel's father was his financial investor so wouldn't he make sure he took Mabel's lessons? Did all those trips to Cambridge reveal to him the kind of life he might like to have with Mr. Hubbard's daughter?

He gave me a sheet of exercises, which I'd copied for him the week before. I tried to study them but my thoughts were full of Mabel and Mr. Bell, and myself and Frank. The clarity I'd felt on seeing the way Mr. Bell had looked at her was gone, and my thoughts bubbled like a film of oil. Mabel had won Mr. Bell's affections but I didn't know where I stood with Frank, or any of the Tanners after Frank's withdrawn mood and Mrs. Ellison's reservations about me.

My essay, I said to Mr. Bell, looking up from the rows of symbols. Have you read it yet?

He frowned. Had he forgotten what I referred to? I wanted to say for *The Pioneer*, but right then I didn't trust my voice.

Your essay, yes, he said. He took out his notebook. This was a matter he wished to be clear about, or else he preferred the distance afforded by a notebook. "I'm afraid I have no time to get the next issue of *The Pioneer* out and I do not know about the one after that."

I looked at him, unsure of what to say. I knew I ought to say Oh, never mind! But the words wouldn't form on my lips.

Mr. Bell looked worried. "I promise," he wrote, "that when I do publish it, it will be the first paper in the journal."

I could see him thinking his way toward some kind of conciliatory gesture. I don't know what I would have done without you, he added.

I felt myself relenting, like a fist was uncurling in my chest, but he continued: The copying has made my workload so much easier. I have been terribly busy.

Copying. My eyes measured the word carefully. There were no homophenes I could think of for copying. I had copied, and with the extra time this had afforded him, he'd been able to teach Mabel.

He leaned toward me and there was that old light in his eyes. He said, That is why I am so pleased that you will be demonstrating at the Institute.

I parted my lips but my words felt like marbles that had been knocked in a hundred directions. I gathered my breath and said, I shall say one word.

His face was dented with surprise. He drew back and said something about Important. When I didn't understand he took up the pen. "The apparatus is just as important as Visible Speech," he wrote. "Members of the Institute are very interested in it."

He tried a smile. Miss Lark, he began, then decided to switch to the pen again. He was using his notebook more than usual.

"I have told you, and scarcely anyone else, what it may lead to. I cannot persuade Mr. Hubbard of it, or even little George Sanders's mother who has been so good to me! I live too much in an atmosphere of discouragement for scientific pursuits, surrounded by 'cui bono' people."

I skated over his paragraph then let my eyes rest on "cui bono." I didn't want to look up. I feared that if I met his gaze, I wouldn't be able to help myself from falling toward the idea he had always offered: that I could be a person of worth in the hearing world. But I was more "cui bono" than Mr. Bell could ever guess. I knew now there was no utility in Visible Speech, or any apparatus he dreamed up in the Institute, even if esteemed men of science flocked to see it.

I took my own pencil from the desk so I didn't need to ask him for his pen. "May I ask a question?" I wrote without showing him the sentence, or waiting for an answer. "You said the Phonoautograph would help deaf people by making speech visible, but deaf people won't be able to use a talking telegraph, so how will it help them?"

I handed Mr. Bell the page. He bent his face down and I was surprised to feel desperation inching through me as I stared at his dark crown. I wanted him to explain that I had simply misunderstood. Of course this was something he had considered.

When he looked up again, I saw that he was the one who didn't understand. But his confusion only made him look tired. He said, Are you saying I shouldn't do it?

He waited but weariness was settling into his face, even as he held himself still in anticipation of my answer. My understanding became full and lustrous. I wasn't supposed to doubt him.

He picked up one of the papers on his desk which I now saw was a letter. This is from my father, he said, then took up the pen. "My father thinks I should publish and sell my plans for the telegraph," he wrote. "He has advised that I take what I can now. I am overworked. My headaches have returned. But he is also concerned that I am not doing my duty toward Visible Speech. I have promised to do all I can to promote it. I will tell you what I have told him. Should I make money from the Multiple Telegraph, or even a human voice telegraph, we shall have Visible Speech put before the world in a more permanent form than at present. There is so much more I can do for the deaf once I have accomplished my ambitions for the telegraph. I shall campaign for day schools, for one thing, so that deaf children may reside with their families and spend as little time as possible in the company of one another."

He handed me the page but I could see his disappointment

in the flatness of his eyes. I had become one of the "cui bono" people, like Mr. Hubbard and his father, refusing to dream with him. When I finished reading, I looked up, trying to find some foothold in his expression into which I could hook my response. But his thoughts were elsewhere: with his teachings, his letters and the telegraph race. With Mabel Hubbard. I was left alone with the shining burn of his dismissal.

Shall we continue? he said.

Of course, I replied, feeling the upward boil of an anger that was as quick and dangerous as laughter. I picked up the exercises in my lap and focused on the symbols.

Cease, I began. Sea, Safety, Savings. My voice began to fill up my throat and mouth like a river. Youth, I said. Yearn, Yoke, Oyster. Roar, I continued. Fissure, Paper, Matter.

I was a torrent of words, and all of them were perfect.

13

[A changing scene]

I COULDN'T help my short temper with Frank in our next lesson together. You aren't concentrating, I told him.

I'm trying hard, he replied, puffing out his cheeks as he signed. His mood had lifted from the previous week and his propensity for distraction had returned.

You are wasting my time, I continued. You are wasting your money. You don't seem to have any interest in speech-reading. I paused then added: You told everyone last week what you really thought of Mr. Bell's methods.

It was the first time I had mentioned Mr. Bell in our lessons. I spelled out his name and then hesitated. Piano Man. That was what Frank's friends had called Mr. Bell. I played my hand along invisible keys. I was pleased to see Frank's nod.

Then he replied, You are annoyed about Mrs. Ellison.

His conclusion was neat and final so I leveled my eyes on him.

Don't worry about her, he continued. She has her own firm beliefs.

I gazed at Frank in all his openness. His good humor was like a vast and silvery lake and my anger skimmed toward it. Wasn't this his fault, anyway? He had asked for lessons and caused this confusion within myself, leaving me alone with it when Mrs. Ellison turned on me.

You agree with her, I signed.

He shrugged and bobbed his head from side to side, a neither-here-nor-there gesture. But it was an ambivalence for my benefit: he agreed.

He reached across and shut my book. He signed, I don't want to learn from Mr. Bell. I want to learn from you. Yes, it's not possible to speak perfectly without the symbols, but this—he pointed at the symbols—is Mr. Bell's voice. It's how he wants your words. They're his, not yours.

I felt the reflexive slam of my pride. Had he asked for these lessons because he thought I was the one who needed instruction? I wanted to tell him that Mr. Bell did value my words since he had confided in me about the telegraph. But I knew it was no longer true. Frank was right in more senses than he realized. Mr. Bell had always been listening for certain words to come out of my mouth. My praise, approval. I thought I could question him but I was wrong.

I got up and went to the window. The mass of telegraph wires was like a canopy over the street below, a dark protective wing. They were filled at this moment, as with every other, with electric signals racing faster than the tread of human feet below. Hadn't my longing for connection sped me to places I hadn't expected? I thought of Mabel standing in the corridor with Mr. Bell, fixed in the mist of his admiration. He was ten years older, her teacher, and not of the same social standing. Was all this eclipsed by what sparked between them? I knew what it was for the space between you and another person to melt into your exchanges so that you became the shared notions that were passing between you. And I knew Frank's touch, the fiery strokes of his fingertips. They had gone no further than my wrist but caused the rest of me to ache from their absence.

When I turned back to him, his expression had changed. The equanimity was gone, leaving the fuzzed lines of his concern. There was almost a quiver at his eyebrows, his jaw. It knocked any thoughts of Mr. Bell right from my head.

I wagged my hand. Come here. Let's watch people from the window.

He frowned, newly uncertain.

You're right, I continued. You cannot learn everything from a book. We will watch and you will tell me what you see. It's all guesswork, right? Let's compare our guesses.

He laughed and came to stand beside me. There isn't anyone, he signed. No one. Look.

We will wait, I replied. He stood with his shoulders less than an inch away, a gap that was easily closed by some small accidental movement. But he was very still as we waited. It started to rain. Frank turned down his smile, matched by a fatalistic shrug, and signed: Let's go out.

Out? In the rain?

Yes, out. We will find people. Isn't that what you meant? To speech-read.

We took one umbrella, which Frank propped against his shoulder so the canopy covered both of us. My gloves were dark like my coat and what with walking along in that huddled fashion, my signs were camouflaged. I took them off and we walked with our hands bright in the gray day.

As we walked, he told me about the Tanners' friends who had been at the dinner. Most of them lived throughout New England and regularly went back to Hartford for reunions. Mr. Olive was the only exception having lost his hearing as an adult. Mr. Brooks came from a black deaf family who were established in New Haven, whereas Clara Brooks lost her hearing when she almost drowned as a child. She would rather not live by the sea, Frank signed, but boats are the Brookses' business. Almena Ellison came from a Southern family and went to Hartford at a time before there were any schools for deaf people in the South. I don't think her family were pleased, he added, to learn that a few free black pupils were in the student body.

He pointed to a cigar store where two men were deep in conversation. Blue Glass, he declared. They are talking about a lecture on Blue Glass.

I studied the pair and saw what Frank had surely spotted: a pamphlet for Tremont Temple stuffed into the pocket of one of the men.

You're just guessing that because of what's in his pocket.

You told me to find the clues.

I laughed. But they aren't even looking at the pamphlet, I replied. "Blue" is easy to see on the lips, and I can't see anything about Blue.

Next, we tried taking guesses from two women who were waiting outside a bakehouse, and another woman buying ice from the driver of an ice-cart. She wants to marry him, Frank concluded.

She does not, I answered. She is asking for the largest block of ice and wants it cheap.

We watched them haggling, and Frank signed: He is agreeing. Do you think he is agreeing? What price is he asking? If it's good I'll tell my friends. He'll have a queue of deaf people all the way down the street tomorrow.

His palms drew out the long queue so it went right back to

his shoulder. I pointed at the ice-seller again. Look, she needs three blocks. That will be heavy.

Frank narrowed his eyes on the pair. Deliver, he said. She wants him to deliver them.

I watched the ice-seller. He was shaking his head but his lips were clear with a flicking *L* and biting *V.*

You're right, I signed. Deliver. But he won't do it. Look how pleased you are to be right!

He shrugged. I don't want you to think you are a bad teacher, he replied, the corners of his smile winking. Then he pushed his arm that was holding the umbrella against mine with a nudge. I felt curved muscle, the point of his elbow, and pushed back against him, bone against bone, fused for the briefest moment.

You're a terrible student, I reminded him.

The Public Garden was deserted. Some early spring buds were pushing through on the trees, but mostly the branches were bare. Frank suggested we walk down Commonwealth Avenue Mall, but I hesitated. Further into the Back Bay was the Institute. My earlier thoughts of Mr. Bell drifted back to me, although I knew he wasn't in Boston. Frank glanced at the sky as if to see what the heavens were threatening. Nothing much, it seemed, although the sidewalk puddles continued to flash with rippling circles. He made a question with his eyebrows: Well? he asked. You want to go back?

I didn't want to go back, but the turning for the Institute—Berkeley Street—seemed to shine out from the rain. But it wouldn't take long to get past the street, and then I could put it out of my mind.

No, I told him. Let's go quickly before the rain gets worse. I've never been further than Clarendon Street, I added. My fingers were starting to feel stiff from the cold.

C? That's not far at all. The houses are the grandest in Boston. Shall we have a look?

Frank started walking and I fell in step. Huge houses flanked either side of the Mall, which was thinly planted down the middle with young trees. There was no dust since the rain had turned it into a dirty paste. That one, Frank signed. I'd like to live in that one.

We were passing the turning for the Institute. I waved my finger at the other side of the street. Did he know the streets were named after English Lords? I didn't know the sign for Lords, if there was one, and could only think of the sign for King, slicing my hand diagonally down my chest.

Kings? Frank asked. He hadn't heard of any kings called Clarendon.

Lords, I repeated, this time spelling on my fingers.

Lord Clarendon? Frank laughed. Boston people see themselves as royalty. Why not? I fancy being a lord. A deaf lord. You can picture it? How about these hearing lords? This is Lord Berkeley.

He puffed out his cheeks and showed his walking fingers swaggering down the sidewalk, his shoulders matched to their rhythm. Lord Clarendon was thin and spindly, and liked to sip his tea through the corner of his mouth. I did Lord Dartmouth, clawing the sign for sleep down my face, then dropping my head dozily to one side, blowing out my lips as if I was snoring. Frank laughed.

We proceeded down the Mall in the passing company of the Lords Fairfield, Gloucester, Hereford. The Institute was behind us now. The spaces grew between the houses, which became walls with no roofs, and then foundations with no walls, and then just empty plots. Soon there would be nothing but gravel pit and swamp.

I stopped but Frank took a step forward, taking the umbrella with him, so I had to shuffle forward. The salt marsh ahead of us stretched on to Gravelly Point, where two dams joined and ran down one side of the marsh, separating it from the river. Mudflats spooled on either side of the dams while wagon traffic plied the tops. Rail trucks brought in the next loads of gravel.

I glanced at Frank. We had come as far as we could. Shouldn't we turn back?

Birds landed on the marsh, and a worker tossed some gravel in their direction, causing them to fly away. We watched them soar against the sky, and when Frank turned to me, I felt his eyes go right into me, a flight path of their own.

Mr. Bell, he began, startling me. He works in the Back Bay. I know there is a scientific building here which he visits. Near Berkeley Street, or Boylston? I saw you glancing. Look, I must give you an explanation, he added quickly, seeing my alarm.

I nodded, unsure with what I was agreeing. Frank continued, Do you remember how we gave him Piano for his sign name at Hartford because he played the piano with his hotel window open? All the hearing teachers said you could hear his music coming into the school. We didn't know. How could we? But he filled the town with music, same as he tried to fill us with speech. All together in a huge hall, our voices shouted those symbols. If Mr. Bell looked happy, maybe some English had come out of us. How could we know that as well? We stood in the assembly hall shouting out his symbols and he told us we were speaking, and then he went to his hotel, and opened the window and played his piano.

Frank paused to check I was following. I nodded again, but it felt like I was in the flood of his pictures. He showed the hall where the pupils had stood, their voices flowing out of them, the piano flowing into the town, Mr. Bell, exacting and precise, the conjurer of both.

Frank dashed a finger between us. You and I. We are the lucky ones. You learned English as a child. I knew signs from birth. But there are children who have no hearing from birth, so they can't learn English, and their parents don't know any sign language. Some of them, they hate the idea of it and won't let them use it. At Hartford, ten-year-olds would arrive with no words, no signs, no concepts.

I nodded again. No language, I signed and shook out the O shapes of my hands: nothing.

Right, nothing. There was one boy, Frank continued. His name was Roy Stamper. He was like that. I was a senior pupil and was made his college parent. I taught him to sign. He understood nothing at first but he was quick, so quick. Our first day we went into the gardens. It was early summer, all the flowers were out. There was so much color everywhere. I named the colors for him as we walked through the garden. It was the young sunflowers he liked best.

He spelled sunflower then made a sign for the flower, but instead of signing *sun* and *flower*, he held up his forearm and with his opening fist showed the flower's head lifting and rotating toward the sun. It showed the boy, the way he was taking everything in.

That's why I gave him his sign name, Frank continued, and he twisted the *y* hand shape—the sign for Yellow—close to his head.

Roy, he signed. *Yellow.* Roy learned quickly. Soon he was signing the same as the other children. He came to spend summer holidays with my parents. I have three brothers, he was like a fourth. I don't think his own parents cared about him. Then, in his second year he got dropsy of the lungs. He refused to go home, because no one could talk to him there. His teachers didn't know what to do. I stayed at his bedside. I promised him he would get better, I wouldn't leave him, and he wouldn't have to go home.

One evening, he did seem better. I was telling him stories, making him laugh, but not too much. There was a full moon, so I opened the curtains, to make the room bright. An hour passed, I left him because I was thirsty. I needed some fresh air, he seemed peaceful. Mr. Bell was in the corridor. He stopped me. He told me how it was the saddest thing in the world. A boy who didn't want to go to his family when he was dying. I told him maybe, but that's what Roy wanted. We were his family now. But Mr. Bell told me that I must persuade the boy to go home. That's when I realized he didn't understand us.

He paused for a moment, and I thought of Reverend Keep, acting as a go-between for Mr. Tanner and his customer. Perhaps the principal didn't convey your meaning properly, I signed.

Frank was looking hard at me. Mr. Bell knows the sign language, he signed. Didn't he tell you?

I couldn't help my disbelief, all my thoughts stalling on this new fact. He didn't tell me, I managed after a moment.

He's not very good, Frank continued, but he thinks he knows enough to decide we shouldn't use it ourselves.

Frank looked across the bay, his gaze sweeping across the flats which were speckled with men and carts. His eyes wavered as if he couldn't make something out in the distance. When he turned back to me, his signs were slower, carefully made.

We argued in signs, he continued, no third person. Just me and him. I lost my temper. The principal saw us arguing. I was just a pupil, Mr. Bell our guest teacher. I wasn't allowed back into Roy's room. I begged but the principal was furious with me. I went into the garden. I thought Roy might go to the window and see me. The moon was bright, he could see me signing in the garden. You know what I saw? Someone had gone into his room and closed the curtains. Left him in the dark to hear nothing, see nothing. I went straight back inside but the principal was coming down the stairs and stopped me. The next day, I learned that Roy had died. Then at lunchtime the hotel window was open. Mr. Bell was filling the town with his music.

Frank's right hand brushed back and forth above his left palm—*music*—then he spanned his sign out as if the music was traveling across the air, out into the Bay. He smiled a little and added, Maybe it was a funeral march? Who knows. We couldn't hear it.

You think Mr. Bell closed the curtains, I signed, and as I drew down my hands, I thought how the sign for curtains closing felt similar to falling darkness. *Curtains, Darkness.* Once I'd confused the same word with Gardens, and it had led to Mr. Bell asking for the paper he'd never read.

Him or the principal.

Did he stay? I asked.

He went back to Boston to be a professor. You know the rest. He set up his own school but I was expelled from mine. I wanted to stay at Hartford and become a teacher like my older brothers. I had a sweetheart, we were to be married.

His eyes switched to the bay again, leaving me with the hovering pictures of his story. Mr. Bell, his hands at the piano, the music rising from the keys and summoned into the bay, swelling through the air, and Frank's sign for Sweetheart hung among those planes of music. He'd never mentioned anyone to me. Did she break things off or stand by him? I wanted to ask but I knew it would do nothing but suggest my own feelings at the wrong moment.

Printing is a good profession, I told him, when he turned back.

Lucky my uncle took me on, he agreed, then turned and cast his gaze back down the Mall. What bothers me, he began, is all the scientists listening to him. His ideas, filling up that building, same as his piano in Hartford. If he gets the multiple telegraph, it will be even worse.

Frank's face looked bare in a way I'd not seen before. It lasted only a second before his expression tightened, pinched by regret. I pictured the boy waiting for Frank, the curtains sealed against any hope of light in the room.

There are lots of men like him, I signed. Women too, I added, thinking of Miss Lance and Miss Roscoe.

He laughed a little. Should that make us feel better? Come on, it is getting late.

As we walked back down the Mall, and the houses began

to rise around us, I felt a growing sense of misery. When we reached the turning for the Institute, I didn't try and breeze past like before. I had been wrong about Mr. Bell, and no longer cared what he did with a telegraph and whether he could make it yield voices or not. At my next lesson at the Oratory School, I would bring the smoked glass with me and return it to him.

I turned to Frank, feeling purposefulness stack up inside me. You don't need to worry about Mr. Bell, I told him. He can't persuade anyone to finance what he really wants. Can you guess what it is?

I smiled, readying Frank for the revelation. He wants to put a voice in a wire, I told him. He wants to make the telegraph talk so that two people can hear each other across a distance. But even hearing people can't see the value, I added. No one is interested!

Frank was watching me closely. There was a sharp light of interest in his eyes. I was taken aback. I'd been expecting his scorn. Had my signs not been clear?

I tried a second time, drawing out the line of the wire and showing how a voice might travel along it, so that it could be heard at the other end, where a listener was located, receiving the sound. Now that I was trying to convey Mr. Bell's idea in signs, I started to think that perhaps it really was absurd after all.

You see? I told Frank. If he doesn't make any money from the idea, then he can't promote Visible Speech.

But Frank was nodding slowly. Tell me that again, he signed. One more time.

I was thrown into confusion. What interest could Frank have with such a device? But I repeated my signs again, more slowly, trying out a different spatial arrangement to see if that helped communicate my meaning.

He told you this? he asked. You?

Yes, I replied, starting to feel my temper rising. He told me all this. He showed me some apparatus in the Institute of Technology. That's the name of the place where he works.

He showed you a telegraphic device?

No, it was for teaching deaf children, but it gave him inspiration for the human voice telegraph. But as I spelled out Inspiration, not knowing the sign, I felt my shame curling up tight inside me, remembering how pleased I'd been to notice the sensitivity of the tiny bones in the cadaver ear.

Inspiration, right. I see. How would it work? he asked. The talking telegraph, I mean. Did he tell you that?

His face didn't show any sign of challenge, but he was affecting casualness, trying to soften the edges of his keenness.

I don't think he fully knows yet, I replied. The idea is that the vibrations of the voice can induce a current. But he has some problems with the voice being strong enough to generate the current. He isn't an electrician. There is a membrane, I added, trying to remember the Phonoautograph. A stylus rests against it, which can conduct sound through the membrane—

My signing had come apart by this point, and I was relying heavily on finger-spelling. Frank had also started correcting me because he wanted to be clear. A stylus, he spelled. A current? It goes where? Here? The membrane? I don't understand. Spell it, don't sign it. I can't follow your signs.

I threw up my hands. Does it matter anyway? I told him. I thought you were worried about the deaf community, not about membranes, and... But I trailed off, unable to repeat the litany of finger-spelled words a second time.

He drew back, holding up his hands in an overdone concession, as if my accusations had been unreasonable. Then he tried a purposefully neutral expression. So he wants to put voices into the telegraph, he signed. What about the multiple telegraph? Did he tell you about that race?

I looked at Frank. In spite of his efforts to hide it, his questions were queued up in his eyes. The conversation over the dinner

table at the Tanners' came back to me. How did you know that
Mr. Bell has rented the attic? I asked.

He stalled. What attic?

The one at the mechanic shop.

That? Well, my uncle sees him there occasionally.

In the attic?

No, no. At the counter downstairs.

He broke eye contact and turned a few paces, twisting foot-
prints in the mud underfoot.

Aren't you worried he will see you? I asked. You were so
worried when we first met. Remember? You asked me not to
tell Mr. Bell about you. Well, he might be here now. There, in
the Institute. I pointed toward Berkeley Street.

Frank shook his head. He's not in town, he replied.

My mouth dropped and my hands lifted—how did he
know?—but at that moment two men turned out of Berkeley
Street and Frank, glancing at them, reached for my elbow. Let's
go, he signed.

When we were at the end of the street, I asked him: Did you
know those men?

He frowned. Which men? Those men? No. But his smile
lifted his cheeks with an effortful joviality. You have a lot of
questions, he signed.

I stopped on the sidewalk. I have a lot of questions? I replied,
thumping my chest twice.

His glance was brief, but something quickened in him. He
stepped up to me, and his signs came out fast, raised in keeping with his string of Yous, as he pointed his questions at me.
You, you, you.

I don't see how Mr. Bell can have told you all this, he signed.
Do you know about electricity? Do you know how sound works?
Why would he tell you?

He was looking at me hard, his gaze like a surgeon's blade,
cutting and lifting away something for assessment. He was try-

ing to see my lessons with Mr. Bell. Did he wonder at our closeness? Suddenly I wanted him to see what I knew was no longer
there. Myself, Mr. Bell's star pupil, to whom he confided more
than he ought. In any case, the swirl of my anger and pride was
making me feel like it might still be true. I held myself straight
and open before Frank's inspection. I meant to show him that
I had nothing to hide, and that all his suspicions were entirely
reasonable.

But then I signed, Mr. Bell needed someone to believe in
his idea.

Believe. It combined two signs, *think* and *marry*. I touched
my index to my temple then clasped my hands together. But
my cupped hands trembled between us, even though my chin
was lifted high with resolution. My signs married nothing of
my conviction, and he saw it.

So you did! he replied. You told him you believed in all those
voices.

He made the voices travel in aimless lines around his head, like
irritating flies. His scorn had arrived, only now it was too late.

You should be thankful! I replied. I told you because you
were worried about Mr. Bell's bad idea catching on. I tried to
reassure you.

He considered me. It isn't just one man, he signed. A bad idea?
Maybe, who knows. But maybe you don't know Mr. Bell at all.
Maybe you haven't stood in a room with hundreds of children,
all of us following one man's determination to have us speak the
same as him. There's you and him, sitting together comfortably,
chatting about the telegraph, chatting away.

He finished on his picture of two people seated and his flat
hand flickering at his mouth, his face straight with boredom and
tipped back against this endless repetitious chatter of myself and
Mr. Bell. He made us look like hearing people, and our easy
talking was a mindless absurdity.

He turned and started walking. I had to follow quickly. He

kept his eyes on the sidewalk ahead, his closed umbrella now
strutting out our haste even though the rain had stopped, and
we might have ambled through more of Boston. Anger made
my steps feel light, as if my chest had ballooned with so much
heat it was surging me along. A new idea was burning brightly.
Frank had lost so much because of Mr. Bell. His future at Hartford, his sweetheart. He'd broken his promise to Roy to stay
with him and that was Mr. Bell's fault as well. Then he met me,
and he thought he could win something back. Our lessons were
a kind of revenge. He meant to destroy my confidence in Mr.
Bell and his methods, and that would be a small victory. How
much did he hope to settle a score with his old teacher? And
win my affections as well? He had succeeded, so now what? My
thoughts carried on swiveling into this darkening hole. Never
mind Mr. Bell's lessons. I was a pawn in Frank's lessons, serving some purpose that I'd not been able to see.

We stopped at the gates to the Public Gardens. From here
our routes home diverged. He turned to me. You are angry, he
signed.

His simple statement of the fact only made me angrier. And I
wanted to cling on to my anger because it was all I had left. His
picture of myself and Mr. Bell nattering away was stuck in my
mind. Of course, we hadn't talked as easily as that! But the truth
was worse. I'd labored over understanding Mr. Bell's words, for
months and months, and pretended I hadn't, and that Mr. Bell
spoke to me like he spoke to all people.

Frank's own anger had dropped away, almost as quickly as
it had arisen. I'm sorry, he signed. I shouldn't have said those
things. I'm a terrible liar. Yes, I did know those men. Yes, I have
many questions about Mr. Bell's work.

For a moment he looked so stricken, I thought he wouldn't
continue. Then he drew a deep breath. I've been so worried,
he signed. I knew I would have to tell you, but my plans went
wrong. Next time I will explain. I promise. But not here, like

this. Look, see? It's raining again. Will you come next Tuesday for our lesson? And I will walk you home?

Dimly, I knew that I didn't want us to part on bad terms, but I shook my head instead. No, I can walk myself back, I told him.

As I turned away, I glimpsed his hand lifting in a T shape, beginning the circle of Tuesday. He still wanted to know if I was coming next week. But my anger had started my steps and I couldn't seem to stop them. I carried on walking, my pace getting faster as I pushed through the rising wall of my regret. My cheeks started to tingle and dampen with the fresh rain, and I was grateful for its coolness.

It was only when I got back to Little St. Clouds that I realized I hadn't put my gloves back on in spite of the cold, even after I'd left him.

14

Believe

MR. CRANE stands under the arcades at the top of the Horticultural Gardens, gazing across the flower walks and the late-
afternoon crowds drifting in from Hyde Park. He looks around
when I enter at the far end, and my boots start striking the paving stones. It's been a long time, I sign, when I reach him, arcing forward the circles of my thumbs and indexes.

I was away, he replies, and draws me farther along the gloomy
corridor. I have new information, he adds, his indexes flying
from his chin. Are you cold? This way. He points toward the
Conservatory at the end of the arcade.

I'm not cold, I tell him, but I follow him into the conservatory which smells of hot paint and new growth. As we seat ourselves behind a large fern, like a courting couple seeking privacy from prying eyes, I wonder again if I should have ignored his latest letter. Weeks had passed without a word from him, even after I'd written to inform him that Harmon and I would be calling on the Bells. They were touring with the Telephone but were due back within a few weeks. I waited, and had almost put Mr. Crane out of my mind, and was starting to wonder how it would be to see Mabel again, when his reply arrived. I must meet him, he wrote, the following day. I toyed with throwing the letter away, but when the hour came, I put on my coat, leaving old Holmwood asleep, and the laundry folded in the sunshine.

Mr. Crane fishes a note from his pocket, and hands it to me. Mr. Gray, he signs. Remember him? His patent application arrived at the Patent Office on the same day as Mr. Bell's.

His expressiveness, as he signs, dispels the sullen twist of his features, so that you would hardly guess him to be hearing. My thoughts skip back to the Thames embankment, and the word on Mr. Bell's lips. Mr. Gray, Mystery. Which one was it? But doubt won't help me now. I remember, I reply. Mr. Bell was awarded the patent.

Read that, he signs. It's copied from Mr. Bell's Telephone patent application. For the first patent, not the second one.

What strikes me, when I open the note, is that it's not Mr. Bell's handwriting. The topic appears to be his, as the author describes mercury or some other liquid forming part of a voltaic current. But I have to read the sentences about conducting wires, and their immersion in the mercury, and the resistance that results, several times, jolted by the long words and strange handwriting.

I don't understand, I tell him. These words—

I space my thumb and index along the page, shaking my head. I look at Mr. Crane, wanting his signs, his pictures to make sense of the note.

His eyes are beaded with excitement. That is the idea of Variable Resistance, he signs, prodding at the paper first. If you can vary the resistance, you can create an undulating current.

I watch his index finger waving up and down for the undulating current, before both indexes line up, pushing back and forth. *Resistance.* The rest of his explanation unfolds in the air, and I can't help smiling to see it. It's an elegance that I'm sure would rival even one of Mr. Bell's most eloquent speeches. I nod, trying to fasten on to a detail that I learned from the newspapers. I've read all the papers closely, looking for the things that Mr. Bell didn't tell me, or that I missed when he talked to me.

The Telephone, I sign, is different from the telegraph. It needs an undulating current not an intermittent one.

I have to finger-spell most of the Telephone words but attempt a matching sign, stabbing out the intermittent current, shaking my head and hands afterward in negation of what the Telephone did not require.

Exactly, Mr. Crane answers. But how do you create such a current? Here is Mr. Bell's answer. Variable Resistance. That is the key principle.

I look down at the note again. Who wrote this? I ask. It isn't Mr. Bell's handwriting.

He smiles as if I've shown a pleasing sharpness. But don't I know Mr. Bell's handwriting almost as well as my mother's? It filled dozens of our class notebooks, along with the schedules and exercises that I copied for him.

Someone in the Washington patent office made a copy of Mr. Bell's patent application for me.

They will do that? I ask, then immediately regret the question because Mr. Crane is smiling again. This time it's for my naivety.

I know a few people there. He hands me another note, written in the same hand, which I now know to belong to a patent officer in Washington. A line of words at the bottom have been circled: "I claim as my invention the art of transmitting vocal sounds or conversations telegraphically through an electric circuit."

This is also from Mr. Bell's first patent application?

He's almost grinning. No, that one is Mr. Gray.

I hold up both notes, looking from one to the other, and my thoughts cast back to the Philadelphia Exposition. It was there that Frank and I met Mr. Gray. A willowy man with gentle eyes: he spoke kindly of Mr. Bell, conceded the Telephone readily, wrote gracious words in my notebook. And now I hold both men's work side by side.

Mr. Gray's patent application, I sign, also proposes liquid to vary the resistance. It's the same as Mr. Bell's. And they both propose an instrument for transmitting vocal sounds.

But Mr. Crane shakes his head. It's not the same. Mr. Bell's first patent application was for improvements in the telegraph. It included noises or vocal sounds as an additional use, and it included variable resistance. He pauses, then adds, In Mr. Bell's patent application all that detail is scribbled into the margins.

I look at Mr. Crane. The margins? I ask, using finger-spelling, to check I have understood the space he has delineated in the air. He taps his fist in confirmation: the margins.

Is that allowed? I ask, wondering how the marvel of the Telephone could be born from the margins of a piece of paper.

If it's written down somewhere, yes, it's allowed.

I look again at the notes which the patent officers had considered side by side, as I had done, before awarding the patent to Mr. Bell. Soon afterward, his financial backers gave him the go-ahead to work on the talking telegraph, not the Multiple Telegraph. His dream could be unleashed, while Mr. Gray had to abandon his. But I no longer had anything to do with Mr. Bell by then, or him with me.

I fold away the notes, and sign, The key principle is what's important, right? Mr. Bell had been thinking about the Telephone for a long time, I add, flickering my fingers down from my shoulders.

I'm about to tell Mr. Crane that it was his backers who didn't believe the idea was worth anything, but I stop myself. The soft bump of pleasure granted to me by this piece of knowledge vanishes. Why am I here? To defend Mr. Bell, or hold him to task? Or is it that circling need to go back, to understand what I didn't before? I remember the Telephone on the Thames embankment and how I pressed my finger inside it, longing for it to speak to me, so I could be amazed like everyone else. I hated the gaps of understanding I was often left with, and here was Mr. Crane, offering to fill some of them in. Then I think of Frank, and my breath scrunches inside me like balled-up paper. With Frank, too, my understanding had come too late.

There's one more thing, Mr. Crane continues. Mr. Bell's legal team have been trying to find the English version of this patent. It came here a few weeks before the American copy was filed. They seemed in a hurry. My guess is that they wanted to find it before the Western Union's lawyers did.

I give him a wry smile. Let me guess, I tell him. You know people.

His thumb tapping his temple in confirmation. Yes, he did know people. People who could get him invited to the house of the man who was managing Mr. Bell's English patents for him.

I got a quick glimpse, he signs. That was all. But it was a big surprise, and I think I know why Mr. Bell's lawyers want it back. There was no mention of the use of liquid to create variable resistance.

Nothing, he repeats, and his eyes blaze at me with triumph. Mr. Bell's English patent application, he signs, doesn't mention mercury or liquid or variable resistance at all. There's nothing. The key principle isn't there.

I think of all the letters and papers I have copied. It would be a poor clerk to omit something that significant.

My guess, he continues, is that one copy came to England and shortly afterward the American copy was taken to Washington to be filed. Mr. Bell could only add variable resistance to the American copy because the English copy had already sailed. That means variable resistance was a very late addition to the American copy. *Late.* He strikes the sign down twice and hard.

You think, I ask, that Mr. Bell copied Mr. Gray's patent application?

Perhaps he's a copy-clerk himself, Mr. Crane remarks, with a teasing smile at me. It might not have been him, he adds. It might have been his lawyers, or other people. You know Mr. Bell has a whole team around him.

Team. His sign emphasizes its size and impressiveness. I hold back on telling him that once Mr. Bell's team was him and I, for I was the one he trusted with his fledgling idea. But I don't say anything in case it seems feeble, or worse, petty. Besides, another thought lurks at the underside of this one, as I recall the times Mr. Bell reached for his notebook because I couldn't follow him. The truth was that voice had never been strong enough for me. It left me reaching after it, always slipping around some corner and out of my grasp. And when I finally came to terms with this, Mr. Bell vanished in the same way. But not until he'd made sure that Adeline knew about my lies.

Mr. Crane is leaning forward, agitated by my distraction. He swings his fingers toward himself. Look at me. This is important. The patent officer said something about showing Mr. Gray's patent application to Mr. Bell. He was in debt to Mr. Bell's financiers. But he is also a drunk. I can't go to the Union until I have definite evidence. I need something about that English patent. You are perfect. You are close to him, and he won't suspect you, because—

He spreads his hands, leaving his sentence unfinished. Not the kind of tact a fellow deaf person would spare me. Because I'm deaf-and-dumb? I finish for him. Is that your meaning?

A confidante, he repeats, spelling the word, then making a sign that looks like the one for information kept secret.

But Mr. Crane is the one entrusting me with secrets now. I try to imagine Mr. Bell at the patent office. Did he turn the pages of Mr. Gray's patent application gingerly or hastily? Was the patent officer there with him? Mr. Bell was neck-and-neck with Mr. Gray in the race for the Multiple Telegraph, and yet there, shining up from Mr. Gray's patent application, was the thing he really cared about, an instrument that could carry voices. And he was desperate, I supposed. He wanted to marry Mabel, and needed to secure their future. I picture his disbelief, his hesitation. I see him pick up his pen, and copy.

You trust a drunk? I ask, thinking now that the patent officer's writing did seem quite messy.

I trust you, he says, slicing his hand firmly into his palm. But his eyes slip away a moment later, embarrassed. He shuffles back a little, as if he's only just realized how close we've been huddled. He looks down to the garden, where a gardener is calling out something. It must be closing time. I study Mr. Crane's flattish profile, which gives nothing away, and my thoughts drift back to Frank standing on the Commonwealth Avenue, promising me an explanation. If only he'd told me then about how he was in Mr. Crane's employ. Would it have changed anything about what happened? An ache starts up behind my breastbone. This desperate racket of calculations. I long to be free of it. Meeting with Mr. Crane has brought me hope.

We have to leave soon, Mr. Crane signs. Okay? He flips his thumbs at me, his brow dropped into a question, trying to extract an agreement from me. You just watch what Mr. Bell says, he continues. Then you tell me. The Western Union's case is about the second Telephone patent, but if I can let them know about this first one, they will reward me.

Us, he signs quickly, flicking his fingers between us in correction, and I can't help my laugh. Your reward, I say, is not what I want.

He gazes straight into my laughter, which is openly enough at him. He has the deaf habit of keeping eye contact easily, and seems to have no shame over subjects that concern money.

You aren't what I expected, he signs suddenly.

My face drops into straightness. What did Frank tell him about me? I knock my indexes together, as gentle an admission as I can manage. You same, I reply, but his eyes drill into me so that I feel a shiver of alarm. The notes, he signs, and holds out his hand.

A thought comes to me as I hand them over. Mercury is only mentioned in Mr. Bell's patent. I remember Adeline's statue of the god, Mercury, at Little St. Clouds, and Frank joking, Watch out for him, and my answering laughter.

Why does only Mr. Bell's patent application talk about mercury? I ask.

Mr. Crane puts the notes in his pocket, then bobs his head in acknowledgment. Mercury is a puzzle, he signs. I don't know why he wrote mercury. Mercury wouldn't work. The liquid must be water.

An expert, I reply, pointing at him. Maybe you should be an inventor, everything you've learned. My fingertips bunch together, drawing toward my chest and downward. *Absorb, take in, become imbued.*

He doesn't smile; instead his signing bounces with his defensiveness. I was in Washington when the patents were handed in, he tells me. I stayed in a boardinghouse with the draftsmen working on Mr. Gray's patent. They said the liquid had to be water.

I hold up my hands in concession. I'm sure you're right, I tell him. That paper, I add pointing at the note from Mr. Bell's patent. I need the key words written down in Visible Speech.

All right, he nods. I'll send them to you. He puts away the

notes and takes out an envelope. This is for you, he signs, handing it to me. Inside are some recent articles about the Telephone,
so you know what kind of things Mr. Bell might be talking
about. They are back next week?

I slip the envelope into my bag, trying to push down the
memory of Mabel's tidy note, which she had added to Mr. Bell's
letter: "We will be very glad to see you," she had written.

Thursday, I tell Mr. Crane.

The household tasks keep me from worrying about our call
on the Bells. There is the spring cleaning to be done. I start on
the upper rooms, dismantling the bedsteads and soaking them in
brine, turning down the chairs and sofas so they can be whipped
and brushed, and washing the mirrors with rainwater made
slippery with ammonia. Then I prepare Mr. Holmwood's ar-
rowroot custard and beef tea, exactly as Mama made them. Her
death was followed by his third attack of apoplexy in as many
years. As far as possible, everything must be made easy for him.
Mama wrote six or seven letters of instructions while she was
still well enough to hold her pen. And one letter for me, the
longest of them all. Do not open this yet, she said. And I promised I wouldn't until Harmon and I were wed.

After luncheon, when Mr. Holmwood is napping, I sit down
with my copy-work. There is another stack of business letters from Harmon. I log them before filing blank copies in the
drawer, not even bothering this time to read them first. When
I get to the bottom of the pile, I find my unfinished paper for
Mr. Bell's presentation to the Anthropological Society. "A Statement of Invention," it begins, but I've not written a single line
beyond this title. It won't be long before Harmon asks for it, so
he can make a translation into Visible Speech.

I can't face the task, and decide to write to Mary instead. I
fetch Mama's travel case in which I keep all my correspondence.
But when I open the lid, the first envelope that springs out is

the one that Mr. Crane gave me in the gardens. I'd thrown it in the case after our last meeting. I glance at the clock. Mr. Holmwood might sleep for another hour. There is time to read the articles and still write Mary. Most of them, when I start reading them, only concern how interest in the Telephone is developing, but one about Mr. Edison makes me pause. The subject is not the Telephone, although Mr. Edison has continued to improve on Mr. Bell's design. Instead, it describes his newest invention, called the Phonograph. Sound is played into the instrument, which uses a needle to scratch corresponding grooves onto a foil, and these are run back through the needle and an amplifier. It is the first instance of recorded sound.

I stare at the page. Phonograph and Phonoautograph. The two words shimmer at opposite sides of my thoughts, as if they are assessing themselves in their reflections. The Phonograph, with its needle scratching out marks, doesn't seem so removed from the instrument that Mr. Bell showed me in the Institute. But wasn't Mr. Bell, and no other inventor, the master of sound? I feel tugged toward something I cannot yet see. A question comes to me: what if I showed Mr. Bell the smoked glass again?

I put the thought out of my head. I've only just got the glass back from Mr. Crane. I don't dare part with it again. Turning to my letters, I try to think of what to write Mary. I know she enjoys reading my accounts of London life. "Harmon is proposing a new telephone franchise business," I write. "We have resumed our acquaintance with the Bells, who do not live far from us. We will call on them tomorrow." But then the desire to tell her about Mr. Crane fills me, and I decide to finish the letter quickly. I can imagine the blunt pragmatism I'd receive in response. "Harmon will not understand or forgive this," she'll tell me. "Mr. Holmwood may let you stay for now, but where will you go once he is no longer with you?" She won't invite me to live with her and Glenn King since she can only abide her husband if his temptations are out of sight, and neither of us wish for me to become one of them.

All the same, my regret makes it difficult to fold the letter away. It is not only for what I cannot tell Mary, but what we can never have again: those days wandering the Pawtucket lanes, our home-signs flying between us, perfect sunlit ease.

The Bells live in one of the tall white stucco houses on Cromwell Road, its storeys rising with the branches of the trees. As we walk past the villas, putting our narrow street behind us, I smooth my skirts from the tuck of my jacket and fiddle with my sleeves. Harmon glances at me but I can't help fussing at my appearance. I expect Mabel to be wearing something finer than the plain brocade of my visiting dress, although it's likely her condition will require a generous fit. The smoked glass is wrapped inside a velvet pouch in my skirt pocket. Before we left, I described it vaguely to Harmon who said, Of course you must remind Mr. Bell of it. It belongs in a museum. I nodded, and kept my ideas to myself. I wasn't sure whether or not I would show it to Mr. Bell. What if he didn't let me have it back?

The weather is warm and bright, perfect for strolling, but Harmon struts as if the shine on his polished shoes is leading the way. My curiosity about seeing Mabel again is so jumbled with doubt that I try simply to focus on staying apace, ignoring the watery tingle of my nerves. When we reach their address, the housekeeper is a while opening the door. To bide the minutes, I spell to Harmon, I often saw Mrs. Bell at the school.

I am sure, he spells back, you will have plenty to remember.

Yes, I say. I'm sure. I look away, thinking of how Mabel and I had run through the Oratory School together. Yet, she never called on me in London. Did it seem childish to her now? Or had Mr. Bell told her about Frank? And if so, did she agree with his views or was she secretly pleased when Mr. Bell decided to visit us in London? Perhaps she even encouraged him. "We would be so glad to receive you," she'd written.

The housekeeper finally opens the door and bids us wait in the parlor. A little dog starts bouncing at our feet. I crouch down to pet the creature and take a good look around the room while I do so. It's smaller than the sort of parlor I'm sure Mabel would be keeping in Boston. Harmon tells me that much of their income at present is from Mr. Bell's lecturing fees, but they totter on the edge of huge wealth. If the Bell Company hangs on to Bell's patents, I think. And I can't help wondering: does this parlor please her? Is she content with their life?

It's an effort to keep Mr. Crane's task in sight. I assess the parlor again. Like ours, it is filled with tables, chairs and ornaments. But the lighting is good, coming from gas lamps and the fire blazing behind the fender. It won't matter which chair Mr. Bell takes, or where I position myself. They all look well lit. And the small size of the room means nobody should be standing too far away. It's as decent a room for taking sight of Mr. Bell's speech as I can hope for.

Harmon touches my shoulder. I leave the dog to find Mabel standing in the doorway. She looks much older than when I last saw her, but it's not only the new plumpness of her cheek and dress line. Her hair is smoothly knotted back, setting off her clever face and gray eyes. She smiles at us. Harmon shakes her hand, introducing us as if we'd never met. Good morning, I say, and my voice feels unsteady.

She glances at the dog, which is sitting at her heel with its chin tipped and tail raking back and forth across the rug. Mabel scoops him up. Do you like him? she says to me. With great care she pronounces his name. The word I see is Blema or Pleba, but I've never come across such a name before, and can't help my puzzlement. Have I misunderstood? Mabel tries one more time, freeing one hand from the dog's belly to trace the shape of the *P* and the *M* in the air: Plema. I smile because only she would know what letters can't be easily seen. I say, Your dog must be company for you when Mr. Bell is away.

Mabel hesitates. It's only when the housekeeper answers me that she figures out my question.

When Lady Jones called, says the housekeeper, and found Mrs. Bell out, she asked if she was out alone. I said no, she has her dog with her!

The housekeeper has a steady manner of speaking, with just enough theater to add touches of meaning to her words without resorting to gesture. Likely she learned it through talking so often with her mistress. Mabel laughs. She says something about Protection and shakes her head, kissing the dog. As if Plema is much protection? She puts him down and indicates the chairs for us to be seated.

There's no sign of Mr. Bell. My husband will not be long, Mabel says, but I don't catch the reason she gives for his lateness. We don't mind waiting, Harmon says to dispel the appearance of our uncertainty. Mabel turns to me. Her look is direct, but her eyes reveal her hesitation. I'm sorry, I see her say, followed by a few other words that include: Your mother.

I nod and thank her. I can tell there is care in her phrasing. Harmon is nodding too much, as if to confirm our grief and sadness. Words stack up inside me, but I don't know how to get them out. I glance about for notebooks on the side tables, but there aren't any. I know that Mr. Bell is uncommonly easy to understand, but has she not even one notebook at the ready? My disbelief mingles into curiosity. I want to ask Mabel: how do you do all this? Command your maid and cook? Converse with the scientific experts and titled gentry of your husband's new acquaintance? Manage the dinner parties to smooth along his business connections? Instead, I take the proffered seat.

Having imparted her condolences, Mabel is looking more relaxed. She says, How do you find London life?

Harmon starts talking. She smiles and nods, so I join in with my own smiling and nodding, while fixing my eyes on Harmon in a bid to slow him down. He blinks at me, then tries to steady his words, but Mabel is smiling so calmly that he's fortified and continues as best he can—if anything picking up speed.

Finally, Harmon finishes his account. I glance at Mabel. She is pausing, her gray eyes thinking, as she sorts through the gleaned fragments of Harmon's remarks for something onto which she can stitch a comment of her own. I'm flooded with relief that she doesn't understand my fiancé any better than I do.

Then she says something about the South Kensington museum. Isn't it fascinating?

It's done with deft skill. I think furiously. Was Harmon talking about a museum? Just as I prepare to add something about Italian sculpture—it's a gamble, but Mabel's remark is enough of a lead, and I don't care to be outdone in this particular matter—Mr. Bell bursts into the room.

The gratefulness at his arrival is palatable amongst all of us. He shakes our hands and embraces Mabel. He says, I've just been demonstrating the Telephone at our local post office.

Mabel says something about a boat and their crossing of the Atlantic and Harmon laughs and says, I'm sure. So I copy him and smile too. Did Mr. Bell set up Telephones on their steamer when they made their passage?

Mr. Bell sits himself on the sofa next to his wife. As he settles into the cushions I wonder if the whole sofa vibrates when he speaks, and Mabel sits within the cradling hum of his words. They look at each other with broad smiles of affection on their faces.

After a moment, he turns to us. I am very glad you called, he says. Mabel tells me I am too much a hermit.

He leans forward and shapes Hermit clearly. Then he adds for clarification: keeping myself to myself.

We laugh, although I'm unsure if he intended any joke. My thoughts circle back on earlier ones. Did Mabel persuade Mr.

Bell to visit us? I don't know which possibility I prefer: that Mabel harked back to our friendship in Boston first, or Mr. Bell did. Seated on the sofa together, glancing between one another, they look like a perfect partnership. The dark lines have gone from Mr. Bell's eyes. Does she even succeed in having him keep regular hours?

Mr. Bell continues, It is true that Mabel is far more interested in other people than I am.

He is talking as much to Mabel as us; they are enacting their fondness for each other in well-worn tales that have doubtless been told many times before. He tells his stories in his lovely clear way, sequencing each event so logically, choosing words that are easy to speech-read.

Mabel says, Whenever Alec tells me about all the people he meets, I feel I have met them too.

Although, says Mr. Bell, our first dinner party was not a success.

On this Mabel looks like she would rather not be reminded, but joins in gamely all the same. Neither of them mind when Harmon, roused finally by a look of confusion from me, skims some of their words across his fingers, although I'm sure Mabel gives them a puzzled glance. Dinner party, he spells. Not a success. He adds a few more details as they relate the disastrous party: the guests turned up early while Mr. Bell was sleeping off a headache and Mabel was pinning her hair, the Floating Islands sank in the custard, there was no gravy for the jugged hare, the water pitcher broke, and the maid forgot to open the damper on the fire, so the dining room filled with smoke.

Next, Mr. Bell regales us with the demonstration of the Telephone for Her Majesty the Queen, at Osborne House on the Isle of Wight. This time I guess most of their account from the one I read in the papers: and the awful moment when Mr. Bell made the mistake of touching Her Majesty's arm to get her attention. These are stories with which Mabel is familiar, for she chips in occasionally, and Mr. Bell seems to have set up the entry points for her; his clear painting of the scene and setting of the context allows her words to slide more easily into view. She speaks inside what he has already spoken.

I glance at Harmon. He is laughing hard, but there are bright points of bewilderment in his eyes. Does he wonder at their ease as well? Harmon and I bounce our finger-spelled words between us with a rapidity that confounds many people. How lucky, they often tell me, that you found him. Yes, I'm always careful to reply. I am lucky. Harmon is at my side if I need the doctor, he'll assist in the shops and when we have visitors. But I saw how Harmon spoke with other people. His quick, tumbling speech that matched the restlessness of his thoughts. His quips and quick-fire comments, and long discussion points. Things I could never grasp, and which he left me wondering about. I'm lucky, I'd say.

It's because Alec is so used to touching my arm to get my attention, Mabel explains, and touches her own arm to illustrate.

Mr. Bell says, So it was perfectly natural for me to touch the arm of the Queen.

We laugh again, and I have to drag myself back to Mr. Crane's task. Mr. Bell is cheerful compared to our last meeting with him. There's no mention of his woes with the foreign patents or his business troubles. He doesn't look like a man whose honesty is threatened with a lawsuit from a rival company, or whose character might be impugned. He is a man simply happy with his wife. If I ever wondered why he chose Mabel, there seems little point going over it now. The fact is laid bare to me. There is her family wealth and charm, but also the thread of a rapport between them that binds them tight. I knew it well enough, because I had it once with Frank. This is my fault, I think. I've come to Harmon with memories I can't be free of, laid down in me like paving stones which I must walk over daily.

Harmon starts his own accounts of our life in London, trying to match theirs. But he's going too fast. Anxiety flitters about him, and I catch Mr. Bell glancing at Mabel, to check if she can follow. Her frown has crinkled, but Harmon doesn't seem able to stop. He starts to talk about the Telephone and the interest he is conjuring with local businesses, but Mr. Bell becomes agitated. Now Mabel is the one glancing at him.

When Harmon begins talking about the deaf schools and the visits he has arranged, Mr. Bell finally sits up with interest. Did I tell you, Mr. Bell interrupts, about a new day school for deaf children in Scotland?

After that I lose track of the conversation. My eyes skip to Mabel. She's watching hard, but I'm sure her expression has sunk on realizing the topic to which her husband has steered everyone. When Harmon tries to bring up the Telephone again, her smiles jumps at the word, but Mr. Bell carries on talking about the school in Scotland.

I put my hand in my pocket. For a moment, I can hardly remember why I brought the glass, but if I don't do something I fear that the Bells will be rushing our call to an end, and I won't have anything to tell Mr. Crane. My fingers encircle the soft edges of the glass's wrappings, as if the velvet is melting into my palm, a warm temptation.

We brought something, I say to Harmon. Remember? I take out the velvet pouch, and hand it to him.

Ah yes, he says, looking relieved. He gives the glass to Mr. Bell and asks does he remember it? I feel like a drawstring is being pulled on my eyes as I track the glass, trying to keep tight the space between me and it. This was no longer Mr. Bell's gift to me but my gift to Frank. A promise I once made him being openly passed between these two men who would have little sympathy for him, or the promise.

Mr. Bell lifts the glass from Harmon's palm. This, he says.

My chest tightens because he might simply hand it back to Harmon, and that will be the sum of it.

Mabel shifts uneasily in her chair. She asks, What does it say? Mr. Bell is too busy holding the glass against the gas lamp. I want to watch his reaction, but I turn to Mabel.

Lemonade, I tell her. Mabel looks confused, and I glance at Mr. Bell to see if he will explain. But he is busy turning the glass this way and that. Is he thinking of what the Phonoautograph could have become? If only the scratches had run deeper? If only he had tried to trace them back? He saw far, but not far enough. Recorded sound. Edison's Phonograph could have been his.

Worried by what he has caused, Harmon stumbles about for an explanation, making mention of history and adding something about a museum. He looks at me for support, but Mr. Bell interrupts. You have heard about Mr. Edison's Phonograph?

Harmon is puzzled. Yes, he replies.

Have you seen it yet?

Harmon shakes his head. Wait here, says Mr. Bell, and Mabel says, Alec, must you? She rises slightly from the sofa, struggling with her weight, but Mr. Bell has already put the glass on a side table and is leaving the room. A bubble of sympathy floats up inside me, but I try to dissolve it from my expression. Mr. Bell has always been chaotic and led by his passions. Once that was part of his charm but it's not my place to show any recognition of it. I was just his pupil; she is his wife. I sense her desire to prove herself in this new role, as young as she is.

Mr. Bell reappears, carrying a long cylinder with what looks like an eyeglass attached to its side and wheels at both ends.

He says, I made this up in my workshop. It was so easy to do!

He puts the device on another side table and heaves the table into the center of the room. I can't take my eyes off the device. Apart from the pictures in the papers, I haven't seen a real working Phonograph before. It is far larger than Mr. Bell's instrument, and horizontal in design while the Phonoautograph was upright like a microscope.

Perhaps I have leaned too close. Mr. Bell looks at me, catch-

ing me unaware, his eyes like a tunnel out of which his memories travel, the things that he told me in Boston swimming over
to me. He was the expert on acoustics. He dreamed of putting
speech into a wire. And now he should be the one to put sound
onto a foil so that it can be recorded for eternity! He'd worked
on the Phonoautograph, staring straight at the idea of recorded
sound, but his dreaming of one thing knocked him from the
course of another.

I brace myself against his look, dropping my eyes onto his
makeshift Phonograph instead. Mr. Bell starts fiddling with the
cylinder. Mabel tries to smile. She says something about how
Alec has taken all the spare rooms over with his workshops, so
there's nowhere to put the baby.

Mr. Bell replies, The rooms are all connected with telephone
wires! The baby can ring us. He turns to Harmon. Can you sing?

Harmon nods, and Mabel tries again with a winning smile.
Alec, it only upsets you.

Mr. Bell ignores his wife. He points at the eyeglass disc and
says to Harmon, You must sing into this. He wraps a sheet of
foil around the cylinder and sets the needle upon it. He nods
for Harmon to begin and starts turning the wheel, making the
cylinder rotate and the foil spin underneath the needle. Harmon
is bent low so I can't see anything apart from his hunched back
and Mr. Bell saying: Louder! Sing louder!

Then he holds up his hand: Stop.

Harmon steps back, and Mr. Bell begins turning the wheel
the opposite way. I watch a cautious smile appear on Harmon's
face; there is evident delight at whatever the wheel is causing to
issue from the device, although he tries to check his pleasure,
unsure how much appreciation he should show. After all, Mr.
Bell isn't smiling.

Is it your song? I ask.

Harmon gives me the sort of nod that means to answer a question while putting paid to any more. It's clear that Mr. Bell is

agitated. He stops turning the wheel. He says, I think it is the most marvelous thing. Marvelous!

His chest heaves with his words. I rest my hand on the side table, hoping to feel some of his vehemence thrumming in its mahogany.

You were there with me, he says to me. We looked at it together. All that time I was looking, looking but not seeing.

His gaze is hot and dark as if he is trying to burn something off my skin, something he needs: reassurance perhaps, like I used to give him when no one else would heed his ideas. I feel myself stiffen and hope that Mabel doesn't notice. There is plenty, I wish to tell him, you didn't see.

Harmon, with his speech slowed by the gravity of his conviction, says, Mr. Bell. You saw the Telephone.

Mabel says Quite and Please, dear, don't think on it anymore. She turns toward me and says, I tell Alec that one cannot be the inventor of everything.

Mr. Bell overhears. He says something about *The Times*. If the people writing letters to *The Times* have their way, he will be the inventor of nothing.

I turn to Mabel. My only guilt at having prompted this havoc is for her. I tell her, Everyone says the Telephone is a wonder.

She smiles her appreciation, and says Yes! adding: It's a pity we can't use it, isn't it? I look at her. There is nothing in the admission to suggest she minds it, and yet Harmon says she has more shares in the Telephone than even her husband.

Meanwhile, Harmon's lips are rushing his reassurances. Mr. Bell holds still to heed them, but his look is rigid as though Harmon's words must be withstood. After a while he heaves a sigh, his eyes still on the Phonograph. I imagine what he's thinking. How can he improve it? Edison has been successful in improving his Telephone, so why shouldn't he take a stab at Mr. Edison's invention? All this work and there's still more to do. He's exhausted, but he can't let the Phonograph go either. An inventor must keep inventing. He starts talking about Edison again, his rival. I see him say rival at least twice.

As I watch him grieving and plotting in equal measure, the column of my own grief starts trembling in me again. The smoked glass I gave Frank lies on the side table, seemingly abandoned. This is how I mend the promise. Right now, I must do something, before the moment swerves away from me. If Mr. Bell is going to say anything of interest for Mr. Crane, his distress is likely to aid it. What do I have to tell Mr. Crane? So far, nothing. And I will have given Mr. Bell the smoked glass for no reason.

I take a breath. Poor Mr. Gray, I say.

Everyone looks at me apart from Mabel who looks at her husband.

Excuse me? says Mr. Bell.

I stiffen myself with horror and glance about at the alarm I have caused. I try to arrange a helpless smile on my lips. I say, Are you not talking about Mr. Gray?

Harmon asks whatever do I mean. It's just as well Mr. Bell is staring at me so severely, for I'm reddening, and it will help convince him my mistake is an honest one. I'm sorry, I try, and feel my words slur and slip. I thought you said something about—

Mr. Bell holds up his hand. You are getting mixed up, he said. Mr. Gray did not invent this. Mr. Edison invented this.

Oh, I say. I thought…

I let myself trail off. I wait, trying to keep my demeanor humbled by my mistake.

Shortly there is more. Mr. Bell is telling Harmon about Mr. Gray. Mr. Gray, he says, which is when I see another word, the one he said before. Mystery. His manner starts with firm insistence, but he says Mr. Gray so many times that the firmness is more like the kind of glossy hardness from which every effort at self-preservation slides.

Harmon nods along, stricken at what we have caused, and I

hardly dare look at Mabel. Exhilaration is singing all the way down to my fingertips, up to the roots of my hair. I've shifted the conversation, and now it seems that Mr. Bell cannot say enough about his rival. I long to tell someone, although there is no one other than Mr. Crane to whom I can relate this. I must keep my eyes steady, and try not to miss anything.

Then I see the words Patent and Office. Does he refer to the odd events that transpired at the Washington Patent Office? Clear differences, Mr. Bell could be saying. The patents have clear differences. Mystery, he says. Or Mr. Gray.

There's a bounce of the sofa cushion. Mabel is sitting right next to me. In her hand she has a brown notebook. I don't know where she's fetched it from. I must have been watching too intently to even notice her find it, and I can't help observing her lovely gold pen, which is quite in contrast to the notebook, and reminds me of the one I had as a child.

"All this Telephone talk!" she writes. "I think you like my pen. It belongs to my mother. My sisters and I were always borrowing it so much, she says she was quite grateful whenever we let her have it."

I force my eyes from the men to her page, as she continues, "I miss many things from America, do you find the same?"

I smile, thinking back to Mr. Bell's visit. "Peaches," I write, when she gives me a turn with the notebook, and the pen, which has a fine weightiness in my hand. "I miss the peaches we grew in our orchards. I do like your pen," I add.

Peaches, yes. Her mouth moves with the words as she reads mine. She starts a new line, but hesitates before writing, "Alec tells me you will be helping him demonstrate Visible Speech."

When she tries to give me the book, I find I can't do more than nod. She frowns, made uncertain by my reluctance. After a moment, she continues, "Before we married, my father told him he must choose between the Telephone and his work with the deaf, but Alec refused. Since he has become so successful with the Telephone, I thought he would not have time for his old work. Now it seems to be distracting him again."

She gives me the book, but I'm not sure what she wants from me. I'm surprised by the forcefulness in her look. Her words have filled most of the page, leaving only a narrow space at the bottom, or the next page. I choose the narrow space, playing safe, as I write, "I understand Mr. Bell has many business challenges."

Mabel takes in my sentence almost with impatience. "Yes, there is so much he needs to achieve in England, but he is losing focus. Did you follow him earlier? He is talking about abandoning everything in London to set up a school in Scotland! He talks about day schools all the time. Over breakfast! He likes the little deaf children so much. Sometimes I worry he will forget to even think of his own child!"

I laugh because she is looking at me with something akin to hope. I tell her, "Surely he won't," although I can well believe that he might.

"He has such a hot head," she writes, "and so many passions. Sometimes I don't know what to do with him."

I pause when the notebook comes back to me, feeling a desire to match her confidence in me. "I don't wish to do the demonstrations," I write. "Harmon thinks we should."

Her shoulders sink a notch. Is this what she was after? Good, she says, forgetting the notebook. Then she remembers and takes up the pen. "You can be an influence," she writes. "When you are married, of course. That's our job, isn't it? To be an influence, a good influence. I wonder if—"

A tremor disturbs us. Ladies, says Mr. Bell, standing over us.

Mabel stands up and discreetly flips the notebook shut as she does so. Whatever she has written has vanished, along with any chance of asking what she hoped from me. She rests a hand on her husband's arm, softening him before she speaks. I don't catch whatever she says to him but awe bends open inside me, as much as I'll allow. Already she is skilled at managing Mr.

Bell, although she cuts a slight figure beside him, in spite of the child, and is barely twenty.

Shall we? says Harmon. He's holding out his arm, so it must be time to go. His gaze cuts into me and his arm is a barricade as much as an offering. Indeed, as I step forward he drops the arm: he doesn't intend for me to take it. He is furious at what I've caused.

As we cross the room, I try to veer toward the smoked glass so I can slip it back into my pocket but Mr. Bell steps up to me. Mabel notices and pauses behind him.

Miss Lark, wait, he says.

He is standing close, moving his mouth carefully. I remember a game we used to play, he is saying. Do you remember? Homophenes. Two words that look alike. Ache, Egg.

I nod and say, I had a bad ache at breakfast time.

He smiles. Yes, yes. He looks about for something to write on, and spots Mabel's notebook on the side table. I almost reach out to stop him, desiring to protect our conversation inside, but he flips it open and starts writing on the first blank page that presents itself. Whatever he wishes to say to me, he doesn't want any mistakes. "Perhaps you saw a word earlier that looked like Mr. Gray. The reason for your error. Like peaches and speeches."

He holds my gaze when I look up, locking me into this version of events.

I was sure it was Mr. Gray, I reply, then add: It's a mystery.

He hesitates, uncertain if he has my agreement or not. Behind him Mabel is fixed on me. She sees my words—Mr. Gray, mystery—and her face tightens with alarm. I gaze back at her, feeling my own rising fascination. What should alarm her?

Mr. Bell crunches a small smile, his frustration evident. One more thing, he says. That smoked glass. It's not the same one I gave you. Or it's been tampered with. Tampered, he repeats, when I frown. Altered, changed. The mark does not say Lemonade anymore.

I stare at him. Tampered? He gives me the glass. You may keep it, of course.

Mabel's dog has run into the room and starts bouncing around Mr. Bell's feet. He glances downward, nudging it away with his toecap, but the dog sinks its teeth into his trouser leg, wagging its tail hard at the game. Soon Mabel has grasped the creature and is trying to tug her husband free. Exertion colors her face, but when she looks at me again her smile drops away into cautious reserve. What did I do to startle her just now?

At the door she gathers herself as the men stretch out their farewells into some kind of business talk. I almost see the moment it happens: from doubt to self-possession. Is this how Mabel lives every instant of her life? Insisting on her self-belief, when everything around her seems to waver.

It was a pleasure to see you, she tells me. The smile is no different from the one she greeted me with, I think.

Same, I tell her, but I feel so rattled by what Mr. Bell has told me about the glass that without thinking, I lift my hand and sign, Same. She glances down at my hand sliding between us, then brushes her eyes to me again, pretending she hasn't seen.

15

Lesson IV

ᎣᏤᏬ ᏫᏨ ᎣᎿ ᎾᏈ ᎾᎢᎣᏏᎾᏬ
[Don't cease to be obedient]

THE GAS lamps were dropping skirts of light along the side-walks when I arrived at the Oratory School. I knocked several times but neither Mr. Bell nor Miss Lance opened the door. The smoked glass was in my bag. I had resolved to return it to Mr. Bell, and decline his request that I demonstrate at the Institute. Then I would tell Frank what I had done. Remorse at storming away from him had caught up with me, and I was impatient to see him again.

Now there was no choice but to leave the glass for Mr. Bell. I removed it from my bag and eased open the handkerchief. It was hardly visible in the dimness, and I found it strange to remember the way the line of my voice had blazed in the sunlight at the Institute. Suddenly I was relieved I wouldn't have to give an account in person of why I was returning it. I placed the glass on the doorstep with a scribbled note then walked away feeling a jaunty exhilaration. My only regret was that I would have to return to Little St. Clouds and sit alone with the feeling. Tuesday's lesson with Frank couldn't come soon enough.

Up ahead two figures were coming down the street. The first was unmistakable. My teacher, returning to the school, but he wasn't hurrying in his lateness and neither was he alone. Miss Hubbard was walking beside him. I ducked back into the gateway, although they were so preoccupied with each other that they weren't paying much attention to what was ahead of them. They paused under each of the lights, making slow progress toward the School of Oratory. Miss Hubbard was smiling and nodding. She answered him and he replied: a conversation, one person speaking to the next, with no strain, just the joy of it.

There were at least three gas lamps until they reached me, and they looked intent on making the most of each one. I watched the toss of light-clad words and laughter between them and a point of certainty began to lengthen inside me. They had their laughter, why shouldn't I have mine?

The print shop. I'd go there directly and think of an excuse on the way. Adeline was at the theater and would be back late, and it was Joan's free afternoon. It was starting to drizzle lightly. I could say I was caught in the rain coming back from Washington Street.

I was two paces from the gate when I remembered the smoked glass. I didn't want Mr. Bell to discover it with Miss Hubbard. Would she inquire after it and have him explain the whole story? Perhaps he would tell her the lemonade joke, and they'd laugh over it. They looked to be merry after all. I didn't want her to know the heights of my hopes when she had seemingly made her own accomplishments effortlessly. Pride soaked through me until I was smarting all over, and I hurried back to the doorstep, fetched the glass and slipped out of the gateway a second time, hoping they were too engrossed in their gas-lamp tête-à-tête to notice me.

When Augusta opened the door at the print shop, her surprise lasted barely a second. Instead, she wagged a hand as if she knew why I was there. Come in, come in, she signed.

I hung up my coat and looked around. People milled everywhere, talking in signs. Augusta introduced me to the guests and waved her hand at the composing room. Frank is through there, she told me.

There were just as many people in the composing room. Some were huddled around the imposing-surface, others stood at the Washington letterpress, or lifted rolls of stereotype and pegged up newly printed sheets. Conversations skipped on people's hands between the lift of the letterpress's lever, the wave of paper, the shuffle of type.

Frank spotted me. He was grasping two corners of a sheet, which was glossy with columns of wet ink and hung limply from his hands like a banner. The title shone out from the masthead. *Boston Silent Voice*. He stared at me for a moment and then his surprise melted into a nod. He pegged up the paper and crossed the room.

Just in time, he signed. You can help at the press. Do you want tea or cake?

I thought I should tell him I couldn't stay. But then why had I come? I don't need tea, I replied. I've been in the rain, I've added.

He nodded, glancing at my hair, which I patted self-consciously, feeling the damp crackle of its frizz under my palm. He smiled. This way, come on.

I don't know how—

But he wouldn't heed me, scooping his hand through the air until I had to follow him over to the letterpress. It was being operated by Mr. Brooks and another man, Mr. Read, and the men worked side by side without stopping, as the crowd milled around them.

Mr. Brooks was rolling ink over the composite of type before placing paper onto it, while Mr. Read turned a lever to slide the paper into the machine whereupon the huge iron platen was lowered. A second later the paper flew out again, this time covered in the long narrow columns of newsprint.

The men paused at their work, nodding at me. I returned the greeting before telling Frank, I should help Augusta.

Truthfully, I didn't much want to stand at the table serving teas. The men looked at Frank. No, no, he signed and addressed himself to the men. Miss Lark is very fast at composing already, but I am wondering about this beast.

He patted the press. One hundred and ninety-two sheets an hour, he continued. That's our best. Here, your job is to take this lever. Turn it like this, the paper goes in. Easy, right? Go on!

Mr. Read moved around to the other side of the machine while Mr. Brooks inked the plate of type, lowered the paper and nodded at me. I pushed the lever in a circular motion and the paper rolled in with surprising ease. Soon it was ejected as a page of Frank's newspaper.

Perfect! Frank took up the sheet with more elation than he had shown with the other pages. He dangled it from one corner and with his free hand waved at the others in the room. They gathered around, including Augusta, wondering at the fuss. Very good, she signed, when Frank told everyone it was my first effort.

I turned one handle, I told her, embarrassed.

Very good, she repeated. Perhaps you would like some cake? she added, looking anxious that I might refuse.

Too busy, Frank replied. One hundred and ninety-one more turns to go. Ready?

Soon I was working at the press alongside the men, and we were settled into such a rhythm, making the English pages fly from the platen, that I hardly noticed the other people around us. I had not seen Frank so cheerful; each sheet was fetched from the press with the satisfaction of a round of loaves from the oven. Between the lowering and lifting of the platen, I asked after Mr. Brooks's wife and was told that between the children and dressmaking, she had been unable to take the time. My brothers keep an eye on the boats, he signed, but when a lady wants a dress made, it must be done.

The men laughed, and I told him, Mrs. Tanner's dresses are beautiful. Does your wife make all the dresses here?

I had meant for the community, but he looked at me with surprise. Behind him Mrs. Ellison had appeared and was going around the room with a tray of cordial. Not everyone's, he signed. Imagine that!

You'd be ruined, Frank signed, by all our haggling and discounts. The men laughed again. You know, he continued, this is the fastest we've worked the Washington. Thanks to you, he added, and his smile skipped over to me. I lifted my hands to show him how spoiled they were with ink, and he laughed again. We only paused when some of the children ran over and wanted to try the levers, and three smudged pages were turned out as a result.

The children's edition, declared Frank, pegging them up proudly.

I went to wash my hands, and when I came back Mrs. Ellison found me, holding out the cordial. There was one last glass, and she waited while I drank it.

Thank you, I signed, returning the glass to the tray, hoping that she would move on.

She put the tray down. Thirsty work, she replied, nudging her head at the press so that I felt suddenly aware of the slicked hair against my brow, the warmth in my armpits. Turn your head, she signed.

What?

To my surprise, Mrs. Ellison took my chin in her hands and turned my head away from her, so I was in profile. Then she let go.

Yes, I see it. He showed me a likeness of you.

I frowned. When had Frank cut my silhouette?

He was very proud of it. He had cut it from memory. That is not an easy thing to do, although we deaf see the world in pictures. I can see now he cut it perfectly.

She sprang a smile and alarm jumped in me. I suppose you are planning to marry a hearing person yourself, she signed.

I haven't thought about it.

Nonsense, she replied. Is there a girl who doesn't think about marriage? I thought about it every day from the age of thirteen. Let me tell you this. Only a marriage between deaf people can be a happy one. I was married for thirty years, all of them happy, a partnership.

She listed several deaf marriages she knew. I wanted to say, Yes, a partnership. The free flow of ideas and conversation, and a mutual dependency of the regular sort that couples had for one another, which wasn't weighted on one person translating the world for the other, so that whatever love they felt was mired in obligation, or worse, bolstered by a kind of validation. All of these things I wanted, and I'd thought about them more than I'd ever let on, but it didn't seem to me that Mrs. Ellison was offering friendly advice, or eliciting my agreement.

She was about to turn away. He had a sweetheart, she signed, pausing. At Hartford. Maybe he told you? She was in Mr. Bell's special class. Left Hartford, decided to marry a hearing man.

I tried to keep my expression light and open, but I felt weighted to the spot so that it was an effort to respond at all.

You, she continued, are Mr. Bell's pupil. You live in the hearing world but Frank belongs here.

She jabbed her pointing hands at the floor—here, right here—

so that anger quickened in me. Frank knows his own mind, I replied.

Her smile, this time, seemed to float up from some great depths within her, a benign tolerance of my defense of Frank. That is true, she signed, but men get foolish and make the same mistake twice.

Her meaning was plain. I was a mistake, waiting to be made.

Mrs. Ellison went around the room collecting the empty glasses, exiting with a neat sweep of skirts. I felt newly giddy, caught between two notions that kept colliding with each other. Frank had memorized my likeness, but my likeness, Mrs. Ellison made clear, was to a girl from his past, another pupil of Mr. Bell, who had chosen the hearing world over him.

Frank was standing on an upturned crate, wiping his arms through the air to get the room's attention. Nudges and slaps rippled through the crowd of gathered guests, as they pointed to Frank. People in the shop outside were waved into the room.

Mr. Read and Brooks will do the last page, Frank told them. Then we will have three hundred copies of *Boston Silent Voice*.

The guests gathered around the Washington, talking with excitement. The paper slid in and out of the press, then Frank floated it from the bed and held it up for the crowd to see. Palms lifted, waving with applause.

He pegged up this final sheet. Thank you all for your work, he began, and started on a little speech, although he was interrupted more or less constantly by various people from the crowd. Then he and Mr. Tanner were handing out folded copies of the paper while protesting at how many were being demanded by each person. You can't have three, Frank was signing. How will I have any left? Augusta was ushering everyone out of the room, sending them upstairs to the parlor where claret cups waited.

I dawdled behind the others. Frank was talking to Mr. Brooks at the imposing-surface. Augusta smiled at me. Come upstairs, she signed. I'll walk you home soon. It's late.

Thank you, I replied, wondering if Frank would be coming upstairs too, or if there was more work to be done. My disquiet had settled, leaving only an impatience to be with Frank.

Augusta went out of the room with a pile of plates but I paused before following her. Mr. Brooks had left through the back door so Frank was alone. I put down the cake tin I was carrying and crossed the room, but when I reached the table, I felt newly self-conscious. Was Frank wondering what I was doing here after our disagreement, or had he assumed someone else had invited me, as Augusta had?

For a moment neither of us knew what to say. I didn't invite you, he began, because I didn't think you'd come.

It's an important day for you. I'm glad to be here.

I tried to hold his answering look, but it was like anticipating the crest and break of a wave, as it swelled up to its highest point. I didn't think I could hold the feeling. There was a pile of folded papers on the table, and I patted them as if they were the crown of a child's head, and then felt foolish for doing so. Did you write something for the paper? I asked.

He shook his head.

You must, I signed. You must make your stories visible, so more people can read them.

Frank had taught me the sign for Visible and I liked it. Two V-shaped hands coming down from the eyes, like the sign for See, and turning into two fists, tapping the air solidly. Sight, becoming real.

But Frank's answering nod was slack.

Visible, he repeated. Yes, many deaf people can write and publish and spread news and ideas across the world, but others can't. How can you write pictures?

He shook his head. English connects us, but it isolates us too. It's a double bind, don't you see? The stories in my head, on my hands, they would be nothing like the words on the page. I want my stories to be visible to the mind's eye. Visual, he finished, making a sign similar to Visible, but without the final tap, his V-shaped hands sweeping forward and wide instead.

He looked down at the pile of papers, dissatisfied, and I felt the bite of my error.

Mrs. Ellison told me, I began, about your girl at Hartford. She says I am like her.

His cheeks were tinged with a blush and he glanced away.

Was she happy? I ventured. In her marriage?

He shrugged. How should I know? She wrote once. Two children now. I am happy for her, naturally.

But it didn't look as though the feeling came naturally to him.

I paused. I don't think I should be happy in her place, I signed.

He stared at me. But you have a chance, he began slowly. The hearing world, out there. All your work. There was a labored insistence to his signs.

Would you choose it?

He smiled and flung apart his hands. Oh, I wish that was easy to answer.

Two hard poles of a question, but weren't we being drawn together? What kind of luck was it that I'd seen Mr. Bell and Miss Hubbard today? I had flown to the Tanners because of the sighting. There was happiness to be found, even if Mrs. Ellison didn't think so.

I fetched my bag and carefully removed the handkerchief, placing the smoked glass on the imposing surface.

This is from the Institute, I told him. Mr. Bell's instrument. The one I was writing the essay for, do you remember? This line is my voice.

Frank looked at the smoky glass and its mark. Your voice? he repeated.

It looks like nothing, right?

He shrugged a little. It means nothing to me.

I made a mistake, I continued, thinking of the mistake on the glass, the lemonade that didn't turn out to be illumination after all, or at least not the one I was expecting.

Frank frowned. A mistake?

It's the connection that matters, I signed, making my thumbs and indexes into linked circles, and sliding them back and forth, while curling my shoulders and pressing my lips together, all of me leaning into that connection. Speech will never be fully visible like signs, I continued. I realize that now. Please take it. It's a promise, I add, not to make the same mistake again.

No more Mr. Bell, no more Visible Speech: this was the promise I was making. Where could that promise take us? Could our union be a small advertisement in the deaf press? The possibility warmed me so quickly it felt like certainty.

Frank smiled. Break your promise, he signed, and I'll do what? I'll send the glass straight back to you. Maybe in a gold frame? On a little red cushion?

I laughed as his fingers fussed in the air with perfecting the arrangement on an invisible cushion. Then he picked up the glass for real, and carefully placed it inside the wooden case with the moveable type. He closed the lid, securing it among his tools of English.

A promise, he signed, but a new worry twitched in the curve of his smile, and his eyes were too bright. I promised, he continued, I would tell you why I wanted lip-reading lessons. I've been dishonest—

But I held up my hand. It didn't matter to me anymore why he had asked for lessons. You don't need to explain, I told him.

I thought he might insist, but he hesitated, resting one hand on the counter next to us. As soon as he had touched the wood, his face jumped with surprise, and he swung his eyes to his hand. Then he slid his hand up the wall, pressing his palm against the lime-washed plaster to which the counter was affixed.

He smiled. Dancing, he told me.

In the walls? I asked.

No! In the parlor upstairs.

I placed my hand beside his. I could feel the faint jump of the thin partition wall under my palm.

Irish dancing, Frank signed. My uncle loves a jig. Augusta wanted him to learn the Boston Waltz, but he refused, and she taught me instead.

He put his hand back on the wall and began to tap out rhythms, overlaying the gentle thrumming with the more strident beat of his own hand. His music went into me, running along my arms and into my shoulder, until my bones began to feel liquid, pocked by the music like a lake by drops of rain.

My mother taught me to waltz, I told him, remembering how Mama and I had waltzed across Lorenzo Papanti's dance floor on our first trip to Boston. It felt so impossibly long ago.

He dropped his hand from the wall. Let's join the dancing, he signed, and spread his hands to indicate the room around us.

I laughed. Here? There's no space.

Of course there's space. From the print shop you can reach every corner of the world. It begins here! He made a formal bow and held out his hand.

I laughed again and took his hand. We set off around the room, swooping between the Washington letterpress and type cases, the buckets of inking rolls and frames of formes, our hands locked together, only breaking once when Frank had to save my skirt from snagging on a corner as we swept past. As we moved together, Frank twisted his face with exaggerated nerves as the next obstacle loomed in our path, so that I could hardly hold myself straight from laughter, let alone remember the steps.

But on the fourth circuit, he settled down, and we kept our eyes only on each other. The jesting was gone from Frank's face. In its place was a look of concentration. There was a fluidness I hadn't known before, as we attended to the rhythm made by our feet knocking against the hard floor, so that I couldn't tell myself apart from the dance. I supposed that these floors had a thunder of their own when the jobbing press was running, but now there was just our feet and the shapes of the waltz and all that we felt flowing between us.

Then he stopped almost as abruptly as we started. We stood next to the wall covered in samples of print, of adverts and flyers and programs, interspersed with slim columns about his community, carefully cut from the silent press.

Shall I do it? he asked.

Do what? Nervousness sprang my laughter into a bounce of breath. I'd not seen this look before, his eyes fixed on me as if the answer to his question could be glimpsed inside of me, strung up like a banner. I wanted to enter his gaze, turn myself on to myself, so I could see what I should reply. I laughed again, no less nervous.

Ask your grandmother for your hand, of course.

Yes and No both stormed my thoughts.

Is she very fearsome? he asked. Perhaps she would prefer a letter. You know, I have quite a fine hand too.

I smiled at the face he made in imitation of Adeline. I know that, I replied, but she won't approve. You had better wait for my mother. She comes to Boston in a few months.

A few months? He flung up his arms. That is forever.

You can wait? I am sure I can persuade her.

I wasn't sure at all, but I didn't think Mama would disown me as Adeline would for wasting all her efforts. And as for Mr. Bell's lessons, hadn't Mama thrown Adeline's cures in the trash once before? And this time I was no longer a child. I only needed to compose a careful letter, and have Mama come to Boston to meet Frank. I was sure she would take my decision gracefully, if only I could talk to her without Adeline around.

Frank took both my hands. His palms were like a warm slip of water. He nodded: yes.

Then the floor really did tremble. Mr. Tanner was standing

in the doorway of the composing room. He had stamped his foot. He seemed so perturbed by what he was witnessing that he took off his eyeglasses and rubbed them.

What are you doing? he signed, when he had put them back on and found we remained standing much as we had before. Mr. Bell is here. He would like to see you, he added, pointing at me.

I felt like the printing apparatus which a moment ago had been spinning around us had slammed us into some cold, cruel logistic. Frank was looking at me, his face grown narrow and pale. Mr. Bell? he asked. Why is he here?

Mr. Tanner shrugged again at me. For Miss Lark. Your grandmother is looking for you, he explained.

Guilt crunched through me. Mr. Tanner didn't know I was here without approval.

Wait, I told Frank. I won't be long.

I went through to the print shop. Mr. Bell stood by the counter, his eyes ranging around the shop. He stepped forward when he saw me in the doorway, but quickly froze, his gaze sailing over my shoulder. Then Frank, who had been behind me, stepped right next to me.

To my surprise, Frank started signing. You don't need to worry, he began. My aunt and myself will make sure that Miss Lark gets home safely tonight.

He was signing slowly and formally. Mr. Bell nodded but he carried on nodding after Frank finished, a sequence of further conclusions confirming themselves in his mind. His lips were pinched tight, his eyes dark with anger, but there was a triumphant glint in them too.

I cannot leave without Miss Lark, he replied, using his voice and hands. I was jolted to see his signs. They were cumbersome and matched to his English, but signs all the same.

Mr. Tanner turned to Frank and asked, What is this about?

Frank was staring at Mr. Bell, his mouth set tight, but with

Mr. Tanner's question, his resolve seemed to collapse. He turned to me and signed, *I think you should go with him.*

I felt the rising clamor of my protest, but he was already leaving for the composing room, vanishing behind the huge type-cases. His hands flickered between the slats as he busied himself tidying up the formes.

I turned back to Mr. Bell, seeing a tremble in his jaw that matched the one I harbored inside. But I was suffused with my own stubbornness too: I'd no intention of leaving with him.

He patted his pockets and fished out a piece of paper, scribbling a note which he passed to me.

"Your grandmother is looking for you," the note began. "You did not return home from your lesson. She came to the Oratory School asking for you. I said you had not arrived for your lesson. She thought you might be here because of your copy-work for this place. Did I know the place, she asked? She was quite aggrieved so I offered to fetch you myself. I think you had better come back with me and give an account of yourself."

For a moment I couldn't answer him. My heartbeat was loose in me. I needed to talk with Frank, but I didn't want Mr. Bell to follow me.

I turned over the note to write on the reverse, but hesitated. How could I explain that I'd come for my lesson only to find him locked in conversation with Mabel under the snug light of the streetlamp? "There wasn't a lesson," I wrote. "I came at four o'clock but no one was there." I held out the note so he had to step forward again to retrieve it. I didn't want to leave the doorway. I felt protective of it, although I didn't know if I was protecting Frank or myself, trying to be some kind of barrier between these two worlds I didn't want to meet.

I could see Mr. Tanner was unhappy. He was smiling more than usual, nodding his head every time the notes went between us, as if doing so might encourage the whole business to be speedily concluded. After all, Mr. Bell was a man of some repute, and reputation was important to the Tanners. Who knew what bad words hearing people could put out there, beyond the reach of Mr. Tanner's eyes? He didn't want trouble, and I'd brought it to his precious shop.

I am sorry, I signed to Mr. Tanner. This is my fault.

Mr. Tanner nodded. I think you had better go with Mr. Bell, he replied.

It is late, Mr. Bell said, and struck the sign for Late down his palm.

The buoyancy of my refusal began to slump inside me. I felt like I was transformed into his pupil again with one strike. Besides, Mr. Tanner was right. I couldn't go home unaccompanied at this hour, not when Adeline was already furious. The Tanners needed Mr. Bell to leave and it didn't seem that he would leave without me.

He was scribbling on the paper again. "There must have been a timetabling error," he wrote. "I'll check with Miss Lance."

I half nodded, although it didn't matter to me any longer, and I knew better than to mention seeing him with Mabel. I was desperate for Mr. Bell to vanish so I could talk to Frank privately, to undo the damage of Mr. Bell's appearance.

I turned toward the composing room, but Mr. Tanner caught my hand.

Please, he signed. I will talk to Frank.

I could see he only wanted to hurry me out with Mr. Bell, so that this difficult business could be finished. But I pulled away from him, back into the composing room. My hands felt hot, I could feel the thump of my heart as high as my throat.

Frank had moved into the gloom of the printing room. His white shirt swam in the dark at the far end of the jobbing press, his arms filled with cylinders, as he shifted rolls of stereotype.

He put them down and came to the doorway. Quick signs, his chin lifted. Still here? he asked.

I tried to smooth out my ragged breath. I couldn't bear for him to see me leave with Mr. Bell.

I must go with him, I signed, but I will come back tomorrow.

He was shaking his head. If you go with him, you won't come back.

What do you mean?

He pushed his hands into his pockets and swung around, pivoting on his soles, as if he meant to retreat again. But he paused in the doorway, half folded into the printing room's shadows, and didn't go farther. He seemed caught between a destructive bent to let fate do its worst, and a struggling hope that somehow everything could be redeemed.

I stepped forward, touching his upper arm. My fingertips pressed through the air beneath his shirt, coming up against his solid body. I wanted to slide my hand farther, encircle the narrow part of his arm beneath his shoulder, feel his cool shirt traveling under my palm. But he resisted me, shaking his head and keeping himself in profile, turned partly away. I had to move myself into his sightline.

I told him, Nothing has changed.

It will change, he replied. He shook his head before continuing. Bitterness suffused his face. I was going to tell you, he signed. I don't know why I didn't.

I didn't know what he was talking about, but I pleaded, It is a good thing. We won't have to wait for my mother now. I'll tell my grandmother everything.

My finger pushed forward from my lips and hovered in the air. Frank's eyes steadied on it as if a tiny chalice was proffered on my fingertip.

The truth—he began, his finger coming out to meet mine. But he stopped, dropped his hands, and slid them into a different thought.

Remember our dance, he began, and I felt a note of panic that this was some kind of farewell. His sign for Dance was softened, gentle, and showed our pairing. There was more intimacy in it, and suggestion, than even the dance itself. He added, Write to me tomorrow and I will know the truth.

Mr. Bell and I left the Tanners' shop and turned onto Washington Street. We kept our eyes ahead of us, walking briskly. Solitary figures pressed through the darkness around us while carriages bounced along the streets, returning people home from theaters and dinner appointments. I wanted Mr. Bell to see I didn't care, I wasn't contrite, it didn't matter to me what Adeline said. I would write Frank tomorrow and tell him nothing had changed.

I stopped under one of the gas lamps, forcing Mr. Bell to halt and turn. We were gloved in the light streaming from the lamp, same as he had been with Mabel. I expected to see anger etched into his face but instead he looked utterly rattled. He glanced up at the streetlamp, as if chastising it for its brightness. Under the pouring light he looked shrunk down in size, and there was a hesitating cower in his gaze, as though the image of myself standing beside Frank was shining in place of my solitary self, the person who he understood to be his most dedicated pupil.

I took out my notebook all the same. "No doubt my grandmother will be grateful that you have collected me," I wrote, "but my dishonesty is a matter between her and myself."

He glanced at the page and looked up. Shall I tell you how I know that man? he asked.

He was using signs, his hands carving out slow shapes in the air. I felt again their queerness, as if he was suddenly moving with new life, freed from the outline of another Mr. Bell I'd once known. Even his poor signs were so much clearer than his speech. I had to remind myself that for nearly a year he'd deemed this clear way of communicating to be unworthy, inferior, a lesser kind of understanding.

Go ahead, I replied in signs, my hands held wide and open to

show I was unafraid of whatever he might tell me. And I was unafraid: after all, I already knew everything I needed from Frank.

He looked hard at me. I can see he already told you, he signed.

I replied by way of a slight nod, annoyed at the rip he had
made so quickly in my show of confidence. I was starting to wish
that he would drop the signing and resort again to our notebooks. His closeness under the lamp, his signs; it was as though
we were collaborators, loyal confidants. Only now the mood
was splintered between us and just this unrelenting beam from
the gas lamp glued us together.

Did he tell you, he continued, about the night he broke into
my hotel room and cut a string out of my piano? Trashed the
whole room, tore down the curtains.

As Mr. Bell's hands flopped about in a messy enactment of
that event—the tearing of the curtains, the chucking of things,
the snipping of a wire—I tried to resist the trickle of misery that
would leak through the whole of me if I let it. Frank hadn't told
me anything about the hotel room or a piano string. He had been
expelled because he defended the boy, not because of vandalism.

He is a thief, a thug.

Mr. Bell spelled the accusations on his fingers, and I watched
them flickering next to his face.

He is none of those things, I replied, but already Frank's story
was coming back to me: of everything he had done to ease the
boy's journey in his last hours, only for Mr. Bell to draw the
curtains and block the moonlight, flinging him into darkness,
before returning to his hotel to play his piano like he did every
evening. And I believed it had ended there.

I went to the principal, of course, Mr. Bell continued. It
didn't take us long to find the culprit. What choice did he have
but to expel him?

I thought of Augusta's signs. Reputation is everything, we
must show the hearing world our value. Vandals and thieves
had no place in the Tanners' idea of an upstanding community.

But wasn't that what Frank was trying to protect? This idea tore through me, leaving a warm trail in its wake.

Just one string? I asked. From your piano?

Mr. Bell seemed baffled by my question. Yes, one string. But you need all the strings to play the piano. And he tore the curtains—and he started rehashing what had happened, although it was no more neatly explained than the first time.

And I wanted to smile at Frank's deed: the music ruined because one string was gone. No musician would accept a piece of music with one note constantly sounding silence. And yet, Mr. Bell thought deaf people should accept a world where human conversation fell away from us endlessly.

Frank loved that boy, I signed. He was like a brother.

Mr. Bell frowned. Which boy?

I made a show of my surprise. He had forgotten already? Roy Stamper, I spelled, and I gave his sign name too—Yellow— if only to test Mr. Bell's familiarity with the very people he claimed to serve. Someone drew the curtains, I continued. It was dark, he could see nothing, hearing nothing when he died.

Mr. Bell gazed at me, his own genuine surprise widening his face. That was the reason? I was trying to help him! The curtains, he added, nodding, a new satisfaction growing. So that explains why he tore down my curtains!

He paused, seeming to consider this idea. I am sorry about the boy, he replied. Truly. I have often thought about him, and children like him. It is a terrible situation. But there is no excuse for that kind of behavior. I have lost my own brothers, real brothers—

He stopped, leaving me with the memory of his brothers. I held on to my resolve, refusing to give up Frank to his certain judgment, his bigger and better grief, although it was uncharitable of me. Anger was starting to tremble in me again. New thoughts were stirring in Mr. Bell's eyes, like the swirl of dark treacle.

That explains the curtains, but the piano string? he mused. That was petty. It was because he couldn't hear the music.

Mr. Bell had spelled Petty. He didn't know the sign for it and no other word was apt. Frank was petty. That was his summation. Frank envied Mr. Bell's world, the world of sound.

Sound. But I was thinking of the partition wall in the composing room, jumping under my palm. *Remember our dance.* My fear started to grow: it was a beat that had prompted our dancing, the rhythms of music felt through our palms. It had flung us toward a horizon of possibility, swinging us into a proposal, or almost-proposal. But now the music had retreated. What else would retreat with it? Would tomorrow bring a cooler, more remorseful perspective?

Mr. Bell wasn't finished with his conclusions. He was looking hard at me, a glint forming from the crystals of his calculations. Suddenly, I felt afraid. He was unnerved, strung-out, his mind was swiveling in new directions.

I have often suspected spies in the mechanic shop, he signed. There is evidence. I have found it.

He carried on looking at me, but it took a moment for his accusation to catch. You think it is Frank?

He has motive, don't you think? You told me yourself.

His expression was musing, even in its hardness, as if he wanted to pull me in step with his reasoning, leading me to his deductions.

Or someone close to him, he pressed on. Your grandmother says you go there regularly, and you did not tell her that the family are deaf. And you have kept information about my invention. I remember now. I wrote something on the back of a piece of copy-work I gave you. And you didn't give it back.

I stared at him. My thoughts were strung up in a net of confusion. What notes did he mean? Then I remembered the copywork, and how once he had left a note about his invention inside. Smiling disbelief sank through me.

I did your copy-work faithfully, I signed, and it is not my fault if you leave your scribbles lying around. My signs felt bouncy, and my face was too rigid. I was remembering all the questions Frank had asked me in the Back Bay. Spy-work. Was this what he was struggling to tell me?

Not you, then, Mr. Bell replied. But perhaps you know something about Frank. Clearly you have become—

He drew his index fingers together. Close, he signed.

But as his fingers approached each other, I remembered Frank and I drawing together for our dance, far closer than Mr. Bell's indexes would allow.

It wasn't Frank, I answered. Nor was it me. How dare you accuse us.

Mr. Bell gathered himself, but I didn't like the smile that winked on his face with this new composure. I hadn't been able to defend Frank, despite my best efforts, and Mr. Bell was finding a foothold in the crags of my protestations. There was a delicate tact on his face: it was the worst of his expressions all evening.

I can see you are serious about your intentions, he signed. That is disappointing. But there are other reasons I should discuss this with your grandmother. Do you know that Frank comes from a long line of deaf-mutes?

Of course, I replied. You saw me with his family tonight.

I tried to scoff but my arms were hot with fury. I wanted to add that Mr. Tanner, one of this long line, had been so concerned about displeasing Mr. Bell and yet Mr. Bell had lumped him into this derogatory category without a thought.

Young lovers think only of themselves, Mr. Bell continued, looking almost kindly. Was he thinking of Mabel? His signs were getting large and generous, although not much tidier. But you wish for your children to suffer the same?

My cheeks warmed. That is our business, I replied.

Mr. Bell was watching me. I feel responsible for you, he signed. How did you even meet him?

I was too rinsed with shame and anger to even give him an answer, but I felt the chiseled edge of one final point. I was teaching him lip-reading, I replied. My paper, remember? You couldn't do anything with it.

Mr. Bell stepped forward. To my horror he took up my hands and squeezed them as if I'd somehow returned to that world of sound where I had spent so much time on the edges, and all I needed to do was show him my upset and he would carry me back to it. My hands were lost inside his, but I could feel his voice humming through them as he said: Miss Lark, I must advise against such a marriage.

I said again, It is not your business, but my voice felt messier than even his signs looked.

It is my duty, he replied, to give an honest account of that man. Honest, he repeated, for clarity. An honest account.

This, finally, was how he was my teacher. For all that he confided in me, he wouldn't hold the same trust in return. It was his duty, an overriding clause. I pulled my hands away. No, I said, or thought I said.

He twisted his lips and looked at me. He said, All right. Well, we should go, don't you think? He indicated the stretch of darkness beyond the cone of light. I hesitated, having already followed him once this evening when I did not wish to. He started walking away, slipped into the dark as if it was a cloak he was simply putting on. When I protested a second time, my words were swimming alone under the gas lamp, and did not bring him back. After a moment, I set off as well, keeping several paces behind him, a distance we maintained all the way back to Little St. Clouds.

16

Connect

HELP, HARMON is saying.

Candlelight brightens his hands as he angles his fork into a cut of cold meat. His lips are busy. Help, he repeats. Help.

I stare at him across the dining table. His Help is the gulp of an *l* and the pinch of the *p*, but I can't figure out what he's referring to. He doesn't look distressed, neither does Mr. Holmwood who sits opposite him, and supplements his nephew's monologue with a series of nods. There are no newspapers on the table to prompt his concern, only an opened envelope with the letter sitting on top. I strain my eyes to get sight of the handwriting and then wish I hadn't. It looks like Mr. Bell's writing.

Help.

Is it help that Harmon is asking for, or help we must offer? Harmon's gesticulating becomes faster, and there is nothing I recognize on his lips. Mr. Holmwood drops his fork. It bounces onto the table and the floor, sprinkling snowy flakes of fish as it descends. I get up and wipe the mess, fetching a clean fork from the dresser. Placing it in Mr. Holmwood's hand, I help him fold his fingers around the handle until he's found a firm grasp.

Thank you, he signs, touching the fingers of his other hand slowly to his chin. The simplest of signs and unlike Harmon, he has no qualms about using it. It's a vestige from the days when Mrs. Ketter was with us, and Mama was dying.

I squeeze his shoulder, and Harmon watches as I take my seat again. His fury at me for ruining our call on the Bells has muted into a cool wariness. He hardly bothers making conversation on his fingers or in our notebooks. Since that afternoon, it's been a litany of notes—short and functional—and long spells of silence.

When I'm seated, he writes a few lines in his notebook, sliding it across the table with the open letter. "We are discussing some correspondence I have just received from Mr. Bell today," the notebook informs me.

I take up the letter and Mr. Bell's words sharpen between my hands, bringing his haste into view. I try not to let my thoughts spring ahead with my hopes, but I can't help myself. What might it contain that I can tell Mr. Crane? At first glance, he appears to be responding to a request Harmon has made about the Telephone franchise. If Harmon wants to pursue the prospect further, Mr. Bell has replied, he would do better to take it up directly with the Bell Telephone Company. He himself is sick of the Telephone and its business and doesn't want to waste a penny nor a minute further on it. "The position of an inventor is a hard and thankless one," he has written. "Let others bear the anxiety and expense of it!"

No wonder Harmon is aggrieved. All those letters he has

written to the schools for deaf children, helping Mr. Bell secure contacts. He's told his potential customers about his close
connection to the inventor of the Telephone, only for Mr. Bell
to declare no especial loyalty and pass him over to his business
partners. Now he finds himself in a swamp of humiliation, and
the only route out is a thin insistence on what can be saved. We
must help him.

But the next passage makes me forget Harmon's concerns altogether. "I shall go," Mr. Bell has continued, "to Greenock in
Scotland where I shall set up a school for deaf-mutes. My assistance there is much needed."

I hasten through the details; in essence a small school for a
select group of children, but in its successful establishment he
envisions a better education for the thirty thousand deaf-mutes
of Europe. After all, he writes, isn't this his life's work?

I can almost see the small classroom in which Mr. Bell stands
at the blackboard, scratching out Visible Speech. His face enlivened with focus while the children gaze upon the symbols,
on this new teacher, this mystery of speech which, they have
been told, needn't be a mystery at all. Their hands are in their
laps, and they know they must keep them still. Not a question
or a thought must stir on them. Their mouths are moving instead, and they are watching for someone to tell them they are
doing well. Isn't that what Mr. Bell is seeking too? He'll go as
far as Scotland to feel useful and find comfort of some kind.
The thirty thousand deaf-mutes of Europe come to his aid, as
he goes to theirs.

"Lastly," the letter finishes, "I no longer require a demonstration from Miss Lark for the talk at the Anthropological Society.
If you desire to see me before I depart to Scotland, I will be at
the Royal Society but it will be my last appointment concerning the Telephone."

I don't dare glance at Harmon. Did my behavior when we
called result in this cancellation? Mr. Bell doesn't trust me once

again. Besides, there is new alarm rising from the waves of my
relief. How can I continue with Mr. Crane's task if Mr. Bell
desires to put more distance between us? I feel a reluctant appreciation of Harmon's anger toward me: my actions on our last
meeting led to this. A wrong move, a false step. Fury burns in
my breast, but this was my doing.

I say, We don't need to help Mr. Bell.

My voice sails between the salt and pepper mills, glancing
off the water jug and coffeepot, the plates and the cutlery, until
it lands with a shiny startle in Harmon's eyes. Even Mr. Holmwood turns his head.

Mr. Bell will calm down, I continue. He always does.

There must be a wobble in my voice because Harmon seems
to think I'm the one who needs calming. He fetches Mr. Bell's
letter and stops to rest his palm on my shoulder as I'd done on
Mr. Holmwood's. His hand is as light as a new lover's kiss. I'm
surprised to feel coils of remorse loosening through me, an answering song to the gentle pressure of his hand. Didn't I bring
this on myself? A split created between us the moment I wrote
to Mr. Crane, and dared glance back at the past. But a quick spill
of anger sours this worry. Mrs. Ketter, and Harmon's dismissal
of her, has been unspoken between us for all these months. Our
notes go to and fro, papering over that particular silence, so now
its shadow goes as long as Mama's death.

I reach for the notebook. "We could offer to give a speech at
the Royal Society," I begin. "A demonstration of Visible Speech
down the Telephone. Wouldn't that be an attraction? It will
make amends for our last visit and show our gratitude for the
favor he has shown us."

With difficulty I pass the page to Harmon. I want to rip the
words away as he nods slowly. He is thinking: what a crowd-
pleaser, what a proposal. But he doesn't trust me, and I can't say
if Mr. Bell will either. I feel an agony of waiting. I want him to
tell me that I don't have to do such a thing, to take the stage and

perform Visible Speech again. But I also want him to write yes, so that Mr. Crane's task may continue, our connection with Mr. Bell restored for long enough for me to complete it. And I want us to be content, but I don't know if a Yes or No will bring it.

His decision comes in one neat line. "I will write to Mr. Bell and see what he thinks."

My last report to Mr. Crane was brief. I didn't tell him what had happened when we called on the Bells, because my thoughts were too clouded by what Mr. Bell had revealed about the smoked glass. Was Mr. Crane aware that Frank had tried to deceive him with damaged goods? Did he know the glass had been altered when he bribed me with it? But it was Frank's mark that I wished to understand. I spent hours examining the craggy contours of this new line. It was carefully drawn, with an exact cluster of peaks in the middle. I tipped it back and forth in front of the window but couldn't make anything from it. Instead, I turned my thoughts to Mabel's face and how she had stared over her husband's shoulder as I said Mystery and Mr. Gray. Her alarm was evident. What had she seen? I wrote Mr. Crane asking for more Visible Speech symbols.

His reply came back to me with a list on a separate sheet. "I enclose the translations you have requested," he wrote, "although I must point out that I have already given you the technical words that relate to the Telephone and cannot see the relevance of a single one of these words bar the last one, which I concede was not included on my original list. Have you had sight of this word?"

The letter showed his nervousness: he fears I've lost the plot.

I take out the list and run my finger down the English words which are set next to their Visible Speech symbols. There's Mystery through to Misery, Obituary, and Big Story. I had tried them in a mirror before asking for translations, since they all bear a similar shape to Mr. Gray.

Finally, the last word: Mercury.

Mabel in the Bells' parlor, her face frowning at mine. The pale horror as she drew back. We had already spoken of Mr. Gray that evening, and what should be so perturbing about the word Mystery? She had seen something else on my lips.

I fetch an envelope from my mother's travel case, which is disguised as one of her letters. After my last meeting with Mr. Crane in the Horticultural Gardens, I made a copy of the note he showed me about Mr. Bell's patent. I wrote down as much as I could remember, grateful for my copyist's memory that could hold on to several sentences. "For instance," my messy script reads, "let mercury or some other liquid form part of the circuit."

In my pocket mirror I start examining the Visible Speech symbols. Mercury, I say, watching the shape press and push out my lips. Mr. Gray, Mercury, Mr. Gray.

There's a flash in the picture-glass hanging in the hallway. I'd forgotten to shut the door. Is someone hiding at the door frame? Hasn't Harmon left for the Department Store? Then I see his gloves on the hallway side table beneath the picture: he has come to fetch them and discovered me saying Mr. Gray's name and Mercury perfectly and repeatedly, apparently to myself.

As if my outburst at the Bells' wasn't bad enough.

I shove Mr. Crane's letters under some papers and hold my breath. Perhaps Harmon won't have recognized my voice since I was reeling off Visible Speech. But who else could have spoken? I wait, frozen in my seat. The reflection hesitates and then he slides into view, taking his gloves and softly whacking his other hand with them, as if he's beating out a rhythm for his thoughts. His brow is lowered and his lips are folded by the jut of his chin. The word Mr. Gray dances in the air between us, for a second time this month.

You are not off to work? I say, but I can't look at his face for long. His thoughts are gathering in his expression. He reaches for some paper, and stoops down to the desk so that his sentences make the same awkward angles as his arms and elbows, which knock into me as he writes.

"I have written to Mr. Bell to suggest that we present Visible Speech at the Royal Society."

Good, I say, trying to sound pleased.

But Harmon only looks irritated. He shoves the paper to me a second time. "I thought you said you didn't know anything about the Telephone," he has written, "and yet you seem to have developed some sort of idea about Mr. Elisha Gray. His name is not even in the papers."

I glance at him, still bent double at my elbow and refusing to look at me; his body spelling out his complaint. See, how he must ask me like this. See, how much our modes of talking are a hindrance.

"Shall I find a chair?" I write back. "You do not look comfortable."

His lips: No.

I look uneasily at his question again. "You told me about him in Philadelphia," I write, after a moment. "And I think in Boston there was an article about his work. That's all I know."

He looks up from the page and says something. He's so close, I can smell the coffee on his breath, but I miss most of his words, apart from the last one. Mr. Gray, he says.

His lips: Mercury.

I look down at the desk. I never told Harmon how I met Mr. Gray in Philadelphia. How could I when I was with Frank, and not where I was supposed to be?

His eyes are flinty, and I sit very still. Sit pretty and sit tight, Adeline used to say. It's your best hope. I didn't care if I was sitting pretty but I was sitting awful tight.

"I have been giving our notebooks some thought," he writes. "Perhaps it would not hurt for me to learn a few signs to use with my finger-spelling."

This stumps me completely. The sign language? A bubble of

hope rises in me in spite of myself. "As it happens," he continues, "Mr. Bell told me that there is a person on his legal team who knows signs but is hearing himself. His name is Crane. Perhaps he can help."

He hands me the note and finally stands up, a victor rearing above the spent match. His gaze presses into the back of my neck, bearing down his satisfaction, but I'm only grateful that he can't see my face, as questions ram my thoughts. Mr. Bell's legal team? Is that how Mr. Crane got sight of the English patent? Because he had express permission to view it? I try to bring to mind everything Mr. Crane has told me as I also try to recall every letter I might have left around for Harmon to see. My travel case. Harmon must have been rooting through it.

"I have never heard of Mr. Crane," I write back, making my lines tidy and neat beneath the scribble of his accusation, "but it would give me the greatest pleasure if you would learn the language of signs. You will find that after some practice its natural expressiveness makes communication a joy."

Harmon picks up the paper to read it, then drops it back on the desk. His lips are in profile but I catch some muttered words. Of course, he says, followed by my mother's name. Then a word that looks like Walnuts. I try to check myself, knowing that my thoughts are in a hopeless spin. Mr. Crane is in them, and this new fact of his relation to Mr. Bell. Has he told Mr. Bell everything? And there are no Walnuts on the table, no nuts of any kind in fact, and the table itself is fashioned of mahogany. Warned Us, I think. Not Walnuts. He is saying my mother Warned us. What did Mama warn us of? I try to stretch my mind back to her warnings, but all I can remember are her assurances and certainty.

He leaves the room and returns a moment later with a bundle of envelopes. Dread thickens through me. He is going to reveal Mr. Crane's letters and show me the extent of my lie. But his lips bear a familiar request. Copy. I am to copy them.

I take the bundle, seeing that the handwriting is indeed his own. Of course, I say, unsure whether to be relieved.

I must go, he says, meaning the Department Store, but his eyes don't move away from mine. He wants something more from me, but I don't know what it is. Once he might have reached for me and all our missed words would have ceased to matter, the touch of our fingers draining them away like a straw empties a glass of water. Have a good day, I tell him, and he nods, but it's a functional farewell, a mere agreement to part.

After he leaves, I look at the envelopes. There are six of them. At least we are back to usual business, although I don't relish the prospect of more of his correspondence. I skim through the contents: potential customers, one school, nothing for Mr. Bell. But the last envelope is thunder in my eyes, bringing my heart right into my throat. This is Mrs. Ketter's hand.

I tear it open, and her words spring up at me. The note is short on news but large in spirit. She never wrote long letters, although literacy was a blessing of her education at the Old Kent Road School. She will be in London next month, she writes, and is desiring to meet me. Could I come to St. Saviour's? My happiness makes a small leap before I remember Harmon: I'll have to go carefully, I think, hiding the letter away in my mother's travel case.

After my mother's death, Mrs. Ketter kept me grounded with housework. The house needed our attention. The months of sickness had let dust thicken on the sills and ledges. We set about with whitewash, soda and carbolic acid. We washed the lace curtains, folded away the carpets and scattered pails of wet sawdust over the floorboards. Mrs. Ketter went about on her knees with a pair of bellows, blowing cayenne pepper into the corners of every room. Some of it came back in our faces, making us sneeze and sputter and laugh. We stood in the yard, shaking and snapping the damp wool blankets until they were ready to hang. We talked from the start of every day to the end, and each task was a navigation of our tools and our signing, what to hold and how to do it, so you could keep up the conversation on one hand, if not two.

You'll be mistress one day, Mrs. Ketter signed, signaling the house as we stood in the yard with the laundry. Mr. Holmwood's health was not faring any better, and we were accustomed to weekly visits from his doctor. I looked at the house, its walls still dirty white from the cut-and-cover works, not even touched pink by the afternoon sun. I didn't tell her what Mama had also said. "Your stepfather," she had written, "promises that you'll have Mrs. Ketter too."

You'll stay here with me? I replied.

She laughed. Leave this thundering house? No, never.

She meant the trains in the nearby tunnels. We felt the shuddering of brickwork and floorboards, as regular as clockwork, traveling up through our soles and into our shins. Mrs. Ketter and I became quite used to it, being in the house all day. I was even comforted by the vibrations. The trains had not stopped for Mama's death and the house rumbled as it had always done. The house talked to us, from deep in the earth. Mrs. Ketter liked to muse on the travelers under our feet, and where they were going. She liked destinations. Her community was small and dispersed, so she was used to traveling long distances to see old friends. She taught me the sign for almost every British town and city. I learned Stoke and Bristol and Brighton in amongst Soap and Careful and Connect.

But Harmon's eyes burned darkly whenever he found us signing. He couldn't fail to notice how my smiles and replies came back faster for Mrs. Ketter's signs than they did for his fingers and notebooks.

Mrs. Ketter even began to stop signing whenever he entered the room, and switched to finger-spelling instead. Sometimes she just curtailed our talk altogether, so that our terminated conversation swung like soft, heavy curtains into his face. He seemed to like that no better.

One day we were folding up the bed linen. It was one of those tasks for which no adaptation could be made to accommodate our conversation. We worked in stillness, feeling the sharp tugs traveling through the fabric as if it was threaded with nerves. Harmon came into the room and started finger-spelling at us. There was a heap of linen still to fold, but we stopped as he was clearly angry. There was some trouble with the household budgets. We were down on money, and the logs showed huge spendings at the market. What was Mrs. Ketter buying there?

I have logged everything, she insisted. It is all there.

Then you have been overcharged, he spelled. They have taken advantage of you and this has happened. He waved the account book to illustrate his point.

Mrs. Ketter protested on her fingers to Harmon, then in letters to Mr. Holmwood, who said Harmon ought to go directly to the market himself and take it up with the stall holders. But by that time Harmon had begun on other faults in her work, and by the following week she was gone.

For a while Harmon insisted on coming to the markets with me, although he hardly had the time. I watched as he talked and laughed with the stall holders. I waited for a better price to be presented to us. I didn't know what had been achieved, as the price appeared the same, but Harmon was happy with it. I knew they hadn't overcharged us. Mama had taught me how to spot the clear, cherry-red color of a fresh cut of beef. She told me what price to expect. It was in her letters. But he refused to heed me when I tried to show him. He said it wasn't the point, but however I studied his lips, I couldn't discern exactly what his point was. And then he found Miss Brindle to accompany me to the market, who seemed pleasant enough but never attempted any other conversation than the brisk ones she had with the stall holders.

I didn't hear from Mrs. Ketter for months. Was she angry, or did Harmon keep her letters from me? As the date of her visit to London grows closer, I become agitated. How would Harmon know if I went? Mr. Holmwood asks no questions of me, and where I go in the daytimes.

Harmon brings me more letters to copy. The franchise is taking its first shaky steps. Invoices, letters, bills and receipts stack up on my desk. He has relented for the time being on writing to the schools for the deaf, so I don't make any more blank copies for the drawer.

Letters arrive from Mr. Crane as well, but I put those in the fire. Anger singes me with each one. I should have suspected him when he told me he'd been able to get sight of the English patent. He was in the employ of Mr. Bell, not the Union. It is no mean feat to get hold of such a document.

Then news comes of Mabel's baby. Harmon is almost as joyful as if the child was his own. I add a note of congratulations to his letter, but I can't stop thinking of Mabel without her mother at her side, and only her housekeeper and husband to help her decipher the doctor's words as the child is delivered. There is the child to be deciphered too, as it gets older and goes from crying to speaking. Harmon and I have never discussed children, and I try to push my own fears away with an image of Mabel, rosy-cheeked and smiling, the infant in her arms. But as I sign off Harmon's letter, I can't help remembering the empty, sunlit top floor of Oratory School, the to-and-fro of our notebook, and suddenly I long for Mabel's confidence again.

"The child has no deformity," Harmon writes in the short note he leaves at breakfast. "Mr. Bell rang a bell at her ears to check."

No sooner have I spotted St. Saviour's than I see Mrs. Ketter standing on the steps. She is chatting to another woman, her fingers flickering slowly with alphabet letters so I suppose her companion is new to the community and its language. I dawdle on the pavement, my mind casting back to my first weeks in London when she signed with me in this way too. Her close-lipped smile is broad and lopsided just like I remember it, and her silver curls bounce defiantly out from her bonnet. She waves both arms when she sees me. I break into a run, taking the steps two at a time and causing her companion to startle at my rapid, ungainly ascent. I fling my arms around Mrs. Ketter's neck and feel her surprised laughter against my chest, her breath in my hair, the pats that come gently down on my back. I don't want to let her go. In fact, I don't for several minutes because my face is wet and her shawl smells like it always did, of primroses and salty-warm butter, and I can't tell if the cotton is mopping up my tears or bringing them forth at the same time. So I cry into her shawl until she pries me from her neck and grasps my shoulders.

Careful! she signs, directing my gaze at a huge bag of oranges at her feet. I bought them just now from a costermonger girl. Turned out she was deaf! Came right up to me when she saw my signs. I bought all her oranges and told her to go to the Old Kent School and give the principal my name. This is Miss Burrows. New to the church. This is my dear friend, Miss Lark.

Miss Burrows has clearly found herself the recipient of Mrs. Ketter's generosity in more ways than she was expecting, judging by the jut of her elbow over her bag which is stuffed with oranges. Her shoulder sags to one side under its weight as she watches Mrs. Ketter's signs carefully. There is a hint of nervousness in her smile as she greets me and explains in fingerspelling that she was just leaving. Come again, I tell her, a broad mood of welcome suffusing through me which belies the fact I've only set foot in St. Saviour's myself once. But the reunion with Mrs. Ketter has flooded me with a giddy abundance. You must come again, I insist.

Miss Burrows goes down the steps, the oranges making a sliver of color against her coat. Mrs. Ketter prods my arm. Here, help me with these.

Gathering up the oranges, I follow Mrs. Ketter into St. Saviour's. This time the place is filled with people. A service must recently have been concluded, and the congregation stand chatting in the pews, hands in motion everywhere, or in circles that break and reform as people move between the groups. Mrs. Ketter takes my arm, leading me toward the door on the far side. It takes us ten minutes to reach the door, since she must pause every three steps to chat to someone and introduce me.

The room we eventually arrive in looks like the club room. It has been recently used, judging by the scattering of pens and crumbs on the tables. Mrs. Ketter goes to the centermost table, places the oranges in a bowl and starts unpacking a picnic of ham, salted silver side and bonbon crackers around it.

The service was good today, she signs. You hungry? I've been looking forward to seeing you for months. She pats the table. Sit down, sit down. Eat, eat. Tell me how you are.

Since there is already a damp patch in her shawl, I hardly dare answer truthfully, so I tell her what I can about my copy-work, and Mr. Holmwood and how he fares. I don't mention Harmon and Mrs. Ketter doesn't ask about him. Instead, she tells me about her four children and eight grandchildren, her new job as a housekeeper at a deaf school, and her husband, Arnold, who is plagued by an episode of gout. She details each of his balms and liniments and pills as we work our way through the picnic, grabbing mouthfuls between our signing, picking things up, putting them down, asking for clarifications, her anecdotes littered with my Rights and Whats?

Then she moves on to her newest grandchild who has been born hearing. Eleven deaf children in the family, she signs, and one is hearing. One! How is it possible?

Did you have the bell ringing? I ask, remembering Mabel, and Harmon's letter about the Bells' new child.

Oh yes, she signs. Everyone came, we had the biggest feast, the biggest party. You know what happened? The girl turned her head as soon as we rang the bell and nobody knew what to say to each other. A hearing child! The mother rang the bell three more times, from behind the door, the screen, even from outside of the room. Each time the baby turned, laughed. Laughing and laughing at the bell. Well, we all had to laugh too.

We pause our conversation to peel the oranges. The juice spreads across my tongue like sunshine. I watch Mrs. Ketter slipping the segments into her mouth, and wonder if she's thinking about the costermonger girl, or her granddaughter, or both.

She wipes her hands on the flannels and with clean fingers spells a name. I have to get her to repeat it twice. Crane. Elbert Crane. Refusal rams through me. This is surely some kind of terrible mistake. Crane? I repeat.

Right, she replies. He wrote to me because you are not answering his letters.

She gives me a reproving look. I suppose my mouth is still open. I shut it. How do you know Mr. Crane? I ask but already I'm dreading her answer. The deaf community's connections are tight and deep, and I don't want to discover Mrs. Ketter and Mr. Crane knotted in the middle of them.

I'm a friend to his parents. But I didn't meet Elbert until recently.

Recently? I repeat. When?

Last year. His grandparents took him away when he was a boy, so he grew up in London. He left for America when he was sixteen, and no one heard about him again. Then he decided to come back, and I met him finally.

For a moment I can't think what to respond. This new fact of his history has re-configured him. Did they take him away because he was hearing? I ask.

She nods, and replies, They worried he wouldn't learn English properly. His brother was deaf like his parents, so he was the only hearing one.

Three of them deaf? I ask.

Right, his grandparents thought they could leave the other child, that was fair and the best way. Elbert rarely saw his parents, she adds, and her index pops up in the air in a scattered fashion, for the occasional and infrequent visits. His signing is good now, isn't it? He spends a lot of time at St. Saviour's, but he must have remembered it from before.

His parents must have been happy, I sign, when he came back from America.

She shakes her head. They didn't see him. It was too late. They had both died.

Died, died, she signs neatly, placing the two deaths side by side, and I feel my chest tighten. His brother? I ask. What about him?

He died when he was a child.

I watch Mrs. Ketter's extended fingers sinking through the air for a third time, and I have to look away, picking at the piths of my orange instead. I try to hold on to the other truth, that Mr. Crane lied to me about his relation to Mr. Bell's legal team, lest it become eclipsed by this new picture of his loneliness. You gave him my address, I sign, after a moment's pause, but my signs are an abrupt burst nonetheless.

Mrs. Ketter doesn't flinch, even at the fierceness of my pointing index. Elbert said he knew you from Boston, she replies. I was worried about you. I couldn't visit, so I sent him instead.

The truth sharpens like needles at my temples. Elbert Crane sought out Mrs. Ketter to get to me, and she fell for it. I close my eyes until the thought subsides. Then I sign, He made no mention of you, shaking out my Nothing so hard that I feel the twinge in my right wrist from last night's copying work.

Impatience jumps across Mrs. Ketter's face. Yes, I understand that now. I don't know what his game is, she replies. But I told him to sort things out. Now you won't answer his letters so I had to come myself. She studies me for a moment. You're worried. What's the problem?

I take a breath. He bribed me, I tell her. He wanted me to spy on Mr. Bell. Because of Frank, I add. He said Frank owed him money and he wanted it back.

Mrs. Ketter nods, her eyes steadying on me so I feel their disquieting brightness. Her concern is not for what she's missed, but for me. She used to look at me this way whenever Harmon said something that I couldn't follow, or a visitor came to the house and Harmon forgot to explain who the person was, or why they were there. A new idea starts rising through me, creeping upwards like floodwater. Mr. Crane knew what happened in Philadelphia, and held me responsible.

Elbert's a funny one, Mrs. Ketter signs. Shifty. I can't get a sense of him. Too much mixing with hearing people, that's my view. He can't sort out a matter in a direct way. Crane isn't even his name, or his grandparents' name. That's what happens, she finishes, when you live in two worlds but don't belong in either. You end up with no idea of who you are.

He blames me, I blurt out. For what happened to Frank.

You blame yourself, she replies. That's why you would never come to this place.

I feel so rigid with misery that the only escape seems to be a reassertion of the truth. Frank was in the penitentiary for one year, I tell her. He lost everything. His new job, his good name.

I wait but the bald statement of this fact appears to change nothing about it.

Mrs. Ketter reaches across the table and touches my hand briefly. Elbert made a mistake too, she signs. He shunned his parents, and then it was too late. I didn't know he was going to lie like this. I'm disappointed, she decides. This is not the deaf way.

She starts rearranging the remaining oranges, stacking them into a bright pyramid, a centerpiece in the club room, so that everyone can help themselves. As I watch, Mr. Crane shuffles into my thoughts with an insistence that is a demand coming from himself; look at me, he's saying, we are the same. What we have been denied. Our closest connections deemed harmful to us.

I tap the table for Mrs. Ketter's attention. My mother went looking for you. I remember her making the trip. Afterwards she told me she had found a housekeeper. But I think she went to find you. She didn't want anyone. She wanted a deaf person.

Mrs. Ketter smiles. Your mother came to this church for a recommendation. Yes, she was asking around. Then she visited me and said you needed some company. I was living in London back then, so I agreed.

Her shrug is quick and light, matching the simplicity of her explanation, but as her shoulders drop down again, the next part of the story seeps into the room like a slow exhale.

About Harmon, I begin, I don't know what to do.

I wait, my breath trapped and tight, as she considers me. I want the certain, decisive strikes of her signs, but she makes them carefully. I agree with your mother's decision for you. But you can always come to Bristol. It's a long journey though.

As I watch her hand arcing westwards, I feel a deepening ache to open Mama's last letter. Perhaps there's no harm. After all, what is the point of advice, if it cannot be called upon when needed? But Mr. Crane must be dealt with first.

Tell Mr. Crane, I sign, to meet me at the Royal Society. Next Thursday evening.

There will be lots of rooms and people, I think. We can talk without drawing attention. But the thought of the speech I've volunteered myself for makes me feel cold all over, so I push it away.

Good! she signs. I'll let him know. Her hand snatches at the air before her brow and swoops down and outwards: a transferring of knowledge from herself to Mr. Crane. It's one of the first British signs she taught me—to let someone know—deftly showing how you slide the contents of one mind to another. And as she packs up our late luncheon, I notice the club room anew. The empty tables with their detritus are suggestive of the previous hour's busy back-and-forth of conversation, seeded with facts, information, advice. The building is alive with knowledge, although no doubt Mr. Bell would prefer that it didn't exist. This is how deaf people meet, make friendships, marry.

His face, shining in the lamplight on Washington Street, comes back to me. His advice about Frank, that he felt was so necessary, he was willing to put it on his own hands. The crispness of my understanding, finally; but it was an understanding I didn't want. The refusal I'd felt at having to heed him rushes through me again, as fresh as the first time, even though I know it's no use, and will change nothing about what happened.

Mrs. Ketter is watching me. Do you remember those newspapers you gave me from America? she asks. The silent press?

I nod, and she stands up, waving her hand, so I follow her across the club room to a second door, which opens onto a small library. Mrs. Ketter crosses to the shelves and starts running her eyes along the books, until she arrives at a section labeled in her own writing: North America.

On the shelf are all the papers that Frank gave me from his collection, which I'd never been able to return. She slides out a few and hands them to me. On the top, by chance, is the paper bearing the masthead *Boston Silent Voice.*

Frank's paper. Wonder brushes through me as I hold the lightness of the pages. For a moment I feel I might look up and find the Washington letterpress and the huge type-cases around me again. Frank declaring there was room enough to dance in the print shop because from the shop you could reach deaf people in every corner of the world. A dance of connections yielding more connections, building into a movement and flow of links and fastenings, people coming together. I'd taken part in this dance myself by giving Mrs. Ketter the papers. And now Frank was touching me again with inked words and all the memories between them. I feel a soft drift of reverence that I can't tell apart from hope, for how the past might be ordered and co tained, and kept safe in a sacred place. I reach out and run my fingers down the spines and each one is like a tendon, taut and ready to dance.

17

Lesson V
ʃɯ ɯʃ əˈɹʏɯʊɥ ɪ ʊʊˈʊʀ
[All the world's a stage]

WHEN WE arrived back at Little St. Clouds, Mr. Bell requested an audience with Adeline alone. I tried to remain in the parlor, but Adeline was already furious at the worry I'd caused, so I went to my bedroom and made my account to my mother instead. The next morning, when Adeline summoned me, it was clear she had the full picture of Frank from Mr. Bell. He was a thief and thug, and his family history was a grave concern, in terms of our union. Mr. Bell was planning some research on the subject, he'd told her, and talked at length about the families on Martha's Vineyard, where an unusually large number of deaf people had been born over the generations. Deaf marriages seemed to him, were more likely to produce deaf progeny, and Adeline needed to be made aware.

But the fact that I'd lied to her was the sharpest thorn. Adeline wouldn't heed any of my reasoning, and wrote Mama to catch the next available steamer to Boston. My classes with Mr. Bell, naturally, would finish. Instead, I would help round the clock with the boardinghouse until my mother arrived. At first, I felt nothing but the brick wall of my own response. Adeline insisted on my selfishness, and I had so little with which to protect myself that I resorted to the simplest method of all: refusing to comprehend. A veil slipped between myself and the world. But I was desperate to get a letter to Frank. Adeline was intercepting my mail, but I pleaded with Joan and plotted as I carried up plates of stew from the kitchen. I was certain that every hour that passed was deepening my betrayal in his mind. I kept revisiting the moment I'd left the shop, Frank watching me go through the rows of type from the composing room. My back, the last of me, as I vanished into Mr. Bell's version of events.

On the third day, I managed to persuade a boarder to drop a letter at the Tanners' print shop for me. Nothing had changed, I told him, and Mr. Bell's revelations did not matter to me. The letter that came back was from Augusta. Adeline's fury that I'd gotten something past her was checked only by her satisfaction at this reply, and she let me have it.

Inside I found a folded sheet of newspaper along with Augusta's letter. I put the sheet aside and read the letter first. Augusta wrote simply that Frank had gone to seek a new job elsewhere and wouldn't be returning to Boston. "I think this is the best course for all parties," she wrote, "although we will always remember our acquaintance with you fondly, and beg that you might do the same."

One thought filled my head like a balloon. I should never have left the print shop with Mr. Bell. That had been my biggest mistake of all.

I picked up the news sheet, which was a copy of the *Boston Silent Voice*. Adeline must have passed it over, since as soon as I opened it, another letter fell out on to the table. I picked it up with trepidation. Augusta's hand was scribbled across the front: "Frank wished you to have this."

"Dear Miss Lark," his letter began.

I do not doubt that Mr. Bell has given you his fullest account of my character. I will not waste your time in attempting to refute it. My only regret is that I have not been honest with you. There is the final matter I wish to have resolved between us. My deepest shame is that I did not inform you of it sooner, and let other preoccupations get in the way of my better judgment.

I will tell you now what I should have told you before. My employer believed that I could become more closely acquainted with Mr. Bell but he didn't know our history and I confess I had motives of my own, and thought you might be able to do some of the work for me. However I didn't anticipate how my own feelings would grow toward you. I am deeply ashamed of my dishonesty right up to the last occasion of our meeting.

I have taken the opportunity of visiting friends in Hartford and plan to look for work elsewhere. My relatives are in support of my departure. My employer occasionally visited me at the shop, so you may imagine the extent of my uncle's displeasure.

The letter ended with his deepest regrets. I rose, thinking that I must get a reply to him immediately. But when I checked his note again, there was no address or forwarding details. And the Tanners, it was clear, wished for the matter to be resolved. I knew they wouldn't want to send on a letter of mine. Augusta was one of the firmest people I knew, even if she was the most gracious. Surely Frank would write again in the fullness of time?

But only one more letter arrived during those last few months in Boston, as I waited for Mama to come from England. It wasn't from Frank, or anyone connected to the Tanners. Our old boarder, Mr. Dupont, wished to tell me about a demonstration Mr. Bell had given at the Institute. "I was wrong in my estimations," he wrote, "of your teacher. He tells me that he is being borne up on a rising tide and I cannot dispute it."

At first, I thought he meant the demonstration of Visible Speech at the Institute, which must have happened without me. Instead, the enclosed article from the *Boston Transcript* described a public demonstration of speech being transmitted along a telegraph wire. "I was in the audience," Mr. Dupont had written. "The transmission was often garbled but occasionally a sentence came out with startling distinctness."

I stared at the article for a long time. The human voice, Mr. Bell had found, was strong enough to generate a current after all. A crackle, a smudged consonant, a feather that wouldn't lift its barbs. He had chiseled through hope and despair, until at last he heard distinct words. It was, Mr. Dupont wrote, a triumph.

My mother finally arrived in the month of June. If her attire had been the colors of autumn when she stood at the Oral School gates, now she wore plainer shades. Her hair was slicked back from her face and she looked older and braver than I remembered. Her arms came forward, as huge as before, as she gripped me and said, I swear you have grown. I said, Mama, I stopped growing long ago, I am sure. She laughed and held me firmly by the shoulders and said, And your voice is lovely.

I looked away, not wanting her to see that I didn't care, even if I had believed her.

Mama indicated the young man behind her in the hallway. He was tall and slender-framed, and the sleekness in his auburn hair, and his suit, gave him a polished, delicate appearance. The blue of his eyes was intense, so he appeared constantly to be making a fascinated examination. She took out a notebook, which looked newly purchased, and wrote, "This is Harmon Bardsley. He is your stepfather's nephew. Mr. Holmwood is in poor health so Harmon has accompanied me instead. He is eager to see America."

I looked up from her words and Harmon bobbed his head. When he started speaking, his lip-shapes were so tiny that I caught nothing of what he said.

Mama's smile was strained as she glanced at me. He is pleased to meet you, she summarized, and Harmon, realizing I'd not understood, started off talking again. I thought it best not to let him get too far a second time, and interrupted. Likewise, it is a pleasure, I said carefully. He smiled, flushed with relief. Yes, yes, a pleasure, he replied and then appeared stuck for a further response.

Mama's index was raised. We stay for one night, she said. Tomorrow we are going on an adventure.

We are not going to England? I asked, wishing we could turn away from Harmon who was watching me closely.

Not immediately, she said. She was so close I was sure I could feel that old hum, an industriousness of love vibrating in her fibers. She drew out a slim wad of papers from her bag and showed them to me. Tickets for the Centennial International Exposition in Philadelphia.

Mama, I laughed. Haven't you read Adeline's letters? I am being punished.

Harmon's eyebrows lifted with a query: Mama had clearly neglected to tell him this, in spite of their long journey together across the Atlantic. Or perhaps he hadn't understood me.

Mama tossed her head and blew out her lips. She took up the notebook, and out of Harmon's sight, she wrote, "I think that we have had enough of Adeline, don't you?"

★ ★ ★

We left in so much haste that I didn't have time to think about my leave-taking. And as the train departed from the city's south-side railroad, something in me began to lift. The trees passing the carriage window slatted the afternoon sun, and the pastures stretched on endlessly. Boston, and everything that had happened, began to take on the hazy, indistinct contours of an old dream.

Harmon sat on the other side of the carriage, studying a post-card Mama had given him of the British Manual Alphabet. He hardly looked out of the window once, as he practiced spelling names, the months of the year, and objects in the carriage around us. By the time the train pulled into Philadelphia, he had managed a slow account of himself. He was the manager of a shop floor in a department store on Oxford Street, London. He expected to be promoted this year, although his real dream was to set up a business selling the latest gaslights. Because he kept muddling the vowels on his fingers, and his *b* with *g*—spelling baslobhts—soon we were all laughing when I asked him what this latest new-fangled invention did.

And when we arrived at Fairmount Park, it was impossible to think of anything apart from the scene before us. The park was blanketed with people flowing from one huge exhibition hall to the next. The brochure was as hefty as a book. Harmon consulted it constantly. He suggested one place then another, pinning the book to his chest with his arms so that he could spell the names on both freed hands: Main Exhibition Hall, Machinery Hall, Horticultural Gardens, Aviary.

The first few days passed happily. I walked with my mother, our arms looped. Harmon was quick and active with his interest in everything. We pored over the guide and plotted our way around the park. In Machinery Hall we looked at sewing machines and projection lanterns. We stood beneath the Corliss Steam Engine, the room trembling from the thundering spin of its enormous flywheel as it powered all the other machines in the hall, spinning cotton, combing wool, sawing wood and pumping water.

In the electrical section we examined tuning forks, hand tele-scopes and eyeglasses. Harmon made a close inspection of each item, asking the exhibitors questions, nodding in his quick way as he listened, as if he was ticking off the points of understand-ing with each duck of his chin.

"It is the entrepreneur in him," my mother wrote. "He is al-ways thinking about what he might sell."

Once my mother caught me watching him and dug an elbow into my ribs. "I can't help staring," I protested in our notebook. "He is impossible to lip-read."

On the fourth day, we stopped by the typewriters in Ma-chinery Hall. Chairs had been arrayed by the stall: a lecture was due to be given. Harmon took out a notebook and patted the cover. Would I care for him to write down the lecture? I ac-cepted. Harmon pressed the notebook to his knee and the lec-ture flashed rapidly under his pen nib.

I couldn't help my glances from sliding up Harmon's hand and arm until I reached his soft, clever face. He had an out-of-place air, and the excessive attention that he alternately paid himself and others seemed like an attempt to dispel it, to fix himself more firmly in the world. He pressed his lips together in con-centration as he wrote. His whole manner was tightly wound, but I liked his strange mixture of earnestness and unease.

I had glanced at him several times when the stream of the lecture was interrupted on the page: "Are you looking at me," he'd written, "or reading the lecture?"

Then he continued writing. I had no means to respond but snatched another glance at him. He was smiling down at the page. A second later, he wrote, "You did it again." I smiled but kept my eyes on his writing.

Back at our lodging house, he copied out the lecture more tidily, and slipped it under my door with a note: "What did you think? Should you like a typewriter one day?"

Mama was at the washstand, smoothing a brush down her hair. Her travel case was in disarray along the counter. She was making a critical inspection of herself, her eyes narrowed as she stroked and patted the curls at her temples. Sitting behind her, I wanted to funnel myself into that gaze, to know what she was seeing about herself. Questions rushed up inside me. Was she happy with Mr. Holmwood? What regrets loitered in her mind? And I wanted her to slide her eyes to the right, to where my reflection hovered at her shoulder, and see me differently somehow. She hadn't once mentioned the Tanners. She clearly thought that it was best to leave everything about Boston behind us.

When she caught me watching, she turned and smiled at Harmon's letter in my lap, giving it a wink. I frowned at her, so she raised her hands and drew back in mock-defensive apology. I went over to the desk and found a clean sheet of paper, which was provided by the lodging house and specially headed with "Centennial International Exposition." But as I started to write, my hand felt heavy, and I couldn't find the energy to reply. I put Harmon's letter away, thinking to answer it later.

When we were leaving the lodging house on the fifth day, the landlady stopped us at the door. She showed a note to Mama who looked puzzled. Acquaintance, the landlady said, nodding at me.

We had to hurry to catch the stagecoach and it wasn't until we were at Fairmount Park that I managed to ask Mama about the note. She handed it to me. "My dear Ellen," the unfamiliar handwriting read. "I spotted you and a lady I would guess to be your mother outside your lodging house yesterday, as we were passing on the stagecoach. A small party from Boston is here at the Exposition. We meet daily at the Cataract fountain and would be delighted to see you. After all, it has been a while. Your true friend, Augusta Tanner."

Augusta. I felt all of Fairmount Park rushing down on me, the sunlight and people swimming around me so fast I had to stop on the path. Was Frank here too? Surely not, since she hadn't mentioned him.

My mother paused. What is it? she asked.

Nothing, I told her, shaking my head. A friend from Boston. We don't have time to meet them.

Mama hesitated, and I could see whatever it was that Adeline had told her crosshatching her thoughts. Are you sure? she asked.

I patted her hand. Yes, I said. Look, we must catch up. Harmon stood by one of the pavilions, examining the guide while his lips moved as if he was softly chanting to it.

But as we entered the Food Hall, I couldn't concentrate on anything, let alone eat any of the foods. I couldn't stop thinking about Augusta's note. And Frank? Was he here and did he know I was too?

We found our way to Horticultural Hall and wandered among the sunken gardens, ornamental shrubs and ironworks. The heat was unbearable. The sun pummeled in through the glass roof. The fairgoers gathered around the fountain in the middle of the Hall, fanning themselves. Harmon went off to find the balconies but my mother said that I looked pale so we went for refreshments instead.

We joined the long queue at the Tufts Arctic Soda, the fountain's ornamental marble towering toward while soda spurted from the seventy-six syrup di base. We paid ten cents for strawberry sodas a seats nearby. I focused on drawing the soda's the straw and ignoring Mama, who was stu

When I finished, Mama was writing so book, which she slid across the table.

grandmother wrote me of recent events," she'd written. "I am of a mind to put it all behind us."

I looked at her. Old worry lines had surfaced under her rouge. She shook her head, saying, I shouldn't have—

Shouldn't have what, Mama? I asked.

I reached for her long-fingered hand. Was she going to tell me she regretted leaving me at the Oral School? With Adeline?

I wanted to tell her that if I'd never gone to Mr. Bell, I'd never have met Frank and I didn't regret any of it, apart from how it had ended. As the months had passed, I'd hoped for a letter from Frank, but it seemed that either they never made it past Adeline, or he was steadfast in his regret and had accepted that there was nothing to be done. It was best to move on. Wasn't the only course for me to do the same? I'd persuaded myself of it right up to the moment the note came from Augusta.

Mama was gazing at her hand beneath mine. Something was troubling her. She glanced at the soda fountain distractedly. I'll get another one, I said, thinking to give her a moment.

When I came back, she had written a short paragraph in her own notebook. "There is a problem," she'd written. "Do you remember Mr. Ackers? He is here at the Exposition. He would like to see your progress under his sponsorship. He very much desired to meet you but you seem somewhat out of sorts today. I have told Harmon to say that you are unwell. But we will need to meet him at some point. I feel deeply obligated. You see, I didn't give him a full account of what has happened with your lessons. I do not want Mr. Ackers raising questions about you because we have avoided him or behaved strangely. And Mr. Holmwood paid for our tickets, of course. I can't think what reason to give him."

I read the paragraph several times. I remembered Mr. Ackers, the Governor, and my grandmother standing in the cramped parlor in Pawtucket. Robinson Crusoe's spiky aloes that I'd so tly lied about.

I didn't see how I could refuse Mama. And I hated to see her at a loss. She seemed so careworn, in spite of her fine clothes, and I didn't want her to feel obligated to Mr. Holmwood on my account.

"Of course," I wrote back. "We should meet with Mr. Ackers."

Mama smiled. Good, she said, and squeezed my hand so my bunched fingertips ached.

That evening at the lodging house, Harmon joined us just as we were finishing dinner. The landlady brought out more plates of hotchpotch and green corn pudding, while Mama and I finished off what had been described on the menu as Centennial Cakes. They were plain sponges crammed with raisins.

As many raisins as exhibits, Mama remarked.

After we had eaten, Harmon started talking with what was coming to be a familiar look of excitement. But as Mama listened, I watched her face cloud with worry. She said, You better ask Ellen.

So Harmon took up his pen, and wrote raggedly for a while before turning the page to me. "Today I have seen Mr. Bell's Visible Speech stand," he had written. "Mr. Ackers took me to see it. The system is extraordinary. I had a long discussion with your old teacher Miss Lance. She is looking after the stall this week and she is to make a presentation of one of Mr. Bell's pupils tomorrow, but the young lady in question has taken sick."

Reading his words, I felt a growing unease.

"Mr. Ackers has offered your help. He said he had been sponsoring your tuition with Mr. Bell. Miss Lance says she has some Visible Speech material you can read."

I felt myself go hollow inside. I looked at Mama. Oh dear, she said, seeing my face. I don't know how we can refuse.

Harmon said something about refusing and why would we? I looked down at the last pieces of the Centennial Cake. Mama had promised me to Mr. Ackers and now Mr. Ackers had promised me to Miss Lance. And I was thinking of the smoked glass

I'd given Frank and the promise I'd made to him about Visible Speech.

But I couldn't leave my mother in her conundrum of refusing Mr. Ackers when Harmon had already made the arrangement. I took up the pen. "Is Mr. Bell here?" I wrote.

"He is not here until next week."

"Were there many people at the exhibit today?"

Harmon looked at my question and smiled, mistaking it for nerves.

"No," he wrote. "It is a small stand in the corner of the Massachusetts Exhibit as part of a display on education. A handful of people passed by while we were there but only two or three stopped. There may be more tomorrow, of course."

"It is fine," I told Mama, sliding the notebook to her. "Miss Lance may present me, but Mr. Ackers will have to be satisfied with tomorrow as I do not want to do more Visible Speech presentations when we get to England."

My mother nodded, relieved. She relayed the contents of my note to Harmon who dipped his chin and said Excellent. All that mattered was that Mama's anxiety was abated. As for my promise to Frank, I would be in England soon and besides, what truly remained of our promises to each other after he'd left Boston?

The following day was even hotter. The sun beat through the windows and the queues for the soda fountains were so long they wound through the other exhibits. Any draft was a relief, although the air came dry and stale. It took a long time for us to work our way through the crowds.

When we eventually arrived at the Massachusetts Exhibit, we found that some forty seats had been arranged in front of the stand. I gazed across the chairs, which were still empty. Harmon had written that Miss Lance wanted someone to illustrate Visible Speech at the exhibit, but that wasn't the same as a formal demonstration, was it? Surely all these chairs weren't for me? I looked around for some kind of escape, hot with panic. But my arm was locked too firmly into Mama's as she moved me forward.

Miss Lance was waiting for us with Mr. Ackers. The dimensions of his beard were unchanged from when I had last seen him, although it was graying like the rest of his hair. I didn't understand a word he said as he funneled his large, forward-flowing energy into handshakes and shoulder pats. Miss Lance's smile was more pinched but it was nervousness, for I saw her lips press out the word Pleasure. It was a pleasure to see me again.

I tried to smile back. I'd long felt bad for my snarkiness in our lessons. Hadn't she been right to warn me? She tried to protect me from the glancing nature of Mr. Bell's attentions. Briefly, he had made me more than a pupil. It might have been better to have stayed as one. Could I have forgiven him more easily when his sense of teacherly duty had finally prevailed, and he saw fit to go to Adeline?

Miss Lance pointed at the middle seat of the front row. Judge, she said. That was where the judge would sit. She began taking brisk steps backward toward a small board announcing my demonstration, where she did a little twirl and landed her folded hands in her skirts as they settled about her. You will stand here, she said. What do you think? She looked girlish, pleased.

I looked at Mama. Judge? I asked.

Yes, she said, but I saw her matching surprise. Harmon had neglected to mention Exposition judges and an audience of forty people. Visible Speech was surely being put forward for an Exposition prize, if there was a judge. My gaze roamed the seats wildly. How could I perform Visible Speech in front of so many? It was all far more than I'd agreed to. An idea skated through my head: I'd tell them I didn't have any worthy material prepared. Then Miss Lance was tapping my arm, and she had a sheet of paper in her hands.

Do you remember, she said, your essay for Mr. Bell? For *The Pioneer.*

I saw that shape clearly, although it'd been months since I'd thought of *The Pioneer.* Dread stiffened my arms as I took the sheet she offered me. Along the top was the title: "The Art of Speech-reading with a Survey of Homophenous Words in the English Language." Underneath there was a whole page of Visible Speech symbols.

I looked at Miss Lance. She was smiling nervously. You wanted it to be published, she said. So I thought—

She fanned her hands at the forty seats. No, forty-one, forty-two: an assistant was adding more.

I tried to smile. Was this some kind of peace offering? Knowing nothing of Frank, she had guessed at my disappointment about Mr. Bell and the forgotten essay. She couldn't know that I had pushed him far from my thoughts and the essay along with him. That I wanted nothing more to do with Visible Speech, but owed this last demonstration to my mother.

I was struggling to concentrate on Miss Lance's lips as she explained how she had translated the whole essay, although I needn't read it all. Then I spotted something on the board behind her shoulder. I pushed past her, leaving her mid-sentence. Next to Mr. Bell's Visible Speech charts was a carefully scissored page of my class notebook. He'd written a title across the top: "A Sampler from a Pupil's Notebook." The page included several of Mr. Bell's exercises in Visible Speech, a few lines of his instructions, and one of my own questions: "Should my voice follow your pencil?"

Coils of dizziness loosened inside my head, and I felt the swelter of my dress. All this time my work had been on open display. I had already been exhibited alongside Visible Speech, and would continue to be exhibited until the Exposition ended sometime in October. All without my permission or consent. Why had Mr. Bell chosen my notebook? I supposed my fine handwriting was one reason. A bloom of nausea began to spread through me. I was about to lie openly about the wonders of Visible Speech and be applauded for it.

I turned to survey the seats. Were so many people really expected? Couldn't I still leave? I looked about for Mama. I'd tell her I was feeling faint, but she was with Mr. Ackers and talking to a gentleman who wore a sash over his suit. The judge. I couldn't think what to do. Other people were starting to arrive as well, so I had no choice but to wait with Miss Lance while the audience took their seats.

By the time of my speech, which I now saw was advertised on a hastily drawn poster, not one chair was left empty. Harmon managed to seat himself next to the judge while Mama was in the row behind him. On the other side of the judge was a young man wearing a matching sash and holding a clipboard, so I supposed he was a judge's assistant. He sat very straight as if he was taking his duty with utmost seriousness. Our eyes locked for a moment, and he offered a smile, but I looked away.

Everyone was here: I couldn't let Mama down.

Miss Lance began her introductions. She waved her hand at the board covered in Visible Speech symbols as she explained them to the crowd. I waited, stinging all over. When Miss Lance finished with the board, she turned and started talking about me. I watched for some sort of cue, wishing she would hurry up so the whole thing could be over with. She kept turning her head back and forth between myself and the crowd, so I had no idea what she was saying. Eventually she wagged her hand at me, stepping back at the same time and narrowly missing the board behind her.

The audience looked to me, and I looked down at Mr. Bell's symbols in Miss Lance's hand. They started to swim and for a moment I couldn't see anything at all. There was a lump quivering in my throat and the upward slide of words seemed impossible. I could feel the crowd waiting. I glanced up but there was only a dark mass of shoulders and hats fluted with pale faces, although Mr. Ackers's face shone out at me and Mama was smiling hard, her head nodding as if she could persuade me out of my silence. Harmon's lips were pinched as if he couldn't guess what the problem was. Anger flashed in me: we'd trusted Harmon to give a full explanation of the event, but he had been neglectful with the details.

I cleared my throat. There was a shift of alarm in the crowd. I paused and cleared it a second time. That unsettled the crowd even more, but it made me feel better. I preferred to see their nerves over my own. It was a trick to look a little afraid myself, so that the crowd feared for me and for themselves. Would this young woman pull off this feat? They didn't want to bear witness to my disappointment.

I opened my mouth and gathered the first symbol in my throat, tightening it there like a bolt. I pictured its shape, and the shape of the symbol after it until, lining up several in a row, I had a ribbon of words ready to speak.

Then I was speaking and there was a little collapse of relief from the audience. I didn't know what I said, but the symbols were going in my eyes, and something was coming out of my mouth because of them. And whatever it was, my voice was softening Harmon's face into a smile, while Mama was practically grinning. The judge was nodding slowly, and other smiles and nods were rippling through the audience as my voice danced across the Hall and into the thoughts of these people who I'd never met. After a while, the sentences were tipping lightly out of my mouth, and I began to feel as if I was on fire with some kind of music I'd never known before. It wasn't entirely disagreeable. The ease, finally, of speech.

The sight of the applause, when it came, made me blink. People rising to their feet and knocking together their hands. Mr. Ackers rushed forward, saying, Sensational! Miss Lance said,

Perfect, perfect. Harmon looked at me for several long seconds
with his blue gaze swimming over me.

Then Mama was squeezing my hand and trying to lead me
away from the crowd. It is enough, she was saying. Let's go back
to the lodging house. But we couldn't escape Miss Lance and
the judge, and his assistant who hovered around us as well. I
answered their questions with my notebooks so I didn't under-
mine my performance, which no one questioned.

ʃx ɑɟɔ ʊʃ ʊʃɜ.
[I caught the thief]

To celebrate my success, Harmon took us to Lauber's German restaurant to eat Hamburg Steak. Miss Lance joined us,
and there was a great deal of conversation: about the steaks,
which were eaten in a split bun rather like a sandwich, and other
things I couldn't follow. The table was long, and I could only see
three faces clearly. Besides, I felt exhausted and empty, scooped
out by the thought of how neatly I'd done it. Forty people had
stormed the room with applause just as they'd once stood for
Theresa Dudley and Miss Flagg. Men and women were gathering in the cause of Oralism, even in the seemingly quiet corner of the Massachusetts exhibit. And I'd only helped them. But
the more I wished for the dinner to finish, the more the others
found something new to talk about.

After a while it seemed that everyone was saying Bell, and
Miss Lance said Two Days. Harmon was sitting to my left and
noticed me frowning. The tabletop was cluttered but he pushed
aside his plate and flattened his notebook. "Miss Lance," he
wrote, "had a telegram from Mr. Bell. He is coming in two days'
time. There has been a last-minute change of plan."

Why? I said, abruptly, because Miss Lance dropped her steak
bun.

He smiled at me. "I expect Miss Hubbard persuaded him to

leave the School. Miss Lance tells me she was terribly anxious for him to attend the Exposition." Then he added with a smile, "And he probably heard how well his rivals are doing."

I remembered the letter Mr. Bell had written to me, which was the first time I'd heard of any of his rivals. Mr. Gray? I asked, as Miss Lance placed her steak back inside its bun and carefully took a bite.

Harmon frowned for a moment. I saw him say, Elisha Gray? Then he wrote it down. "Yes, Mr. Elisha Gray is here with the Western Union. He has been demonstrating his harmonic Multiple Telegraph."

"But Mr. Bell is no longer his rival. He has invented a talking telegraph instead. The electrical transmission of speech. It was in the *Boston Transcript*."

Harmon seemed surprised by my response. "That is quite possibly true," he wrote, "although I remember reading somewhere that Mr. Gray also hopes to invent a device called a Telephone which would do exactly that."

I mulled this over as the dinner continued. My exhaustion began to spiral into a kind of conviction, as if all my thoughts could only spin in one direction. Mr. Bell was coming to the Exposition and most likely, he'd thank me for the demonstration. It would be a pin in his assurance that he'd done the right thing regarding myself and Frank. And I wasn't going to give him the pleasure. Instead, I was going to find Frank.

As it happened, the next day Mama felt unwell and decided to stay at the lodging house. She insisted that I go into the Exposition with Harmon. We wandered through Main Exhibition Hall, as Harmon struck up long conversations with the exhibitors. We spent nearly fifteen minutes at Mr. Muspratt's stand with its beautiful bottles of soda ash lined up inside a glass cabinet. "Soap, glass, paper," Harmon wrote. "Mr. Muspratt says British production of soda is greater than any other country."

I nodded and attended to his long discussions on the potential of the British markets as best I could, while trying to think how I could make my excuses to slip away and join the Tanners at the Cataract fountain. Finally, we reached Memorial Hall and its arts exhibits. There was a sculpture of a Dying Lioness outside the main entrance. I looked at it, thinking of Mama. It was so unlike her to be unwell. Hadn't she become paler since arriving in Philadelphia? Perhaps the crowds were too much. Harmon studied the statue for a long while, as if it could be understood by careful inspection.

I fetched my notebook. "It is too hot," I wrote. "I would like to return to check on my mother. I will take the stage car back to the lodging house."

Immediately he replied, I will come with you. I shook my head. No, no, you go on. I wrote, "You said you wanted to see everything. I shall be fine."

He hesitated. I felt the opportunity slipping from me. "It is not far," I wrote. "You can watch me until I am at the stage-car stop."

He nodded. All right, he said, so I went down to the sidewalk and waited under the awning, relieved that there wasn't a stage car already waiting. I waved back to him and eventually he turned and went into Memorial Hall. I put the Dying Lioness behind me, her cubs scrambling over her back and the arrow that had pierced her and wound my way through the crowds: not to Mama, but to Frank.

The Cataract was a huge hydraulic display shooting jets of water in arcs that almost reached the ceiling of Main Exhibition Hall. I squinted through the spray. Framed by overlapping arcs was Mr. Tanner. He stood with a group of people, all of them talking in the sign language. I saw Mrs. Tanner next and several people I recognized but whose names I couldn't remember and others who I didn't know at all. I didn't see Mrs. Ellison or the Brookses.

Frank wasn't with them. I searched the group one more time, feeling disappointment drop through me like a stone. I didn't know what to do. I realized how hasty my plan had been and how strange it would appear for me to announce myself unaccompanied, but I couldn't bring myself to leave the Cataract.

The group set off, led by Mr. Tanner. They carried on signing, breaking into pairs as they rounded the fountain. It was only as they moved clear of the water that I saw him. He was in deep discussion about something with a stout young woman who I recalled as Miss Lizzie. His hair was shorter than I remembered, and he seemed thinner, as if a new maturity had thrown him into sharper relief. I felt as if my heart was coursing blood through me with a force that matched the water jets.

Miss Lizzie saw me first and turned to Frank with my name on her fingers. Frank glanced over and his gaze tingled across me.

A ripple of commotion ran through the group as my name passed from one pair of hands to the next, shoulders being tapped in turn. Eventually the news had reached the Tanners at the front, and a moment later they were standing before me. I was almost relieved that Frank hung back, for it gave me time to deal with the hugs, welcomes and questions, as Augusta asked the inevitable: Why are you here alone?

My hands dealt with the question with more agility than I'd expected of either my signs or my poor planning. My mother was feeling unwell, I told them, but I had to see them before we left. I felt that I'd been terribly rude in not answering her note.

It wasn't exactly a lie.

I am sorry to hear that, Augusta replied. We guessed that you were with your mother, she added, looking at me carefully as she signed Mother, so that I wondered if it was only the prospect of Adeline that had stopped her writing again. After all, I'd told her so many favorable things about my mother.

You must join us, she continued. Only we can't decide where to go next. Everyone has a different opinion.

My preference is Agricultural Hall, signed Mr. Tanner.

I don't want to look at swine and tobacco, Augusta returned.

Let's continue through the Main Exhibition Building, he suggested. Have you seen everything here?

Yes, I told him. But there's always more.

They laughed. Augusta patted my arm and confided, I feel the same. I'm exhausted. I'm ready to go home but he says we must see everything.

Mr. Tanner turned to the group and everyone stopped. He seemed to have the only copy of the guidebook and Augusta held it for him so his hands were free. He had to sign slightly aloft, holding his hands high, as the group was large.

We have a decision! he told them and began translating the guide into signs. There were exhibits from thirty countries and we would see all the countries in order. He made a map in the air, placing each nation in its rightful tower in the building; France in the North East central tower, the Teutonic nations in the Southwest, and so on, with the United States in the middle.

Everyone was happy with the plan. The group set off again. Frank was still at the back with Miss Lizzie but the Tanners were busy telling me about the Elevated Railway trip they had taken the day before. Then the couple behind them, the Fishers, wanted to introduce themselves. There were interruptions of Take care and Look there. And all the time I was trying to catch sight of Frank. He was no longer at the back of the group, but in the middle, and then, as we arrived at a vast array of silks hanging from wooden racks, he was next to me. His gaze skimmed the fabrics while I made a show of being interested in a peacock-blue one that I distractedly thought Mama might like. The fact of his sudden departure from Boston, and the reasons for it, felt draped over us with the same heavy delicacy as the silks.

My new job, he began, is at the Pennsylvania School. I'm teaching printing to the pupils. The Tanners have come to visit me. Everyone has come! My good reputation outlasted my bad one, he added.

I'm happy for you, I told him. It was what you always wanted.

Yes, he nodded. To teach.

The Brookses are not here? I asked.

He hesitated. No, they didn't come. Did you hear about Mr. Douglass? The police tried to refuse his ticket at the opening ceremony. They couldn't believe he was invited to join the President on the stage.

Did Mr. Douglass speak? I asked. I hadn't seen many black people at the Exposition although Mama and I had passed a group gathered around a statue, The Freed Slave, in Memorial Hall. A man with an easel was making a sketch of the scene.

No, he wasn't invited. He had to sit at the back, just sit there. You didn't arrive in time for the ceremony? My aunt interpreted the President's speech for the group, and she had quite a crowd of hearing people around her by the end. Everyone thought she was one of the exhibits!

We lingered at the table for a while, pretending to be interested in the silks. What about you? he asked.

I leave tomorrow, I told him, and the fact came to me in a starker light, somehow too large to be comprehended. I'm moving to England, I finished.

With your fiancé?

I'm sorry?

Frank reddened slightly. I saw you three days ago, he admitted. From afar. A gentleman with you. Thin, tall. Always talking, clutching his guidebook. British, I think. He was spelling on two hands.

I tried not to smile at the description of Harmon with the

guidebook clasped to his chest. How far away had Frank been standing, I wondered, to see him so accurately?

No, I said. Not fiancé.

Suitor, he tried.

I made a noncommittal shrug. Frank had been the one to put the past behind us so why shouldn't I have him think I'd done the same? It was a petty revenge that I regretted even as I signaled it.

An exhibitor was trying to tell me about a piece of silk I'd picked up without even noticing. I saw no recourse but to pretend I could understand what he was saying in the hope he would soon stop.

Frank signed, Why don't you tell him you're deaf? Poor man. Look how hard he's trying.

The exhibitor saw Frank's signs. His face creased with smiles of dawning comprehension. He began circling his hands extravagantly before commencing on a sequence of gestures that we supposed concerned the silk. Frank held up a hand to slow him down, and then started copying his gestures, trying to clarify the man's meaning. Their gestures went between them until Frank understood that the blue silk on display was of the best quality, and the exhibitor understood that Frank didn't want to buy it regardless. When they were finally finished, Frank flipped up his thumbs. The exhibitor, delighted, did the same. They both stood there, their thumbs erect atop their fists like cavalry spears. Frank broke the well-meaning impasse, diving forward and shaking the exhibitor's hand. Then Frank took my arm and we walked off, leaving the exhibitor with a fading grin.

Should I have brought the silk? Frank signed. He was trying so hard.

I could feel the smile in the corners of my mouth, but I shrugged, and replied, He was charging too much, don't you think?

Far too much, Frank agreed. Not a bargain at all.

Between exhibits he began to tell me more about the Pennsylvania school, his pupils, the editions of the silent press they
had printed in the school's print shops. By the time we reached
Japan, we had become separated from the group.

Frank scanned the Hall briefly. Don't worry, he replied. Deaf
people always find each other.

I laughed. It's a small world outside, I told him. But not in
here.

Frank shook his head. Wrong, he signed. I know exactly
which exhibits my uncle is visiting for the next three days. He's
been planning this trip for months.

He looked at me and I felt my breath and heartbeat bump together. He signed, We don't have to join them.

Lacquer boxes were laid out on a table, each one covered in
intricate birds and trees. Their golden fruits made me think
of our Pawtucket orchards. I examined the boxes for a while,
feeling suddenly fearful. Then I looked up. All right, I nodded,
but I held Frank's gaze so that he understood: we couldn't keep
skirting around the past like this.

Frank signed, Let's go to the giant hand sculpture. Did you
hear about it? After the Exposition, they're going to put the hand
on a statue in New York Harbor. Imagine that! Frank made his
whole forearm into the statue, his hand sculpted into a clench-
ing fist at the top.

Doesn't your uncle want to see it?

No, he wants to see Agricultural Hall. I want to see the
Hand. Come on. You aren't interested in harvesters, are you?
Or furniture?

I would need to return to the lodging house soon before Harmon discovered I wasn't there. It was already past one o'clock. I
felt grief creeping through me. Everything that was unsaid between us still seemed too vast for me to leave Frank yet. A desperate notion filled my head that we could find a way to meet
on the morrow, but even if I could conjure up an excuse, I was

leaving on a scheduled steamer for England and Frank was returning to his new job. An hour alone together was better than
nothing. It might yield some reason to hope and promise of future contact. It didn't matter, I thought, what explanations we
gave each other, if they could just get us to the point where none
of it mattered anymore. I looked around one more time but
couldn't see the Tanners and their friends anywhere, so Frank
and I set off for the north exit of the hall.

We never made it to Bartholdi's Giant Hand. If we had had
a copy of the guide, we would have learned that the sculpture,
which had a staircase to a viewing platform so you could see
across Fairmount Park, wasn't due until the final month of the
Exposition. If we had known this, perhaps we would have left
the Main Exhibition Building by a different exit and the way
we parted would have been entirely different.

As it was, we were almost out of the hall when Frank stopped.
He was looking down the main aisle to where a large placard
was raised above the exhibits. Although it was at some distance,
the huge lettering was impossible to miss. It was the area of the
hall belonging to the Western Union. Most prominent amongst
its exhibits was the Western Electric Company. A crowd was
gathered around its table, which had a signboard describing the
equipment as telegraphic apparatus.

When the people shifted, I glimpsed the exhibitor. He was
older than Mr. Bell, with a gentle bearing, his hair neatly combed
across his head and small eyes glittering under the prominent
fuzz of his eyebrows. A placard gave his name: the inventor,
Mr. Elisha Gray.

I looked at Frank. He caught my gaze. What? he signed.
Come on. This way. I think we need the east exit actually.

He turned on his heels, but I didn't move. When he looked
back, I signed, I'd like to see Mr. Gray's Telegraph.

He stared at me. Why?

I didn't know how to answer but I felt an odd twang of kinship for Mr. Gray. If what Harmon had told me over dinner about the Telephone was true, then both of our hopes had been dashed in different ways. Both of us had fallen into the shadow of Mr. Bell's success.

Frank squinted at me, hesitating, and I remembered, suddenly, that Mr. Gray was one of the Western Union's inventors. Were they behind the business with Frank's mysterious former employer, who was collecting information on Mr. Bell?

Quickly, he signed. It's hot in here, I want to get outside.

We approached the table. Mr. Gray was demonstrating a series of little black boxes and cones, which were connected by short lengths of wire. There wasn't much for us to see. People were striking tuning forks at one set of apparatus and appeared to be listening to sounds coming out of the other.

But we were watching so intently that Mr. Gray spotted us. He waved for us to come closer. Frank hesitated and shook his head, raising his hand politely. There was an anxious humility about his behavior that was uncharacteristic. I studied Mr. Gray. He clearly didn't recognize Frank so whatever he might know about the spying business, he didn't suspect that Frank had any part in it. His bearing seemed so honest and gentlemanly it was hard to imagine he had any involvement. Frank started to turn, but it was too late, as Mr. Gray was upon us.

Frank produced a notebook, not dissimilar from my own. From it he unfolded a page with an explanation—he was deaf-and-dumb—although the page was printed in type, rather than written by hand. The page was well-thumbed.

Mr. Gray nodded and asked if he might have the notebook. "Welcome to my exhibit," he wrote. "Can I demonstrate for you the multiplex transmission of Morse Code down a wire?"

He returned the pen and notebook to Frank, and I watched his careful handwriting appear. He told Mr. Gray we would very much like to see his device, in fact his uncle ran a printing business and demand was such that a multiple telegraph would be of great use.

Mr. Gray was delighted. "Yes," he agreed by way of Frank's notebook. "The commercial application of the Multiple Telegraph is enormous."

He showed us how the device worked. "Forgive me for suggesting it," he wrote, "but I have noticed that the noise in the Hall is such that it is best for everyone to rely on touch rather than sound when transmitting the code, so perhaps this is something yourself and your wife would like to try?"

I looked at Frank. His wife. But he took the notebook and underneath the sentence that called me his wife, he only wrote that we would love to try his invention.

He positioned himself at one end of the wire, with myself at the other, as Mr. Gray showed us where to rest our fingers and tap off samples of Morse Code displayed on a notecard.

Gd afternoon, Frank tapped. It's hot tday.

V hot, I replied. Do you need yr hat?

Frank removed his hat and waved it, so I laughed. As he came back over to me, I couldn't help the thought: why not his wife, even now?

Frank had begun to write "I would like to thank—" when I signaled for the notebook. I didn't want to use my own notebook, because it would bewilder Mr. Gray to have both of us assailing him with pen and paper.

I wrote, "Forgive me for asking, but is it your intention that one day this device will transmit the human voice?"

Frank stared at me. What game was I playing? I wasn't sure myself. Perhaps I was hoping that somehow this kind man could still be the inventor of the telephone, not Mr. Bell. If this history could be altered, couldn't the same happen for mine with Frank?

Mr. Gray startled and his shoulders bounced as if he'd emitted a stunted laugh. His alarm softened into a smile although his eyes retreated from us. He paused, before writing: "I wasn't awarded that patent, although I believe I was very close."

When we looked up from the notebook, his face looked stiff as though he was trying to keep his smile in place until we had finished reading. He asked again for the notebook. "If you want to see such a device, I believe the inventor Professor Bell will be setting up his apparatus for the judges of the Electrical Section tomorrow. The Exhibition will be closed for the Sabbath, but you will be able to see his work next week, if you're still around."

Frank frowned. Was he troubled by the appearance of Mr. Bell's name, or because I'd disturbed Mr. Gray's equanimity? He seemed almost obsequious as he wrote, "Thank you but we have no interest in a device that can transmit voices."

"We are of a similar mindset then," Mr. Gray wrote back. "I had hoped to achieve such a feat, but I do believe the talking telegraph only creates interest in scientific circles. As a toy it is beautiful, but its commercial value will be limited. We shall see what the judges have to say tomorrow."

More people arrived to see Mr. Gray's work, so we bade him farewell and continued toward the north exit. As we walked, I thought about what Mr. Gray had written about the talking telegraph. Mr. Bell had wanted to put a voice in a wire for so long. Could it really be of no consequence?

Frank stopped by the exhibit for typewriters, where Harmon and I had visited a few days before. He was making an elaborate inspection of the type and suddenly I was angry. I tapped his arm sharply. You didn't correct Mr. Gray.

About the Telegraph?

About me being your wife.

Humor suffused his face, but it was a defensive attempt to keep my question at bay. He pointed at me and signed, Now you have a suitor—

You should have corrected him.

He carried on looking at me. You're angry. I understand.

But his color rose, and he looked away, pressing a few keys of the typewriter. After a moment, he continued, My brothers and cousins all graduated from Hartford. I'm the only one who didn't. Most of them became teachers, that was my dream although I know printing is a good job for a man like me. I felt like a failure. Everything was one bad choice after another bad choice. Something lifted when I met you, and I thought if I could only hold on to it—

His hands clutched the air and then he was shaking them, and his head: he didn't wish to carry on.

I wanted to reach out and hold his shoulders, but I didn't think he would let me, he looked so jumpy. And people were all around us, some of them glancing at our signing. We moved on toward the exit, which was a bright square of daylight at the end of the main aisle.

I didn't care, I told him, about what Mr. Bell told me. But you left, and how could I take your side when you had gone? I didn't even know how to write you.

The sunlight was pouring through the doors. Frank stepped away from the exit but couldn't find a space clear of the blinding light, so I sank back against the wall, behind an empty exhibit, allowing him to move out of the glare. My eyes didn't immediately adjust to the new gloom and when Frank signed—I'm sorry—he looked shrunk into the shade around us, as if he was disappearing into his apology, and the hand rubbing on his chest.

It doesn't matter now, I told him, and added, Look at this! For we were standing amongst an array of kicked-in boxes, scattered pamphlets and upturned packing cases. He smiled and reached for my hand, but didn't quite take it, letting his fingers brush against mine. After a moment, he signed, I saw your Visible Speech demonstration.

I stared at him, feeling a cold rinse of horror. You were there?

He was still smiling. You look like you've seen a ghost! I saw the advert the day before. I didn't think it would be you, surely it was another pupil, but there you were! There were some ex-hibits to the side, here—and he recreated the Massachusetts Ex-hibit in the space between us and showed exactly where he had been standing—and you just kept your eyes glued to the paper, reading and reading. Everyone was impressed, he added, and clapped his hands gently in the way hearing people did, as if he was trying it out.

I was still staring at him. The other girl was sick, I managed eventually.

Sick? Maybe she knew there would be a huge crowd. Did you know? I felt for you, you looked so nervous. Unhappy, he added. He paused, watching me. Then he signed, It doesn't mat-ter what you do for Mr. Bell.

I felt the jump of my defenses. I didn't, I started telling him, wanting to explain it was for my mother, not Mr. Bell. But my reasoning suddenly seemed watery, even to me. Instead, I asked, What do you mean?

I think Mr. Gray is wrong, he replied, and Mr. Bell will be-come rich and famous. His smile deepened on his lips, and he signed, I'd like to be rich and famous. He drew himself up tall and dropped his chin like a dignified gentleman, ghosting one of our Lords from the Back Bay into the hall.

It was the old Frank, but I couldn't smile back. I had broken my promise, and he had witnessed it, and now he was trying to make light of it all. I tried to gather myself and turn my thoughts in the same direction as his, although my body was still sting-ing with shame. I had made a mistake, only I didn't know how to come back from it, if I could at all.

You're going to be a great teacher, I told him. Better than Mr. Bell.

He smiled, but it looked rueful, I thought. Look at all this progress, he signed, spanning his arm at the room. Progress ev-erywhere! Speech is progress, not signs. That's what the oral-ists believe. Sign language is a primitive language. It's not even a language! Gestures, pantomime. The world is changing, and they think that communication is something you can make in Machinery Hall.

My aunt and uncle were right, he continued. They didn't know about the spying business, but they knew how angry and unhappy I was after I got expelled from Hartford. They said to me the best fight is to live a normal life. That offends hearing people more than anything. People like Mr. Bell, they don't like that our community is self-sufficient. Strange, because it is our community that stops us being a burden on society. I look at the Brookses and think, that is how I wish to do it. A family, a job, no need to be dependent on anyone. He laughed. Well, maybe Reverend Keep.

I gazed at Frank. A normal life. I tried to keep the notion in view; I wanted to hold on to the pictures of understanding he'd shown me, as if it was a dream that had only been in hiding, and he was gently teasing it out again.

Where are you going? he asked, looking alarmed.

To Mr. Bell's Visible Speech stand.

Why?

I smiled at him, as if it ought to be obvious. There's a page of my notebook on display. I'm going to take it down, I answered.

What's the point?

But I was already stepping past the packing cases and walking back down the aisle. I couldn't undo the speech I had given, but I could prevent my work from being displayed all summer. Frank tried to stop me, but I ignored him, although I was glad of his company, and what I would have him witness.

We never made it to the Visible Speech stand either. It was a day of diverted journeys. Like the Western Union placard, I saw Mr. Bell's Telegraphic Exhibit before Frank. I hadn't noticed the table, marked out with Mr. Bell's name, when we walked through Massachusetts the day before. What is it? Frank asked.

Nothing, I replied, but he spotted the exhibit. His eyebrows lifted but he made no remark.

No one was in attendance. The exhibit looked as if it was in the process of being set up, with boxes stacked under the table. I didn't know if I was disappointed not to see the apparatus for myself. Mr. Bell had made me promise not to tell anyone about it, and yet here it would stand, before the crowds of the Centennial.

A wire had been stretched from the table across the East Gallery. Was this for the judges' demonstration? I followed the wire as far as I could, until it disappeared behind a large Hastings Hood further up the gallery. I could already imagine the men stamping their feet in joy at his demonstration. Wonderment at a voice detached from one person's throat and appearing in another person's ear. But it wasn't the voice that mattered: it was the connection. As I turned back to the stand, I knew I could never have that with hearing people like I had it with Frank.

On the table was a pair of clippers. They didn't look very strong, but I picked them up anyway. I felt very calm and clear in my thoughts as I stepped over to the wire.

Frank came after me. What are you doing?

Cutting the wire.

What?

Didn't you do the same once? The piano wire.

He stared at me, and I felt I was leaning into the force of his gaze. Then he seemed to rouse himself; he had his hands on my arm, but all his attempt to restrain me did was excite my own resistance. I could feel the blood in my ears. I pulled against him, wanting to be strong and for him to be stronger, until something broke, I didn't know what. It didn't even have to be the wire, but I had the clippers in my hand, and something had to go.

Frank was signing quickly, his fury at me tempered only by his panic that I should stop. I was a thief, he signed. For one night I was a vandal, and it changed everything. I don't want the same thing to happen to you.

But his signs glanced off me. Mr. Bell couldn't get me expelled. Our lessons had finished long ago. I could imagine Mr.
Bell's annoyance. He'd be starting the demonstration on a back
foot, if nothing else, while his assistants fussed around for a new
wire. His composure would be ruffled. He might even lose a
few notches of authority from his voice, as he addressed the impatient audience. A hoax, a charlatan, wasting their time. If that
was the only result, it was worth it.

Frank's exasperation melded into his alarm. He reached for
my wrist again, and his sudden move prompted my own, and
by the time his hand was grabbing mine, I'd already found purchase on the wire with the blades. All Frank achieved, in tugging my hand, was aiding the clippers to make their bite. The
wire fell limply on to the floor. We were lucky that there was
no one nearby. Frank's eyes chased the wire until he couldn't
see it any more, and then he turned to me aghast and furious.

Stupid! You can't stop him by cutting one wire. They'll just find
another one. Then what? You can't cut every wire in the world.

I felt calm roaring through me, as if the aftermath of what
I'd done had left a huge space inside me for the truth to spread
in any direction.

He was shaking his head. A small victory, he signed. I thought
the same. What did I learn? One small victory, one large consequence.

I bent down and unraveled the end of the cut wire from where
it was attached to a hook on the table. This left me with about a
yard of wire dangling loose in my hand. I wanted to go to the
Visible Speech stand to fetch my notebook page, but there was
no time. I coiled the wire into my pocket and allowed Frank to
hurry me from the Main Exhibition Building.

Outside in the sunshine, Frank let go of my arm. We were
standing on the Avenue of the Republic. People were pushing
past us in both directions, trying to access the building from

which we'd just left. I looked around for somewhere quieter, but Frank started hurrying along the avenue in a westerly direction. I managed to catch up to him. Where are we going? I asked. There was a pavilion a short distance off, flags flying from its wooden turrets: the Judges' Pavilion, I'd later learn.

He didn't look at me when he answered, so I had to read his signs sideways. The French restaurant, he replied. The group is meeting there for lunch. Then he stopped. No, I should take you to the stage-car stop.

No, I replied, feeling the bulk of my refusal like a sandbag at a door frame. I knew he was right and that by now Harmon had probably raised the alarm, and Mama would be in a state of rising panic. But I was shaking my head anyway; not at his common sense, but at everything, that it had to end like this.

The three men appeared from nowhere and surrounded Frank. At first, just one of the men was talking at him, then a second joined when Frank started shaking his head and waving his arms. I saw him feel around for his notebook and realized that I still had it from when we met Mr. Gray. I scrambled to pull it from my pocket. The crowd had moved between myself and the men, so I had to push through them. The men's mouth-moving became more rigid as did Frank's arms in response. They were a standoff of limbs and words. Then I couldn't see them anymore, as the crowd flowed into the space between us.

I thought it was the crowd who had knocked Frank over. It looked like the men were trying to pull him up. They were holding on to Frank's hands and arms, and he was struggling hard. I had to tell them to stop: they were as good as clamping his mouth with their hands on his wrists like that. They were shouting. He wouldn't stand like they wanted him to. He was twisting, using his weight to pull against their grip, digging in his heels as best he could, although his feet kept slipping. His hat was knocked off. The crowd continued to press around us.

I tried to get closer. I had to explain. They had to let go of his hands. I had a notebook, if they would just let me give it him, he would explain, or I would. If they could just let me explain.

I grabbed the shoulder of one of the men who wasn't shouting. He ignored me, perhaps thinking it was just the shove of the crowd. So I prodded and tapped until he turned around. Immediately, I recognized him. It was the judge's assistant from the Visible Speech demonstration. His face jumped with surprise. I was about to tell him that Frank couldn't hear him, but the man seemed to think I was in want of an explanation, for I saw his mouth shape out the word Thief. He pointed at Frank.

Then I realized. Someone must have seen me cutting the wire, but why was it Frank they had grabbed?

I opened my mouth. I would explain everything. It wasn't Frank, I began and my voice came out loud and huge, because I could feel it humming in my nose and cheeks. I carried on for a little while, but the man didn't seem to understand, so I tried more force from my throat, in case the noise of the crowd was a problem. This caused him to step back with a look of alarm. I decided to take the wire from my pocket instead. That would help. And I showed it to this man—this judge's assistant, who was surely of sound reasoning—and told him it was me, I was the one who cut the wire. But my throat was beginning to feel ragged, so I waved the wire at him, making him look at it.

The judge's assistant peered at me, then the wire. He took it and held it up almost triumphantly. Relief flushed through me. Finally, he understood. He said something to the men, and I waited for them to release Frank. But instead, they were taking him away. Frank was standing now, but with the men on either side of him. He only just managed to turn his head to look back. What he saw was the judge's assistant holding the wire with a grin on his face, and me standing next to him. Did he see my meek disbelief? I was too slow by a matter of seconds. By the time I raised my hands to sign an explanation, he'd been forced to look away.

The crowd was foaming around Frank in a sea of parasols, hot faces and brochures. I pushed after him, but a hand was pulling me up short. It was the judge's assistant. He was drawing me firmly away from the Avenue and toward the Judges' Pavilion. I looked around but couldn't see Frank anywhere. I saw no recourse but to let myself be led since the best option now was my notebook. I'd explain everything and clear up the confusion, and they would release Frank. When we finally sat down, I wrote several pages, adding in every detail I could think of, and how Frank had been the one who tried to stop me.

The judge's assistant—his name was Jim Waterford—seemed amused by my account. He shook his head, and I watched as he told me that Frank had a reputation. Someone saw him near the exhibit and had told a member of Mr. Bell's party.

He had to jot out all the trickier words as he spoke, and eventually resorted to the paper itself. "Tomorrow's a big day for Mr. Bell. It's the judging of the Electrical Section. Someone will fix that wire but we don't want Mr. McKinney hanging about."

"But you don't understand," I tried. "He was the one who tried to stop me."

Mr. Waterford managed to keep his smile polite as he waited for me to finish. I sensed his pity for my desperation, but he was unmoved to do anything about it. When he didn't appear inclined to respond, I asked instead, What will happen to him?

"Police station," he wrote.

Horror chilled me. Which station? I asked.

He shook his head and shrugged. He didn't know which station.

You must take me there, I said.

What?

I wrote it on the paper and tapped the word. You must take me, I said, to a police station.

Miss, he said smiling, and wrote, "The only place I am taking you is to your lodging house."

I stared at him. Augusta. I had to find her. She would be able to interpret for Frank. I would tell her everything so she could relay it to the constables at the station. Too bad she was a woman but at least she was hearing. I needed to get to the French restaurant where Frank had said the group were having lunch.

Mr. Waterford was writing something down. He turned the page for me. "The judge is going to award Mr. Bell a gold medal," he'd written, "for your demonstration of Visible Speech. It was a magnificent feat. Don't you think Mr. Bell will be pleased to hear of it? I won't tell him about any of this, of course. It would be such a shame."

I looked at Mr. Waterford, appalled. A prize? I felt nauseous. If only I'd ignored the wire and heeded Frank, we might be taking our seats in the French restaurant, none of this having happened.

Tell Mr. Bell, I said, tearing the page with my account and waving it in Mr. Waterford's face. Show this to him.

Then I rose from my seat and ran toward the door of the pavilion. I glanced back once. He wasn't following me; instead he was scrunching my account into a ball, and looking for a trash can.

The afternoon passed in a hot daze. I couldn't find the Tanners in the French restaurant or anywhere in the Exposition although it was ridiculous to hope that I might. When I returned to our lodging rooms, expecting a hailstorm of anger and relief, I found Mama asleep with the landlady at her bedside. She gave me a reproving look.

"She had a nasty spasm of the lungs," she wrote for me. "The doctor has visited. It has exhausted her as you can see. I'm certain it's the heat, it's too much for a person of her constitution. Mr. Bardsley didn't want to trouble her about you. He has gone back to the Exposition to look for you again."

I collapsed in the chair next to Mama's bed and the landlady got up. I saw her say Booked Up and Tomorrow. They were booked up for tomorrow night. I fussed about Mama although she was asleep. What constitution did the landlady mean? I refilled her water, dabbed at her brow, patted her hand uselessly. I was frightened by this susceptibility of her health. I'd never known Mama to be ill. But I couldn't help the awful thought from forming that if Mama wasn't well enough for the journey home tomorrow, then I'd be able to return to the Exposition. I'd find the Tanners or other members of their party at the Cataract, explain what had happened and offer them my help.

But the landlady had warned me that the lodging rooms were booked, and besides I couldn't sit about doing nothing. I got my notebook and made five copies of the explanation I'd given in the Judges' Pavilion, improving them slightly and addressing one to Augusta. I went downstairs and gave them to the landlady with coins sneaked from Mama's purse, asking her to send them to the Philadelphia police stations, except for the last envelope, which was for the Tanners. They had come looking for me before. Surely they would do so again. Perhaps they would even call later. I waited all evening and through to the next morning, sitting at Mama's side, but they didn't come.

18

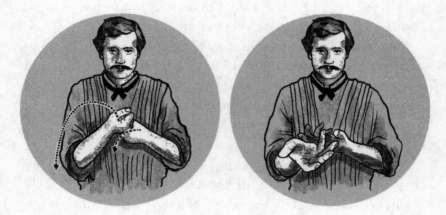

Express

MAMA'S WORDS are a river, her final letter spread open in my lap. Her voice turns through me, her sentences wide and flowing. Pages of advice, all of which she's given me before, but everything she fears I might forget. I don't want her words to finish, as I resurrect her in the back-and-forth of my eyes. At the end is an instruction: "I have left a gift with your stepfather for the occasion of your wedding. May it serve you well."

Downstairs I knock on Mr. Holmwood's door, scribbling out the best account I can of how I opened my mother's letter before I was supposed to. When he hesitates, I point out that he has already opened all the ones she left for him. He looks up from the notebook and smiles, tapping his bent hand in the air. It looks like the sign for Future. He's picked up more from Mrs. Ketter than I realized. He swipes his hand against his chin. Future. He doesn't have one. Not like me. I infer the rest: what was the point in him saving up his letters?

He considers me, trying to assess any cause for concern. I hold myself resolutely calm, doing my best to ignore the smoking guilt that I might be giving him reason to worry after all. Then he takes a small box from his drawer and slides it across the table.

Inside is the long gleaming blade of the past. A gold pen, identical to the one I had as a child. On the tag, Mama has written, "For all the words that are yet to come."

I ease the pen from its velvet pillow and test its weight along with my own disbelief. Surely it can't be the same? It would be impossible to have fetched it from the depths of the well in Pawtucket. Mama must have remembered it exactly and sought to purchase a replica. I look at Mr. Holmwood, who confirms my guess with a smile.

It's perfect, I tell him, making the sign for perfect. But my chest tightens as I do so. Our last day in Philadelphia, Mama's health was only slightly improved. She was still too unwell to bear the burden of my account, so I told her nothing. Harmon showed his dismay at my waywardness before I'd even dared tell him what I'd done. I couldn't trust him to help me, and he was insisting we move on to acquaintances in New York where Mama could recover in time for us to sail to England. All my hope was funneled into the landlady and her promise to give my letter to the Tanners, as well as a forwarding address. I waited weeks and then months until eventually a reply came to me with news that Frank was confined in the Philadelphia penitentiary. There'd been an incident at the police station, Augusta wrote, which caused further trouble. She didn't elaborate, but I guessed at it. How long was it until someone arrived to interpret for him? I wrote letters in response to the Tanners, asking how I could assist them, but got no answers. It was Mrs. Ketter who found out a year later that he'd been released.

There's a movement from the far side of the room. Harmon is standing in the doorway, holding a brochure of some kind. He glances at the pen but doesn't see anything worthy of inquiry. I'm relieved that I don't have to explain that it was a wedding gift, and I've opened it early because I have started to think that the wedding may not happen. Instead, I focus on the brochure he proffers, which is for the Royal Society of Arts. Harmon watches as I read:

Visible Speech and the Talking Telegraph
Two Great Inventions
In Deaf-Mute Education and Telephony
A demonstration by Professor Alexander Graham Bell

I nod while making a casual pucker of my lips, meaning to show him that I'm unconcerned and ready for the occasion. But he's scribbling something in our notebook. "I do not think you should come with me to the Society tonight," he has written. "Having reflected on the matter, I think it would be better if we cancel the demonstration."

I look up from his words to find an unexpected quiver of concern in his cheeks. No, I say. I want to attend.

The suggestion that I give a speech at the Royal Society was received with cautious welcome by Mr. Bell. He had passed on the idea to Mr. Price who was organizing the event. Certainly, it was a novel idea if I was willing. However, he added, Mrs. Bell was anxious to advise these events were often crowded and may not suit a person of sensitive disposition.

That was the verdict they had chosen after our last visit. My disposition was to blame. I picture Mr. Bell standing before his wife with Harmon's letter in his hand, as Mabel studies his lips. Now she must manage a querulous baby at her shoulder, as well as her husband and the little dog at her heel. No, she is saying, shaking her head. It is inadvisable. Her husband's insistence: but think, my dear, what an audience it shall be for Visible Speech. Miss Lark, he'll say, is regretful of her behavior last time.

"We promised Mr. Bell," I write for Harmon, "and it is poor form to break a promise."

But it's the old, already-broken promises that are calling me. Forty pairs of ears at the Centennial Exposition listening to the marvel of Visible Speech. I had seen my error too late and impulsively cut the wire, but that was a mistake too. Isn't Mr. Bell right to call me regretful? We are more alike than he would care to acknowledge, if his own actions are any indicator. He flies to Greenock, abandoning his own wife and baby as well as the Telephone business. No kind of "inadvisable" from Mabel is likely to stop him either.

A conversation with Mr. Bell on the Telephone before an audience of hundreds. What errors could be undone? But nerves crunch through me when I picture the large, attentive crowd, and for a moment I'm tempted to accept Harmon's suggestion and let him go alone.

Harmon watches me with strained effort. He cannot take the measure of me. It was Harmon who arranged for me to be presented to the Exposition judges without giving me the details, because a snatch of information is what most people think I should be content with. And now he finds himself similarly mired in guesswork and doesn't like it one bit.

"I have chosen my dress," I write, "the earrings you gave me that I have not yet worn."

I am presentable: this is the idea, I present.

No—

Harmon is shaking his head although the edges of his Yes haven't fully retreated. He hates to let Mr. Bell down, especially when he learned that Mr. Ackers, a man of prestige and government who is setting up a school for teachers of the deaf in Ealing, will be there too. He will even be taking a delegation to an international congress in Milan next year to promote speech-teaching. Perhaps Harmon has already pictured for us a cabin on a steamer to Italy, so that we might join the great debate. Will Mr. Ackers's daughter be there too? She was the reason Mr. Ackers visited me in the first place, the wellspring of his blinkered dedication.

"I will go alone," Harmon writes, to give his decision a finality afforded by ink, "and after tonight there will be no more Telephones."

Not long after he leaves, I pack my finest notebook and the gold pen into my bag, and set out on foot myself. When I reach the Royal Society, the crowds are spilling onto the street, trying to enter the building. A wire has been strung between a first-floor window and the doors of the Adelphi Hotel opposite, and several guests are gathered at each end, hollering into the Telephone mouthpieces, so their delight travels over the queues on the pavement. Once I'm inside, I realize that the Society is filled with even more of them. There are wires tacked everywhere, snaking along corridors and through doorways to Telephones in the lobbies and foyers.

In the Great Room, the guests spread out under the murals, so that the crowd below seems to be mirrored by the ancient crowds depicted above. A Telephone stands polished and aloof on a raised lectern. This one is surely the centerpiece of the Society, but is it my Telephone? From which I will converse with Mr. Bell in Visible Speech?

But there will be no Visible Speech tonight. On that I'm decided.

In a chance moment the crowd drifts apart, giving me a clear view of the instrument. It waits for me like a dancing partner at the far end of the room. I could walk right up to it and brush my fingers along the handle as if it were a lover's cheek. What will I whisper into its mouthpiece? An honest voice must run down these wires this evening. A voice of flaws and imperfections that usually earns jests and blank stares, not prizes. A voice that persists even after I'd labored for months on Visible Speech, trying to be like Miss Dudley, Miss Flagg and Miss Jennings. Girls who had no doubt stepped down from the stage and—out of earshot, out of sight—slipped into their own natural voices or even quick-handed signs.

You exist because of us, I will say to the Telephone. We are the voices that made you.

It's Mr. Price, the event organizer, who I need to find. Has Harmon already tracked him down and canceled the demonstration? I look around for Harmon, relieved that at least all these people will prevent him from making a scene. Nonetheless, dread jumps into my stomach as a hand takes my elbow. But I turn to find Mr. Crane, not Harmon, standing next to me. His face is arranged into a smile as he grips my arm, and his lips stir with a word. Is it Fancy? Fancy seeing you here?

I pull loose of him, heading for the main doors. I haven't a notion of where I'm going. Mr. Crane catches my sleeve before I reach the stairs, his hand firming this time around my wrist. He guides us into a narrow corridor, standing so close to me I can smell his tobacco.

Why have you come? he asks.

I make confident circles of my fists, my thumbs pointing up. To complete my task, I tell him.

For the Western Union? I thought you'd dropped that. You didn't answer my letters.

I level my gaze at him. There's a new softness in his face, or else regret has been loosening through him as well, and the desire to make amends. I didn't answer your letters, I tell him, because I don't wish to work for Mr. Bell's legal team.

His eyes tighten with consideration, pressing out more wrin-

kles. After a pause, he signs, I'm not on his team. Mr. Bell's lawyers in America asked me to get his English patent. I was useful
to his lawyers a few years ago. They think I am being useful
now. That's all.

Very useful, I reply. Lying to everyone.

He holds up his hands to stall my assertion, then circles his
palms out from his chest. I'll explain, he signs. A few years ago,
I was staying in Washington. Every evening I had dinner with
Mr. Gray's draftsmen in the boardinghouse. One day Mr. Bell's
lawyers approached me. They wanted some information, and I
needed money. At that time Mr. Gray wasn't working for the
Western Union, so I didn't owe him anything. It was a one-off.

Even with his upper arms tucked to his sides in the cramped
space, he maps out the events clearly. The evening conversations
with the draftsmen, the approach of Mr. Bell's lawyers.

When he finishes, my conclusions fly from my hands so
quickly I can't tell if the confidence is in what I've deduced or
in the simple joy of expression. I sign, You told his lawyers what
was in Mr. Gray's patent application.

Three places marked in the air—Mr. Crane, Mr. Bell's lawyers, Mr. Gray—and the web of Mr. Crane's deceit dancing
between them.

I only told them, he signs, that Mr. Gray's caveat was about
the telegraph and the human voice, and that he was filing it
soon. Nothing else. It's what the draftsmen were saying. And a
talking telegraph was different from a Multiple Telegraph, so it
seemed like a small bit of information. They paid good cash. I
left Washington after that. But I guess the information worried
them. They smelled an interference. Then Mr. Bell's application
arrived at the patent office the same day as Mr. Gray's. And it
mentioned liquid, the same as Mr. Gray's.

I gaze at Elbert Crane. How does one live a life of endless calculation? I suppose I should know. Endlessly guessing at words,
at speech. And yet what I learned was that everything useful to

survive and love in the world was taught to me by deaf people or people who saw their value. And every one of them had been taken away from me. Frank, Mrs. Ketter, the pupils at the Oral School. People had been thieving from us our whole lives, insisting that we would only be lowly people if we kept each other's lowly company. Mr. Crane was stolen goods himself, the second lost son of his parents. Is this what compels him? A desire to take back something? For himself, his parents, his brother?

Your thieving, I sign, might have lost Mr. Gray the Telephone.

A queue of people has formed at the end of the corridor, heading in the direction of the Great Room. Perhaps Mr. Bell has started his speech, his voice threading through the wires and across the Society. A family catch my notice as they inch forward. The parents are talking to one another while behind them their son and daughter are spelling furiously on their fingers. The mother glances back and the children drop their hands immediately. The girl is quicker.

Both deaf? Mr. Crane asks, when the family have gone on their way.

The boy maybe, I reply and look at Mr. Crane. Did he and his brother once sign in that same close way? I remember Mary, our home-signs, and feel the notch of an ache in my breast.

But Mr. Crane's eyes slip from me. It's a topic he won't broach. He looks at the floor for the first time, thrusting his hands in his pockets. After a moment he continues, I didn't say anything about the wire vibrating in the liquid. I didn't tell the lawyers about that. I don't know how it got into Mr. Bell's patent. Truly I don't. I knew about it from his draftsmen, but I said nothing. His lawyers must have got their hands on Mr. Gray's caveat and seen it for themselves. Everybody at the patent office was in each other's pockets. Do you understand? he finishes.

Is it his guilt I must understand? For that's what I see. Timing was everything, I reply. You told me yourself. If the patent applications hadn't arrived at the same time, it would have been impossible for the officials to overlook the normal rules. And now Mr. Bell's lawyers have the English patent. Won't they hide it? Keep it from the lawsuits?

That's why I needed you.

The people in the corridor are now trotting with haste. Perhaps they can hear Mr. Bell from the Great Room. Does Mr. Crane hear him also? The air feels heavy and warm, thickened with all the hushed conversation and summoning: quick, hurry, it's starting. I feel a longing to see those two children spelling secretly on their fingers again. What do they make of the crowds, the commotion of lips?

But Mr. Crane's attention is bent on me. I brace myself against what I fear he'll tell me, and the name I can see forming on his hand, even before it begins the downward slice from his nose: Frank.

When I was in America, he begins, I was trying to get far away from my family. Frank was a friend of mine. I was fond of him. Well, everyone is fond of Frank. He was supposed to take lessons with Mr. Bell, get close to him. That's what the Union was paying him for. But I guess he didn't want to do it. He suggested that you would be a better person to do the job, if he could persuade you. You were already close to Mr. Bell. I gave him the Union's money, so he could take lessons with you. I had my doubts about the whole thing, but the people at the Union were intrigued. Frank told them you were good at lip-reading. They liked the idea of a spy who could lip-read!

He shakes his head. That was my mistake, he signs. I shouldn't have agreed. Later, Frank told me the business was finished. He left Boston, never wrote again. Took all the leftover money, and I had nothing to show for it apart from that piece of glass he sent me.

A sour pucker gathers at the corners of his mouth. Mrs. Ketter told me everything, he continues. You, Frank. Then I understood.

The twitch of annoyance I feel at Mrs. Ketter's easy sharing of information vanishes with this flicker of his index. His understanding, like a bright flame in his mind. To my alarm, I blush at what his understanding might contain.

Imagine my humiliation, he continues, when I had to tell the Union! All that money gone and nothing to show for it! I'm not a rich man, he adds, stiffening himself straight. Frank lied to me. You same.

I didn't know about the Union, I reply, but it feels like a thin, watered-down truth. Hadn't I pushed aside my queries about how Frank was paying my fee?

Mr. Crane's nodding is impatient. Sure, but I didn't know that. I thought you knew everything. Taking the money, taking Frank for a ride too.

His signs become rough and abrupt, as his fist swipes through the air—Taking money, taking Frank—and I feel anger and shame burn me up. That smoked glass, I sign. Frank changed the mark. He altered it. You're right, now it really isn't worth anything.

Mr. Crane's eyebrows lift with surprise. Changed? he repeats, and to my surprise, my anger melts into disappointment. I was hoping this was another secret he'd be able to account for. He didn't tell you anything? I ask.

His face darkens, a slumping of his cheek and brows. History, he signs. He told me it was history. Important history because that device helped Mr. Bell get to the Telephone. I asked him about the line. Was it a word? He laughed and said does it look like a word? Hearing people always look for words. Sometimes we should look for pictures instead. That's what he said.

I feel my mind yawning open, and I stare at Mr. Crane until even he looks taken aback. My thoughts have slipped, scrabbling frantically. Pictures, not words. Of course, a picture!

That's all? I ask, but he's still locked into his own ideas. He is, I realize, the kind of person who imagines keenly how people rally against him. His temper has reached his jaw, crawling color into his face. He's made a fool of me, he replies. He has a wife and son now. You would think he would learn how to be respectable, not these games. Before you ask, a deaf wife. His son the same. One big happy deaf family. Here, wait.

Before I have time to adjust to this news of Frank, Mr. Crane is taking a slip of paper from his pocket. When I see the handwriting, I practically snatch it from him.

The glass was wrapped in that paper, he signs and pushes his fists toward me, following the trajectory of the note. Keep it. I don't want it anymore.

I sink my eyes on the note, overflowing with hope. Frank's writing once again. How bright and solid was the greeting sweep of his hand through the air. Now I read his single penned sentence.

"A Likeness of Miss Ellen Lark."

Likeness, Mr. Crane spells on his fingers. I thought he meant your voice. A likeness of your voice.

I nod—yes, yes—while trying to bury my disappointment at the note's brevity and summon the glass to mind instead. Pictures, not words. But the precise pattern of the mark is too hazy to hold in my thoughts, which instead are flooded with images of Frank, his son and wife. I can't make out their faces, only the movement of three pairs of hands in conversation over the white of a dining room tablecloth. I see printed papers arrayed along a side-cabinet, and a mess of cutlery, correspondence and children's toys in amongst the breakfast things. I try to pick out the details of this busy little home scene. I want to see the fullness of his contentment and feel how deep my remorse will go. Shouldn't I be happy for him? Frank freed from the penitentiary, making a life for himself again. Did I think that he was living in a state of suspension like my own, and that somehow, we would come together again? That I might find a way back to him.

Elbert Crane's watch of me has hardened. There is still unfinished business, he begins. I gave you that glass, whatever it was worth. His curled fists, knuckle to knuckle, rock in the air. Worth. But it looks like a plea. The money is still on his mind, after everything. I told the Union, he persists, that the matter was still ongoing.

I look from Mr. Crane to the corridor. It's empty, Mr. Bell's introductory speech has surely started. Then I pat my hands soothingly at his angst. Don't worry, I tell him, I have some information.

His whole body leans toward me. Mercury, he spells. You saw Mercury.

Do you know Mr. Price? I ask.

No, why?

I have an appointment, I sign, tapping my hooked fingers into my palm, with the Telephone.

The lecture in the Great Room is finished and the smaller rooms are filling with people. They elbow their way with polite insistence to the Telephones on the tables. Listening, speaking, listening again: voices fly along the wires and between the rooms. The crackled words of jokes, quips, psalms, Shakespeare perhaps. In the walls, along the skirting boards, up and down the marble staircases.

You can cut one wire, Frank had said. It'll make no difference.

I check the program, my pocket watch: half an hour until my scheduled speech, or the announcement that it has been canceled. I go from room to room, looking for a steward or somebody who might be Mr. Price. When I find myself at the staircase for a second time, I realize I'm going in circles. I stop by a tall, gilt-framed picture of a Society president and think of the smoked glass again. Was I forgiven, and that's why Frank gave Mr. Crane the smoked glass? It was an important item, he had told him. This new possibility slides into view. Could his forgiveness bring this evening to an end? I could simply walk out of the Society's doors and go back to Harmon, and try for a new life, same as Frank.

Through a doorway I glimpse him: not Mr. Price, but Mr. Bell standing next to a plinth and talking with a small group. I take a few steps forward. There's a shine on his suit that comfortably covers his expanded girth while new strands of gray wind into his hair. He nods, he smiles, he listens: his eyes slide to the left and he sees me. But he carries on nodding while his gaze fixes me in the doorway. No matter the thump of my heart: I've been spotted and so would be my retreat.

A few words to the group, a smile and laugh, a gentle slap on someone's shoulder: he dispatches of them and their praise.

Alone? he asks, when he reaches me.

Harmon, I say, and wave a hand generally at the crowd by which I mean to convey: he's in there somewhere. I don't know how loud or soft to make my voice with all these people in this room. Then I remember Mama's letter and the gold pen that I brought with me. I take out my notebook, unable to help the well of pleasure as I grip the lovely pen and put down my words. "Mr. Bell," I begin, "I think I have discovered what the mark is on the smoked glass. Do you remember you told me it was altered?"

His eyes lift from the page, as he gives me a wary glance, but I continue anyway. "A likeness," I write. "A silhouette."

But he doesn't understand. "It was always a likeness," he writes, his large fingers wrapped around my gold pen, so I can't help wishing he'd use his own pen. "Illuminate and Lemonade. Although they are not exactly the same. The 'U' sends the lips narrow, which you do not see in Lemonade. So they are not homophenes, just likenesses."

Yes, a likeness, I say, nodding to suggest my comprehension. To be a likeness of a hearing person, I want to add. That is the goal of the oralist education. But look more closely and you will see our straining eyes, the false nod, the weary expression, as we search out the narrow-lipped *U* in Illuminate.

"I remember Miss Dudley," I write, "Miss Flagg and Miss Jennings. Perhaps you know if they found the illumination the gentlemen were speaking of?"

Mr. Bell hesitates. He says but does not write: Miss Flagg does well, I believe.

"Those girls," I continue, "didn't know what they were saying, although their voices were perfect. You told us yourself."

He studies me for a moment, and my thoughts flip to the smoked glass. Frank's little joke in history. I can't help the crinkle of laughter in my chest. The likeness of my voice changed into a likeness that Frank preferred: a picture.

"Mr. Bell," I write. "I have been remembering our lessons, and our old game with the homophenes. I have a new sentence if you are willing? Perhaps you will be able to guess the homophene correctly."

He looks up from the notebook. Go on, he says, but his agreement stirs across his lips with a matching mistrust in his eyes.

I gather my words carefully, thinking of Mr. Crane's Visible Speech translations, and make sure I don't use my voice for the key one: Mystery. There is no mystery, I say, in the lost patent.

His eyes are fixed on my lips and the shape of the word that flickers there. I see him repeat it: Mercury. The lips push out in a degree slightly less than that of Mystery, but they are close likenesses nonetheless. Mercury, he says, and looks around, as though he fears others might have detected the silent word.

"What patent do you mean?" he writes, stabbing his words so I know he is angry.

"Have not several patents been lost? In Europe," I add.

"None of them mention that liquid." Mercury, he says, when I look up, puzzled.

Mercury? I ask, then laugh. See? I have won. Taking the pen

from him, I write, "I said Mystery, not Mercury. But I thought you might see Mr. Gray. I didn't think of Mercury."

His cheeks have reddened although his eyes are still dark-cool, like nighttime puddles.

I give him a reassuring smile. "That is a good one," I tell him. "Perhaps you didn't need my help writing that paper on homophenes after all. I would never have seen Mercury, although I make mistakes all the time. Is it of some significance to you?"

He takes back the notebook. "It is not relevant. That liquid would never have worked in the Telephone."

I nod, to show my comprehension, while remembering Mr. Crane's words. It was the liquid principle that mattered. Mercury was a broad illustration. Did his lawyers recommend the insertion to ensure the two patent applications weren't too similar?

He continues, "I appreciate the game, but these are complex matters which are best left to experts."

The gold pen is resting in the centerfold. I can feel Mr. Bell waiting for my reply. Some confirmation that I have understood. Only experts are of use to him now. But I have no answer for him. Once I earned him a prize for Visible Speech, and I must take it back.

Around us the stewards organize the turn-taking at the Telephones. People crowd the tables and don't seem to notice the Telephone's inventor himself, partly hidden behind the plinth. Mr. Bell's eyes slip over my shoulder. His smile springs open just as a hand presses my elbow. This time I know it's Harmon. He's managed to ball his mouth tightly shut, but his eyes are gaping.

Good evening, I say.

What—

But he stops himself. Mr. Bell is still smiling at him, and doesn't know my misdemeanor, that I came here alone. Mr. Bell spans a hand at the busy rooms and says, Easy and Lost.

It is easy to get lost in the Society.

Yes, replies Harmon, fixing his gaze on me.

Then he bends his head to Mr. Bell. The demonstration. They are discussing the matter of my speech. I try to single out the words on his shaded mouth. That I will give a speech or that I should not? That he has spoken with Mr. Price or he hasn't? Mr. Bell tucks in his chin as he considers Harmon's proposal or account, whatever it is.

I'm about to interrupt. Since I am here, I might as well do it, surely? But the two children I saw earlier enter the room, distracting me from Harmon and Mr. Bell's huddle. They follow their parents with their hands folded in front of them, until the mother stops to talk with some acquaintances, one of whom bends down to the children. The girl is ready with her answers, but the boy's eyes fix on the gentleman's questions, his face pulling close in a frown. It's a look I know so well.

Then Harmon is saying All right. He takes my arm and says, Mr. Price. We'd better talk to him. His grip feels rigid as he says, This Way. Mr. Bell watches me go, his hands looped at his back, his chin dipped, the darkness of his gaze like a slick down my neck.

Well? We fold ourselves into the corridor and I rotate my palms upward in question.

Harmon takes out his notebook and pen. "Your speech is due in fifteen minutes so we better find Mr. Price. I told him it was canceled because you were unwell. What will he think of me now?"

I look up from the page. The surprised anger at seeing me here has lifted from his face, leaving an imprint of bewilderment. A scratch of guilt lodges behind my breastbone. Not for the lines I may cross, but from the growing sense that it is too late, and I may not be able to cross back from them. He suspects none of it.

"Mr. Bell says that he would like to hear it," he adds. "He expressly said that to me."

I'm a long time lifting my eyes. Is it a challenge or a peace offering? Does Mr. Bell wish me to forget about mercury and have no qualms with him? To let me take the stage and join him in thrilling the crowd. Or does he prefer to remind me that once I'm on that stage, I will be no more than what I have always been, his pupil? Harmon snatches back the notebook in frustration. "But what will you read? You don't have any Visible Speech. You haven't asked me to translate anything. I don't think Mr. Bell realizes that. If you give me your speech now, perhaps I can try to remember enough symbols to do the first few sentences."

"My speech is ready," I write for him. Then I gesture with my hand at the doorway: is it this way?

He stares at me, his face taut with concern. He wants us aligned, in harmony, wedded and happy. That is his desire and duty. You don't have to do this, he spells on his fingers. But I'm already taking out my notebook, the gold pen poking up from its inner pages like a tongue. Wherever, he asks, did you get that pen?

His whole face is a question. From the bottom of a well, I reply, the notebook and pen tucked under my arm as I leave the side room and make my way over to the Telephone.

The Great Room is filling with people again. I climb onto the podium and turn to face the audience. Harmon stands near the front, looking miserable. I can't see Mr. Bell anywhere. Does he wait in an anteroom with another Telephone pressed to his ear, listening for my voice?

I prop my notebook with the little speech I've prepared on the lectern next to the Telephone. Mr. Price glances at the page and frowns. He may not know much about Visible Speech, but he can see that what I've written is regular English.

I nod to show I'm ready. His puzzled face lingers before he turns to the crowd. I watch his mouth, imagining his introduction of me to match the declarations of an advertisement or newspaper report. He says Visible Speech and Mr. Bell's name and Miraculous. I don't catch the rest. Is he more like a circus ringmaster? Ladies and gentlemen, he might be saying. I give you Miss Ellen Lark!

His fingertips extend in my direction, and he drops his head, bowing his way backward across the stage.

The crowd starts leaving the Great Room, and it takes me a moment to remember why. The audience is following Mr. Price's instructions to relocate to whichever Telephone is connected to the one in front of me. That is the promise of the evening. Visible Speech and the Telephone: two great inventions of the voice to meet along the wires.

A small group remains in the room with Harmon. I spot Mr. Ackers standing in the middle, the shadow of a smile under his thick beard, and the hand of a young woman pressed into the crook of his elbow. She looks about my age, fair-haired and sturdy, a light frown of concentration on her face. Is this his daughter? I try to remember her name. Edith, I think. Edith Ackers.

Near the back of the crowd, Elbert Crane shifts into view. I manage a smile, which causes both Mr. Ackers and Harmon to look around. But Elbert has that ability to appear insignificant. Shortly the men look back to the stage, just as I open my mouth and take a breath, readying myself for the first word of the plain English in front of me.

But when I look at the crowd again, a fresh problem arises. Not only is Edith in attendance, but I spot the boy with his sister and parents. He stands close in his mother's skirts, holding her hand, his face grave. Neither Edith nor this boy will understand my speech. All they will see is the bob of my head and a flicker of tiny shapes on my lips. They'll search out the crowd's approval and find alarm and confusion. What understanding will that leave them with?

The boy straightens himself, suddenly conscious of my gaze.

His mother glances down, as if she too is surprised that her son has caught my notice. She puts a protective arm around him and looks at me with her eyebrows lifted: not a question, it seems, but a challenge.

I want to tell the boy and Edith Ackers that their eyes are their gifts. They must let their sight have all that it can. But you cannot make sense of the world on lips alone. The pictures they make are scant, barely pictures at all. You will confine your eyes to the same silence as your ears, until your body becomes a grave of lost connections.

What happens next is quite simple. Mr. Price, having stepped down from the stage, crosses to the Telephone and extends the butterstamp mouthpiece so it hovers before my lips. A red-brown wooden disc, polished so thoroughly that stripes of light wobble between the six brass screws. In the middle is a small, dark hole just large enough for a probing finger. It leads down into the mechanisms of the Telephone, fashioned precisely by Mr. Bell's assistant according to Mr. Bell's design. The current sends its quarry of the human voice onward, along the wires fixed to the skirting boards, and into the paired Telephones in the other rooms, setting a tremble in the eardrums of the audience. My audience.

Mr. Price lifts his eyebrows, creasing his brow with worry. Go on, he says. Yes?

My notebook is open on the podium. I glance again at the first line but instead of speech, I feel a burst of thoughts and before I even have time to consider them, they've run down my arms and into my hands.

Good evening, I sign to the Telephone.

And, signing, continue with my speech.

I want to tell you a story, I sign. About a young boy. As my finger brushes my chin, I think of Frank and the boy he befriended at Hartford, and how Frank tried to comfort him as he lay on his sickbed.

I've no skills in presentation, and fresh and lively are not descriptors that I'll ever be awarded although it feels as if my words could not be fresher or livelier, flowing as they do from my hands. My arms are unlocked, freed, and what rises in my chest has no need to navigate the mechanics of my throat and mouth to be uttered.

Astonishment shivers across the small crowd, but the hole of the butterstamp receiver stares back at me darkly. I picture Mr. Bell at the other end, straining to hear.

Mr. Price stands there gaping. He's still holding the Telephone receiver although in his amazement his own hand has dropped until the receiver is level with my hands, instead of my mouth.

I try to unfold the story of the boy in the sign language. It is Roy, Frank's friend, but it could be the story of any deaf child. Baby is an easy sign to grasp: a babe swinging in its mother's arms. Then I grow the babe into a young child, running and playing, gazing up at the world and adults around it. I show its encounters with other children, and the setting of a classroom in which the child is made to sit and stare and study. The appearance of speaking: the child moves its mouth, but from the expression on the child's face, you know its struggle and confusion. The punishment: the child made to sit on its hands, or those hands tied to a chair. The child grows up and I level my head and straighten my neck as the child, now a young adult, regards a world of people its own height. But something is wrong, missing. The world is receding, not coming closer. The isolation becomes deeper, thicker.

How, I ask the crowd, can you have rich notions of the world if you don't have a rich language? Did you not flock to the Society this evening because you felt the true appeal of the Telephone? The magic is not the disconnected voice. The magic is the making of a connection across space and time. The immediacy of another person from afar. The pulse of your own response in making your reply.

The Inventor of the Telephone knows it, I tell them. He knows why you have come.

For several minutes the words in my hands are the only movement in the Great Room. They're as full and clear as I can make them. If Edith Ackers and the boy understand nothing, then at least they'll have no less understanding than the others.

People are trickling back into the Great Room with puzzled faces and the same question on their lips. Why is there silence on the lines? Some of them inform Mr. Price of the situation at their end.

The Telephone, they say, is broken.

Mr. Price is staring at me, his grip loosened on the butterstamp handle so it's practically dangling. His hand is about to drop away completely when Elbert Crane steps forward and takes the Telephone from him. He signs, I will voice your speech, and takes the butterstamp from Mr. Price, wagging his eyebrows at me: Continue.

But I shake my head. This is a silence for the audience and one in which Edith and the boy are not alone. I carry on with my signs, and the crowd gaze at me, and start glancing at one another. Distantly, I'm aware of Harmon, his jaw trembling. Mr. Ackers made pale. I hardly dare look at the boy's mother.

When I've finished, Elbert Crane passes the Telephone back to Mr. Price who looks so astonished at the proceedings he doesn't seem to recognize the butterstamp handle when it's returned to him. Elbert waves his hands in applause. A few people copy him, and slowly the wave lifts around the room like birds taking flight, blocking my view of any person in amongst the crowd who is frowning or sneering, or worse.

I step down from the stage and push my way toward the doors. I don't know if Harmon or Elbert Crane are behind me. The corridors are thick with people. I push through them as if they're the crowds at the Exposition again, and I'm following Frank once more through the sea of shoulders on the Avenue of the Republic, trying to reach him.

This time, I'll get there. If not to Frank, then to St. Saviour's, where Elbert Crane will think to find me. Isn't today the church's social night? Will it be cards, bingo, a play or debate? One night's shelter, and a train journey to Bristol and Mrs. Ketter. I try not to picture Harmon's face when he reads my letter of explanation, and finds the blank copies I stowed away in my drawers. Will he rage at the discovery? A white bower of paper about him as he hurls the copies into the air. But we both broke our promises to Mama, and he is freed of them now, same as me. He'll rise at the Department Store, find new fancies and enterprises. He'll be free again in his quick-lipped world.

In London, as Telephones are wired into the city, Frank's newspaper will sit on the shelves of the St. Saviour's library. Perhaps I'll write Augusta for more editions of the silent press, so that St. Saviour's will be paired with the little print shop on Washington Street. Can't I make a normal life like Mrs. Ketter? Paired to the one that Frank has found in Connecticut with his new wife and family. We will live like two Telephones at either end of an Atlantic wire, and the wire will be made of memory.

Outside the Society, I look up and down the road, trying to figure the direction of Oxford Street. A waving arm catches my eye. A gentleman standing in front of the Adelphi Hotel has a Telephone pressed to his ear. He waves and cries out: Over there!

I follow his pointing finger back to the Society building. Mr. Bell hovers in the window above the entrance, which still has wires draped over its sill. He's holding a Telephone transmitter to his mouth while the Adelphi fellow presses the receiver to his ear, nodding his head as Mr. Bell talks. The man bends down to a piece of paper and after a moment of hasty, one-handed scribbling, hands it to me.

Thank you, I say, taking the note. The message is brief: "I would have your good opinion of me."

I look up at the window. Mr. Bell is watching me, his mouth and face in shadow. He raises his arms and makes a British sign: Good Night. First his thumbs flick upward and then his arms and wide, flat palms circle down in front of him. Night. A setting sun, the curtains closing, the darkness falling.

He drops away from the windowsill, and back into the halls of the Society. I turn and hurry on down the street, putting the crowds and their chatter behind me. The night air is starting to cool but I don't falter. My steps are carrying me, as voices different from the ones in the wires travel toward me. They come out of the dark streets, a summoning that I answer with my feet, my body, and quickening heart.

★ ★ ★ ★ ★

Author's Note

A SIGN OF HER OWN is a work of fiction inspired by historical events. While broadly following the chronology of the telephone's invention, I have compressed some stretches of time in
the historical record to shape the story's narrative.

Many deaf people's stories are missing from the records but
I'm grateful to the following places for the resources and archives
which they have made available about the Deaf community in
the 19th century: Gallaudet University in the US; University
College of London; UCL Ear Institute & Action of Hearing Loss
Libraries (now closed) and blog; and the University of Bristol.

Several books were invaluable in exploring emerging Deaf
culture in the US and UK, and the campaign against sign lan-
guage, in particular: *A Mighty Change* edited by Christopher
Krentz; *Damned for their Difference* by Jan Branson and Don
Miller; *Forbidden Signs* by Douglas C. Baynton; and *Words Made
Flesh* by R.A.R. Edwards.

The Brooks family are based on my readings about the lives
of Black Deaf Americans at the time, specifically the Boardwin
and Metrash families in R.A.R. Edwards's book. The limited

research in this area suggests that a small number of Black Deaf Americans were admitted to certain schools in the early-to-mid 19th century, but it should be noted that many educational establishments and associations for deaf people excluded Black Deaf Americans until later in the 20th century.

Ellen Lark is a fictional character. Her story took root in my mind when I first read about Alexander Graham Bell's demonstration of Visible Speech with Theresa Dudley and her peers. Ellen's lessons with Bell are based on the class notebooks he used with Theresa which can be found online, along with Bell's letters, at the US Library of Congress. Her essay for *The Pioneer* stems from a well-received paper that Mabel Bell wrote called "The Subtle Art of Speech-reading." Her revisionist involvement with the telephone is inspired by another of Bell's students, Jeanie Lippitt, who claimed that Bell was completely absorbed by his invention. Jeanie wrote, 'It was while training my voice, as well as the voices of his other deaf pupils, that the vibration of our voices gave Professor Bell the idea, the missing link, and then his machine really talked.'

The Visible Speech symbols and extracts are taken from Alexander Melville Bell's textbooks on the subject. Examples of lip-reading exercises, and many of Ellen's collected homophenes, are taken from Edward Bartlett Nitchie's early 20th century textbooks on lip-reading.

Adequately representing the richness of sign languages in English is a challenge. This is especially so for historical signing, since sign languages, like all languages, have evolved over time. For descriptions of American signs, I have cross-checked early 20th century dictionaries with modern day usage. British signs have been informed by my experience of learning British Sign Language as an adult. I am also grateful to Jenna Beacom for her advice on how sign languages are represented in this book. Any shortcomings and errors are mine.

I first encountered Bell's controversial role in deaf education in Harlan Lane's book on Deaf history, *When the Mind Hears*. Other biographies provided an overview of his life and inventing work, in particular Robert V. Bruce's biography *Bell: Alexander Graham Bell and the Conquest of Solitude* and *Reluctant Genius* by Charlotte Gray. Bell's reaction to the death of a boy whilst he was teaching at the school in Hartford is described by Bruce although I have fictionalized the events surrounding the incident.

The legal suit referenced in this story, which is known as the Dowd case, was settled out of court awarding all rights to Bell. The controversy surrounding Bell's first telephone patent surfaced in later legal suits when the English copy of the patent application came to light, but again the courts ruled in Bell's favor. These events are detailed most comprehensively in *The Telephone Patent Controversy of 1876* by A. Edward Evenson. In his lifetime, Bell's two telephone patents were challenged around 600 times, making the telephone one of the most contested inventions in history.

Bell moved on from the telephone to pursue his many ideas and interests in the fields of science and technology, but he remained passionate about the education of deaf people. Elevated by his wealth and fame as the telephone's inventor, he campaigned for articulation teaching and oralism throughout his life. He regarded the superiority of speech over sign languages to be so great that he said, in 1884, 'to ask the value of speech…is like asking the value of life.' In sending Ellen on her journey, I have hoped to ask that question again, and to show how it might be possible to arrive at different answers.

Acknowledgments

I OWE a debt of gratitude to many people for this novel. I'm particularly grateful to Paula Milne and Mónica Parle for their encouragement. My deepest thanks to my brilliant agent, Nelle Andrew, and to Laura Brown and Mary-Anne Harrington for having a vision for this book beyond anything I could have hoped for. My gratitude to the team at Park Row Books, and at Tinder Press in the UK, for their skill and dedication.

I would like to thank Deepa Shastri for invaluable guidance and insight as a British Sign Language consultant during the book's production stages, and Jenna Beacom for her detailed sensitivity read. My thanks also to Park Row Books' design team for working with Jenna to bring American Sign Language to the page in the beautifully illustrated chapter headings.

The London Library's Emerging Writers Programme provided me with space, a peer network, and resources which informed the sections on 19th century printing, amongst others. I'm grateful to the Lucy Cavendish Prize for shortlisting me in 2019 and for all their support for new writers.

Many readers helped me on the long journey of writing a

novel. Special thanks to Mark Cockshutt, Jay Bhadricha, Chez Cotton, Claire Griffiths, Stephen Hepplestone, Sophia Morris-Jones, Yosola Olorunshola, Sarah Pickthall, Lisa Smith and Katie Waldegrave.

For support and advice while I was writing, my gratitude to David Cross, Kim Helman, Sylvia Puchalska, Faye Stewart and Rosie Thomasson. I would like to thank all my teachers of British Sign Language (at City Lit, Proud Hands BSL and Remark!) for their dedication and expertise, in particular Sue Birkin and Alison Wherry-Alimo.

To my family, Henry Marsh and Kate Fox, Katharine Stockland and William Marsh, Amadis Cammell, Sue and Andy Walker: thank you for your love and support. To Tom, who with my two daughters created many joyful distractions from writing, thank you for your patience and advice, and for holding everything together so I could write this book.

Lastly, to my mother, Hilary Marsh, and aunts, Vivienne Pozo and Josephine Leppard, thank you for your wisdom, and the gifts and lessons of deafness. I'm grateful for this inheritance.